700013623 5 AF
(Fantasy)

NORTH
LINCOLNSHIRE
COUNCIL

Library items can be renewed online 24/7, you will need your library card number and PIN.

Avoid library overdue charges by signing up to receive email preoverdue reminders at

http://www.opac.northlincs.gov.uk/

Follow us on Facebook
www.facebook.com/northlincolnshirelibraries

www.northlincs.gov.uk/libraries

Max and the Gatekeeper

Book II

The Hourglass of Souls

James Todd

Cochrane

Special thanks to all my family and friends for their help and support. Thanks to all the kids who motivated me to keep writing. Thanks to the following schools for their help with a number of characters.

Auke Bay Elementary
Riverbend Elementary
Mendenhall River Elementary
Meadowbrook Elementary

All rights reserved. Published by Dark Moon Publishing Inc.

Copyright © 2008 James Todd Cochrane
Hardback Published April 4, 2009
Originally Published June 4, 2009
Second Publication July 1, 2010

Cover by Kalen O'Donnell
Sketches by Beth Peluso

www.darkmoonpublishing.com

Library of Congress Control Number: 2009905875
ISBN 978-0-9797202-3-9

CONTENTS

CHAPTER 1
Surprise Visitors · 1

CHAPTER 2
To Uncle's House · 10

CHAPTER 3
Not One Hair · 20

CHAPTER 4
The Demonstration · 29

CHAPTER 5
The Channeller · 37

CHAPTER 6
A Message · 49

CHAPTER 7
Cindy's Showdown · 63

CHAPTER 8
Ell's Perception · 75

CHAPTER 9
Pekel's Secret · 88

CHAPTER 10
An Important Discovery · 102

CHAPTER 11
Sladkor · 113

CHAPTER 12
The War Begins · 126

CHAPTER 13
Max Disappears · 137

CHAPTER 14
Battle for Putooee · 149

CHAPTER 15
Out of the Frying Pan into the Fire · 165

CHAPTER 16
Monsters and Rivals · 178

CHAPTER 17
Larry's Trap · 193

CHAPTER 18
Max's Plan · 205

CHAPTER 19
The Arrangement · 220

CHAPTER 20
The Feather in the Enemy's Cap · 233

CHAPTER 21
Battles Everywhere · 247

CHAPTER 22
Happy Reunions, Unfinished Business · 258

1

Surprise Visitors

Thirteen-year-old Max Rigdon sat in class, staring out the window, his green eyes fixed on the stranger in the alley on the far side of the playground. He made Max anxious. The man wore black clothing, and a large hood hid his face. Since spending last summer with his grandpa, the sight of dark-clad people worried Max, especially after they tried to kill him.

By outward appearances, Max seemed the same as everyone else in his class. He was thin and a little above average height. With his wavy, light brown hair and tanned complexion, some of the girls in his class said he was cute. What separated Max from the other boys and girls his age was something much deeper; something to do with his heritage. A secret no one at school knew. Max was involved in a battle that had been raging for centuries. Last summer Max was unwittingly caught up in a magical war between good and evil after he discovered his grandfather possessed a powerful gateway. This gateway opened paths to other dimensional worlds where lived a host of other peoples and creatures, many bent on controlling life everywhere.

The mysterious man leaned against the building and gave Max a creepy impression; the stranger stared directly at him. *He almost looks like a Night Shade.* Max shivered as he remembered the pitch-black skin and hissing voices of the evil creatures. On several occasions last summer, Night Shades had attempted to destroy him, his grandfather, and his best friend, Cindy, as they ventured into other worlds.

Max glanced around the classroom. His teacher sat at her desk grading papers, while the other students busily worked on their assignment. *Only three days of school left and she still gives us stuff to do.* He went back to watching the dark figure outside, thinking of the evil powers this figure possibly possessed.

I wonder. Max had an idea. He fished around in his pocket for the small crystal his grandfather gave him last summer. Marko, a man Max had believed to be his friend, but who later betrayed him, had shown Max how the crystal would give off a flash of light on anyone in a dimension not their own. Max peered around the classroom again to make sure everyone was concentrating on the homework, and not on him. Satisfied no one would notice, he waved the crystal toward the stranger across the street. The result was quick and terrifying. The crystal gave off a small twinkle of light, confirming Max's fear. The man across the street didn't belong in this world.

Max's heart started racing and his palms grew sweaty. *A Night Shade! What's he doing here? Is he waiting for me?* Max glanced at his watch and noticed the bell was about to ring. *What should I do?* He peered out the window again to see someone approaching the stranger in the alley. It looked like a drunk or a homeless person seeking a hand out. The stranger's quick movements were like those of a striking snake. A crooked knife blade glinted in the sun as he held it high over the beggar's head.

As the knife swung down, Max screamed and stumbled and tried to get out of his seat. He knocked over several desks, sending papers in all directions. The entire class watched as a hysterical Max landed on his back between two rows of desks. "He killed him! He killed him!"

"What? Who killed who?" Max's teacher rushed to help him into a sitting position.

"Outside!" Max struggled to breathe. "A man—a man in the alley just got stabbed!"

Everyone's attention went from Max to the alley, as the students scrambled to the windows.

"Where? I don't see anything but a man standing against a building," one student commented.

"He's right. There's only one guy," added another.

"No one's been stabbed," several added, with a hint of annoyance.

Max climbed to his feet and pushed his way to the window. The stranger stood against the building as if he had never moved. There was nothing out of the ordinary. There was no sign of the beggar. "That can't be."

"Are you sure you didn't doze off?" His teacher looked mildly concerned.

The ring of the bell filled the air, and the disappointed students gathered up their things and filed out of the classroom.

"I swear. I saw a man get stabbed," Max emphasized to the teacher, who gave him a disapproving look.

She shook her head, looking more exasperated than concerned now. "I think you fell asleep and had a dream."

As the teacher went back to her desk, and the students emptied out of the classroom, Max waved the crystal in front of the stranger. Again the crystal responded with a soft, white light confirming what he had seen earlier. *He killed someone and somehow he got rid of the body.*

Max ducked to the side of the window as the stranger stepped out of the alley. Once again, the stranger appeared to be looking right at him.

"Are you all right, Max?" the teacher asked, looking up from her papers.

"Uh, yes," Max added, as he moved back to his desk and began to pack up his things.

How could they have found me? Max wondered. It had been almost nine months since he spent the summer at his grandfather's house. From that time he hadn't seen anyone from his grandfather's town, let alone another world. Max had minimal contact with his grandfather during the school year. His grandfather felt it would help hide Max and his mother from the enemy.

Max walked through the main hallway toward the front doors of the school, as students jostled in all directions, excited for the end of the school day. As he approached the glassed-in foyer of the school, Max could see another stranger standing across the street. This figure appeared to be intently watching the school. He wore a deep hood, which cast a shadow over his face, just like the man outside Max's classroom. Max flattened himself against the wall of the corridor to let other students go by. The stranger's head swiveled back and forth, clearly searching for someone among the groups of students scattering into the surrounding streets. *Do they know what I look like?*

"Hey, Max," Max's friend, Brian, yelled, as he wandered up the hall towards him.

"Are you walking home?" Max asked.

"Yeah, you want to go together?"

"Sure," Max said, feeling a little better at the thought of having company. He took his baseball cap out of his backpack and pulled it low over his eyes to hide his face.

Max and his friend proceeded out the front doors and strolled towards the main sidewalk. Max kept his friend engaged in idle conversation, while keeping an eye on the strange man, as they exited the school grounds. The stranger casually fell in line several yards behind them as they turned left down the street.

"What's with the hat?" Brian jovially asked, with a slightly puzzled expression. "You on the run from the police or something?"

"I have a headache and the sun's hurting my eyes," Max lied.

"Do you have to go to your grandfather's for the summer again?"

"Yep!" Max said with a smile.

"You sound excited," his friend added. "You won't be playing baseball here again. Last year you were totally bummed about going there."

"I," Max started, and jerked to a halt when he spotted another unusual man waiting at the end of the block. He didn't know what to do.

"What's the..." his friend began, and then he, too, noticed the strangers. "Who are they?"

"You need to get out of here," Max stammered, as he looked for a place to run. "There, between those houses. Go!"

"Uh, Max, I think you're over-reacting." Brian looked at him as if he was crazy.

Several strange, unrecognizable words littered the air. Max's friend immediately stiffened and fell to the ground, unconscious.

"Maxsssssss," the figures hissed in unison.

"Who? Who's Max?" Max acted as if he didn't know what they were talking about.

"We knows who yous are. You can'ts fools usss," the approaching Night Shade hissed.

"I don't know any Max," Max continued, taking a small step back to keep the Night Shades at a safe distance. "My name is Marko." Max flinched as the traitor's name rolled off his tongue.

"Holds outs your handsss, and proves usss wrongs, Maxssssss," the second one hissed.

"Yessss," murmured the first. "Shows usss your handsss."

"*Premakni!*" Max shouted, and thrust a hand out toward each Night Shade. The spell caught the Night Shades and threw them several yards backwards. Max bolted down the alley between the houses. As he looked back to see the Night Shades racing after him, Max banged his knee on some garbage cans, and stumbled.

Max picked up a trash can and threw it towards the Night Shades as he clambered to his feet. Turning and fleeing down the alley, a high-pitched screech echoed off the walls and almost froze his entire body. A black-winged creature flew across the sky, following him from above. It was one of the gargoyle-like beasts he had encountered last summer. *What are they doing here, where everyone can see them!*

Down the street screams rang out, followed by shouts of fear and confusion from people passing by.

"What is it?" a voice called, followed by a child's scream.

"Some kind of devil with wings!" cried another.

I'll never lose them if I stay in the open. Max emerged from the alley onto another street. People screamed and pointed at the winged beast descending from the sky.

A third Night Shade came from Max's left so Max ran to the right. The two trailing Night Shades closed in fast. *How can they be here? It can't be good if they're willing to let everyone see them.*

Sharp pain exploded in Max's shoulders as the flying creature's talons punctured his flesh, and the weight of the winged horror drove him to the ground, asphalt painfully scraping the skin from his hands and knees. Screeching tires and crunching metal filled the street as several cars collided with each other at the sight of the strange winged creature.

The car wrecks and the frightened spectators gave Max the distraction he needed. The commotion startled the creature enough for Max to break free. Ignoring the searing pain in his shoulders, Max rolled onto his back and thrust his hands forward. "*Prizgaj*," he called, and a fireball engulfed the winged nightmare.

The beast roared in pain, silencing the spectators.

Max jumped to his feet and raced through the traffic jam of smashed cars. He made his way down the street and into an apartment building. Max knew what he needed to do as soon as he passed through the front doors. He headed for the stairs. Suddenly, breaking glass and flying debris thundered through the building. A violent force threw Max down the stairwell, as the glass doors to the apartment building burst inward behind him. Shards of glass, metal, brick and dust filled the air.

The Night Shades stormed into the building. A cloud of debris helped Max avoid detection as he rolled around a corner and down another flight of stairs.

"Maxssss," the leading Night Shade hissed. "We wills findsss youss."

The landlord rushed out of his apartment to see what was causing the disturbance. A spell from the Night Shades thrust him back into his living room.

"Searchss everywheresss," one Night Shade ordered.

Max reached the lower level of the building and entered the parking garage. Running in a crouched position, he hurried along a line of cars. He tried to steady his heavy breathing and pounding heart. He could feel blood running down his back where the flying attacker had pierced him with its claws.

At the sound of loud footsteps rushing through the garage, Max ducked down between two cars. He dropped to his stomach and crawled under a parked car, then watched a frightened couple get into their car and speed away. *I need to get out of here! I have to get home and call Grandpa.* He waited in silence for several minutes before deciding to move.

He slid out from under the car, noticing that he ached all over. After pausing to make sure the parking garage was empty, he climbed to his feet and hustled to the exit. Max could still hear sounds of fear and hysteria outside. He hesitated before daring to sprint blindly into the street.

Max peered around the edge of the wall, his eyes darting up and down the street. He couldn't see any Night Shades or winged creatures. After several moments gathering his courage, Max decided remaining motionless was worse than moving, and he ventured out into the open. *It's now or never.* He hugged the wall of the building before dashing across the street.

A loud shriek penetrated the already chaotic noises from the street. Max knew the enemy had spotted him. People fled in all directions at the sight of the terrifying creature diving into the crowd. Max sprinted into the middle of a group of people, feeling guilty about endangering others, but needing to confuse his pursuer.

The gargoyle-like monster hovered over Max and the hysterical people. A gunshot echoed off the buildings, followed by another high-pitched scream. The wounded beast fell to earth and smashed into several parked cars. A police officer had shot the attacking nightmare out of the air. Before the officer could fire his gun a second time, there was a bright flash of light, and the winged monster disappeared.

Max didn't hang around with the astonished crowd. The Night Shades were still somewhere behind him, and he had to get out of sight.

He weaved in and out of people and cars until he reached the end of the street.

Max thought he was never going to reach the safety of the apartment where he and his mother lived. He took alternate routes and doubled back to make sure no one was following him. Down back alleys and through empty lots he ran, always looking over his shoulder for pursuing Night Shades.

When he finally reached his own neighborhood, he stopped behind a car parked across the street from his apartment building. Sweat streamed down Max's forehead as he gulped down several deep breaths to regain his strength. He scanned the surrounding area for anything out of the ordinary. He even searched the sky and the tops of the buildings. *I definitely don't want them to know where I live. What if they already know?* The thought sent a shiver up his spine.

They know what city I live in. "I need to call Grandpa, right now," he murmured, as he determined whether the coast was clear. He rounded the fender of the car while still glancing in all directions for any hint of the enemy.

He was halfway across the street when a woman's scream caused all the fine hairs on his body to stand on end. "Mom!" he shouted in a panic, and sprinted towards his apartment.

He entered the building and bounded up the first flight of stairs. More screams, mingled with the sound of furniture smashing, filled the hallway, along with a strange sulfurous smell. "Mom!" Max yelled as he grabbed the doorknob, only to find the door locked.

"Mom, Mom," he cried, as he fumbled in his pocket to find his key and unlock the door.

"Max!" his mother screamed from inside the apartment. "Max! Help me!"

Max finally got the door open, but a spell propelled him backwards across the hall, where he thudded into a neighbor's door. His mother struggled against the two Night Shades who were binding her arms and legs. A third Night Shade stood in front of her with its arms extended. A strange, thin light hovered above the kitchen floor behind his mother and the Night Shades. It stretched from just above the ground to the ceiling and was only an inch wide. Every few seconds the light would pulsate in different areas along its vertical axis.

"*Premakni*," Max called, with extended hands. The spell caught the Night Shade standing in front of his mother and slammed him into a bookshelf.

The small crack of light grew more intense and changed into a man-like shape. When the light shrank back to its original size, another Night Shade appeared before it. A moment later a fifth Night Shade emerged from the light.

"*Pridi*," Max called. The spell yanked his mother from her captors' hands towards the open doorway. As Max's spell propelled her through the air, her head collided with the doorframe, knocking her unconscious. Max raced to her side, but before he reached her another spell sent him back across the hall. The tremendous collision with the wall stole the air from Max's lungs.

Max struggled to breathe as he tried to cast another spell. Before he could speak another word, the Night Shades lifted his mother off the floor and carried her towards the strange light.

"*Pridi*," Max gasped. This time the Night Shades held tight to their prisoner, but the whole group of them slid several inches backwards. Their wicked laughter filled the apartment as the light grew and shrank, swallowing the Night Shades and Max's mother.

Max dashed towards the kitchen, desperately hoping to follow his mother. Just as he reached the light it disappeared in a shower of sparks.

2

To Uncle's House

"She...she's gone! They took her!" Max stammered into the phone, as he tried to catch his breath. His hands shook uncontrollably, making it hard to hold onto the phone.

"What? Who's gone? Who took who?" Grandpa tried to sound calm.

"Mom!" Max gasped for air, looking around the apartment for answers. "Night Shades came and took Mom!"

"What? When? How?"

"Just now! Th-they came through a t-type of gateway and took..." fighting back tears, Max couldn't finish the sentence.

"Relax, slow down," Grandpa said. "Take a deep breath."

Max inhaled and exhaled several times. His hands and knees continued to tremble. "Some N-night Shades entered our world through some kind of gateway and took M-Mom," his voice cracked.

"Gateway? What are you talking about?" Grandpa sounded nervous. "I need you to tell me everything. Don't leave out a thing."

Max drew air into his lungs, and tried to picture the events leading up to that point. He relayed everything that had happened from the moment he saw the stranger outside school. "What should I do?" Max felt the helplessness of his situation.

"You need to call the police, if some neighbors haven't already."

"What? Call the police. And what do I tell them?"

"Tell them that some men broke into your apartment and kidnapped your mother," Grandpa explained. "You need to dial 9-1-1 immediately."

"What about me? What should I do? Where do I go?"

"Go with the police after they arrive. You should be safe with them. I'm on my way. I'll be there in about an hour."

"How?"

"Don't worry about that. I'll be there. See you shortly. And Max, try not to worry; we'll get your mother back."

Max felt as if he was falling. Every inch he dropped seemed to take him farther from his mother. He hung up the phone, but it rang before he could pick it up again to call the police.

"Hello, Max," an oddly familiar voice came from the receiver.

"Grandpa? Who is this?" Max asked.

"I like to think of myself as an old friend," the voice continued.

"Alan," Max hissed through clenched teeth. His hands tightened around the receiver as his blood began to boil.

Alan, one of the enemy, had the nerve to call. Alan had been among the people involved in the plot that tried to destroy Max and his friends last summer. Max hadn't missed him or his bully of a son, Larry, one bit since leaving Grandpa's house at the end of last summer.

"What do you want?" Max demanded, his blood pressure rising. Somehow he knew Alan was involved in the abduction of his mother. Why else would he call? Alan had killed his father, and now he had taken his mother away.

"To give my condolences to you on your mother Rachel's disappearance," Alan said in a cool, aloof manner. "I do hope nothing terrible happens to her."

Max had no trouble imagining Alan's sinister grin, certain to be present, which enraged him even more.

"I also called to tell you something very important, and if you want to see your mother again, you'll do exactly as you're told and nothing else."

Max suddenly had a flashback to last summer when Hudich's followers kidnapped his best friend, Cindy. They used this situation to help bring Hudich, the most evil creature alive, out of his prison—a world called Pekel. Grandpa Joe had thwarted Hudich's followers from complete success by placing a collar around Hudich's neck that prevented him from performing magic. The device also allowed Grandpa to track Hudich at all times. "You want the key," Max spat.

"Yes, but not in the way you expect."

"What do you mean?" His whole body shook with anger.

"For now, you need to do as you're told. We don't have much time. The police are already on their way. I want you to tell the police whatever story you, and that fool you call a grandfather, decided on. Then, you will ask them to take you to your Uncle Frank's house. You will stay there until I contact you again."

"What about Grandpa?"

"You will not contact him until I say so," Alan paused. "That includes your communicator that allows you to send messages from different worlds. You won't like the consequences if these directions are not followed completely. If you choose to ignore these instructions, your mother will be the one who suffers"

Max's heart sank into his stomach, he felt nauseated at the thought of Alan mistreating his mother in any way. It was hard enough when they took Cindy captive, but it was unbearable for them to have his mother.

"Max," Alan brought him out of his thoughts. "If you don't do as you're told, your mother's body will be found somewhere in the city. Just go to your Uncle Frank's and wait for more instructions."

It was as if Alan had punched him in the gut. His mouth was dry, and he couldn't believe what was happening. He wanted his mother back and would do anything to make it happen. The joy of wrecking the enemy's plans last summer disappeared. He hated Alan and vowed to ruin whatever scheme they had developed and to get his mother back safely.

"Tell me you understand," Alan ordered.

"I understand," Max replied, his voice low.

"Max."

"Yes?"

Knock. Knock.

Max started at the sudden thumps on the door. "Hello? Alan?" he said into the receiver, but there was only silence. "Who is it?" Max hollered, as he hung up the phone.

"This is the police," a gruff voice answered from the other side of door.

Grandpa Joe arrived at the police station early in the evening to retrieve Max. He approached the front desk where a heavyset balding officer was answering a ringing phone. Joe waited for the officer to finish his call. Max's grandfather was an elderly man with a thin build. His thick wavy-white hair and mustache reminded people of Mark Twain.

"May I help you?" The officer put down the phone and looked up.

"I'm here to pick up my grandson, Max Rigdon," Joe replied.

The officer moved to the computer on his desk and tapped in the name.

"Max Rigdon," he paused, reading the screen. "He's no longer here. He's been released."

"What? Where did he go?" Grandpa ruffled his mustache.

"You say you're related?" the officer asked.

"Yes! I am his grandfather. I told him I'd be here to pick him up in an hour." Joe felt uneasy, and small beads of sweat began to form along his brow.

"I'm sorry, sir, but he isn't here anymore."

"Can you tell me where he is?"

"I am sorry, sir, I can't release that information."

"But I'm his grandfather!" A sense of dread poured over him like cold water. "I told him I was coming."

"I will need some proof of your relationship before I can give out any information. You must understand, we need to protect him."

Another officer, apparently concerned with the ruckus, approached the desk, peering at Joe with a questioning eye.

"May I help you, sir?"

"I'm just trying to find my grandson." Joe sighed in frustration. "He was supposed to be here, waiting for me."

"What's his name?"

"Max Rigdon, but apparently he's already been released, and I just want to know to whom."

The new officer stared at the computer screen and then exchanged a look with the first officer. "Do you have any proof that you're Max's grandfather?"

"Umm, no," Grandpa stated, taken aback.

"We're going to need to see some identification," the first officer said.

Grandpa extracted an old ID card from his wallet and handed it to the officer. He had an uneasy feeling Max was in trouble, and that he was about to have some difficulties of his own. Max should have been waiting for him, and since he wasn't here, something had gone very wrong. He put his fingers to his temple and tried to rub away the beginnings of a headache.

"Sir, this driver's license is over twenty years old! We can't accept this as a valid ID." The second officer edged around the desk to stand next to Joe. "Do you have another form of identification?" he asked, as a third officer moved in behind Joe.

"No! I haven't driven a car for years, so I've never bothered to renew my license."

"Well, we need some *current* form of ID. We've had a very unusual day, with strange sightings and such. A lot of people are very frightened. This could somehow be connected with your," the officer made quote signs with his hands, "'grandson's' mother's disappearance. People in the apartment building reported seeing some very odd things."

"Do I look like some sort of pitch-black life form that hisses when I speak?" Joe said, his palms starting to sweat.

"How do you know what they look like? And sound like?" asked the officer behind the desk.

"Just a guess," Joe swallowed. A sharp pain exploded in his chest as the officer behind him forced him into the desk. The other one seized him by the arm and yanked it up behind his back painfully.

"We also had a report of a white-haired man matching your description, fleeing the Rigdon's apartment complex." the officer behind breathed in his ear.

"Argg," The officer's blow pushed the air from Joe's lungs.

"Don't fight it, old man," the officer behind the desk said, as he reached forward and grabbed the back of Joe's neck to hold him in place.

"*Zaspite!*" Joe called out, before the officers could put handcuffs around his wrists. The room went silent. The officers and the people in the lobby went limp. Those standing fell to the ground, while others slumped over in their seats; everyone was asleep.

Joe glanced around to make sure the spell had worked on everyone, but his gaze brought him right into the security camera. His heart almost stopped. He needed to hurry out of the city. Worse than the prospect of fleeing, he didn't know where Max was or what was happening to him. He snatched up his ID and put it in his pocket.

"*Unichi,*" he called, pointing his fingers at the camera. Sparks and pieces of broken camera flew everywhere before crashing to the ground. Joe exited the police station as fast as his old legs would carry him.

"I'm in real trouble." He rushed down the steps, shielding his face with his hand as he passed a couple of cops entering the station.

###

An officer dropped Max off at his Uncle Frank's house. His Aunt Donna and cousin Martin waited for him on the sidewalk in front of their house. It was a modern, rambler-style home in a small suburb just outside the city. As the police left, Max's Aunt trembled as she embraced him. She was a short plump woman with curly brown hair.

"Oh Max, we've been so worried!" Aunt Donna hugged him close. "Are you all right?"

"Yes," he snapped. Max ordinarily liked his relatives; their house was the place where he and his mother spent most of their holidays. Today, though, seemed different. He couldn't hide his suspicions about his aunt, uncle, and cousin. Alan sent him here for a reason. Max wondered if one or all of them worked for the enemy.

"Hey, Max," Martin attempted to reach out to his cousin, but Max shot him a keep-your-distance glare. Martin was two years younger than Max; a quiet boy with brown hair and a friendly face. Max always thought his shyness was a result of his height; he was short for his age. Now, Max considered that Martin had been playing him all along.

A pungent, rotting odor stung Max's nose, tainting the air he breathed. He could actually taste the bitter aroma on his tongue. "What's that smell?" he asked, covering his nose and mouth with his hand.

"I wish I knew," his aunt added, eyes watering. She waved a hand in front of her nose and pulled a face. "I've been wondering if the city opened a dump nearby. The smell has been getting worse for over a month now. Let's go inside and get you settled. It usually doesn't stink as bad inside the house.

Max followed them up the sidewalk, his senses working overtime. Something was going on at this house, and he wanted to know what. His aunt and cousin acted the same as always, but today Max didn't trust them.

Once inside, Max's misgivings grew even stronger. His aunt's personality changed suddenly, and a harsh presence seemed to squeeze all happiness from the place. Martin's behavior remained mostly the same, though he now looked fearful of something.

"Do you want anything to eat?" Aunt Donna vented angrily.

"I-I'm not hungry," Max stammered, shocked by his aunt's tone of voice. He had sensed the change in her attitude immediately upon entering the house, but he was confused. Max had never before heard her use such a sharp tone.

"Well, then you can spend the rest of the evening in your room," she snarled, her round face twisting with lines of anger.

Max sat on the bed in the guestroom and kept the lights out. He wondered where his mother was, and if she was all right. He decided she must be safe because Alan wanted something, but that didn't make him feel any better. Hospitality and comfort for hostages weren't high on the enemy's list of priorities. "Grandpa, what are we going to do?" he whispered to the room with a sad sigh. Just then, a car drove up, followed by the opening and closing of the front door, announcing his uncle's arrival.

Max crept to the bedroom door so he could hear.

"Where is the little brat?" The muffled sound of his uncle's voice reached him.

"In the guestroom," his aunt fired back.

Max listened for several more minutes, but he didn't hear anything that hinted at what was happening with his mother. He was convinced his relatives weren't willfully working with the enemy, but rather under some sort of spell. His aunt seemed genuinely concerned out in the yard. After they entered the house she turned into another person.

It was past midnight and Max hadn't managed to fall asleep. Shortly after lying down on the bed, he thought he heard a scream outside, followed by some strange growling noises. Something just felt wrong in this house, and he knew he wasn't safe. He lay in the dark, trying to figure out how to help his mother, when someone or something moved outside his bedroom door.

Max's heart jumped into his throat, but he tried to calm his breathing so he could listen. He pulled the covers tight around his shoulders, feeling somewhat safer than he would out in the open. The doorknob twisted and the fear of what may happen next turned Max's blood cold. *This is it*, he thought as the door creaked opened. Max brought his hands forward to cast a spell, when Martin appeared in the doorway.

"Max," Martin whispered.

"What do you want, Martin?" Max asked, with annoyance tinged with fear, as he sat up in his bed.

Martin entered the room, closing the door as quietly as he could behind him, and then moved to the edge of the bed. He eyed the door nervously as if expecting someone else to come in and catch him there.

"What do you want?" Max asked again.

"Max, we're in danger," Martin said, still keeping watch on the door.

"Danger!" Max exclaimed, with too much volume for Martin's comfort. Martin put a finger to his lips to quiet him.

"Yes," Martin emphasized, his eyes stuck on the door. "Didn't you notice the way my mom changed when we came in the house?"

Max nodded. He couldn't deny the difference. It reminded him of the transformation Larry and his father went through after Yelka put a counter spell on Cindy's house last summer. Max believed he couldn't trust anyone in this house, but here was Martin, acting like something was terrifying him.

"It started a couple of months ago," Martin paused as a noise from outside caught his attention. Seemingly satisfied that no one had heard, he continued. "My mom is different when she's in the house. Her temper and moods are completely the opposite from the way she used to be… the way she is when she's outside."

"I noticed that too," Max said flatly, not wanting to let his cousin know what he was thinking or feeling.

"That's not all," Martin said. "My mother is herself when we're not in this house, but my father isn't my father."

"You mean he's acting different too?"

"No, I mean he isn't my dad. He looks like him, but that man isn't my father. I don't even think he's human."

"What? What do you mean? How do you…"

"I think he's some kind of alien or creature. Every night, he leaves when it gets dark. I don't know where he goes, but when he returns he always goes into the shed out back."

"You *have* seen him!"

"Yes and no. Because it's dark I can't say for sure, but he doesn't look like my dad. And he sometimes brings things back to the shed with him. I've seen him carrying or dragging what look like bodies." Martin swallowed, his eyes darting back and forth from the door to Max.

"What?"

"That stinky smell is coming from our shed. When he was gone I tried to open it, but I couldn't get in. We need to get help."

Max softened a little towards his younger cousin. "Go back to bed, Martin. I'll think of something."

After Martin left, Max remained wide-awake. Martin's words kept repeating over and over in his mind, *"that man isn't my father."*

Who or what could he be? Max realized he had only scratched the surface of strange and frightening creatures with his gateway adventures last summer.

After a night of little sleep, Max awoke late. He really wanted to stay in his room and sleep longer, but hunger forced him out. The house was empty, so he fixed himself something to eat. He was happy to be alone, even though he felt there was something wrong in the house.

After breakfast he went outside where he found his aunt and cousin working in the front yard. The change from his aunt's indoor personality to outdoor personality was like night and day. Out in the yard she was kind and genuinely concerned about him and his mother, but inside she was hateful and downright mean.

"How are you feeling this morning?" She asked, with a sad smile.

"A little tired."

"Well, I'm sure the police will come up with some leads soon," she added. "You will be back with your mother in no time."

Martin gave him an "I-told-you-so" look, as he continued plucking weeds from a small flowerbed.

"Do you need some help?" Max offered.

"No, you just take it easy." Aunt Donna smiled at him. "We've got it covered."

Max sat on the porch steps and watched his aunt and cousin plant some ground cover. He wondered what Grandpa was doing. *He must be worried sick about Mom and me.*

Martin stopped working and stared up the street. He had a look of fear on his face, and the color disappeared from his cheeks. Max followed his line of sight to an approaching car and recognized it as his uncle's.

"Dad's coming," Martin said in a shaky voice. "He has that weird man with him."

"Shh," Aunt Donna warned. "That's not nice."

Max watched as the car drew near. It pulled up to the curb, and his uncle got out of the car, followed by his passenger. Max's heart sank as he recognized the second man.

"Hello Max," Alan said, with a wicked smile.

3

Not One Hair

Max glared at Alan as they sat across the kitchen table. He seethed, and wished with the heat of his stare he could melt the horrible man. The constant pacing from his uncle, or rather the impostor who had replaced his uncle, only added to the unbearable tension.

Alan was a tall strong man, and except for the gray mixed in with his brown hair, would look younger than his years. He wore a business suit, which Max assumed was to portray himself as having important status.

Max knew he would see Alan at some point this summer when he went to visit his grandfather, but he had hoped it would be under different circumstances. Sitting across the table from the man who had tried to kill him and his friends last summer was not what Max expected. Not only had Alan tried to murder him, but is the main suspect in his father's death.

"What have you done with my mother?" Max spoke through gritted teeth; under the table his hands balled into fists, nails digging into his palms.

"She's safe for now," Alan responded pleasantly. He had an air of complete control, and Max could tell he was enjoying the situation. "But, that could change at any moment. You see, your mother is in prison in a very dangerous world, and I don't know how long I can protect her."

"Well then, just bring her back here!" Max's blood pounded in his temples.

"Oh, she will never be returning home," Alan cackled. "I could, however; be persuaded to move her to a more pleasant situation."

"I don't know what you want," Max said, "but I won't do it just so my mother can be moved to another prison. I will only do it if you release her. Here, in our world!" Max rose out of his chair and was almost yelling.

"Max, Max," Alan sighed, and shook his head. He uttered some garbled word, and the spell drove Max back down through the chair, smashing it to pieces.

Max convulsed on the floor; excruciating pain erupted in every nerve of his body. He clenched his teeth, holding back the cry that wanted to escape his lips. When the pain finally subsided, Max couldn't see. A loud ringing in his ears blocked out all sounds. The darkness before his eyes gradually faded, and Max saw Alan and his uncle standing over him. Fear, and the lingering results of the spell, left him shaking.

"The time for games is finished," Alan spat, towering over him as he lay gasping on the floor. "We are at war, Max Rigdon! A war in which people will die. Our victory will place Hudich in control of countless worlds. So, Max, you are going to do as I say, or your mother will be a casualty of war instead of a prisoner of war. Do you understand me?"

Max debated his response a moment too long so Alan hit him with the spell again. This time Max screamed as he thrashed about the floor as though set on fire. He closed his eyes to hold back the tears, and it seemed as if Alan wasn't ever going to release him.

"Do you understand me?" Alan repeated.

Max could barely hear him over the sharp stabbing sensation in his ears. "Yes," Max gasped, as he struggled for air, "yes."

"Good, I want to make sure everything is perfectly clear. I'm in control and you will do as you're told," Alan smiled. "Now, are you ready to listen to what you must do in order to keep your mother alive?"

Max nodded hazily as he tried to get control of his limbs. There was a deep, throbbing ache in every part of him, and the incessant ringing in his ears made him dizzy.

"Grd, give Max another chair," Alan said to Max's uncle, who yanked Max up off the kitchen floor and slammed him into another chair.

"First, and probably the most important thing, is that you will tell no one about our little conversation. Second, you will give me your communicator."

"My communicator?" Max stammered, it felt like all the blood drained out of his body. This was the one possession that gave him comfort. It was his only link to his grandfather.

"You didn't think we forgot about that, did you? After all, it is how you managed to escape the world of the Zeenosees. I do not trust you with it. Hand it over." Alan held out his hand.

Max took the communicator out of his pocket and stared at it.

"Now! It will be returned when we're done with you." Alan grinned.

Max's hand shook as he extended it across the table.

Alan grabbed the device and placed it in his pocket. "The third thing you will do is steal the key to the collar your grandfather placed around Hudich's neck. We'll remove the collar from Hudich, you will place it on your grandfather's neck, and then you will give me the key. You will do these things, or your mother will die."

"How do you expect me to accomplish all that?" Max glared at Alan. He gently rubbed his arms and legs to help relieve the pins and needles in his limbs.

"Grd, give Max some water," Alan ordered.

"Grd?" Max raised his eyebrows as his uncle filled a glass with water and placed it on the table. Max's eyes nearly popped out of his head as his uncle flashed a wicked smile, and his flesh melted away to reveal a reptilian looking monster. He had smooth, silver scales, almost like mercury, yellow eyes with black slits for pupils, and sharp hooked teeth. A forked tongue flicked out of his mouth, flipping slimy, florescent-green saliva everywhere. A putrid smell of decay wafted across the kitchen, causing Max to gag. A second later, the human-like form of his uncle reappeared.

"Where's m-my uncle?" Max asked with horror, as his cousin's suspicion was confirmed.

"He's with your mother," Alan said. "Not only do you have your mother to worry about, you also have your uncle and his family as well. Grd," Alan motioned to his uncle, "has a hunger for human flesh that's not easily satisfied. You wouldn't want anything to happen to your aunt or cousin, would you? We are in complete control. You can't do anything without us knowing about it. If you displease us in any way, your mother's and your uncle's discomfort will be increased, to put it mildly."

"I will need to go to my grandfather's to get the key," Max said. "How am I going to explain why I was here?"

"Oh, we will keep you here for a few more days," Alan stated. "Then, we will let you use your communicator to call your grandfather. You'll tell him you've been kept a prisoner. That we took your communicator but you managed to get it back to contact him. He and his friends can perform some kind of rescue. However, let me burn into your little brain, they are never to know about any of this."

"How will you know what I tell them?" Max's mind raced with the consequences of doing what they want, and also with the horrors of not doing as they demand.

"We have ways of knowing," Alan smirked. "Disobedience will not go unpunished. Now, in a few days I will give your communicator back so you can make your call. Grd will set it up. Tell your grandfather that your aunt, uncle, and cousin now serve Hudich and held you prisoner. I will make contact with you from time to time to check on your progress. Tell me you understand," Alan commanded.

"I understand," Max spat.

"I don't think you really do." Alan sneered. "Believe me, before we are through, you will. Grd, punish Max for breaking your chair."

Grd's approach was quick and silent; Max had no time to react. Sharp pain burst inside Max's head as Grd backhanded him across the face, knocking him out of his chair. Then, every inch of his body burned as if molten metal scoured his skin. He wanted to scream as he had never screamed before.

###

Max lay completely drained and dispirited on his bed, not wanting to move. Any little twitch caused him pain. His muscles and joints were hot and swollen; he felt like someone had thrown him into a pit of hungry rats. He listened to the eerie silence of his relatives' house as if death waited in the shadows. Nothing moved, and only the occasional creak of the old rambler broke the stillness. Max's lip quivered so he bit down on it and took a deep breath. He hadn't cried in three years, and he wasn't about to start now.

A twinkling of light outside his bedroom window caught his attention. He slipped out of bed onto the hardwood floor and crept to the window. He paused as a floorboard groaned in protest under his weight. In the back yard a small shadow approached the house. The way it jetted in and out of the limited light, and used objects to shield it from view, suggested it wanted to avoid detection. It hesitated several times and ran in a hunched position. The cautious figure hustled from one place of hiding to another. Max's heart rate increased as his senses went into high gear, magnifying the footfalls of the approaching shadow.

It can't be one of the enemy. If it were, it would come through the front door as a welcome guest.

Suddenly, the small figure turned and sprinted towards Max's bedroom window. The corner streetlamp cast a light onto the figure; it was Yelka. For the first time since the Night Shades had kidnapped his mother, a smile crossed Max's face. He quietly slid the bedroom window open, his eyes shifting from the door to Yelka.

Yelka, Max's magic instructor and friend from the world of Svet, was a short elfin woman. She had long blond hair, which she always kept braided. Tonight, instead of her usual work dress, she wore a black velvet cape pulled tight about her shoulders. The hood to her cloak hid her soft pixie face with its tan skin, pointed ears, and blue eyes.

Her head swiveled back and forth as she delicately picked her way across the neatly trimmed lawn toward Max. "Hello, Max," she whispered, as she stopped below his window, craning her neck to look up at him.

"Yelka, I'm so glad to see you," Max said in a hushed voice. "How did you get here?"

"Through the gateway, of course," she responded. "You didn't think it only opened doorways into other worlds, did you?"

"Actually, yes!"

"Never mind that. Are you all right?"

"Yes, but they have my mother," Max said. The emotions he fought so hard to restrain pushed their way to the surface, and a tear rolled down his cheek, as he choked down the lump in his throat.

"We know," breathed Yelka, a look of sympathy and worry crossed her brow and briefly darkened her features. "And we're doing everything we can to help her. We have been trying to reach you on your communicator. We must get you out of here. Take out the screen and come with me. The gateway is just a short distance away."

"They have my communicator and I can't leave, at least not yet." Max's mind raced. He wanted to tell her everything, but didn't know where to start, and also didn't know if he should. Trusting Alan was something Max would never do, but he was terrified of doing anything that might jeopardize his mother's life.

"I have to stay—for a while," Max said in a hushed voice.

"What? Why?"

"If I stay, I may be able to find out more about my mother and where they're keeping her. I'm sure I can get more information, if I stay a little longer," Max offered. It was a partial lie, but it did have some truth. He did want to learn more about where his mother was being held captive, but Max knew Alan well enough to know that he couldn't simply leave with Yelka without putting his mother's life in grave danger. "I'm going to stay—a few more days. I think I can get a message to you if I'm in trouble. I just need more time."

Yelka stood below his window, staring up at him. Max could tell she was thinking about what he said. "Are you sure…?"

"Please, Yelka! Tell Grandpa I'm all right," he pleaded.

"Max, there is an evil curse on this house, and something dreadfully horrible has been going on in that shed. I don't think you should stay here very long. It's not safe. After prolonged exposure, the curse will start to affect you," Yelka warned. "Without your communicator, how will you reach us if you're in trouble?"

Max looked at the shed with a shudder and remembered his cousin's tale. "I'm pretty sure I could get to a phone to call Grandpa if I need to," he said, his eyes still on the shed. "Can you use a counter curse on this house like you did last summer at Cindy's? It is affecting my aunt and cousin." A creak in a distant part of the house caused Max to glance at the door.

"Remember, I gave Cindy that charm before the enemy had cast their spell. It may already be too late for your aunt and cousin. The spell on this house has been working unhindered for who knows how long, and the damage may be irreversible. As for the shed, it is filled with darkness and stinks of death. I fear an extremely evil creature is near. It is probably guarding this house."

"I don't believe it's too late. My cousin knows something is happening to his mother and father, but it hasn't affected him as much. When my aunt is outside, she's her old self again. We must do something."

A light clicked on in the hallway and filtered under the bedroom door.

"Yelka, you have to go!" Max urged.

Yelka hesitated a moment. "Very well. I will have something figured out when you call. I do not believe Joseph will be happy about you staying, but if it will help your mother, I understand. However, I'm only giving you a couple of days, and then I'll be back to fetch you," Yelka cautioned, before she turned and hurried off into the darkness, glancing in every direction.

Max jumped into bed and endured several anxious moments as the sound of footsteps reverberated in the hall. Whoever it was passed his door a couple of times before the light in the hall finally clicked off again.

I have to tell Grandpa. He felt desperate. Giving into Alan's demands was out of the question. *But I can't sacrifice my mother or my relatives.* The weight of the situation made his head throb more than the wounds left by Grd's beating and Alan's spells.

The night seemed to press in on Max as if the darkness could penetrate his mind. Even his dreams were gloomy, full of dreary places and horrible monsters. Death surrounded him with its eerie claws, and Max tried to run. His heart raced and he struggled to breathe. As his doom appeared sealed, and he wanted to give up, a light appeared. Out of the light a familiar voice called. "Don't give up. Fight! Fight them at every turn."

"DAD!" Max called, as he sat up in bed.

It was late morning, and the light of the sun filled the entire room with a warm hazy glow.

"Dad," Max sighed, the pain of his two missing parents strangled his heart. He lay back down in the bed as the words his father spoke spread through his mind like the wind whistling through the tall grasses of an open field. "FIGHT!" It gave him new life as it spilled out of his thoughts and through his body, reviving him.

He climbed out of bed to find the house empty once again. He stepped out the back door where, to his surprise, he found his aunt and cousin playing catch. Not only was his cousin small for his age, but he was uncoordinated. Max's aunt gave Martin encouraging words despite his fumbling of the ball. Seeing this made Max yearn again for his own parents, and for the simple time of summers past when baseball had been his only concern.

"Good morning, Max." Aunt Donna paused as she noticed Max on the porch.

"Morning, Max," Martin added with a smile, waving his glove in the air. "One day I'm going to be as good a pitcher as you are."

Max couldn't stop the smile from crossing his face. "Not throwing like that you won't," he said, as he went down the steps towards Martin. "You're not using your legs. All power comes from your legs."

After a little coaching, Martin could throw the ball with more accuracy and power. Max was so focused on Martin that, for a short time, he forgot his own problems.

"Good job," Max said.

"Nice throw," added Donna, and shot Max a wink.

Martin beamed with pride.

Max's bliss lasted until the paperboy rode by and threw the daily newspaper at his feet. The headlines jumped out at him, as Max picked up the paper. "Woman Abducted after Strange Sightings."

Donna hurried to Max and read over his shoulder. "Who's hungry?" Aunt Donna gave Max a sympathetic look. "What do you say I fix a nice big lunch? Martin, why don't you give me a hand?" she said, and they hurried into the house.

Max couldn't take his eyes off the paper as he staggered over to the porch. He sat on the steps, feeling lost, and wondering what to do. Once again, he battled with his emotions like a swimmer against the riptides. Tears stung his eyes, and he wanted to scream as loudly as he could; scream out the pain, terror and helplessness. *I must do something, but what can I do?* He flipped blindly through the paper, not reading, but vaguely looking for anything to take his mind off his mother. As he turned a page, another headline caught his attention, "Citizens Fight Back with Anonymous Tips." Max scanned through the article describing how everyday people had helped solve crimes by giving information to the police.

Max used the back of his hand to wipe the tears from his eyes as a mischievous smile spread across his face. *I can't help Mom at the moment, but I can help Martin and Aunt Donna.*

"I've been slaving away fixing your lunch, so get your lazy hide in here and eat it, you little brat! If you don't come now, you can go without lunch for the day!" Aunt Donna screamed furiously through the screen door.

The only thing that kept Max from going to pieces was his plan to help his aunt and cousin. After lunch he went to his room, took out a piece of paper from the small desk in the corner, and began to write. He jotted down an elaborate note tying his mother's and other people's disappearances to the shed behind his uncle's house. *Don't know what I'll do if I get caught.* Max decided the risk was worth it, folded the paper, and tucked it into an envelope addressed to the newspaper. After placing the envelope in his pocket, he went outside to escape the oppressive feeling of doom prevailing in the house, and to scout out a place to mail his letter.

Late into the night, hoping that everyone was asleep, Max slid out of bed and tiptoed to the bedroom door. After a short pause to listen, he crept to the window and popped the screen out. As quietly as possible, he climbed out the window, dropped down to the grass, and went in search of the mailbox he had spotted earlier. *Take that, losers*! Max thought with delight as he dropped the envelope in the slot.

He hurried back to his uncle's house and scrambled back through the window. He just replaced the window screen when the hall light clicked on.

Max dove under the covers to make it appear he had been sleeping when the door exploded into splinters. Several shadowy, twisted shapes poured into his room. Max's heart jumped into his throat as he flung back the covers. "*Premaknite.*" His spell threw two attackers into the closet. Before Max could cast another spell multiple hands seized Max's body pinning him to the bed, while blows from all directions hammered him like a meat tenderizer.

"Let me go!" Max twisted and squirmed as they lifted him off the bed. His body screamed in pain as the attackers continued the assault.

"Quietssss." The familiar speech of a Night Shade rang in Max's ears, and the hairs on the back of his neck stood on end.

The Night Shades forced Max's hands behind his back and wound a rope tightly, painfully, around his wrists. He continued to struggle as they stuffed a gag in his mouth.

"That shouldss silence the little bratss ups."

Max kicked and flopped as the attackers dragged him into the hall, where a crack of bright light filled the hallway. The light stretched and grew as if it was a living, breathing entity. They forced Max towards the light as several dark muscular arms with sharp, yellow nails reached out. Max screamed into his gag, as the disembodied arms grabbed him and pulled him into the light.

The light seeped in around him, and he felt a sharp pain erupt at the base of his skull. Thousands of tiny white flickers popped in front of his face, and then he lost consciousness.

4

The Demonstration

When Max awoke, he was lying on his stomach in darkness. The only light was a soft, red glow that outlined what appeared to be the crack of a door. His head ached and a strong sulfur scent stung his nose. The sound of a muffled cry started Max's heart pumping. He remained motionless, straining his ears to hear more. After a few minutes of waiting, the stifled wail came again. It didn't sound close by, but its desperate plea was easily recognizable. "He—hello."

"Who, who's there," a familiar voice answered, from somewhere in the darkness.

"Mom, is that you?" Max said hopefully.

"Max, oh Max, is it really you?" Her voice was full of panic mixed with relief.

"Are you okay?"

"So far!"

Max pushed himself up onto his hands and knees. Flashing sparks flickered before his eyes and the room spun. After waiting for the dizziness to subside, he crawled in the direction of his mother's voice. Rough stone, and what felt like loose, matted straw shifted in Max's hands as he maneuvered across the floor. Bong! Swirling stars joined the sparks in front of his eyes, and Max dropped to his stomach, cradling his head in his arm.

"Max, what was that? Are you okay?"

"Yes, Mom, I'm okay. I didn't realize we were in cages. I just hit my head on the bars." He gently massaged the swelling bump on his brow. "How long have I been here?"

"I would guess a couple of hours," his mother answered.

"How long have you been here?"

"I'm not sure. I've been here since they abducted me," his mother's voice cracked.

"Two days then." Max's eyes adjusted enough to make out shadows in the direction of the red glow. In the opposite direction there was complete darkness. Seconds later the outlines of bars and cages materialized between him and the faint red light. Max wasn't sure if they were in a warehouse, a basement, or even a cave. A rotten egg smell choked Max's nose and mouth. The creepy wailing came again, raising the hairs on the back of Max's neck. "What is that?"

"I don't know, but it comes and goes," his mother answered worriedly.

"Who's here, Rachel?" The gravelly voice of Uncle Frank drifted through the darkness.

"Frank's here, too?" Max breathed a sigh of relief.

"Max?" Frank asked. He sounded so weary. Max wondered what had happened to him.

"Yes, Max's here," Rachel said.

"Wherever 'here' is. I don't understand what's happening. I think my family is in danger," Frank said.

"They ARE in danger," Max stated.

"Max!" his mother rebuked him. "No!"

"He has the right to know!" Max grasped the bars of the cage and pressed his face up to the cold metal, trying to get as close to his mother and uncle as possible.

"To know what?" Franks voice quivered.

"The truth! That evil things, nonhuman things are happening, and not just in our world," Max stated.

"What? You're just talking crazy."

"We have some explaining to do, Frank, but this is not the time," Max's mother interrupted. "Max, do you know why we are here?"

"I know a little," Max mumbled.

"Well?"

"Do go on, Max," Alan's smooth inflections interrupted from the heavy darkness behind Max, causing him to nearly jump out of his skin.

"Alan," Max dragged out the name, as if exhaling foul air.

"Tell them everything, Max," Alan said, with wicked delight. He then uttered an unfamiliar word causing a faint emerald glow to flow over his body, giving him a ghostly look. "They will never leave this place, so it doesn't matter if you tell them. It might help your Uncle Frank deal with his new life here." A sinister grin spread across Alan's face.

"My new life?" Uncle Frank gasped. "Why are you doing this?" He was on the verge of losing it.

Max could tell his Uncle Frank had hoped this horrible nightmare was just that, a nightmare. The light from Alan's body gave dimension to the small prison. There were four cells, two on one side and two on the other, with a walkway between. Max's mother and uncle sat in the two cells across the aisle from Max. Alan entered the walkway between the cells from the open cell next to Max. There were two large metal doors, each on opposite ends of the room. One of the doors had the crimson light glowing underneath. Max guessed the eerie intermittent wailing came from beyond the other door. He didn't want to try to imagine what frightening creature Alan had imprisoned there.

"The police will find us," Frank said.

Alan threw his head back; his laughter was almost a cackle as it echoed off the stone walls of the prison. "I know you're a part of the ignorant public, Frank, but you are about to join the ranks of the knowing minority. Unfortunately for you, you have become a prisoner of war before you even had a chance to fight. And no, the police will never find you here." Alan shook his head almost pityingly at Frank. "There are no police here. In fact, the only laws are ours."

"A war, what war? What are you talking about?" Frank looked completely baffled.

"We are in a different world, Frank," Max's mother said gently.

"How can we be in another world?" Frank demanded. "I don't understand."

"There are things going on, Frank, that you imagined only taking place in a fantasy book or a motion picture," Alan said. "And I am afraid that the excruciating pain you are going to suffer is something you can never comprehend until you feel it. That is, if Max doesn't do as he's told."

"Leave my son out of this," Max's mother shouted.

"Don't worry, Mrs. Rigdon. Frank is not the only one who will wish for death if Max disobeys our instructions."

"He's just a boy," Mrs. Rigdon whimpered.

"A boy who can turn the tide of war in our favor." Alan strode to the front of Max's cage. "Tell them what you're going to do, Max.

Don't leave out the smallest detail, especially what will happen if you fail."

Max was so angry that he could not bring himself to speak. Fury blazed in the pit of his stomach like a raging volcano. He hated Alan with every cell in his body, and he wanted nothing more than to reduce him to a pile of rubble.

"Tell them!" Alan demanded.

"I won't," Max rumbled through clenched teeth.

"Your attitude problem, Max, is precisely why you've been brought here. You need to see things from a different perspective. Guards!"

The door with the red glow flew open, and several Night Shades entered, some with torches and others with crude-looking metal devices. There were knives, hooks, needles, and what appeared to be large florescent nightcrawlers. The Night Shades unlocked the doors to the cages holding Rachel and Frank. They yanked the sobbing Rachel and the struggling Frank off the floor and fastened them into wall brackets that hadn't been visible in the darkness.

Max's heart raced as sweat moistened his body. "No, wait!" He desperately thrust his arms through the bars of his cage and tried to reach his frantic mother.

"I thought you said you wouldn't help us," Alan sneered. He retrieved a wooden-handled, round metal object and walked into Rachel's cage. It resembled a screwdriver, but instead of a flathead it had a flat steel plate with a razor-like edge on one side. Alan placed a small metallic disc which had a symbol engraved on it, in a slot behind the blade of the strange tool. Max recognized the symbol as the same one that Alan and his cohorts had used to mark his hand a year ago. "I think we should start with the branding, don't you?" He looked at Max as if seeking his approval. "There are other ways to mark people without using magic. Either way, we need to tag our prisoners so we can keep track of them."

"I will do whatever you want," Max cried, tears rolling down his cheeks.

"I know you will," Alan flashed an evil grin. "But I'm not sure of the depth of your conviction." He spoke a strange word, and the tip of the steel device with the symbol glowed fiery red, then white-hot.

Max screamed louder than his mother as Alan placed the tool on the inside of her left hand and turned it sharply. The tool sliced the symbol into her flesh and the heat cauterized the wound. Max shook the bars of his cage as hard as he could in an effort to reach his mother.

"One more." Alan moved to Uncle Frank's cage.

Frank shrank away and tried to keep the hot instrument from touching his skin, without success. He roared through gritted teeth as the smell of burnt flesh filled the small prison.

Alan uttered another strange word and Max's mother and uncle gasped sharply, eyeing their palms. "I needed to start the absorption process. Since I didn't use magic to install these marks, I had to activate them. Now, the marks will put off a signal that tells us your location at all times. Max, the one we used on you last summer immediately infused with your tissue, which instantly triggered the device. The marks today will take a couple of weeks to fuse with the flesh of their owners." Alan turned towards Max. "Now, tell them what you're going to do."

Joe stood expectantly next to the control panel with Cindy's mother, Mrs. Carlson, as Yelka stepped through the gateway into the third floor of Joe's house.

"Where's Max?" Joe asked. He felt a twinge of fear pulling at his spine.

"He wouldn't come," Yelka said.

"What? Why?" Mrs. Carlson asked.

Joe could hear the same concern in Mrs. Carlson's voice that was building in the pit of his stomach.

"He said he needed more time to gather information about his mother," Yelka frowned.

"Well, that could be a good thing," Joe tried to add a positive spin to the situation. "From what Max told me on the phone the night of her disappearance, it sounded like the enemy has developed a type of gateway. We know what it means if they have one."

"That isn't what concerns me, Joseph," Yelka said.

Joe had seen that look on Yelka's face several times before, and he always trusted her instincts. "What's the problem?"

"There's a tremendous amount of evil where he's staying. Not simply a curse, but something else. A creature is watching over that house. No one is safe there. I told Max I would try to think of a way to help his relatives, but I don't know what I can do."

"Is it anything like the curse they put on my house last summer?" Mrs. Carlson asked. "Are they trying to convert them—his relatives?"

"It is a little different. Instead of converting the family to their side, it's as if Alan and the others are only trying to control them. I have never encountered such a curse before." Yelka glanced towards the gateway as if trying to avoid their stares.

"I saw that look, Yelka," Joe said. "What are you thinking?"

"It is nothing." She continued to watch the gateway.

Joe flicked the power switch of the gateway, the light faded and the force field dissolved.

"Yelka, what's bothering you?" Joe asked. "You've got something unpleasant running through your mind."

"My thought was," she took a deep breath, "if one's goal was to control them rather than converting, what happens to them when they are no longer needed. The presence of the creature disturbs me. The smell of death surrounds their shed, I have a feeling the creature that guards the house hungers for human flesh. It doesn't take a genius to figure out what will happen to Max's uncle, aunt, and cousin once their usefulness runs out."

Mrs. Carlson placed a trembling hand over her mouth, and Joe gasped.

"I hadn't thought of that. They will be disposed of." Joe struggled with the words.

"Exactly."

"What else happened?" Joe asked, the panicky feeling growing more intense.

"Max said he would contact us once he had more information."

"Cindy comes home tomorrow," Mrs. Carlson said. "What am I going to tell her?"

"She doesn't know?" Joe asked.

"No, she's had a hard enough time since she was sent to boarding school. I didn't feel I needed to add any bad news."

"A good choice," Joe agreed. "I felt horrible when she was sent away because the enemies were controlling the school. At least she won't have to go away next year."

"Don't worry about Cindy." Mrs. Carlson put a comforting arm on Joe's shoulder. "Max, his mother, and their relatives are the ones in real trouble."

"All we can do is wait for Max to contact us," Joe said.

"Meanwhile, we have other things to do," Yelka stated.

"Like what?" Mrs. Carlson asked.

"We need to think of a way to rescue his relatives, as well. I believe it would be best to bring the rest of them here," Yelka said.

"We also need to find out how they got their hands on a gateway," Joe added.

After Max finished explaining what he was supposed to do to keep his mother and Uncle Frank alive, he glared at Alan. "I hate you," he spat.

"Hate me," Alan sneered sarcastically. "You've only scratched the surface of the depths your anger can go." Alan approached Max's cage. "I think it is time to extend that scratch to a cut."

"Leave them alone!"

"Oh, I'm not going to do anything else to them today. I'm going to do something to you. I want you to have a taste of what they will suffer if you fail." Alan turned to one of the Night Shades. "Bring me a pair of gloves and a flare worm."

"If you lay a finger on him!" Max's mother threatened, her voice filled with venom.

Alan ignored her as if she were a bothersome insect. He uttered an unfamiliar word, and the mark on her palm blazed white hot through the skin. She screamed, and sagged within the confines of the shackles.

A Night Shade carrying a pair of steel mesh gloves and a glass jar with the nightcrawler-like organism stopped next to Alan. Alan drew on the gloves and gently persuaded one of the strange worms from the container. A small blue flame danced up and down its long narrow body as the worm twisted and turned like a small snake.

"Hold out your arm," Alan ordered Max.

Max's eyes met his mother's and she shook her head. Max's throat was dry. His entire body trembled.

"I said, hold out your arm or I will put this worm on your mother," Alan ordered more forcefully, as he kept rotating his hands for the worm to slide through.

Max extended his right arm through the bars of his cage.

Alan's eyes focused on the scar on Max's right hand. "Maybe you should hold out your left hand." A sinister grin spread across Alan's face. "This way you can have matching scars."

Max withdrew his right arm and stuck out his left.

"Palm up," Alan ordered pleasantly.

Max opened his hand and turned his palm up.

"Do you know how these worms got their names?" Alan asked.

"No," the word was barely audible as it escaped Max's parched mouth. He stared into Alan's eyes willing himself to not break contact.

"When they come in contact with any type of flesh, the blue flame you see gliding along its body turns red, and they melt through your skin. Don't fret, Max, it happens so quickly the worms barely have time to go in any direction other than the way gravity pulls them. Of course they bounce off bone, so that can change their course. There have been some occasions where they have managed to turn on their own and go through at an angle." Alan giggled with wicked mirth, and the Night Shades joined in, grunting.

Max clenched his jaw and stared with terror as Alan's gloved thumb and index finger held the worm in position above his palm.

"Just get on with it," he forced through his teeth.

"That's the spirit," Alan said. "It will not cause any permanent damage." Alan released the worm.

The worm fell in a straight line, and true to its name, it flared a bright red color the moment it touched Max's palm. Searing pain caused Max to yank his hand back, but the worm was already through. It hit the ground and the blue flame returned. Alan quickly picked it up and placed it back into the container.

Max staggered backward until he bumped into the wall. He managed to stifle his scream, but he felt like he was going to vomit. The horrible, muffled moaning penetrated Max's senses. The room grew dark and he could sense himself falling.

5

The Channeller

A cold wave of water washed over Max's body, pulling him awake. He gasped and saw Alan standing next to his cell, holding an empty bucket. His stomach did back flips and his hand throbbed. His hand shook as he inspected the burn that went all the way through. He tried to move his fingers, but they wouldn't work properly. Two of his fingers wouldn't close; it felt as if a large nail had been driven through his palm.

"Painful isn't it," Alan chuckled.

A pool of anger, like molten lava ready to erupt, swirled in Max's stomach. He gritted his teeth, closed his eyes, and pulled himself to his feet. He wanted to attack, to crush the man before him. He might have risked it, if it wasn't for his mother and uncle. Supporting his left arm with his right hand, he staggered to the front of his cage. His momentum carried him into the bars before he crashed to his knees.

"Now, imagine if I had placed the flare worm on your foot or knee, or your stomach as you lay on the ground. Perhaps, while chained to the wall, I put it on your shoulder." Alan crouched outside Max's cage so his hateful face was only inches from Max's. "The pain would be incredible, and who knows what damage would be done. This is just a taste of the things we will do to your mother and your uncle. Believe me, we have worse things than flare worms."

Max's chest rose and fell as he fought back the rage coursing through his veins.

"Let me paint an uglier picture. After we have experimented with the worms on arms and shoulders, we will end it over the heart or eye.

I'll let you imagine what would happen if the worms were dropped there."

"You wouldn't—"

"Dare me? Let me demonstrate what I wouldn't dare to do," Alan jeered. He turned to the Night Shades, "Shackle the uncle to the floor."

The Night Shades laughed their snake-like laughs, hissing as they entered Frank's cell. He twisted and screamed as he fought for freedom. The Night Shades chained him to the floor of the cell with his arms and legs spread-eagled. In the next cell, Max's mother was screaming hysterically.

"Don't, don't, please don't!" Max pleaded, tears already blurring his sight.

"You see, we have your mother so we really have no need for your uncle." Alan entered Frank's cell with the container of worms.

"No, No." Frank tugged violently against his restraints. Sweat rolled down his forehead and his chest heaved in panic.

"I'll do everything you want," Max cried. "Just don't hurt him."

"I know you will," Alan said without emotion, as he used the special gloves to pull a worm out of the jar. He dangled the worm over Frank's chest for a moment.

"No! Please! Stop!" Everyone screamed in fear.

Cindy stepped out of the car onto the sidewalk in front of her house. Her chin-length blond hair stuck out from under a red woolen beret as her big blue eyes strayed to the new housing development behind the three-story house next door. She pursed her red lips. "When did they start building those?" She snapped her gum as she pointed towards the new neighborhood.

"They started construction shortly after Christmas. It went up in a hurry," her father said, as he closed the driver's side door.

"So, now we're surrounded on all sides by losers?" Cindy scrunched her face.

"It's not what you think."

"What do you mean?" she asked.

"They're on our side. Several things have gone on since you've been away. It looks like you won't be going back to the boarding school."

"What if I want to go back?" Cindy folded her arms across her chest and eyed the old three-story house. "So, where's Max? I thought he would be here slobbering all over me."

"Cindy," her dad began, and lines of worry appeared on his forehead.

"What? What's happened to him?" she asked.

"His mother was kidnapped by Night Shades."

Cindy's heart dropped into the pit of her gut. "Where is she?"

"That's the problem, we don't know. They must have a gateway or something. We have no idea where she is. Max is at his aunt's house, which is under a spell and controlled by the enemy."

"What?" Cindy dashed towards the neighbor's house, her loose chain belt jingling like a reindeer at Christmas.

"Cindy, wait." Her father ran after her.

Joe almost fell over from the shock of Cindy's appearance as she rushed in the front door. The shy tomboy was gone. Her baggy clothes and black eye liner reminded him of a troubled teen. "Cindy," he tried to keep the surprise out of his voice.

"Grandpa, where's Max? What's going on?" she demanded, as her father joined them.

"Come back to the kitchen for a glass of lemonade, and I'll tell you what we know." Joe waved for them to follow as he led them through the house to the kitchen.

Alan placed the worm back in the jar and approached Max's cell. "Follow orders, or I'll finish what I started here." He reached into his pocket, pulled out Max's communicator, and handed it to him through the bars.

Max glanced at the device and then at Alan. He continued to clutch his sore hand against his chest. "What do you want me to do with that?"

"I want you to call your grandfather."

"And?"

"Tell him you think you can escape tonight," Alan sneered.

"That won't work," Max looked from Alan to his mother, who was still shackled to the wall.

"What do you mean, 'it won't work'? You seem to forget you're not in charge here. We make the rules, and if you do not follow them, there will be severe penalties." With a look of twisted pleasure, Alan held up the jar of flare worms.

"Yes, but I have to take my aunt and cousin with me when I go." Max fought to stop his body from shaking. He had to tell Alan about Yelka's visit, but he didn't want Alan to punish his mother or his uncle because of it.

"Why in the world do you believe we would let them go with you?"

"Because, Yelka came to rescue me the other night. They know about the curse you've placed on their house. They also know that the thing living there isn't my uncle. Yelka won't let them stay."

Alan's brow furrowed and his eyes glowed with anger. "I warned you what would happen if you told anyone," he uttered through gritted teeth.

"I didn't tell anyone anything." Max met his glare. "But you couldn't have expected my grandfather to do nothing when I wasn't at the police station."

"What exactly did you tell Yelka?"

"I said I wanted time to find out more about my mother."

Alan nodded at a Night Shade who immediately came and retrieved the jar of flare worms. "We should make an example of your Grandfather's mistake. He must realize that the rules pertain to him as well." A wicked smile flashed across Alan's face.

"But I haven't disobeyed you," Max stressed. "And Grandpa couldn't possibly know!"

Max's mother and uncle watched Alan's every move with trepidation. They were sweating profusely as their breathing came in quick gasps. The ever present muffled wailing from behind the second metal door added to the tension.

"The fact that I told you about Yelka should earn a little trust." Max was desperate. He figured being honest with Alan was the best thing to do right now.

"This could work to our advantage," Alan said, more to himself than anyone in the room. "If they rescue all three of you, they may think your escape is genuine."

"Yes, they would," Max agreed.

"Take the communicator," Alan said, and Max accepted the device.

"What do you want me to tell him?"

"Tell him you overheard me and your 'uncle' speaking, and that we will be gone for a couple of hours tonight around 1 a.m. Tell them this might be your only opportunity to get away. Of course, you'll need to figure out how you are going to get your aunt out of the house."

"What about my mother?"

"What about her?"

"I told them I wanted to stay so I could learn more about her. What should I tell them? I mean, wouldn't they be suspicious if all of a sudden I want to leave and don't have any information about her?"

"Tell them you discovered where she's being held."

Everyone looked at Alan with surprise.

"You want me to tell them where she is?" Max's voice barely escaped his lips over the shock. "But I don't know where we are."

"Tell them you overheard that your mother is held captive in a world called, Zemlje. Mention we are seeking a trade, your mother for the key."

"Zemlje," Max repeated, knowing it was a lie.

"Now, send the message," Alan ordered.

Max's fingers moved over the dials as he obeyed Alan's command.

As Joe, Cindy, Yelka, and Cindy's father sat around the worn kitchen table, Joe told Cindy the details about Max and his mother. He paused to see if he had forgotten anything.

"What are we going to do?" Cindy asked.

Joe could detect a little of the old Cindy underneath the hard exterior she tried to portray. "Well, we're waiting for Max to contact us," Joe replied. "And Yelka is working on a plan to help his aunt and cousin."

"So, we're just going to wait," Cindy snapped, with her eyes wide and her lips pursed, as if to say they should be doing more.

Joe felt the urge to say something in response to Cindy's unspoken accusation, but decided to let it go. "We're doing all we can at the moment. We have people searching for his mother and uncle."

"Joseph!" Yelka pointed to the counter where Joe's communicator flashed with an incoming message.

Joe almost fell out of his chair as he scrambled for the device. "It's from Max," he said, as he read the message.

Everyone crowded around Joe, eager for information.

"What's he saying?" Cindy pressed.

"He wants us to get him, along with his aunt and cousin, tonight. He has information about his mother. It looks like they will be alone around 1 a.m." Joe continued to study the message.

"Is there more?" Mr. Carlson asked.

"No." Joe typed in his reply. "But I find this very interesting," Joe added. He handed his communicator to Yelka, who began reading the device as well.

"What? What's so interesting?" Cindy bounced on the balls of her feet.

"I find it interesting that Max has the information he needed in less than two days." Joe gave Yelka a short nod.

"He agreed," Max said, as he read Grandpa's response. He started to place the communicator in his pocket.

"No!" Alan's hand shot through the bars. "You can't keep that yet."

Max dropped the communicator into Alan's open palm.

"I will give you a few minutes to say your good-byes. Unshackle them," Alan ordered the Night Shades as he turned to leave. "This could be the last time you ever see each other." He and the Night Shades laughed before Alan left the room.

Max was grateful the Night Shades left the torches burning after they unchained his mother and uncle and departed. He preferred seeing his mother, even if it was in a ragged state. Max wanted to reassure her everything would be fine, that he would get them out of this situation, but no words would come. A lump in his throat kept him from speaking. He blinked to clear the tears.

"How are Donna and Martin?" his uncle asked, breaking the silence.

"Th-They're okay. Or at least they're going to be." Max tried to reassure his uncle. He didn't want to give his uncle anything else to worry about. "They'll be safe at Grandpa's house."

"Tell them I'm all right."

His uncle's voice sounded anything but all right. He shook as if on the verge of a breakdown; as though the ordeal had compromised his sanity.

"Max, how's your hand?" His mother asked, as she leaned against the bars at the front of her cell.

"Probably about the same as yours. Don't worry, mom. I'm going to get you out of here, I promise." He tried to reach her hand, but the distance between their cells was too great.

"I don't want you to worry about me. I want you to keep safe; don't do anything foolish," Max's mother said.

"I can't leave you here. I won't leave you here. I won't let Alan win." Max's face grew warmer as his anger started to rise. He never believed he could dislike another being as much as he hated Alan.

"This isn't about letting anyone win or lose," his mother scolded. "This is about living or dying. I don't want you to worry about me or Frank."

"What?" Frank interjected, drawing Max's attention.

"Max," his mother said forcefully, pulling his eyes back to her. "There are more lives at stake than mine or Frank's and you know it. Forget about us. Don't give in to them."

Tears rolled down Max's cheeks. "I can't lose you. I've already lost dad. I…"

"Max, you're so brave," his mother cried as well. "I need you to be strong. I love you and I always will."

"I love you too." Max sobbed.

Again the wailing from the other room brought the hairs on the back of Max's neck on end. "I wonder what's making that sound."

"I'm not sure I want to know," Frank answered.

They all sat in silence for a few moments.

"You can't expect him to leave us here." Frank broke the calm, his voice cracking.

"Yes, Frank, I do. There are many things—bigger things—going on than you know. The lives of countless people are at stake."

"What are you talking about? Max, you need to go to the police," Frank pleaded.

"Frank," Max's mother said, "the police can't help us. We aren't anywhere they can find us. I'm sure Max doesn't even know where we are. I doubt it's Zemlje. Even if we escape from this prison, we wouldn't be able to get home."

"I think you're all crazy," Frank mumbled, as he sat crossed-legged on the floor and hung his head. "None of this makes any sense."

"I'm sorry, Frank, but you're just going to have to deal with it," Max's mother said, as she brushed her long dark hair away from her brown eyes. She looked tired and dirty, as if she had been hiking in a dust storm for days.

"I won't leave you here to die," Max said. "I will find a way to save you. I promise."

"Max, think of the consequences of giving into them," his mother warned. "You know what could happen."

"I'm thinking of what will happen if I don't give in to them."

"You shouldn't do that. I know how difficult it is, but you mustn't obey them. I don't know that you'll ever be able to save us."

"I can't..." Max couldn't form any more words; the lump in his throat had grown to the size of a baseball and kept him from speaking. The helplessness of the situation pressed down on him like a crashing wave. If he wasn't careful, it would crush or suffocate him. Even now he was short of breath.

The door to the prison opened with a sound like nails on a chalkboard as its metal frame slid across the stone floor. Alan entered, once again accompanied by two Night Shades. "Has everyone said their goodbyes?" He looked smug, as if he was enjoying the moment. "I hope it wasn't too heart-wrenching." He smiled as his eyes swept over the three prisoners.

Max wanted to wipe the smile off Alan's face. He desired to cause Alan more pain than he had ever felt.

"Any final words?" Alan rocked back and forth on his heels as if everything was right in the world.

Max exchanged looks with his mother and Uncle Frank.

"No?" Alan smiled. "Then it's time to go." He nodded to the Night Shades, who moved to Max's cell and unlocked the door. Max staggered to the back wall. He tried to make his muscles work, but with all he had been through during the last few days, they wouldn't respond.

"Leave him alone," his mother screamed, as she desperately tried to reach him through the bars.

"Don't worry, Mrs. Rigdon. Max is going to his grandfather's house."

Max locked eyes with his mother. He was about to leave her, and he didn't know if or when he would see her again. He gathered up all his strength and rushed through the advancing Night Shades. His sudden burst of energy propelled him past the Night Shades and into his mother's arms at the front of her cell. They held each other tight, kissing each other's cheeks.

"I love you, Max."

"I love you, too."

The Night Shades grabbed Max and tried to pry him from his mother. One yanked him by the hair and the other backhanded his mother in the face through the cell bars. The blow landed with such force his mother released her grip and fell to the floor of her cell.

"No," Max screamed, as he was dragged away from her.

"Max," his mother's cry echoed off the walls.

The Night Shades dragged Max through the door, with Alan a step behind. Alan silenced Rachel's pleas as he slammed the prison door behind him.

"Struggling is pointless," Alan proclaimed, as he cast a spell that paralyzed Max.

Max felt hopeless as the Night Shade lifted his stiff body off the floor and marched at a quicker pace. *Just like last summer.* Max remembered how Alan had used the same spell to immobilize him in the world of Mir. No matter how hard he tried, he couldn't move.

The red glow that filtered in under the prison door was now a wave of light that covered everything. The Night Shades' normal black attire appeared dark red in color, as well as the prison and the floor. They walked next to multiple large pools of red-hot lava giving off waves of steam. Several rock formations rose from the floor, giving the impression that volcanic activity had created them. Slow rivers of lava bubbled and boiled with blurbs and plops as they flowed around the stone protrusions, giving off the red glow. The heat and smell of sulfur was almost overpowering, stinging Max's eyes and nose.

The Night Shades followed a path between a few stone buildings, with Alan trailing a little behind them. The red glow that had been all encompassing gave way to a soft white glow as they exited the lava-and-steam dominated area. Stars dotted the sky, but what amazed Max more was the sight of two moons. One full and the other half full hung above the jagged tops of a stretch of mountains. Between the light of the moons and the rivers of lava, one could easily travel by night in this world.

The Night Shades carried him into an area where large stone slabs formed a circle thirty yards across, reminding Max of Stonehenge. In the center of the large stone slabs were three tall thin pillars forming a smaller circle. The tops of these pillars slanted inward and touched at the center of the circle forming what looked like a three-columned archway. The lava rivers crept around the outer circle, with several stone bridges providing access to the circle within.

Max's escorts dropped his body on the smooth floor next to the archway, and then headed back towards the prison. Alan stood over him and spoke the counter spell, releasing Max from his invisible straight jacket.

"You're going back to your uncle's house now. When your grandfather comes to rescue you, you'll need to figure out how to get your aunt out of the house without a fight." Alan chuckled.

"What is this place?" Max asked, running his hand along the smooth stone floor. In the middle of the three center stones, the floor had a hole nine inches in diameter.

"We call this place the Channeller. It is our gateway. It's how we brought you and your family members here."

"How did you find it?"

"We didn't find it," Alan scoffed in such a way that Max knew he was lying. "We created it. The question you need to ask is: where did we discover the magic to make it work? Unfortunately, that is not your concern."

Max climbed to his feet as several cloaked figures entered the circle from the bridges across the lava. Each figure took up a position in front of one of the larger stone slabs forming the outer circle. The last figure entered the circle and approached Alan, carrying a large unusual hourglass. The figure passed the hourglass to Alan and went to the last open stone slab. Once in place they began to chant.

The hourglass, which was unlike any Max had ever seen, seemed to be responding to the chanting. Alan held the hourglass in front of him as it started to flash a rainbow of colors. It was a foot tall and a little over half that in width. The outer casing was made of ornately decorated gold symbols. Inside the glass were marble-sized balls with a hazy white appearance. The ghost-like spheres were the source of the colorful lights, and the chanting increased the brightness and intensity of their glow.

Alan stepped into the center of the stone archway and turned the hourglass upside down. The little lights started to tumble through the narrow strip of glass separating the top from the bottom, just like sand in an ordinary hourglass. Alan slid the device into the hole in the center of the floor. A bright white light filled the archway as Alan exited it to stand next to Max. The chanting was now loud and strong.

"Time to go," Alan said, as he handed Max his communicator. "Remember the consequences for disobedience."

Max took the communicator and dropped it into his pocket. "How will I contact you?"

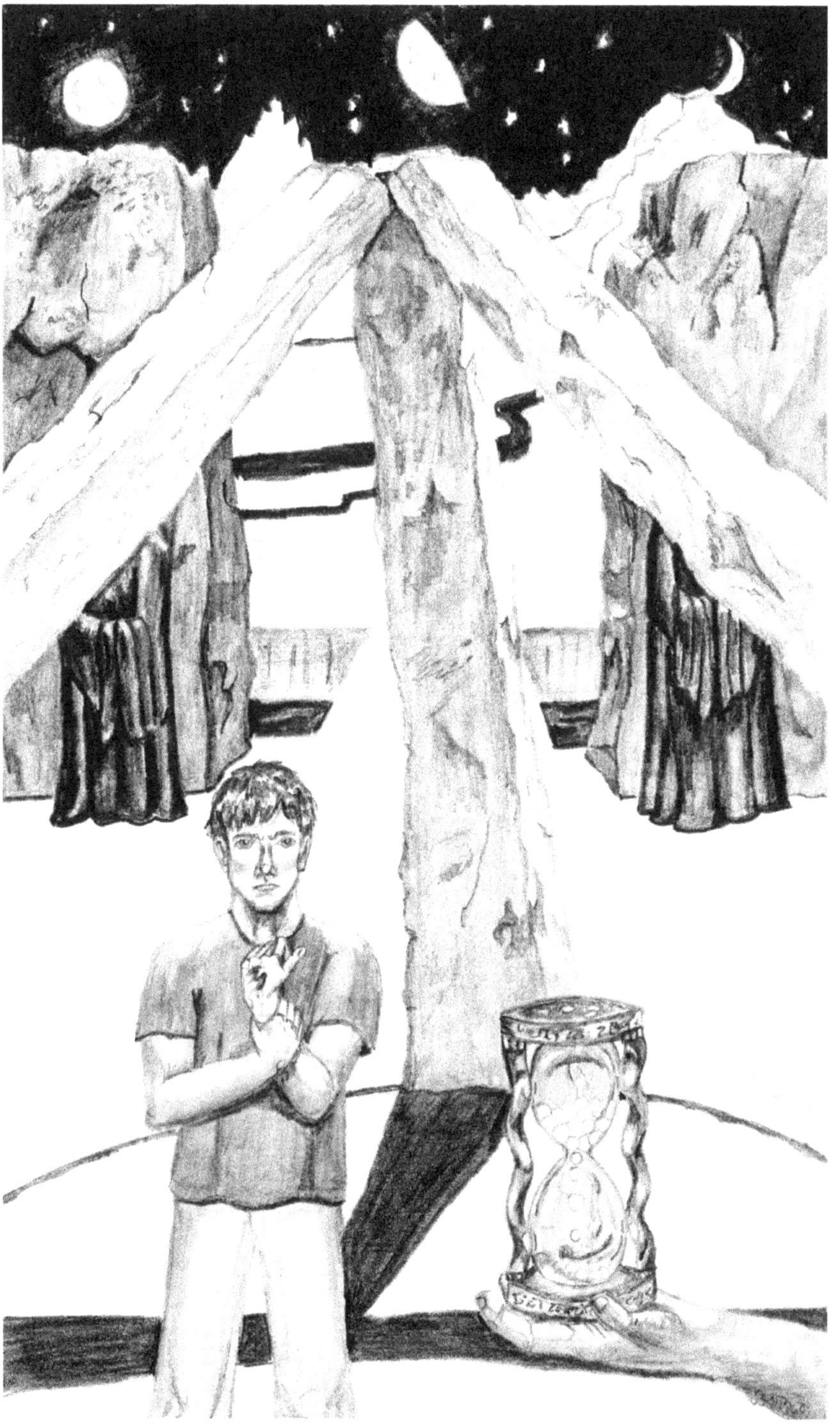

"Don't worry. We will contact you." Alan nodded towards the archway. "Remember, we have eyes everywhere."

Max stepped towards the archway. He took one last look at the man he hated more than any other, and then entered the gateway.

When Max disappeared, the cloaked figures stopped chanting, and the light in the archway faded. One of the figures approached Alan and lowered his hood to reveal his gargoyle-like features. "Is the plant in?"

"Yes," Alan said. He entered the archway and retrieved the hourglass.

"Are you sure they won't discover the spy's identity?"

"Yes, with all the people joining their cause in the last several months, they won't be able to figure it out." Alan handed the hourglass to the gargoyle.

"Everything is going as planned."

"Yes," Alan smiled.

6

A Message

Max exited the light to find himself in the guest bedroom of Uncle Frank's house. The sliver of light that stretched from the floor to the ceiling hovered in the air for a couple of seconds and then vanished. The alarm clock by the side of the bed glowed, 12:01 a.m.

Max took out his communicator and entered a message. He started to pace around the guest bedroom, impatiently awaiting his grandfather's reply. His pulse pounded in his temples and wounded hand with each step he made. The horrible damage to his hand, caused by the flare worm, induced agony every time he moved his fingers. With some effort, he discovered he was slowly regaining function.

The tension he felt subsided a tad when his grandfather replied that Yelka would be there within the hour.

I wonder how I'm going to get my aunt out of the house. He left his room and headed for Martin's. *I shouldn't have any trouble convincing Martin to leave.*

Max entered his cousin's room to find him sleeping in a fetal position. The covers were tightly tucked in around him as if to protect him from the monsters in his closet or under his bed. Max placed a hand on Martin's shoulder and gave it a gentle shake. "Martin, wake up."

Martin jerked away from Max with such force, Max flinched in surprise.

"What, who's there?" Martin sounded groggy and disoriented, but also fearful.

"It's me, Max."

"Max, what do you want?" Martin asked. Max could see Martin's eyes darting back and forth between him and the bedroom door. Even in the dark, Max could tell Martin was afraid of something.

"We're getting out of here."

"What do you mean?"

"I mean, we're leaving. You, me, and your mom."

"When? Where?"

"Tonight. We're going to my grandfather's house."

"How are we going to get there?"

"I'll explain later, but for now we need to figure out how to get your mom out of the house. You need to get up, now," Max stressed. He knew his cousin must be confused, but they didn't have time to waste.

Martin climbed out of bed and started to get dressed. While buttoning up his shirt, he noticed Max's wound. "What's wrong with your hand?" he asked, staring at Max's injury.

Max looked down to see that he was holding his injured hand close to his side protectively. "It's nothing. Just hurry." Max moved to the door to listen for anything out of the ordinary.

"What about my dad?" Martin whispered, as he joined Max by the door.

"You were right. The man in your house isn't your dad."

"How do you know that?"

"Because I saw your dad; he's with my mother. Look Martin, there's a lot of things going on right now, and I don't have time to explain it. You're going to have to trust me. First thing we need to do is to get your mom out of the house."

"Why?"

"Because, like you said, she isn't herself while she's in this place." Max opened the door, peeked out, and then waved Martin to follow him into the hall. Max slunk down the dark corridor, his eyes straining in the blackness. As they entered the front room, a horrible stench, like the smell of decaying flesh, caused Max to crinkle his nose. "Ahh, what is that?" Max's voice cracked, as he struggled to breathe.

Martin started coughing uncontrollably. "I don't know," he said as he pulled his shirt collar up over his face, covering his mouth.

"WHAT ARE YOU TWO BRATS DOING OUT OF BED?" Aunt Donna screamed, as she turned on the front room light and stormed in carrying a leather belt. "IF YOU AREN'T IN BED IN TWO SECONDS I'LL TURN YOUR HIND-ENDS BLACK AND BLUE." Max thought

Cruella de Vil had entered the room, seeing Aunt Donna with her blue bathrobe, pink fluffy slippers and curlers in her hair.

Martin's face looked like a melting snowman's in the hot sun as tears rolled down his checks. He crumbled to the floor and started to sob.

"I'LL GIVE YOU SOMETHING TO CRY ABOUT!" Donna raised the belt above her head as she advanced on them.

"*VSTANI*," Max yelled, with his hands extended towards her.

Aunt Donna froze like a bronze statue, and Martin went from a whimpering puddle of tears to a terrified animal. He started to shake and his eyes bulged like a giant bullfrog's as he stared at Max.

"Y-You k-killed my mother," Martin stammered.

"She's okay, trust me. She's not dead." Max held out his hand to help him off the floor, but Martin scrambled away, bumping his head on the end table. "Martin, I need you to help me get your mom outside, we only have a few minutes."

"I—I'm not going to help you do anything." Martin shook his head. "You're—you're not normal."

Max was desperate. Yelka would be here soon. The situation, along with the rotting compost smell burning his eyes and nose, made Max nauseated. "Martin, we need to get out of here," Max pleaded as he grabbed his aunt around the waist and began dragging her towards the front door.

"Leave my mother alone," Martin howled, and seized his mother's ankles, slowing Max's progress.

"Martin, you don't understand. I'm not going to hurt you or your mother. I'm trying to help you. We have to go, NOW!" Max struggled with his throbbing hand to drag Martin and his aunt towards the front door.

Martin acted terrified and clung to his mother like a newborn chimp. His behavior shocked Max. He had expected Martin to help him willingly, but now he was more of an obstacle. If he didn't convince Martin to help him in the next few minutes, he was going to have to use a spell on his cousin as well. "Martin, get up!" Max said it with such force Martin stopped crying and looked at him. "You were right about your dad, and the creature is going to come back. If he catches us here we're going to be in big trouble. Now, I need you to help me."

"Are you really my cousin?"

"Yes, I am!"

"What did you do to my mother?"

"I used magic. Now, help me get her outside before she regains control of her muscles." Max's eyes locked onto his aunt's. He could tell the spell was wearing off. He pulled his aunt towards the door with Martin trying to lift her feet off the floor. Although Martin assisted, his pale face and wide eyes showed he was still very frightened. Max wondered if he was only obeying because he was more terrified of his father's imposter than he was of Max.

They managed to get Aunt Donna out the front door and onto the porch before Max's spell wore off.

"What's going on?" Donna asked in a stern voice which was more pleasant than the one she used in the house.

"I don't have time to explain but we need to get out of here," Max tried to remain calm. "None of us are safe in your house."

"What are you talking about?" Donna asked. The lines of anger in her face changed to creases of concern. Martin continued to hold tight to his mother's bathrobe with eyes as big as saucers. "Is there a fire? Did you hear something?"

"You just have to trust me. If we stay here something bad is going to happen. My Grandpa Joe is coming to get us." Max could hear the desperation in his voice and hoped it would convince his aunt. He took her by the hand and led her and Martin out into the yard.

As they approached the main sidewalk, the impostor posing as Uncle Frank stepped out onto the porch. "What are you doing?" he asked in a concerned manner, as if seeing them outside at such a late hour surprised him.

Aunt Donna looked from Max to her husband. "I don't know, but Max insists that we aren't safe in the house."

"What are you talking about, darling? There's nothing wrong. We don't need to go anywhere. Come back into the house," the impostor continued his soft voice, as if he didn't have a clue why Max would leave with his wife and son.

Max's heart leapt into his throat. He was in complete shock. He expected some kind of resistance to the escape but he didn't think it would be his uncle's impersonator playing on the emotions of his aunt. Martin seemed to be the only one who wasn't fazed by his father's words, and held even tighter to his mother.

"Max, tell me what's going on?" Donna demanded, putting her hands on her hips.

"Honey, have I done something to upset you? You're not leaving me?" The impostor said with watery eyes, as he walked down the steps.

"Frank, I'm not leaving you. Max seems to think we're in some sort of danger."

Max felt as if he was falling into an endless nightmare. Just when he didn't think the scene could get any worse, Yelka showed up. She wore a long green cloak with her blond hair tied in a single braid. Everyone had a look of utter surprise as the short, tan elf-like woman jogged up the sidewalk towards them.

"Is everyone ready?" Yelka asked, as she reached them.

"Not quite," Max sighed.

"Who is that?" Martin asked, as his eyes locked on the strange little woman. The confused look on Donna's face indicated she wondered the same thing.

"Who's that with you, darling?" the impostor asked, moving towards them with an outstretched hand.

"Yelka, I need some help." Max pleaded.

Yelka gasped as she eyed the impostor approaching from the house.

"Donna, don't leave me. Come back in the house." The impostor had just about reached them.

"*Odkri*," Yelka said with her hands extended towards Frank. Suddenly, it wasn't Uncle Frank standing there. It was a reptilian creature with shiny, grey scales for skin and sharp hooked teeth. The averaged sized body of Uncle Frank became a body of solid muscle under the tiny armored plates. Even the fresh evening air changed, filled with a rancid smell of decaying carcasses. Clawed hands reached out towards Donna's throat as a forked tongue flicked across the creature's lips.

Donna screamed with terror as Martin clamped his arms around his mother's waist for protection.

Max yanked Donna and Martin away from Grd with such force that she avoided Grd's grasp. Yelka cast a second spell that threw Grd crashing into the front of the house.

"Come on! The gateway is just up the street." Yelka called to them.

Max continued pulling his aunt and cousin. "Aunt Donna, we have to get out of here. That thing will kill us!"

A roar echoed down the street, as Grd climbed to his feet. It appeared he no longer cared for his disguise as he ripped off his clothes to reveal a body of scaly armor. A long silver tail whipped around behind him as he shot forward with incredible speed.

"He's going to catch us," Max yelled to Yelka, who was leading the way.

The sight of the beast, plus its cry, was enough to frighten Donna and Martin into fleeing with Max. "Where's Frank? What is that thing?" Donna gasped, while sprinting behind Max.

Martin let out a high-pitched shriek as Grd closed the distance between them. Grd's arms went forward and he began running on all fours like a cheetah. The light of the street lamps flashed off his slick, silvery, body and reflected in his yellow eyes.

"*Premakni*," Max yelled, his hands extending towards the creature.

Grd collided with the spell with such force it was like he smashed into a brick wall. The spell rebounded, knocking Max and the others to the ground.

Yelka had a crystal in her hand, and it flashed a white light as she waved it in front of the gateway.

Donna's face was as pale as a sheet, and her hands trembled as she helped Martin off the ground. "Where did you learn that?"

"I'll explain at Grandpa's. First, let's get out of here."

"How? Where?" Donna asked.

"Follow Yelka!"

Max's spell seemed to have dazed Grd, who was staggering around and wagging his head from side to side. He hoped it would give them enough time to get through the gateway.

Yelka reached the gateway first, and waited for the others to join her. "Here! You have to step up to get through."

"Get through what?" Donna looked baffled.

"Max, you go first and help them through," Yelka ordered.

Max jumped into what looked like thin air and disappeared for a second before his head and upper body reappeared. He beckoned Aunt Donna and Martin to follow.

Grd charged again, as Max helped his aunt and cousin through the gateway. Yelka quickly threw out a wall of protective fire that stopped Grd's advance, before she entered the gateway herself and disappeared.

Donna and Martin looked like a couple of gazelles surrounded by lions as they huddled in the corner of the third floor at Grandpa's house. Their eyes were wide and they trembled from head to toe. Max saw how afraid they were, and recalled memories of last summer when he, too, had first encountered a fearsome creature bent on destroying him.

He remembered his first night and being marked with an evil curse by black-hooded strangers; his grandfather disappearing into that ball of light; and then later learning about magic and other worlds.

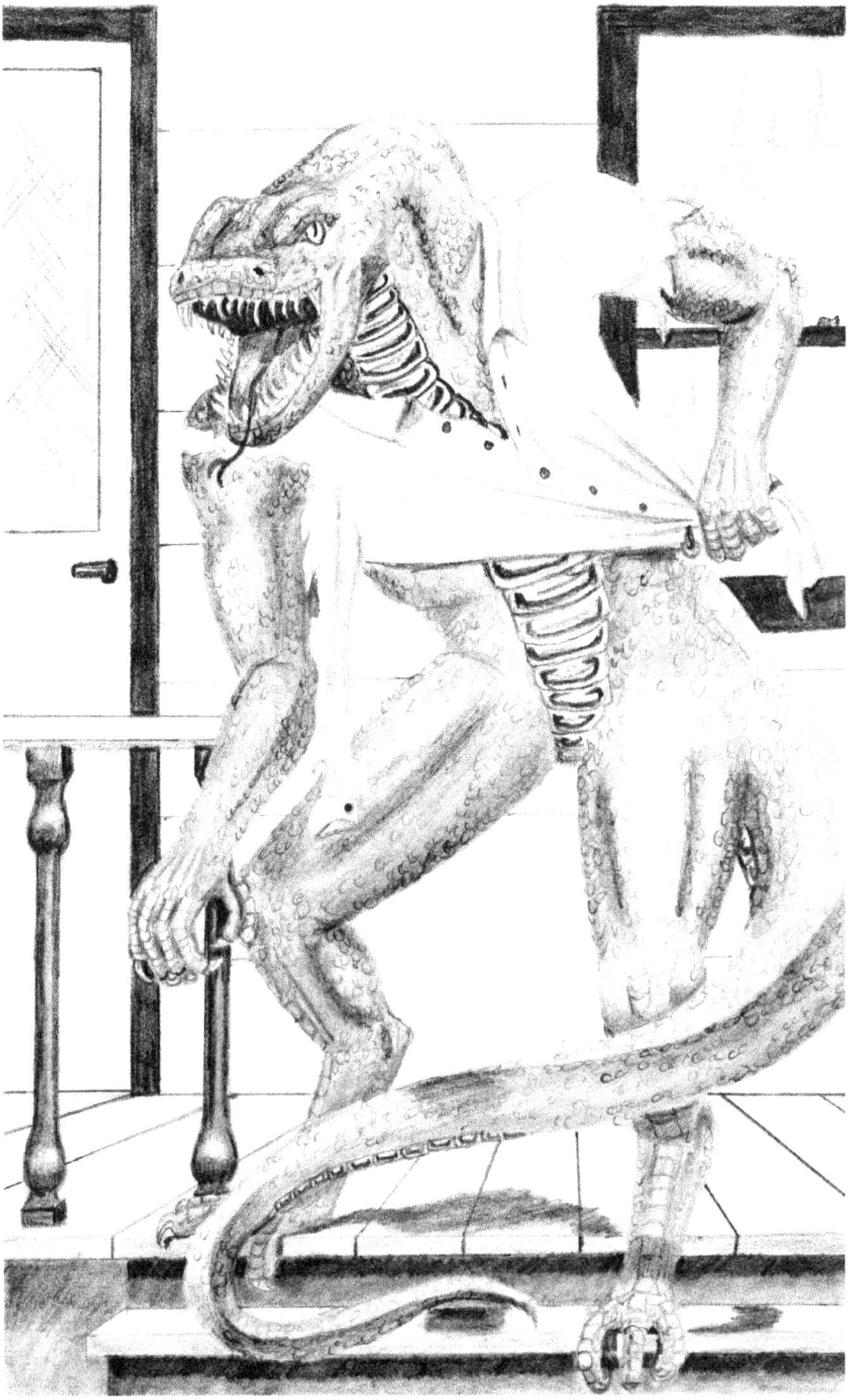

"I understand how you feel. I felt the same way last summer," Max tried to offer some comfort and sympathy to his aunt and cousin.

Grandpa and Yelka stood by the gateway control console discussing something in whispers.

"Max, what's going on?" A tear rolled down his aunt's pale face. Her hair was still in curlers, and everyone was extremely disheveled after their frantic flight from Grd.

"A lot of things are going on. The important thing is: we are safe right now."

"Hello, Mrs. Smith," Grandpa said, as he and Yelka approached. "I am Max's Grandpa Joe."

"Where are we?" Donna asked. Her arms wrapped protectively around Martin as they sat on the bare floor in the furthest corner of the room.

"You are in my house." Grandpa Joe smiled warmly. "You must have a lot of questions, and I think we would all be more comfortable downstairs with a nice mug of hot cocoa."

###

Surrounding the wooden table in the kitchen, Grandpa, Yelka, and Max tried their best to explain everything to Donna and Martin.

"I can tell you that Frank is alive. I have seen him," Max said. "But that thing at your house definitely wasn't your husband. I don't know how long it's been there, but I would guess at least a couple of months."

Max thought his aunt appeared a little more relaxed now that the initial shock had worn off. With everything she had seen in the last couple of hours, she seemed to believe what she was hearing. Martin, on the other hand, still seemed to be frightened. His chair was so close to his mother's that he was practically in her lap.

After answering many more questions, Grandpa said, "Mrs. Smith, Martin, you've been through a great deal tonight and it's getting late. You look exhausted. Why don't we call it a night and continue our conversation in the morning? You are perfectly safe here. Yelka, will you please show them to the guest bedroom we prepared for them? Max, I need a quick word."

"Of course, Joseph," Yelka said, getting to her feet. "This way, Mrs. Smith, Martin." Yelka ushered them down the hall and out of sight.

Once they were gone, Grandpa turned to Max. "Let me see your hand. I noticed it was wounded from the way you were holding it."

Max extended his arm across the table for his grandfather's inspection.

"How's the pain?"

"With everything that's happened, I kind of blocked it out. Now, it's really starting to hurt."

"I think Olik should have a look at it," Grandpa added, as he pulled out his communicator and typed in a message.

"I saw Mom," Max stammered, as tears filled his eyes; no longer able to hold back the sobs. Grandpa hugged him close, and Max couldn't remember much after that. It was as if he was floating through a dream. He knew Olik had shown up to look at his hand, and Grandpa escorted Max back to his room. Other than that, Max couldn't recall much of any conversation, except that Grandpa said they would talk in the morning. He lay on his bed and drifted off to sleep.

The sunlight woke Max late the next morning. He glanced at the alarm clock, which read 10:20 a.m. As he got out of bed to get dressed, something outside his bedroom window caused him to do a double take. Where there had once been a large field that separated Grandpa's house from the surrounding hills, now sat a sprawling new community. Several new roads and houses spanned the area. It looked like a couple more subdivisions were under construction.

"When did this happen?" he muttered to himself, and rubbed his fingers through his thick brown hair. The idea of being surrounded by the enemy twisted his insides like a rope. The image of an old castle besieged on all sides flashed before his eyes. For several moments he watched a crew of construction workers putting the roof on one of the buildings, then he headed downstairs.

As Max scuttled down the stairs, letting his feet fall on each step, he noticed a girl with chin-length blond hair dressed in baggy black clothing and a bright red beret. She leaned against the banister, picking at her black-painted fingernails.

"It's about time you got up," Cindy's familiar voice gave a sharp rebuke. "I've been waiting all day."

Max stopped in midstride as he recognized Cindy's blue eyes surrounded by heavy black eyeliner. "Cindy?"

"Uhhh, yes," Cindy said sarcastically, while tilting her head, her eyes widening. "Who else?"

"What's with the Goth look?"

Cindy pursed her lips, and the redness of her cheeks told Max he had asked the wrong question.

"And I might ask you what's with the bed head!"

This wasn't how Max had pictured his reunion with Cindy. She wasn't the same person he had left nine months ago. Grandpa had told him how she'd been shipped away to a boarding school to protect her from any influence or control by the enemy.

"So," Max changed the subject quickly, "when did you get back?"

"A couple of days ago." The tension in Cindy's face vanished. "Come on. Breakfast is waiting, and then I'm supposed to take you to some stupid council meeting."

"Council meeting?"

"That's what I said! You need me to repeat it?" Cindy rolled her eyes, but had a grin on her face. "Apparently, a lot has happened in this town since we've been gone. You probably noticed all the new houses."

"Yeah, I saw them from my window this morning."

"Well, I guess we aren't as alone in this fight as we thought. All those new people are on our side."

Max took a breath. "That's a relief. I thought we wouldn't be able to make a move in any direction without being hounded." His earlier anxiety subsided a little. "Where are my aunt and cousin?"

"They're already at the meeting place. Grandpa asked me to wait around for you."

"I suppose you heard about my mother?" Max asked, as he descended the rest of the stairs. Even with her new dark look, Max found Cindy as pretty as ever.

"Yes," Cindy flashed a sad, apologetic smile. "It's awful." She put a comforting hand briefly on his shoulder. "Let's get something to eat and get going." Cindy motioned towards the kitchen.

###

After breakfast Cindy led Max to the new school building. A small gathering of kids played basketball on the outdoor court in the playground. They stopped and watched as Max and Cindy entered the front door of the school.

"Who are they?"

"Kids," Cindy said. "Kids on our side."

"At least we won't have to play by ourselves all summer."

"Yeah. How great will *that* be?" muttered Cindy sarcastically.

Cindy ushered Max into the cafeteria where the lunch tables had been folded and stacked against the wall. Several rows of occupied chairs faced Grandpa, who stood at the front. Cindy and Max came in at the back of the room. Martin and Aunt Donna sat to the side while Grandpa Joe spoke to the group.

"Max," Grandpa said, as his eyes fell on Max and Cindy. Everyone in the room turned to look at them as they stood in the back of the room.

Max felt a little uncomfortable being in this group of strangers. There must have been at least forty people in attendance and every one of them stared at him. Cindy edged over to a wall and leaned against it in a no-big-deal manner. She even pulled out a cell phone and began sending a text message to someone.

"Max, I want you to come up here and tell everyone what has been happening." Grandpa waved him to the front of the room.

Max's heart pushed its way up into his throat. Alan warned him he would be watched, and now who knows how many traitors occupied the room. Any one of them could be a spy for the enemy. Marko's betrayal jumped to the front of his mind. If Marko had been his friend and then betrayed him, how easy would it be for one of these people to be one of the enemy?

"Grandpa," Max cleared his throat. "May I speak to you out in the hall for a moment?"

"Certainly," Grandpa smiled cheerfully. "We'll just be a moment," he reassured the group.

Max exited the cafeteria, and Grandpa joined him a moment later. He waited for the door to shut before he began. "Grandpa, I kind of hoped we could discuss things in private first. I mean, I don't know any of these people. Are you sure you can trust them?"

"Max, I know you have been through a lot, but these people are here to help."

"I was just thinking about Marko." Max swallowed and looked at the floor.

"Listen, just give them an overview. You don't have to tell them anything you don't want to. I trust these people. They all want to know about the enemy's gateway. They all know that's how your mom was taken. Just tell them what you know about that."

Max let out a sigh. "I guess that would be all right."

"Good." Grandpa patted him gently on the back and escorted him back into the cafeteria.

Max found talking about the enemy's gateway easier than he had pictured. He told them about the day they took his mother and then meeting Alan at his aunt's house. The pain on his aunt's face, when he mentioned his uncle, was difficult for Max to watch. He couldn't imagine what she was thinking after watching the man she thought was her husband turn into a horrible creature. He wished to give her some hope so he told them about Zemlje, the world where his mother and uncle remained prisoners. Max still didn't think that was where they really were, because it was Alan who had said it.

Max didn't want this to turn into a question and answer session but that's what happened. The people continued to query Max until he had told them everything he could remember about the enemy's gateway.

After he finished, he felt anxious, as if he had done something wrong. He hadn't planned to tell them as much as he did, but it seemed to help his aunt. Max was sure the knowledge about her husband being alive had lifted her spirits. Even Martin seemed to be coping better. He was no longer clinging to his mother like a baby koala bear, and his eyes no longer held the fear they had the night before. Perhaps just being out of his parents' house made a difference.

"Can I go now?" Max asked his grandfather, as the crowd of people began breaking off into small groups to discuss the latest information.

"Yes, why don't you take your aunt and Martin back with you?" Grandpa pulled Max closer. "I think they're beginning to understand," he whispered in Max's ear.

Max moved to his aunt, who gave him a hug. "I would never have guessed," she said.

"I just knew something was wrong." Martin's speech was low. "Do you think we can get my dad and your mom back?"

"I think so." Max tried to give his cousin some comfort. Deep down, his stomach was a storm of doubt. He felt that at any moment it could drown him. "Let's go home."

They passed Cindy, who hadn't looked up from her cell phone the entire time. "Are you coming?"

Cindy finished typing in a message and placed the phone in her pocket. "Whatever."

Max didn't respond. This wasn't the Cindy he remembered, and he missed the old Cindy something fierce. He needed someone to talk to, but he didn't think he could share anything with the new Cindy.

They walked home in silence. Max wondered how much his aunt and cousin had learned before he had arrived at the school.

As they entered the front gate, he spotted Larry and his gang riding their bikes towards them. The absolute last person he wanted to see today was Larry, Alan's son, who also happened to be the town bully. Max had his fill of Larry, and his gang of rabble, the previous summer. It wasn't just the ordinary group of misfits. There was a new member, but not one Max would have expected. It was a girl.

Not only was she female, but she also had bright pink hair. She appeared to be Max and Cindy's age. The snarl on her face and her narrow smoke-colored eyes suggested she was as mean as Larry.

"Hey twerp," Larry called, as he stopped his bike on the other side of the fence.

"Don't mess with me, Larry," Max threatened. "You'll only wind up with another broken nose."

Cindy snorted at this remark.

"What are you laughing at, Cindy? Oh, and, nice clothes. Where did you get those? Did you steal them off a corpse down at the mortuary?"

A roar of laughter filled the street.

"My clothes aren't half as bad as bubble-gum top over there." Cindy pointed to the girl with the pink hair.

The new girl dropped her bike and headed towards the fence.

"No." Larry grabbed her by the arms to hold her back. "We'll deal with them another time."

Cindy started towards the gate but Max blocked her way. "What do you want, Larry?" he asked.

"I brought you a little present," Larry smiled his same old evil grin. "You were warned that we would be watching you and my dad thinks you talked a little too much about things you shouldn't have."

Max's heart started to race and he felt dizzy. *How could they know? How could they know so fast?*

Larry pulled something black out of his pocket and threw it over the fence. "This is a warning," he shouted out, before he and his gang hopped quickly onto their bikes and pedaled away.

"I'll see YOU later," the pink haired girl snarled at Cindy, as she followed after the others.

"Come on, Jo," Larry called over his shoulder.

"Jo," Max and Cindy crinkled their noses.

"That freak has the same name as my grandpa." Max said, as he eyed the object on the ground.

"What is it?" Martin asked, as Cindy picked it up.

"It's someone's hair," Cindy said holding out a large bundle of black hair tied together with a red bow.

"It's my mother's," Max gasped.

7

Cindy's Showdown

Max lay on his bed, staring up at the ceiling. He held the smooth lock of his mother's hair in his hand, rubbing it between his thumb and forefinger. It felt like a giant weight sat on his chest, squishing him into the mattress. The pressure of the situation was more than he thought he could withstand. *Who is the traitor?*

It could have been anyone in the room, except Grandpa, his aunt, Martin, Cindy.... *Or could it be Cindy? She seemed to be texting someone the entire meeting. Who was she texting? Could it have been the enemy? Maybe that isn't even Cindy.*

Max made a mental note. He would have to pay attention the next time Cindy entered the front gate at his grandfather's house. He knew that with the gate closed, a spell protected his grandfather's property, keeping the enemy out. If Cindy wasn't "the real" Cindy, she wouldn't be able to pass through the gate unless it was opened for her.

A knock at the door startled him out of his thoughts.

"Who is it?"

"Cindy."

"What do you *want*?" He said it with a little more edge to his voice than he had intended. He couldn't help feeling that somehow Cindy was involved.

"To see how you're doing?" Cindy shot back with annoyance.

"I'm fine," he retorted. "I'll be down in a minute."

"Okay." A dejected tone replaced the annoyed one.

Max waited until he could no longer hear her in the hall. He got out of bed and went to the window. He wondered how many people in this town were really on their side. Last year it had only been his grandfather, Cindy, and himself. The traitor could be anyone.

He went downstairs to find Cindy sitting on the sofa in the front room.

"I'm sorry about your mom," Cindy said, staring out the front window. "You haven't had a good summer so far."

"That's an understatement. Where are my aunt and cousin?"

"I think they're in the kitchen eating lunch. I expect their summer is worse than yours."

"How can theirs be worse than mine?"

"Well, at least you know what's happening in the world. This is all new to them."

"We went through the same thing last summer!" Max could feel blood pumping to his face.

"No, we didn't. We didn't have a relative kidnapped. We didn't see a family member turn into a monster before we knew what was happening," Cindy snapped back. "We had a couple of surprises but not like that!"

"I guess you're right," Max sighed. "So, is Grandpa back from the meeting?"

"Nope."

Max decided to act as normal as possible around Cindy, until he could determine whether or not she was the traitor. He didn't plan to take his eyes off her.

"Have you met any of the new kids?" he asked.

"Not really. We've been trying to figure out how to get you back."

"Do you want to go and meet some of them?"

"Why?" Cindy took out her cell phone and started to send a message.

"Who are you talking to?"

"What are you, my mother?" Cindy raised her eyebrows as if to say: none of your business.

"No, but. . ."

"But what?"

"Nothing." Max dropped the subject for now. "I'm going to see if Martin wants to go outside for a while. I think he's still rattled by what's happened." As Max walked towards the kitchen, it dawned on him he had something else to figure out. The key. Where was the key to Hudich's collar? He had to find it to save his mother. He needed a plan on how to search for it without anyone noticing. To know where it was would be to his advantage, even if he didn't give it to Alan.

Another thought brought Max even lower than he already was. What lies would he have to tell his Grandpa to protect his mother? He didn't know if he could handle any more pressure than he was under now. The only people who probably felt worse than he did were his aunt and cousin.

It took Max more than a week of coaxing, with the help of his aunt, to convince Martin a little fresh air would be good for him. Martin followed alongside Max and Cindy as they navigated the new neighborhoods. Max noticed that Martin hadn't lifted his eyes above ground level since they left Grandpa's house.

"How long have you been able to do magic?" Martin's voice was almost a whisper.

"About a year," Max answered, as he watched Martin slowly lift his head. Out of the corner of his eye he could see Cindy looking off in another direction, staring at the house they were passing. She didn't seem interested in being with them. They hadn't gotten along very well over the past week, and Max's suspicions about her continued to grow.

"Did you learn magic from your grandpa?"

"Yes and no. I, I mean we," Max shot a quick glance to see Cindy finally looking at him, "learned it from Yelka, the short woman who helped us escape from your house. She and Grandpa made us practice all the time."

"Do you think I can learn?"

"Since you know about the war, I think it's probably a good thing."

"What did Larry mean last week by 'you were warned' and that you were being watched?' Cindy asked, staring pointedly in the opposite direction.

The question landed like a slap to the face. The last thing Max wanted to talk about was what had happened between him and the enemy. His distrust of Cindy, and the fact that his cousin was with them, made it less than ideal to discuss anything that could get his mother or uncle injured. *Oh, Mother! What am I to do?*

"Are they holding your mother hostage?" Cindy continued, in an unconcerned manner.

"I don't want to talk about it." Max spat. He said it with such force that Cindy met his gaze. For a second, she looked hurt, like the Cindy from last summer, but then a cold expression crossed her face.

"Fine!" Cindy turned and began marching up the street. She whipped out her cell phone and started texting again.

Yeah! Tell them I didn't say anything. Max's blood pumped with such force his temples twitched. His best friend Cindy was a traitor. She held the life of his mother in her hands!

"What's wrong?" Martin asked, hustling to keep up with Max as he stalked after Cindy.

"Nothing," Max tried to sound casual, but knew he wasn't doing a very good job.

They turned onto a side street to see Grandpa marching at a crisp pace, heading straight for them. Cindy was so busy texting she almost collided with him when he stopped just in front of her.

"Grandpa," she squawked, and stumbled backward to avoid hitting him. "Sorry, I didn't see you."

"No problem." He smiled. "I can see you were absorbed with your cell phone."

"Ummm-yeah." Cindy blushed a little, like she had been caught doing something she shouldn't.

"Cindy, I wonder if you would do me a favor. Would you show Martin around while I speak with Max for a few minutes?"

"Sure, Grandpa. Come on Martin." Cindy looked at Martin and nodded for him to follow.

"It's okay, Martin," Grandpa added.

Returning to Grandpa's house, Max sat on one side of a small table Grandpa had brought up to the third floor. Grandpa and Yelka occupied seats facing him. Aside from the table, the room looked just as it had last summer. The five metallic stands surrounded the control panel and the antique-looking mirror that was the gateway. Boards covered every window, keeping unwanted eyes from peeking in.

"Well, Max, you've had a busy start to your summer," Grandpa said, concern on his face. "I've given you a little time to cope with the situation. Now, what can you tell us?"

Max glanced back and forth between Grandpa and Yelka. They looked very worried. *What can I tell them without endangering my mom?* "Where to start?" Max took a deep breath.

"We know you are being watched," Yelka spoke up. "And with that little incident last week, with the lock of hair, someone is not who they say they are. Believe me, nothing you say here will go beyond this room."

"I know," Max said. *Can I be sure? With all these new people, things are bound to get out.*

"What do they want?" Grandpa leaned closer, his eyes intense.

"Th-they haven't told me yet." Max lied, but he was sure his grandfather could read it on his face. "They said they would be in touch with instructions. I'm supposed to do something for them." Max's stomach launched once again into back flips, he felt lightheaded and was afraid he might throw up. He hated deceiving his grandfather, but he couldn't risk his mother's life.

"They're probably testing you, to see if you will do what they want," Yelka piped in. "They may ask you to do a couple of small things first, but then, with your mother as leverage, you can be sure they want something big."

"Well, I'm not to talk too much about them. They didn't like what I said at the school last week."

"I promise you, Max. Anything said here, stays here," Grandpa said, with Yelka nodding in agreement.

Max tried to steady his nerves. *How much do I tell them?* "What else do you want to know?"

"Tell me, again, everything about their gateway."

"I wouldn't call it a gateway, exactly. It is more like a tear or a rip into another world."

"How do they operate it?" Yelka asked.

"Is it a machine?" Grandpa questioned, his eyebrows pointed upward in a curious matter.

"No, it wasn't a machine. It didn't use electricity. It used magic."

"It would take a lot of magical power to be able to move objects permanently," Yelka said.

"Max, tell us what you know about it," Grandpa urged. Max could see both concern and curiosity in his eyes.

Max described the enemy's gateway to the best of his ability. He talked about the rough stone arch with its three adjoining pillars, the group of robed chanters, the flat, bowl-like stone platform, and the hourglass with its rainbow colored lights that seemed to respond to the incantation.

"How did they discover such a place?" Yelka asked.

"Not only that, but the magic to operate it. That isn't something you would find without help."

"You think someone told them about it?" Max asked.

"I'm not sure, but I don't think it is something they just happened to stumble into. With all of the elements needed to make it work, it seems nearly impossible to discover by luck." Grandpa rubbed his chin and stared at nothing in particular. "You say they turned the hourglass upside down and inserted it into the floor just under the archway before it worked?"

"Yes."

"What are you thinking, Joseph?"

"I'm thinking that something must have recently happened that allowed them to discover this gateway."

"But what?" Yelka asked.

"Hudich is no longer in Pekel," Max suggested.

"Brilliant! That has to be it! Hudich is able to discuss plans with his followers. Either he knew about this gateway before we trapped him in Pekel, or he somehow discovered it in Pekel. I have a strange feeling it is the latter. His followers would certainly have known about it if Hudich had already been aware of it before his exile."

"What if whoever invented that gateway had traveled to Pekel and met Hudich?" Yelka offered.

"That seems like a possibility."

"How can we be sure?" Yelka asked.

"I think there is only one way to find out. And that is with a trip into Pekel and back into the Trogs' castle where Hudich used to live."

"It's too dangerous!" Yelka interjected.

"Yes, but it may be the only way to figure out how they got their gateway and the answer to destroying it. I'm hoping that they don't fully understand how it works and can't duplicate it."

"I want to go with you," Max said.

"I don't think that will be possible," Grandpa frowned.

"Why not? I'm supposed to be your replacement. Right? How am I going to learn about these places if I don't go?"

"He's got a point." Grandpa looked at Yelka, as if seeking her approval.

"Max, how is your magic coming along?" Yelka asked. "Have you been practicing like you said you would?"

"Yes! I have been, and I've made progress."

"I'll be the judge of that." Yelka seemed to have a look in her eyes that doubted Max had progressed as much as she wanted.

"*Izginem se*," Max called, and vanished before Grandpa and Yelka's eyes. Yelka gave an audible gasp, and Max could tell they were both surprised and impressed.

"*Prikazi se*," Max said, and reappeared.

"You *have* been practicing," Yelka beamed at him with her wide blue eyes.

"You see? I'm serious. If I am going to be the gatekeeper one day, I think I need to know everything," Max said. "I need to know things like Hudich's movements. Is the collar still in place? Where is the key and is it safe? Are we keeping an eye on him?" Max hoped they wouldn't see him hold his breath. He wanted them to think this was all part of preparing to take his grandfather's place and not that he was following Alan's orders.

"We are definitely keeping tabs on Hudich. The collar is still securely around his neck. And the key is safe and sound. You should know everything, and you will, but in time." Grandpa informed him.

"Why not now?" Max almost pleaded. He still hadn't heard the most important piece of news that concerned his mother. *Where was that key?*

###

Cindy and Martin strolled down the street towards the new school. Cindy had just put her phone in her pocket when she noticed Martin staring at her.

"What?"

"Can you do magic?" Martin asked.

"Yeah, a little."

"As good as Max?"

"Probably not. I didn't have much time to practice during the school year. I had to live in a dorm where people would have seen me. I'll bet Max practiced every day."

"Have you been practicing since you got back here?"

"Yes, Yelka has been giving me lessons. So, it's coming back."

"Do you think she'll teach me?"

"I'm not sure. There is a person in the new neighborhood that teaches all the kids. You might be taught with them."

As they passed the school, Cindy decided to head back towards Grandpa's house. They went down a new street where the owners hadn't yet finished landscaping their yards. The grass still had that checkerboard look where new sod had been laid. The trees were small and surrounded by stakes and rope to give them support.

"Are you mad at Max?" Martin asked, as Grandpa's house came into view.

"No!"

"Then how come you both act like you're mad at each other?"

"Max might be mad at me, but I'm not mad at him," Cindy huffed, her voice going up an octave. "I mean, what makes you think I'm mad? Just because Max stayed with his mother all school year, and I ended up being sent to a boarding school, why would I be mad?"

Martin stared at Cindy with his mouth agape and eyes like saucers. Cindy felt her face flush red with embarrassment as she realized she had raised her voice and let her true feelings out.

"Sorry," she added, and looked away.

"Hey, Cindy," called a voice from the street in front of Grandpa's house.

Jo, the girl with the bright pink hair, approached on her bicycle, followed by Larry and his group of troublemakers. Her eyes locked on Cindy as she drew near.

"What do you want, *Pinky*?" Cindy asked.

Jo stopped her bike a foot away from Cindy, with Larry and the others right behind her. "I want to see how tough you are when you're not hiding behind that fence." She nodded in the direction of Grandpa's house.

Martin stepped behind Cindy.

"It looks like your new boyfriend is an improvement over Max," Larry laughed, and the others joined in.

"He's not my boyfriend, catcher's mitt!" Cindy snapped.

This remark, a reference to when Max had broken Larry's nose a year ago, caused Larry's face to boil with anger. "Thump her, Jo!"

"Yeah Jo, kick her @#!" the others shouted and cheered.

"What about it, Cindy? Want a lesson from your superiors?" Jo asked, ruffling her thick pink hair.

Cindy snorted right in Jo's face. "Superiors? You can't mean you, *Pinky*!"

Jo's eyebrows became one sharp line as her brow furrowed in rage. Her reddened face made her look like a deranged clown with pink hair. "You wouldn't stand a chance, Cindy!"

"Don't worry, Cindy, we'll take good care of your little boyfriend while Jo drops you," Larry laughed.

Cindy could feel Martin shake as he cowered behind her. She threw quick glances in the direction of Grandpa's and her house to see if anyone had noticed what was happening.

"Oh, looking for a way to back out?" Jo said, in a whiny, mocking voice. "Are you scared, Cindy?" Jo laughed. Not an ordinary laugh. It was a hysterical cackle on the verge of madness that spewed from her mouth. "Do you need your mommy?"

"No," Cindy barked as a rush of adrenaline pumped through her veins causing all the little hairs on her body to stand on end. "I'm just making sure no one will be around to stop me from kicking your face in."

"Cindy," Martin tugged at the back of her shirt. "I want to go home."

"Is Cindy's new boyfriend afraid? Is he going to cry?" Larry rubbed his eyes with balled up fists, pretending to cry. He and his entire gang roared with laughter.

"Martin, you can go home," Cindy said.

"No, he can't!" Larry rode his bike around behind Cindy and Martin to trap him. A couple of the other boys blocked them on the sides. "We wouldn't want him going home and telling Max and that crazy old man."

"If we do it right here in the street, somebody is bound to see us," Jo snarled, her narrowed eyes boring into Cindy's.

"Cindy, I really want to go. Please, let me go." Martin said, with tears pooling up in his eyes.

"Where can we go?" Jo asked, ignoring Martin's plea.

"How about the sandlot field?" one of the boys suggested.

"Yeah," Larry agreed. "How about it, Cindy? Are you willing to take that mouth of yours out of your little protective community to get your hiney kicked?"

"Cindy," Martin whimpered.

"Look, little boy." Larry loomed over Martin. "You're not going home, so quit crying or I'll knock your teeth out."

"I'll only go to the sandlot on one condition," Cindy said.

"What's that?" Jo tried to intimidate Cindy by getting right in her face.

"You have to promise to leave Martin alone."

Larry and his friends exchange confused glances. They looked as if someone had just broken their crayons.

"Well," Cindy asked impatiently, folding her arms across her chest.

"Okay. Okay. We won't touch him," Larry said. "Be at the sandlot field in ten minutes or it will be open season on you and your little friend."

Jo stared Cindy down for a couple more seconds before getting on her bike.

"Come on," Larry ordered, as he led the group away.

"Cindy, we should go home," Martin urged.

"No, I need to teach that little girl a lesson."

"It's not going to be a fair fight. There are a lot of them and only one of you," Martin pointed out.

Cindy took out her phone and typed in a number. She handed the phone to Martin. "If anything goes wrong or you're in trouble, just hit the send button. It's programmed for Grandpa's house."

"Please, don't do it."

"Come on. It's going to be all right."

Cindy hurried past Grandpa's house and then her own, glancing at each, hoping no one would see them. As they entered the enemy's side of town, people watched as they made their way to the field. Something in their looks gave off an oppressive feeling as if the air wasn't clean to breathe. For the first time in a long time, she was worried. Her mouth was dry and her palms wet. Maybe *Martin's right. This could be a trap.*

Martin seemed more frightened than ever. He was visibly trembling, as if he expected something to attack them at any moment.

Relax. You've been in fights before. She took a slow, deep, calming breath as the sandlot field gradually came into view. Larry, Jo and the rest of the gang huddled together in the center of the field.

"If it looks like I'm in serious trouble, call Max," Cindy whispered out of the side of her mouth.

"Can I call now?" Martin pleaded.

"No! I can take her with one arm, if magic isn't involved," Cindy smiled, even though her insides squirmed with anxiety. It felt as if someone was playing tug of war inside her stomach. *How did I get myself into this?* As they reached the field, Cindy instructed Martin to wait by the road.

Jo, Larry, and the others were like a den of hungry lions as they watched her approach. There was nothing but hate and loathing in their eyes.

Cindy stopped a few yards out into the field, keeping her distance from the entire group. *No turning back now.*

"Stand back guys, while I teach this skank a lesson!"

"Go get her, babe," Larry said.

"Babe," Cindy laughed. "She's your girlfriend? Wow!"

"Okay, witch!" Jo growled, as she raced towards Cindy. With her pink hair flying and her bloodshot eyes, she looked to be on the verge of insanity.

Cindy cocked back to throw a well-aimed punch, but before she was in reach, Jo uttered something strange and disappeared. Another unfamiliar word rang out which launched Cindy through the air. She landed flat on her back on the hard ground of the sandlot, with the wind knocked out of her. She could only lay there struggling to breathe, when several blows landed in her stomach causing her knees to jerk into a fetal position. A hard crack to her face brought a fountain of blood flowing from her nose and upper lip.

"Not so tough now, are we?" a bodiless voice spoke from somewhere behind her, followed by laughter. Cheers from Larry and his gang filled the sandlot field.

I'm going to get killed if I remain still!

Another kick to the gut reveled Jo's location. Cindy rolled as fast as she could in the direction of the blow. Her plan worked and she collided with Jo's legs knocking her to the ground. Cindy scrambled on top and started punching as hard and as fast as she could. Jo kicked and screamed as Cindy's blows made contact with her face.

Cindy's aggressiveness caused Jo's invisibility spell to fade. "Take that, you little pink freak!" Cindy landed another punch to the chin that made Jo cry out.

Something hard hit Cindy in the chest and threw her off Jo. She searched for her new attacker. Larry stood in front of his gang with his arms extended. Jo lay on the ground, crying. As Cindy struggled to stand, another spell flattened her again. The second she hit the ground pain erupted all over her body. She screamed under its intensity. She could see Larry and his gang laughing as they stood over her.

"Call this payback for breaking my nose," Larry sputtered.

He uttered another strange word. Cindy thought a truck had parked on her chest. She squirmed on the ground to free herself from the weight pressing down on her, once again stealing her newly regained breath. No matter what she did, she couldn't release herself. Everything was turning black. Just before she lost consciousness, she saw a bright flash of light that seemed strangely familiar.

8

Ell's Perception

"You mean she's been texting herself?" The hushed voice of Mrs. Carlson reached Max's ears from the hall. He sat next to Cindy's bed, feeling as if he were drowning. Nothing had gone right this summer and he wondered if anything would. At least Cindy wasn't a spy, which meant his best friend hadn't betrayed him.

Cindy had been asleep since he and Grandpa brought her home. If Martin hadn't called she might be dead. Her swollen face resembled a small pumpkin. It looked like she had been in a car wreck without her seat belt and collided with the front windshield. She whimpered and thrashed under her covers, startling Max.

He reached under the covers and took her hand. Several cuts and scrapes made her hand rough and puffy. "I'm sorry," he whispered.

"Sorry about what?" Mrs. Carlson asked as she entered the room.

Max's face grew warm and his cheeks turned blotchy. "I haven't been all that nice to her lately." Max lowered his head.

"I think you've both had a couple of hard weeks."

"I've only had a couple of weeks, Cindy's had about nine months."

"Well, with the new neighbors, she won't have to go back to that school." Mrs. Carlson gave him a quick smile. She took a damp cloth and gently patted the cuts on Cindy's face.

"Can I ask you something?" Max ventured.

"Of course."

"Cindy hasn't been texting anyone but herself?"

"Yes, apparently her father knew about it from the bills he's received but didn't tell anyone. He thought it would hurt her feelings. She was trying so hard to put on this tough exterior; he thought he would cut her some slack because of being sent away to school."

"She is tough."

"What do you mean?"

"That Jo girl didn't walk away unharmed. She looked as bad as Cindy did. I wasn't there, but from what Martin saw, she didn't let them get the better of her."

"She did let them get the better of her ego. She should have never gone to that field with only Martin. She put both their lives at risk."

"Martin said she didn't agree to go until they promised to leave him alone."

Mrs. Carlson sighed and gazed down at her daughter. "A noble gesture, but she shouldn't have trusted them in the first place. Once she was out of commission, what was to stop them from attacking Martin?"

Max didn't care what Mrs. Carlson said, he was proud of Cindy for at least beating that pink-haired freak to a pulp. *If only she could have broken Larry's nose again.*

"What are you smiling at?" Cindy asked in a harsh whisper.

"Cindy," Max jumped at the sound of her voice and released her hand.

"What are you smiling at? And what happened?"

"Max and his grandfather rescued you from being killed," Mrs. Carlson said sternly. "Why did you meet those kids with only Martin?"

"Sorry!"

"You better be, young lady. You'll be lucky if I let you out of the house the rest of the summer. We were so worried! I'm going to get you some Tylenol."

Cindy winced as she tried to sit up then collapsed back into bed.

"What were you smiling at?" Cindy asked again after Mrs. Carlson had left the room.

"I was just imagining how funny it would have been if you would have broken Larry's nose again."

Cindy didn't seem to find that thought as amusing as Max. "How did I get out of that mess?"

"Martin used your cell to call Grandpa. Grandpa cast some spell that sent Larry and his gang running for cover."

"I wondered what that flash of light was."

"That was Grandpa. We arrived to see that Larry had you pinned to the ground with a spell. You were struggling to catch your breath."

"It felt like I had a house sitting on my chest."

Grandpa entered the room, followed by Mrs. Carlson and Yelka.

"How are you feeling?" Grandpa asked with a smile.

"Sore." Cindy struggled to sit up. Her face twisted in a grimace as she managed to arrange the pillows and lean back in a more comfortable position. "And what are you smiling at?" Cindy continued portraying the attitude she had been putting on the last couple of weeks.

"I was just thinking of how well you and Max fit each other's personalities. Neither of you backs down when faced with trouble. A quality I greatly admire."

Cindy was clearly holding back a smile as the corners of her mouth twitched a little. "What do you guys want?" The hard edge returned.

Grandpa, Yelka, and Mrs. Carlson exchanged glances, and Grandpa coughed slightly. "Well, we want to straighten a few things out," Grandpa said.

"Like what?"

Max was puzzled. Everyone seemed to be in on the news except for Cindy and him. All of them stared at Cindy, ignoring Max's gaze.

"We want you to drop the act," Mrs. Carlson answered.

"What act?" Cindy's tone grew colder.

"The one that could interfere with what needs to be done this summer," Mrs. Carlson responded. "Max's mother is in real danger. The enemy has somehow developed a gateway. We need to figure out how to fix these situations, which means all of us are going to have to work together."

"Cindy, I need your help," Max said softly.

"You know you can count on me," Cindy said. Little puddles of water formed along the bottom of her eyelids as she locked eyes with Max.

"I know," Max answered.

"Now that that's settled, we need to get moving on a plan," Grandpa said.

"Like what?" Max asked.

"First, we need to start your training again. There are new spells to learn, science and math to study, and you need to practice your self-defense. Second, we need to start working on how to destroy the enemy's gateway and rescue Max's mother and uncle. Third, we need you to get integrated with this new community."

"Why do we need to get integrated?" Max asked.

"Max, one day you will control the gateway, and you'll need all the help you can get. The war is spreading and reaching into more places. These people will need a leader," Yelka said.

"Leader?" Max swallowed the lump in his throat. Just contemplating Alan's orders made his nausea return. *How can someone who is about to betray them, lead them?*

"I have confidence in you, Max," Grandpa said. Max thought for sure his Grandpa could read his mind at that moment. His eyes had a questioning look that suggested he knew Max was hiding something.

###

A couple of days later, Max sat in a classroom in the new school with Martin and fourteen other kids. The other students ranged from ages eight to seventeen, with nine girls and five boys, not counting Max and Martin. The teacher, Mrs. Ryan, was a tall red-haired thin woman in her late forties. Max and Martin occupied seats at the very back of the class, listening to the teacher discuss a spell to reveal an enemy.

Martin seemed glued to the lesson, his eyes focused intently on the teacher. Max could hardly contain his excitement. He had waited almost nine months to learn a new spell, and this sounded like a useful one.

The teacher explained how the person who receives the spell doesn't know about it. "The spell doesn't inflict any damage, and the recipient is unaware the spell is even cast. Others around the person may see the glow, but since it only lasts a couple of seconds, it often goes unnoticed."

Max put his hand high in the air. "What's the result?"

"If the person is evil they will give off a hazy, red glow for a moment or two. The spell identifies whether or not the individual has magical powers and how they have used those powers. I'm going to teach you the spell but, unfortunately, it won't work in this setting because we aren't the enemy. I will also teach you the spell to reveal if someone is good. The results are almost the same. Good people will cast a blue colored glow. To reveal an enemy, the spell is pronounced *razkrij zlo*. For someone good, it is *razkrij dobro*. Now let's all say them together."

The class repeated the spells in unison.

Max shifted around at his desk, examining the room for possible suspects. *Now, I will be able to find the traitor!*

"What are you all excited about?" Martin whispered to him.

"If there is a traitor among us, this spell should reveal who it is."

"Okay, I want everyone to pay attention to what we are trying to do. You want to find out who uses magic for good. They will be revealed with a blue glow," Mrs. Ryan emphasized. "I will demonstrate the spell on someone first."

Seven hands shot into the air as numerous students wanted to be the volunteer. The teacher glanced around the class and her eyes fell on Max. "Max, I hear you've got a lot of magical talent. You should give off a nice glow. Will you please come forward?"

Max's cheeks flushed as all of the students turned to look at him. "Sure," he said, so softly he wasn't sure the teacher heard him. He cleared his throat and walked to the front of the class.

"Face the students, please," the teacher ordered, making Max feel even more vulnerable.

Max tried not to stare at anyone in particular as he heard the teacher cast the spell. The students' faces went from mild curiosity to surprise.

"Wow," Mrs. Ryan exhaled.

"What?" Max's face burned, and even more blood rushed to his head.

"I haven't before seen such a bright glow on a student."

"What do you mean?"

"That you have more magical talent than any student I have ever taught. How long have you been using magic?"

"Not even a year."

"That's impressive. Okay, class, let's divide into groups and practice the spell."

Max found himself surrounded by a group of students eager to work with him. "Join our group," an older boy named John said. "No, join ours," a group of girls implored.

"How about I decide," Mrs. Ryan said. "Max, you work with Phil and Sam." Mrs. Ryan indicated two older boys who had been sitting next to Max in the back of the room. "Martin, why don't you come up here and work with me? I understand this is your first magic lesson."

Max walked towards Phil and Sam, while the other students gathered into their own little groups. The room suddenly sounded like somebody had disturbed a beehive. The soft buzzing of spells filled the small classroom. Out of the corner of his eye, Max tried to judge the success rate of the other students, which didn't appear to be very high.

Phil was a gangly sixteen-year-old with blond hair and blue eyes, and Sam was a plump fifteen-year-old with red hair and freckles.

"Shall we get started?" Max offered, after a short introduction. The boys had a weird look of awe on their faces as they eyed him. "What?"

"Is it true? You've seen him, Hudich?" Phil asked in a low voice.

"Uh, yes."

"Wow," they both said, their eyes round with wonder.

Max felt a little embarrassed and shot a quick look around the room to see various students watching him. His mouth went dry and his palms grew damp as he turned back to Phil and Sam. "Should we get to it?"

It took Max three tries to make the spell work. Max couldn't decide if it was the spell that was difficult or if the boys didn't have very much experience or magical talent. Max cast the spell at the teacher, who glowed a soft blue; Max resolved it wasn't that difficult of a spell. Neither of the boys could get the spell to work on Max or the teacher. They were still eyeing him with amazement as he and Martin departed for Grandpa's.

###

Max entered Cindy's bedroom, grinning from ear to ear. Her face was now a swollen rainbow of dark blue, green, black, and purple. The slits between her eyebrows and cheekbones barely revealed her blue eyes. "Get up!"

"What? Where're we going? And what are you smiling about?"

"It's a surprise."

"What is?"

"Actually, all of it! Get up. Get dressed. I'll wait outside."

After a short wait on the whitewashed wooden steps of Cindy's front porch, the door opened. Cindy moved gingerly as she kept her arm pressed against her side and used the other for support on the steel railing. She gasped several times as she proceeded down the steps.

"Where to?" Cindy asked.

"To Grandpa's house." Max pointed. "Do you need any help?"

Even with her battered, swollen face, Max caught the roll of her eyes that suggested she could manage by herself. Max hurried ahead of her to hold the gate open to her yard and then again into Grandpa's yard.

"Settle down, will you. You're acting like a spaz," Cindy said, as she struggled up the steps towards Max before he could open the front door.

"I can't help it," Max smiled. "You're going to love this surprise."

Cindy passed Max in her caveman posture. "What? Are we going to see Ell?"

Max stopped. The excitement he had been holding back escaped from his body like air from a rapidly deflating balloon. "How'd you guess?"

"Do you really think I'm that stupid?" Cindy smiled.

Max could see she got pleasure from ruining his surprise. He could feel the corners of his mouth moving back to a smile.

"What?"

"That's the Cindy I remember," Max said, as he bounded up the stairs. "Do you want help up the stairs?"

"What do you think?"

"No."

"You're not as dumb as you look." Cindy chuckled.

On the third floor, Grandpa stood next to the gateway control panel as Cindy entered the room. "How are you feeling?"

"Sore," Cindy responded, as she crept towards him.

"I can see that. Well, I hope this little trip will cheer you up."

Max glanced around the room. "Where are Martin and Aunt Donna?"

"We'll take them another time." Grandpa made several adjustments to the silver control panel, and the force field spread from the five metallic stands around the room to form a dome. The antique mirror started to revolve and pick up speed. Soon, the light of the gateway replaced the old mirror.

"Max, you go first, so you can help Cindy down." Grandpa suggested.

Max stepped through the light into the lush green rolling hills of Yelka's world to find Yelka and Ell waiting for them. He turned and took Cindy's hand as she emerged from the gateway. After he helped her down, Grandpa came through.

Ell looked like an enormous excited dog. His shaggy black fur flapped up and down to match his enthusiastic leaps. Ell was the size of an elephant, and a terrifying sight to those who didn't know him. He had rows of razor sharp teeth and a long black nose, which separated his yellow eyes.

Cindy released Max's hand and headed towards Ell. She placed a hand on the creature's side and stood motionless in conversation.

Max waited for Cindy to finally step back from Ell before he placed his hand on Ell's side. *Hello.*

Max, it's good to see you.

You too, my friend.

After they had spoken with Ell, they placed Cindy on Ell's back and made their way towards Yelka's house.

Ell waited outside the house as the others went inside to discuss what they were going to do this summer. Grandpa told Max and Cindy he wanted them to study spells at the school and have personal sessions with Yelka. He also informed them they would continue their science lessons with Olik, and he had found them another self-defense teacher.

"And then there are still the missions," Grandpa said.

"What missions?" Max and Cindy asked at the same time.

"Don't worry, we have several. The enemy isn't sitting still and neither are we. We have to constantly keep watch of Hudich and figure out how to rescue Max's mother and uncle."

A twinge of panic started to pump through Max's veins like thick honey. It didn't spread quickly, but it was thorough, leaving no part of his body untouched. His improved mood, which had been getting better each day since he discovered Cindy wasn't a spy, had vanished, and his uneasiness returned. *Should he tell them here? Now? But will the traitor find out somehow? I can't do what Alan wants. But I can't sacrifice my mother, either.*

"Max, are you all right?" Yelka asked. "You look pale."

"Just worried about my mother."

Cindy reached over and took Max's hand. "We'll get her back."

"I hope so." Max fought the urge to hang his head and stare at the floor.

"I think we need to keep busy," Yelka said. "And since you have mastered the invisibility spell, I'm going to let you pick the kind of spells you want to learn."

"You did?" Cindy asked, with her eyes as wide as her swollen face would allow.

"Yes."

"Cindy, you're going to have to work extra hard to catch up," Yelka said. "I'll give you some more roots like I gave you last summer, to help your magic."

"I want to learn the spell to transport myself into another world," Max spoke so quickly he shocked himself. Grandpa and Yelka's faces looked as if they were about to slide off as their jaws dropped. Max couldn't quite make out Cindy's reaction because of the swelling. He had been playing with the idea of using the gateway to find his mother, but if he could go to other worlds without the gateway, he might be able to locate her.

"Well." Yelka gave a slight cough as if to recompose herself after the jolt. "You certainly are going for a big one."

"May I ask why you want to learn that particular spell?" Grandpa queried.

"I've wanted to know how to do it ever since we were trapped in Mir. And I think it's important to understand how the enemy travels." Max knew these weren't the main reasons he wanted to learn the spell, but they were both good arguments.

Just breathe normally. Max wondered if Grandpa suspected his real motivation by the way he held Max with his gaze.

"Fair enough," Grandpa replied.

"How about you, Cindy? What spell would you like to learn?" Yelka asked.

"I don't really know. I haven't thought about it. Can I have some time to decide?"

"Of course you can, sweetie," Yelka responded.

Grandpa stood and stretched his legs. "Well, it's time we get going. Ell has a job to do."

"Ell has a job?" Max asked. Max could tell Cindy was as shocked as he was.

"Yes, you don't think we brought you here just to discuss things we could have talked about at home?" Grandpa responded. "Who do you think is spying on Hudich? Max and I have a job to do also."

"But if Ell is caught, won't he be *killed*?" Cindy argued.

"Calm down, Cindy. Yelka has been working with Ell. He has mastered the invisibility spell. He only has to worry about his size, since people can't see him. He also knows several other spells to aid him if he gets into trouble," Grandpa said.

"But why Ell?" Cindy pleaded.

"Nobody knows the land of the Zeenosees as well as Ell," Yelka explained.

Max remembered that Ell was from the same world as the Zeenosees, where they trapped Hudich at the end of last summer. They had only moved Ell to Yelka's world for his safety.

"Besides, Ell wanted to go," Grandpa added. "He asked to help."

Max was as concerned for Ell as Cindy, but he heard what else Grandpa mentioned. "What do you and I have to do?"

"You're going with me, to Pekel."

"Pekel? Why?"

"I have been thinking about the enemy's gateway. As you said, the thing that has changed in the past year is our removal of Hudich from Pekel. I find it interesting that it wasn't until we took Hudich out of Pekel that the enemy found this gateway. I'm convinced the new gateway is tied to Hudich and Pekel."

"I want to go," Cindy spoke up.

"I know you do, Cindy." Grandpa smiled at her. "But you're still recovering. Once you're healed you'll have plenty to do. While we're gone you can work on your spells with Yelka."

Yelka was nodding her head in agreement. "We need to get your magic skills equal to Max's."

"Does Ell's job also have something to do with the enemy's gateway?" Max asked.

"Yes, we haven't sent him to check on Hudich for a couple of months," Grandpa replied.

They made their way outside and placed Cindy on Ell's back. In no time they were back through the gateway and on the third floor of Grandpa's house.

Cindy stroked Ell's head affectionately while Grandpa made several adjustments to the gateway's control panel. As Yelka listened to Grandpa's instructions, Max walked over to Cindy. "He'll be alright."

"I know he will," Cindy tried to smile through her fat lips. "I'm not worried about him as much as I'm worried about you."

"Me!'

"Yes. Ell says there's something wrong with you. He doesn't know what it is, but he thinks you're in trouble," Cindy spoke quietly so only Max could hear.

Max found it difficult to look Ell in the eye. He knew Ell had sensed something when they spoke in Yelka's world. *I can't touch him without giving myself away?*

"He says not to worry. He won't say anything. He just wants me to watch out for you. I think we need to have a talk when you get back." Cindy held Max's gaze. Her stern look gave him the feeling he was staring at his mother after having done something wrong.

Max's insides rolled and squirmed like a barrel of snakes. He wanted so badly to confide in someone, but he didn't want to risk his mother's life.

"Well?" Cindy asked.

"Well what?"

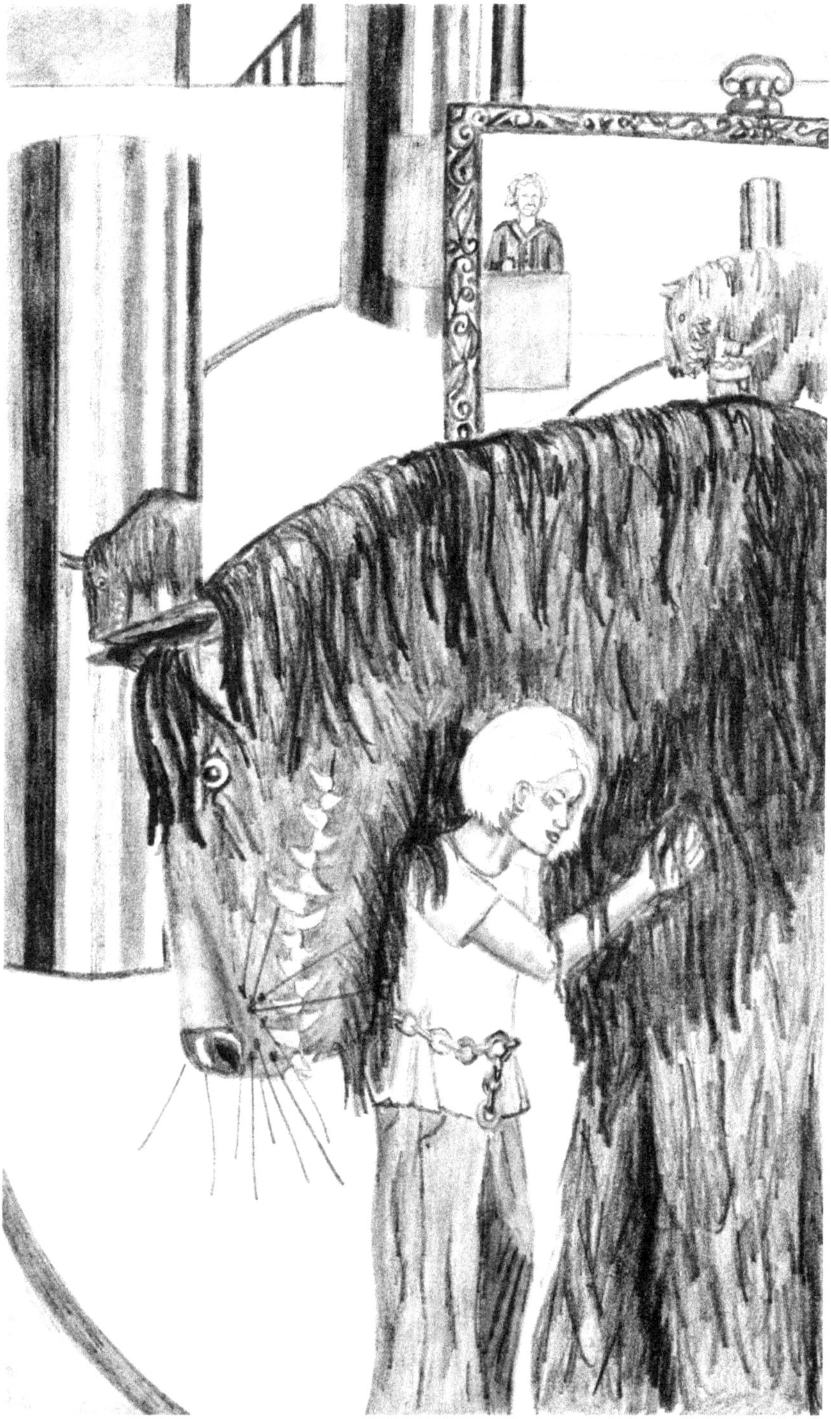

"Are we going to talk about this when you get back?"

Max didn't think he could get out of it. Cindy was holding him fast with her eyes. "Okay," his voice barely audible.

"Are you ready, Ell?" Grandpa asked, as he turned to face them.

"Good luck," Cindy said, patting Ell on the side.

"Be careful," Max added, placing his hands in his pocket.

Ell walked over to the gateway, turned to look at them, and vanished. The light of the gateway grew in intensity as Ell entered. Once the light diminished, Grandpa went back to Yelka and the control panel.

"Max," Grandpa called over his shoulder. "Are you ready?"

A quick flicker of light from the gateway indicated it had changed to another world.

"Yes."

Grandpa picked up two backpacks that were lying at the base of the control panel and handed one to Max. "There's a gun inside. Get it! Here is the translation device you used last year." Grandpa handed him a small device the size of a pinto bean.

Max put the device into his ear. "A gun?" Max shot Cindy a glance when he found the weapon in his pack. It was silver and similar to the one Olik had given Grandpa a year ago. "Do you think I'm going to need this?"

"I hope not, but it's better to be safe than sorry. I don't know how much you know about Pekel. Its atmosphere makes it difficult to use magic. As you now know, it takes energy to use and control magic. Something about Pekel robs us of the energy needed to perform magic. Our magical powers will be extremely limited. That's why the guns."

"Sounds like Pekel would be a great place to practice magic," Cindy said.

"What makes you say that?" Yelka asked, her eyes wide with shock.

"I was just thinking that if you could master it there, you would be very powerful elsewhere."

Grandpa's jaw dropped open. "That's brilliant, Cindy."

"What is?"

"That part about training in Pekel. I think that's something we should look into. Last year Hudich showed great improvement in his magical abilities there."

Cindy's swollen lips spread into a smile. Max thought she was blushing, but the swelling and bruises made it difficult to see.

"I'll signal you when we're ready to come back," Grandpa said to Yelka.

"We'll be waiting."

"Are you ready, Max?"

"Yes."

Grandpa walked into the gateway and Max followed.

The minute Max stepped down he felt a hand clamp around his mouth as Grandpa pulled him to the ground. Campfires burned all around them, and what looked like large green muscular men lay sleeping everywhere. What appeared to be a sentry sat only a few yards away with his back to them. He had a sword strapped across his back and a spear in his hand.

"We seem to have entered into the camp of the Trog's army," Grandpa whispered in his ear.

9

Pekel's Secret

Max and Grandpa huddled quietly in the dark amongst the sleeping Trogs. Max's heart was thumping like a base drum so loudly in his chest that he was certain someone might overhear it. The guard, sitting a short distance away, appeared to be struggling to stay awake. His head bobbed several times before he shook it back and forth to revive his senses.

Max could feel Grandpa moving next to him. He figured Grandpa was looking for a way out. Max couldn't tear his eyes off the sleepy Trog.

"Follow me, stay low to the ground, and keep quiet," Grandpa whispered in Max's ear.

Max got into a squatting position without making a sound. Sleeping not three feet away, the Trog stirred, causing Max to freeze and all the hairs on his body stood on end. Grandpa hesitated and watched the restless Trog as well. After a few seconds of silence, Max followed Grandpa as they crept past the sleeping Trogs.

There were several tents, which Max presumed held either the important Trogs or more dangerous creatures. All the campfires had burned themselves down to glowing embers that popped every once in a while. A couple of sentries stalked about to keep themselves awake, while others appeared to be sleeping at their posts.

Grandpa led Max towards an area of the camp with rows of weapons: armor, swords, spears, pikes, and bows with arrows were leaning or hanging on wooden structures under canvas lean-tos. After that were rows of catapults, battering rams, trebuchets, and vats of oil.

They proceeded through the heavy weapons section, staying low enough to avoid detection. They halted when they heard a sudden movement at the end of the row. Another sentry patrolled the border of the camp behind the weapons area. He kept his head turned towards the trees beyond the camp, as if he expected trouble from outside the camp.

"I'll bet there's more than one," Grandpa whispered.

"What do you want to do?" Max's voice cracked in his dry throat.

"We're either going to have to create a distraction or you're going to have to master the invisibility spell here in Pekel."

"You can do it?"

"Yes, but it took a lot of practice, and I can only maintain it for a little while. Let's move a little closer before we decide." Grandpa continued towards the edge of the camp in his crouched position, with Max right behind him.

A short distance before the end of the camp, they took refuge behind a large wooden catapult. A guard patrolled the area right behind the weapons, while several others huddled around a small fire, separating the weapons area from the forest beyond. The raspy voices of the Trogs near the fire could be heard complaining about having the night watch.

"Let's move a couple of rows away from the fire. When the Trog walks past the fire, we'll run for the woods," Grandpa said in Max's ear.

Max held out a thumbs-up and they snuck over catapults to move away from the fire. As Max climbed over a catapult wheel, his foot hooked a chain that was dangling from a spoke. He dragged it from its perch and across the ground like a ghost carrying chains in a haunted house. The clanking broke the silence of the night, catching the patrol's ears.

Max froze at the noise. Grandpa grabbed him by the front of his shirt and pulled him into the back of a wagon filled with supplies. They huddled quietly under a loose tarp.

Several Trogs rushed up and down the aisle between the war machines. They pointed their guns as if they were ready for battle. Their heads swiveled back and forth like bobble-head dolls as they searched for the cause of the disturbance.

"Guns," Grandpa whispered.

Max peered through a crack in the wood slats that made up the back of the wagon. Two Trogs stood next to the chain Max had dragged. Sure enough, they carried guns similar to the one Grandpa had used to get Hudich out of Pekel. The same as the gun they had left behind when they escaped from the world of the Zeenosees.

One kicked at the chain with his foot. "This here must have been what caused the racket. It musta fallen off a wagon."

"Why we out here anyway?" the other Trog complained. "We ain't at war with no one."

"I heard it was orders from Hudich," the first replied.

"Hudich, he's been gone a year. How we gettin' orders from him?"

"I heard from someone up top that a human showed up and says he's got a message from Hudich. He'd been meetin' with the generals for several days, and said we need to start preparin' for battle. Says we gonna control here and elsewhere."

"Where's elsewhere?"

"That's the bugger; they say there are worlds without number and we'd be a dominatin' force in a major takeover. Where do ya think we got these weapons?"

"You know what I think? I think they been swiggin' too much fire drink. They sound all screwed up in the head."

"Yeah, but these weapons helped us conquer the Laffs in only a couple of weeks."

"You said it. Let's get back to the fire."

"Okay," was called out to the other Trogs, and they went back to their normal patrols.

Max adjusted his feet and noticed he was lying on several large crates loaded with guns. "Grandpa," he whispered signaling to the crates.

"Looks like a lot has been going on here that we weren't supposed to find out about," Grandpa replied.

After waiting several minutes for everyone to settle down, Grandpa and Max crawled out of the wagon.

"Did you hear that part about Hudich?" Max asked in a hushed voice.

"Yes, come on." Grandpa waved Max to follow as they headed down the aisle towards the edge of the camp. They paused for the patrolling Trog to pass the fire, which was now several aisles away, then dashed into the forest.

"What were they talking about, and where did they get the guns?" Max wanted to know, as soon as they were away from the camp.

"Ever since we learned about the enemy gateway, I've had my suspicions about Hudich's involvement," Grandpa said, as he marched through the forest with Max right on his heels. "I suspect they didn't get the gateway until after Hudich was released from here. It's my guess that other people or creatures discovered a way into Pekel with a gateway of some type. Hudich learned about it but couldn't tell anyone until he was set free."

"You're hoping we can find out what Hudich discovered by coming here?"

"Exactly! We've already learned that the Trogs are preparing for something big."

"We've got to stop it!"

"I know."

"So, where do we start?"

Grandpa stopped so suddenly Max almost ran into him. They had reached the end of the trees and were standing on the top of a rocky hill. Below them sat a large, bowl-like valley, a well-lit stone castle with crumbling pillars was in the center. A vast river crept along the valley floor like a slithering snake, surrounding the castle on all sides, forming a protective barrier.

Grandpa dropped to the ground, which was riddled with stones, yanking Max with him. As they lay on their stomachs and looked out through the sparse, high grasses, they spied more Trogs traveling up a dirt road leading from the castle to the top of the hills surrounding the valley. Torches burned all along the road like cars on a major freeway.

"We start in the castle." Grandpa pointed to the dilapidated structure with his bony finger.

"How are we going to get in there?" Max raised his eyebrows.

"There's a tunnel. Hudich and I used it to escape last year. The Trogs didn't know about it, and I'm hoping they still don't. We need to find it from this side." Grandpa took a pair of night vision binoculars out of his pack and used them to scan the area.

The Trogs appeared to be escorting prisoners from the castle, as well as carrying out weapons and other supplies. A massive Trog with a whip snapped the cruel device across the backs of several slaves pulling wagons.

"It looks like they're moving out," Grandpa said, still spying through his binoculars.

"Getting ready to invade some other world," Max said more to himself than to Grandpa. Max felt Grandpa's eyes on him and turned to see Grandpa staring at him. His face looked white like he had seen a ghost. "What?" Max asked.

"What did you just say?"

"It looks like they're preparing to leave. To invade another world."

"We need to hurry," Grandpa said, and began scanning the hills again.

Suddenly, the weight of the unfolding situation hit Max. They're going to invade. War is starting. Life is going to change or end for some unsuspecting world. "I'll bet it's going to be a world that won't be able to fight back."

"I agree," Grandpa said, as he handed the binoculars to Max. "I think the tunnel is behind that large boulder about ten yards down from the top of the hill. The one with the weeds growing all around it." Grandpa pointed to the spot and then retrieved his communicator from his pocket.

Max spied through the glasses and was amazed how the landscape looked as clear as noonday. The night vision allowed him to spot the stone Grandpa had described. "Who are you calling?"

"Yelka, we need her to get the word out. We need to find out which world they're going to attack. Maybe someone in another world has seen the Trogs. Who knows, we might get lucky. If not, you and I will have to find out. Come on. Let's move back into the trees. We should be able to get to the top of the hill right above the rock without the Trogs noticing. From there, we'll decide on our next move."

Crawling through the tall grasses on their hands and knees, Max followed Grandpa until they were back in the trees. It didn't take long to circle around to the hilltop that was directly above the rock.

"At least we're further from the road than we were before," Grandpa said. He got out his water skin and took a drink before handing it to Max.

Max quenched his thirst with the cool water and gave it back to Grandpa. "What do we do now?"

"Well, let's hope they haven't been given any other advanced weapons besides the guns." Grandpa tucked the water skin back in his pack.

"Like night vision glasses," Max added.

"Precisely." Grandpa slid his feet over the edge of the hill and started to climb down towards the stone.

Max watched the Trogs moving along the road to see if they noticed Grandpa's descent. After a few moments without any change in the Trogs behavior, Max followed his grandfather. They reached the rock with ease, and Grandpa began to search around the boulder.

"There should be a latch of some kind," Grandpa whispered. "See if you can find anything."

The creaking of carts and the wail of slaves under the taskmaster's whip reached their ears as they groped around in the dark.

"Ouch!" Max said, a little louder than he would have liked, as a sharp thorn pierced his index finger. He and Grandpa glanced around to see if anyone had heard Max's cry. The Trogs were too far from the hill to hear. Max pulled out the barb and stuck his finger in his mouth to stop the bleeding.

A loud snap, like a sledgehammer hitting stone, launched Max's heart into his throat.

"Found it," Grandpa said, as he held onto what looked like a tree root.

"I thought they'd spotted us," Max whispered, as he took a deep breath to calm his nerves.

"Help me get this open," Grandpa grunted, pushing his weight against the stone.

Max lowered his shoulder into the boulder and shoved with all his might. Stone grating on stone drowned out the other night sounds. Max wondered if the noise had been as loud as it seemed, or if it was just that his senses were on high alert. One. Two. Three times they labored, until the opening was wide enough for them to enter.

They stepped into the complete darkness of the tunnel Grandpa and Hudich used to escape the year before. Grandpa turned on a flashlight to reveal a short hallway at the base of a steep, descending staircase. "There's a flashlight in your pack. Get it. You're going to need it on the stairs."

Max took out his flashlight and clicked it on. He followed Grandpa to the top step, and they both shined their lights into the black hole that was the stairs. The open door created a draft which carried a damp, musty smell to their noses.

"You go first." Grandpa motioned with his flashlight. "Go slow and use the rail. The stairs are steep and some of them are broken."

"Why am I going first?"

"So, you can break my fall," Grandpa chuckled.

The corners of Max's mouth turned up into a smile. It was the first time this summer he heard his grandfather laugh, and for one quick moment it felt like everything would be all right. Suddenly, saving his mother, and the betrayal necessary to do it, came crashing back down on him. It pressed him like a vice squeezing his insides. He didn't know if he could do it. Betray Grandpa! Steal the key! How could he?

As Max started down the crumbling staircase, he couldn't stop the feeling he was descending into his own personal grave. He hoped they would find something that would lead them to his mother without setting Hudich free or making his grandfather a prisoner of the enemy.

When they reached the bottom of the stairs, Max realized the moldy smell had come from water dripping on the pocked and cratered surface of the cave. Max tried to pick a course that would keep their feet dry, but there were puddles too wide and too long to be avoided.

"We're under the river that surrounds the castle, aren't we?" Max asked.

"Yes. The water is seeping in much worse than last year."

"That's comforting," Max said sarcastically. The thought of a deteriorating ceiling supporting millions of gallons of water added to his darkening mood. The constant dripping and plopping of water, joined by Grandpa's labored breathing, throbbed in Max's ears like a balloon ready to burst. Waves of fear grew with each step, about to crash upon him and crush him like a bug. Just when he didn't think he could take anymore, they reached the other side.

Max paused at the bottom of the stairs to let Grandpa catch his wind. "Are you okay?"

"Yes, just getting old and out of shape," Grandpa gasped, as he took several deep breaths and wiped the sweat from his brow with a handkerchief.

"What's the plan once we reach the top?" Max nodded towards the stairs.

"Well," Grandpa took another gulp of air, "Olik gave me a little device that uses sound waves to map out a building. I hope to get some idea where to look for records or histories from the layout of the castle."

"You hope we can find what Hudich found?"

"Yes. Okay, I'm ready." Grandpa turned Max towards the stairs.

Max was glad to be out from under the river. The small tunnel that made up the stairway caused Grandpa's struggles for air to echo loudly. They paused multiple times and climbed at a snail's pace. Suddenly, Grandpa gave him a hard yank on the back of his pack, which caused Max's heart to leap into his chest. For a brief moment he thought they were going to fall.

"Turn off your light! And don't make a sound!" Grandpa whispered in his ear, as he doused his own flashlight.

Max quickly switched off his flashlight and waited for his eyes to adjust to the darkness. In a matter of seconds, Max could see a pale, yellowish light at the top of the stairs. He tried to be as quiet as possible. He couldn't tell which was louder, his heart beating a panicked rhythm in his ears, or Grandpa trying to control his breathing. The light didn't appear to be growing or fading in intensity, giving Max the impression it wasn't someone coming or going.

"You wait here and I'll sneak up and take a look," Max whispered.

"Be careful," Grandpa responded.

Grandpa surprised Max by agreeing to the idea so quickly. He wondered if Grandpa realized he would be the quieter of the two. Max crept up the stairs, gently placing each foot onto the next stone step to avoid making any noise. Before he reached the point where his head would ascend above the top step, he paused to listen. He heard a faint, raspy, gurgling sound, indicating some life form waited nearby.

It took all of Max's self-control to keep from shaking as he popped his eyes above the edge of the top step. Light filtered in from a door propped open at the end of a short hallway. Beyond the door was another flagstone-floored hall with the shadow of a sleeping guard reflected in the entrance. Other than the slumbering watchman, the intersecting hallway appeared to be empty. The only thing Max could hear was the Trog's snoring.

Max snuck back down to where Grandpa waited. "The light is coming from an open door. There's also a guard who seems to be asleep," Max whispered. "What do you want to do?"

Grandpa dug around in his pack and produced an electronic device. It was a flat-screened instrument that was four inches wide and four inches long. Five small buttons ran along the one side. "This is the mapping device Olik gave me. You turn it on with this button." Grandpa pushed the top button, bringing the device to life. "Then start the process with this one." Grandpa pointed to the next button, holding the thing up in the faint light for Max to see. "It needs to be on the floor we want to map. You need to go up the steps again and set it on the main floor." Grandpa pointed up the stairs as he handed it to Max.

Once again Max went up the stairs, until his head was above the last step. He turned the mapping device on and gently placed it on the floor. After pausing to check for any other signs of movement, he started the mapping process. A green three-dimensional holographic image of the castle started to build in the air directly above the small screen. The image contracted in the corridor space to accommodate the rapidly expanding map hovering above the small screen. Not only did the map show rooms and hallways, but it showed furniture, rugs and other objects as well. The ghostly picture's light wasn't strong enough for Max to worry about as long as no one entered the doorway.

After a matter of minutes a small light adjacent to the process button turned orange, and the model stopped growing. Max assumed the light meant the process had finished. He quietly picked up the device and hurried back to Grandpa.

Grandpa took the mapping computer from Max and started to do his search through the castle's layout. His fingers tapped and turned several small buttons on the side of the machine, which brought rooms in and out of focus. The rooms grew and shrank, replacing the image of the entire castle a section at a time, as Grandpa probed for information about the building's floor plan.

Max watched with interest as the entire castle came and went before his eyes. "Why doesn't it show us the Trogs?" Max whispered.

"It only shows the inanimate objects in a building. If someone happens to move an inanimate object after we have run the process, then our data is incorrect."

Grandpa continued looking at the map for a little bit longer, when his fingers came to a stop. The room before them looked like a vault filled with books and scrolls. "I think this is what we're looking for. We can get going after I map a path to this room." Grandpa pressed a few more buttons and the three dimensional image disappeared. Replacing the image was a small map with lines and arrows pointing the direction they needed to go.

"Let's go," Grandpa whispered.

Max led the way up the remaining steps. For the third time, he stopped at a point where he could poke his head above the final steps to take a peek. The soft sounds of the sleeping guard continued unceasing, and his shadow covered the floor through the open doorway. Max climbed the last few steps and slunk towards the door. He swallowed the lump that had been building in his throat as he approached the opening and peered around the corner.

A large Trog slumbered in a wooden chair against the wall. His legs stretched out in front of him almost blocking the passage. Max finally got to see a Trog close up. The Trog's porous green skin looked like the dimples on a golf ball. He had a large bulbous nose with a bulky round chin and pointed hairy ears. *Nightmare!* Max shuddered.

Max waved Grandpa into the hall. Grandpa indicated they had to cross over the Trog's legs. They carefully stepped over the Trog, leaving the guard undisturbed by their passing.

They hurried down the hallway, ducked into a darkened corridor, and paused against the wall. The castle was warm, too warm. Sweat built on Max's back where his pack rested. The air was close and musky and reeked of body odor. Max figured personal hygiene wasn't a high priority with the Trogs. He kept an open eye on the adjoining hallway. "Where to?"

"We need to go down this hall and take the second corridor on the right." Grandpa stared at the map.

Max started to go when Grandpa grabbed him by the sleeve. "Listen. If we hear someone coming you may have to use the invisibility spell."

Max nodded, but Grandpa continued to hold him fast. "It will be a lot harder to make this spell work here. It will take all of your concentration. If you think of anything, I mean anything else, it won't work."

"I understand."

"If there is a place to hide, use that option first."

"What about our guns?"

"That's the last resort, especially since they have guns now. We don't want to have to shoot our way out."

Max left the corridor and crept down the hall. They navigated the castle with relative ease, only stopping a time or two at the sound of voices. No one appeared in any of the hallways. The castle appeared to be almost deserted, as if the Trogs had moved out.

The journey through the castle was silent. Grandpa would tug and point the directions he wanted Max to follow. Grandpa stopped in front of two massive, wooden doors. Time had faded the door's brown stain and the wood was decayed and cracked. Grandpa handed Max the mapping device and pressed his ear to one of the doors. He remained still for several moments and then flashed Max a reassuring smile. Grandpa gently cracked one door open and peered through the small slit.

"Come on," Grandpa whispered, as he opened the door the remainder of the way.

Max followed Grandpa into a dimly lit room the size of a basketball court. Rows and rows of books stretched from wall to wall. The only light filtered in through a few small windows along the back wall. The thick layer of dust that had accumulated everywhere suggested no one had entered the room in quite some time. Piles of leather-bound books and rolls of parchment were stacked on tables and in heaps on the floor.

"It could take weeks to find anything in here," Max commented, a dust cloud billowing as he pulled out a book with crudely drawn pictures of creatures being tortured. The gruesome pictures turned Max's stomach, and he returned the book to its previous spot.

Grandpa had his flashlight out and moved up and down the aisles at a rapid pace. "You have to know what you're looking for, otherwise it could take forever."

"You know what we're looking for?"

"Sort of."

"What does that mean?"

"It means, I know the Trogs. They're not big on reading, so it wasn't a Trog who built this library. My guess is Hudich was the only one to come in here, maybe a couple of others. I'm looking for an area that looks used. Granted, with all this dust it doesn't look like anything has been touched in a long time."

"So, look for something out of the ordinary?"

"Yes."

"Okay, you take the left and I'll take the right," Max suggested, and started searching the aisles on his side of the room. As far as Max could tell, none of the sections seemed different from any of the others. Everything appeared undisturbed.

As Max looked at a row of shelves, Grandpa rounded the corner, shining his flashlight in Max's eyes. "I think I found something," Grandpa whispered, and waited for Max to join him at the end of the row.

Max followed Grandpa into an aisle with several neat stacks of books, a wooden chair, and a number of parchment scrolls which littered the ground. Dust still covered everything, but it did look different from the other aisles. Several of the shelves above the chair were empty or contained only a few books.

"Now, we just have to figure out which book, or books, contain the information we are looking for," Grandpa said, as he sat in the seat and snatched a book off the top of a pile.

Max picked up a book and started to thumb through its pages. The text was in a language Max didn't understand. "You can read these?"

"Yes, the language is that of the Tujec's. I have studied Pekel and its inhabitants for years."

"How many languages do you speak?" Max raised his eyebrows as he realized the depth of his grandfather's knowledge.

"Thirty-two, give or take. A couple of the languages I know only a few words and can just get by."

"Where did you find the time to learn that many?"

"Magic can help you learn and retain at a much faster rate than you ever thought possible. Now, I want you to go to the end of the aisle to keep watch on the door. We don't want to be caught."

Max walked to the end of the row and sat with his back against the wall. From this vantage point he could see both Grandpa flipping through the pages of the books, and the door through which they had entered.

Alone and sitting cross-legged on the floor, Max reflected on his situation. He didn't like it when there was nothing to keep his mind occupied. Every time he had nothing to do, he thought of his mother. Where is the key? Max hated the idea of betraying his grandfather and giving into Alan's demands. If it came down to saving his mother, though, he would do practically anything. He could see her and his uncle sitting in the dark, confined in those small cells. He wondered if she had endured any torture.

"Max," Grandpa whispered, as he signaled Max to join him.

Max hurried to his grandfather, who was holding an old leather bound book.

"I think I found what we're looking for." Grandpa patted the book.

"What does it say?" Max leaned over it for a better look.

"We'll talk about that when we get home, but it tells about some wizards who had visited Pekel a couple hundred years before Hudich or I came along. Turn around."

Max turned around and Grandpa stuffed the book into Max's pack.

"Let's get out of here before we're discovered," Grandpa prodded, and led Max to the door.

They carefully made their way back in the direction they came. The castle seemed even more deserted than when they entered. As they slipped cautiously out of the cave entrance and back up the hill, they spotted the last of the Trogs along the dirt road; they were leaving the castle.

"I wonder where they're headed." Max whispered, as they reached the tree line.

"Me too. In fact, we probably should find out. Who knows what trouble they're going to cause? If they're traveling to another world we need to find out which one." Grandpa removed the water skin from his pack and took a drink.

"Are we going after them?"

"Yes, follow me." Grandpa started to jog in the direction of the Trogs, Max right behind him. They stayed in the trees as much as possible in an attempt to get as close as they could without being seen. The creak of the great wagon wheels mingled with the tramp-tramp of marching Trog feet and grew steadily louder. The only noises to break the constant rhythm were the occasional crack of a whip, followed by wails of pain.

Grandpa and Max reached a spot close enough to observe the Trogs safely. They hid behind a group of bushy shrubs. The racket of the Trog army made it impossible to overhear any conversations that might indicate where they were heading.

"What are we going to do?" Max asked, as he wiped the sweat and dirt off his face.

"I'm not sure yet." Grandpa continued to study the army as it marched along the road. "I have a feeling we aren't going to get what we want by eavesdropping."

"What do you mean?" Max struggled to stifle a cough caused by the dust created by the Trogs and slaves on the dirt road.

"I think, I might have to go undercover as a slave," Grandpa said, more to himself.

"No way!" Max gasped.

"It's the only way to find out which world they are going to invade. Once I move through their gateway, I'll be able to use magic to get away. Then I'll call you and let you know where I am."

"I don't know." Max felt uneasy about letting his grandfather become a Trog's slave. "I'd hate to think what will happen if you're discovered." The lines of determination across his grandfather's forehead told Max his grandfather had already made up his mind. "Okay, but how do we get you in there without being discovered?"

Grandpa and Max moved from one hiding place to another, keeping pace with the Trogs. They watched a group of slaves pushing several heavily loaded carts. The slaves were similar to humans, but not enough for Grandpa to pass as one of them. They were a tall lanky race with leathery pale skin that stretched over their bony frames. They all had gray wiry hair and long narrow faces. They wore tattered robes of a rough burlap-like fabric, cinched in at their waists with a bit of rope.

"Some of them keep their hoods up." Grandpa pointed to one particular slave struggling to carry an oversized backpack.

"But he's the only one," Max added, unable to hide the concern in his voice.

While following the Trogs for hours, they noticed that several of the slaves' strength would periodically give out. The slaves would collapse into a heap of rags, holding up the procession because they were bound to each other by a chain around their ankles. A Trog would kick them several times, trying to get them up and moving, but with mixed results. It appeared that many slaves simply could not go any further. When this occurred, a Trog would unchain them from the others, leaving them to die by the side of the road.

After the army had unshackled another slave and started to proceed on their journey, Grandpa and Max remained behind. Once the army was out of sight, Grandpa put on the clothes of the fallen slave.

Grandpa took his communicator out of his pack and gave the pack to Max. "I'm going to fall in with the rest of the slaves. You'll go back through the gateway and tell Yelka to wait for my signal."

"But,"

"I'll be all right!"

Before Max could argue, Grandpa had sent Max through the gateway out of Pekel.

10

An Important Discovery

As soon as Max disappeared through the gateway, Joe moved into the woods and continued tailing the Trog army. It didn't take long to catch up with the last of the creeping procession. The marching troops and wagon wheels wafted dust everywhere. Grandpa coughed several times into the sleeve of his robe to muffle the noise. The hazy air wreaked havoc with his breathing.

The Trog army continued its journey until it reached the same camp Joe and Max had dropped into the night before. He studied several groups of slaves in an effort to link up with one of them undetected. As the sun began to set, Joe selected the group he would join. They were in the process of packing suits of armor. In a small clearing fifty yards to his left, the enemy gateway opened.

The gateway wasn't what Joe expected. Instead of a round ball of light, it looked like a tear in space. In the dim light of the early evening, the ragged opening shone with an intense, burning light that grew and shrank continually.

Joe noticed that not only had the gateway drawn *his* attention, but everyone else in camp was staring at the strange phenomenon as well. This was the distraction Joe needed. He snuck into the camp and began working with the group of slaves packing armor.

Soon Trogs, slaves, and supplies began to be loaded into the strange rip in space. Many of the slaves fought against their chains and the whips of their masters in an effort to avoid vanishing through the light. Their shrieks of terror echoed through the forest.

Terrified of the unknown, Joe thought.

One slave who had fallen to the ground in his effort to dodge the frightful gateway, was dragged into the light by the chain around his ankle.

Joe busied himself by placing shields into the back of a wagon. An ice-cold shot of terror rushed down Joe's spine as a deep voice bellowed out. "How come you ain't got no shackle round your leg?"

Joe turned slowly, keeping his head down to hide his face from the massive Trog standing next to him.

"Well?" the Trog barked.

Joe shrugged his shoulder and glanced at his ankle, hoping the Trog would understand the gesture.

The Trog spit on the ground. "Those lazy, no-good guards," he said in an irritated voice. "Wait here, you."

Joe lifted his head high enough to watch the Trog stomp towards a cart loaded with various objects. After a minute of digging through the cargo, he produced a chain and a shackle. "Put out your leg," he said as he returned.

Joe hesitated, worried about revealing his human leg to the guard, and received a hard kick to his knee that caused him to crumple to the ground with pain.

"I gave you an order and you'z best be obeying," the Trog advanced on Joe. "Give up your leg."

Joe extended his leg and pulled his robe up high enough for the Trog to fasten on the shackle. Joe gritted his teeth to stifle the grunt of pain as the Trog viciously tightened the clamp. The Trog proceeded to take the end of the chain attached to the shackle and locked it to another chain that united Joe with the other slaves. The Trog then went about his business, mumbling something about incompetent guards.

Joe continued to perform various tasks with the other slaves into the evening. It was past midnight when he and his group accompanied a catapult through the enemy's gateway.

On the other side of the gateway they stepped into the middle of a large stone area. Max's description of the enemy's gateway had been so detailed that Grandpa recognized it immediately. There were cloaked figures standing in a circle around the area chanting a strange spell. As soon as the last slave popped through the gateway, the chanting stopped and the light of the gateway went out, revealing the stone archway.

Grandpa kept his head low as soon as he recognized Alan standing next to the archway. Alan stepped into the archway and removed the strange, colorfully lit hourglass. He turned the hourglass upside down and the little balls of light started to tumble through the narrow neck. Another cloaked figure rotated the stone archway to point in a different direction and Alan dropped the hourglass back into the hole as the surrounding figures chanted once again.

The archway disappeared into a ragged light as orders for the slaves to haul the weapons through rang out. As Joe's eyes adjusted to the dark of the new world upon emerging from the gateway again, he muttered under his breath, "Sladkor."

###

When Max emerged from the gateway, Yelka continued to stand next to the control panel, expecting Grandpa to jump out next.

"He isn't coming," Max stated, as his eyes met Cindy's.

"What?" Cindy and Yelka shrieked together.

"Why?" asked Yelka. "Has something gone wrong?"

"Yes, but it's not what you think. You can close the gateway."

"What is it?" Cindy pressed, as Yelka adjusted some dials and the light of the gateway faded.

"The enemy is using their gateway to move the Trogs into another world," Max said. "Grandpa thinks they're about to attack an unsuspecting world. He went undercover as a slave to find out which world."

"That's very dangerous," Yelka's voice rang, as she shook her head disapprovingly. "I hope he knows what he's doing."

"Did you find what you were looking for?" Cindy interrupted.

"Yes. Grandpa gave me this to bring back." Max took the old book from his pack. "We found this in the Trogs' library."

"You actually snuck into the Trogs' library?" Cindy's eyes were wide with wonder.

"It wasn't all that hard. They were abandoning their fortress for their journey to another world." Max proceeded to tell them what he could remember about the excursion into Pekel.

"So, I guess all we can do is wait for Joseph's call," Yelka said, as she glanced nervously at the gateway-mirror.

"Can you read this book?" Max handed it to her.

Yelka took the book and began examining the pages. After a minute of thumbing through it, she said she could read it. "It will be slow going. It is in a very old language."

"Well, what do we do while we wait?" Cindy wondered aloud, as she exhaled a long breath of boredom.

"You two can practice your magic or self-defense, there is plenty to learn," Yelka said, not looking up from the book. "Cindy, have you thought of any specific spells you want me to teach you?"

"I want to learn the spell that will let me travel to other worlds," Max interrupted, a little more eagerly than he intended, and flushed as both Yelka and Cindy turned to stare at him. He gave a slight cough.

"I know. You've already told me. I was asking Cindy," Yelka said.

"Really?" Cindy eyed Max suspiciously while Yelka seemed to study him, as if trying to read his thoughts.

"I just don't want to have another incident like last summer when we got trapped in Mir," Max explained, trying to hide his real reason for learning the spell. If he could find his mom and uncle, maybe he could rescue them without having to give Alan the key to Hudich's collar. *I can't let Hudich go free, but I will if I have to, to save my mother.*

"That is really an advanced spell," Yelka said.

"Actually, I think learning that spell sounds like a great idea," Cindy piped up. "I think it is important to understand how the enemy travels."

"Please, Yelka," Max pleaded, trying not to sound desperate. "If you teach me that one, you can choose the other spells you want me to learn."

Yelka examined him for another few moments before she agreed. "Very well."

"Wow." Cindy had excitement written all over her still-swollen face as she bounced on her toes.

"All right. I shall teach you the visualization and the words, but you will have to practice on your own. I don't have a great deal of time to help you, because I need to work on this book." Yelka raised the book into the air.

"We understand," Max said, and Cindy nodded in agreement.

"The most difficult part of this spell is to find the location of the world you wish to enter. I think you should start by trying to enter my world, Svet. You have been there before and it is relatively safe. I can give you the location of Svet off of the Gateway." Yelka walked to the control panel and waved for Max and Cindy to join her. "We are currently at this position," she said pointing to the dial. "Svet is here." She adjusted the dial to a new spot to show them Svet's location.

"The transportation spell is somewhat similar to the invisibility spell. Like the invisibility spell, this spell works on your own body.

You need to picture your body dissolving out of this world and materializing in the destination world. Do you think you can do that?"

"We'll have to learn," Cindy responded.

"You need two spells to make this work. The spell to leave is a difficult one and the spell to return is easy. The spell to leave is *preselim se*, and the spell to return is *vrnim se*. Let's repeat them together."

They pronounced the spells out loud together for several minutes.

"So, why is the return spell so easy and the other so difficult?" Max asked.

"Because when you travel by magic your body is tied to the world in which you reside. It is difficult to break that bond, as Joseph probably explained."

"He told us that when you travel by magic, you have to eventually leave because you become weak."

"That is because it takes a lot of energy and concentration to break that bond and keep it broken. That is why the other spell is easy to master. The pull to reunite the bond of your body and its original world is so strong that the return spell requires almost no energy. That's what makes the gateway such a powerful weapon. It makes it possible to travel without magic because the gateway creates a passage between the worlds. When you travel through the gateway, the new world becomes the world you are bonded to. If you travel through the gateway to Svet and then used magic to go elsewhere, when you speak the return spell, you would return to Svet, not Earth."

"That makes sense," Max said.

"It also helps me understand the enemy's interest in the gateway." Cindy added.

Martin and his mother burst into the room from the spiral staircase. "There's been a murder!" Martin shouted.

"What?" they all asked.

"It's true," Aunt Donna confirmed.

"Is it anybody we know?" Max asked.

"I don't think so. No one has reported anybody missing." Aunt Donna stated.

"The body was found in the bushes on the hill behind the Verrelli's house." Martin said. "It wasn't recognizable. They've called the police."

"The *police*." Max spat.

"What's wrong with the police?" Martin inquired.

"They're part of the enemy in this town." Cindy said, exchanging a worried look with Max and Yelka.

"You'd better go and find out what you can," Yelka said. "I need to stay here and wait for Joseph's signal."

Max, Cindy, Martin, and Aunt Donna raced down the stairs and out the front door.

"They're meeting at the school," Aunt Donna pointed in the direction of the red brick schoolhouse.

They hadn't gone very far before it was obvious something big had happened in the small town. The lights from the police cars swirled through the air, glinting red and blue off houses, crowds of people, and the school. It was the first time Max had seen the enemy mix with the new inhabitants of the town. A large crowd of people stood outside the school, talking among themselves.

Larry, Jo, and the rest of Larry's gang sat on their bikes a few yards away. Cindy and Jo glared at each other as if they were two wild animals getting ready to square off over the invasion of one's territory.

"I knew these people were killers," Larry scoffed, as Max and the others passed by.

"I'll bet it was that old kook, Joseph Rigdon," one of the other boys called.

"I think it was Cindy," Jo hollered.

Max grabbed Cindy's arm to keep her from spinning around to face Jo and Larry. "She's not worth it. Besides you need to practice your spells before you take on that witch again."

They ran to Cindy's mother, who was conversing with several people Max recognized by sight, but he didn't know any of their names.

"What's going on?" Cindy asked. Her mother turned to them as they approached.

"They discovered a dead body," Mrs. Carlson said.

"We know that! Is there anything else you know?" Cindy demanded.

"Well, the police are in there with the Verrellis. Apparently, their dogs found the body in the sage brush just beyond their property."

Max looked around and spotted the schoolteacher, Mrs. Ryan, waiting alone, off to the side of the crowd. Lines of worry creased her forehead, and she stood like a petrified tree, unmoving, staring at the school. While Cindy continued to badger her mother for more information, Max sidled towards Mrs. Ryan. As he got closer, he could see tears on her cheeks.

"Mrs. Ryan, are you okay?" Max asked.

"No," She said so quietly Max barely heard her.

"Is there anything I can do to help?"

"There's a very evil presence here in our town. I can feel it," she said, still staring straight ahead at the school. "I don't know what you've heard about the body."

"Nothing! Except where and how it was found."

"What they won't tell you is that it had been partially eaten."

"Eaten!"

Mrs. Ryan turned to look at Max. "I'm telling you this because you're going to have to stop this thing that has entered our town. We don't know whose body they found, but they said it probably wasn't any one from around here. Whatever did this is probably going to do it again. If it is here in our town, who knows who's next?"

"Could it have been a wild animal?"

"NO! There aren't any wild animals around here that size. I saw the remains and whatever did that is not from this world." She returned her stare to the school. "Of course, the police are going to try to blame this on the Verrellis. What frightens me the most is the majority of the enemy seems scared. They don't appear to be aware of what it is."

Goose bumps spread over Max's body as if some horrifying creature had breathed on the back of his neck. He remembered Yelka's concern the night she came to rescue him from his Aunt's house. "Something horrible is going on in the shed," she had said. Then there was that creature pretending to be his uncle.

Max almost strained a neck muscle as his head swiveled back and forth searching for the creature, Grd.

"What are you looking for?" Mrs. Ryan asked, her eyes upon him once more.

"I think I know who, or what, did this," Max said.

"What!"

"There's some type of chameleon that has been impersonating my uncle," Max said, before he could stop himself from giving too much away.

"Where is he?"

"I don't see hi…" Max's eyes locked with Grd's.

Grd, in the form of Max's uncle, leaned against a tree all by himself, and a wicked smile spread slowly across his face, revealing not the human teeth of his uncle, but the sharp, hooked teeth of the creature within.

"*Razkrij zlo*," Max said, and the fuzzy red glow looked like flames as it flickered up and down Grd's skin.

The fact that Grd stood, unaware of what had happened to him shocked Max. Mrs. Ryan gave a sharp gasp, causing the majority of the crowd, including Max to look at her. Max could barely hear the words as she spoke from an obvious state of shock. "That's a very evil creature. I didn't need the spell, I sensed it."

Max spun back towards Grd, who was gone.

"I've never seen this spell cause flames upon the enemy's skin before," she stated, as some of the crowd arrived to see what happened.

Max moved through the crowd until he found Cindy. She, Martin, and a small group was listening to Mrs. Carlson convey what she knew about the mysterious dead. "We need to talk. Privately!" Max whispered in Cindy's ear.

Cindy gave a slight nod and then slowly backed away from the crowd. Max led her back to the house where they locked themselves in Max's bedroom.

"What are you looking for?" Cindy asked, as Max began inspecting the room.

He made sure the window and door were secure before looking under the bed and in the closet. "You have to swear that you will tell no one what I'm going to tell you."

"I swear."

Max proceeded to tell Cindy the details of what had happened to him. He told her about the mission Alan had sent him on, and his trip into the other world where his mom and his uncle were prisoners. "That's what my mother's hair had to do with this," he said. Then he revealed his suspicions about Grd, and his conversation with Mrs. Ryan.

"Oh Max, what are we going to do?"

"First, I'm going to master the transportation spell so I can start searching for my mother. Then, we need to come up with a plan. Don't repeat what I've told you. I can't risk my mother's life. There is a traitor among us, and until we know who that is, we have to work in secret."

"I don't think it's Grandpa, or Yelka, or my parents."

"Neither do I. I think it's someone new."

###

Once Joe was sure the other slaves were asleep, he worked on releasing his ankle from the shackle. He had the information he wanted, and it was time to get out of there. The moment he stepped through the gateway, he knew he was in the world Sladkor. With the bright, vivid colors of flowers and plants, it almost looked like a candy land.

Joe needed to warn the people of Sladkor. The Trogs were prepared for war, and unless help could be sent to the inhabitants of Sladkor, they were doomed. Not just Trogs, but armed Trogs with other, unknown types of weapons.

Joe fiddled with the lock for several hours before coming to the conclusion that he needed the proper tools to be able to free himself. He tried several spells without success. The only thing he could figure was that the metal came from Pekel and somehow it, like the world itself, resisted magic. The longer he took to get free, the less chance the inhabitants of Sladkor had to prepare. After glancing in all directions to make sure no one would see what he was doing, he took out his communicator.

###

Max lay awake on his bed, staring up at the ceiling. He hadn't slept a wink. His mind wouldn't rest after the events of the evening and finally telling Cindy about the mission the enemy gave him. Even with all the new distractions, his thoughts drifted back to his mother. He wiped his eyes as tears started to form. *Be strong!* He must start practicing the transportation spell and start searching for his mother. Besides mastering the spell, he still needed the key. Max gave up trying to sleep and got out of bed. He went upstairs to find Yelka struggling to stay awake.

"No word yet?" Max asked.

"No. I am extremely worried."

"I can take a turn waiting for the call. Why don't you go and get some sleep."

"Are you sure you don't mind?" Yelka asked, with a wide yawn.

"Of course I'm sure!"

"Thank you." Yelka stood and stretched. "Are you feeling all right?"

Max could feel her eyes studying his face. "Yes, just can't sleep."

"If you become tired, come and wake me." Yelka patted his shoulder and then left the room.

The Hourglass of Souls

Max looked at Yelka's communicator as it lay on the control panel and then at the chair she had brought up to sit in while she waited for Grandpa's call. Max let himself fall down onto the seat. He sighed and wondered about his mother's safety. If these chameleons came from the world where she is now a prisoner, how long would she remain unharmed? If he didn't do something to bring her back, Hudich might really go free. *That can't happen*, he thought, as he gritted his teeth and clenched his fists.

He relaxed his hands and took a deep breath. Focusing all his thoughts on Yelka's world, Svet, he whispered, "Preselim se Svet."

After a few minutes of nothing happening, Max stood and walked around the room, shaking out his hands and feet. *I must concentrate harder.* He went to the control panel to see if he could figure out what the coordinates meant. He adjusted the dials for Svet so he could read the settings. There were four coordinates. One of the readings with the title of "Distance" displayed a huge number; another, with the title of "Location" had the number fifty-six showing; the third, with the title "Direction" showed the number thirty-three; and the last switch "Angle" read one hundred and ninety-seven.

He turned the dial back to Earth and noticed the numbers. "Distance", "Angle", "Direction" showed zero but "Location" read one. There were several other dials for the gateway, but Yelka didn't mention them in the instructions for the spell.

He sat back in the chair and assumed the most comfortable position he could find. *The coordinates! How do I use them? Why didn't Yelka explain them better? Wait a minute.*

Max jumped to his feet and raced to the control panel. He adjusted the dials for "Angle" and "Direction" until they stopped on the point which read three hundred and sixty. "Angle" must be the "Angle" from the house's position and "Direction" is the same. That means "Distance" is how far from here.

Excitement raced through Max's veins like a runaway rollercoaster. He resumed his relaxed position in the chair. Concentrating on the coordinates for Svet, Max whispered the spell, "*Preselim se* Svet."

Suddenly Max felt cold, like a freezing wind slammed into his body, penetrating his very flesh as if he wasn't solid anymore. The room started to fade and his vision grew dark. Then there was a ringing in his ears. The ringing blocked out the wind, and the room of Grandpa's house came back into focus. The ringing came again and Max realized it was Yelka's communicator. *Grandpa!*

Max struggled to reach the control panel. He labored to gulp down air as he stood on shaky legs. Little lines of sweat rolled down his forehead and he felt exhausted. Max almost dropped the communicator on the floor with his his trembling hands. *Yelka wasn't kidding when she said that spell takes a lot of energy!*

He read Grandpa's message and quickly responded that he understood. Then he went to wake Yelka.

"Yelka," Max said, as he gently shook her. "Grandpa called and he needs our help."

"Wha... What did he say?" Yelka asked, looking a little confused from being awakened.

"He said he is in a world called Sladkor. He also said he has been shackled, and he needs us to bring the skeleton key to free him. He gave me the directions where to open the gateway. He also wants you to send a message to Sladkor about the threat of war."

"Did he say where the skeleton key was located?"

"It's hidden down in his office. I'll go get it."

"After you get the key, start gathering supplies and meet me up at the gateway."

"Okay," Max agreed and he sprang down the stairs to the den. He turned on the light to reveal a large oak desk standing in the middle of the room, with family pictures displayed on top of it. Walls of bookshelves encircled the room. He went to the window and made sure the curtains were pulled shut. Then he pushed a ladder in front of the bookshelf directly in front of the desk and climbed to the second level. It took him only a second to find "The Hobbit" by J.R.R. Tolkien. He pulled the book from its resting place, which released a lever.

A section of books supported by a hidden door popped open and Max looked inside. He found the skeleton key, just where Grandpa said it would be. Not only did he find the skeleton key, he also found the key to Hudich's collar.

11

Sladkor

Max descended the ladder, his mind racing. He now knew where Grandpa kept the key to Hudich's collar. *I need to come up with an idea to free my mom and uncle. That plan must involve a scheme to keep the key while pretending to give it away. It has to be flawless.*

Head down, deep in the thoughts of his new discovery, Max walked out of the study and collided with Cindy. They bumped heads, and he fell to the floor; the walls seemed to swirl around him.

"Ouch!" Cindy cried, as she too landed on the floor.

"Cindy, what are you doing here?" Max asked, rubbing his forehead to ease the pain.

"Sorry, I couldn't sleep after our conversation. I saw the light on in the den, and thought I'd see who was up. Did you hear from Grandpa?"

Max climbed to his feet and helped Cindy to hers. "Yes, we have!" Max explained that Grandpa was in a world called Sladkor and that he was going there to help him.

"I want to come," Cindy said, as they ran up the stairs to the second floor.

Suddenly they heard a hum coming from the third floor. Max and Cindy exchanged looks and raced down the hall and up the spiral staircase to the third floor. They came to an abrupt halt in the doorway of the tower when they saw a stranger standing next to Yelka. It was a woman unlike any they had seen before. She was a head and shoulders taller than Max and Cindy and had long blond hair. Even though her pale milky-white skin gave her a look as though she were deathly ill, she was beautiful. She wore two swords across her back and an array of daggers in her belt. For some odd reason she gave Max the impression of a cat ready to pounce, and he knew she was not someone to mess with.

Max couldn't stop himself from staring at her smooth, chalky face and full red lips. She had a kind of soft glow that Max imagined an angel would cast.

"You can stop drooling," Cindy snapped, and elbowed Max in the side.

As Yelka shut down the gateway, her eyes met Max and Cindy's. "Max, Cindy, I want you to meet Sky," Yelka said, as Max and Cindy approached.

She gave them both a firm handshake. "Pleasure."

"She's going to be your self-defense teacher and will go with you to help Joseph," Yelka sang.

"She's the new self-defense teacher!" Cindy said, as she crossed her arms and crinkled her nose.

"Wow!" said Max with a smile. She definitely wasn't what he expected Marko's replacement to be. Not only was she a woman, but she displayed her weapons for everyone to see. Max had liked the way Marko hid his weapons. It was always a surprise when he brought them out. Marko had an air of mystery about him with his black cloak. Sky was quite the opposite. Her tunic and pants were forest green, and her tall boots were brown. Max cleared his throat as Cindy rolled her eyes at him. "I mean, cool."

"When do we leave?" Cindy asked, with her arms still folded.

"We?" Yelka asked, turning towards Cindy.

"Are you human?" Max asked, feeling a little lightheaded being around Sky.

"Of sorts. Your grandfather calls me a genie, but I'm not like a genie as you know them. I don't live in a bottle and I don't grant wishes," Sky said.

"Then, how are you like a genie?" Cindy asked her eyes locked on Sky.

"Joseph rescued me from a horrible fate. Like a genie, we are bound for life to the person or creature that helps us. It's the same as your belief that genies are tied to those who set them free. We are very magical. So magical in fact, I used my powers to become a weapons master."

"How did my grandfather save you?" Max asked.

"Cindy, I'm afraid you won't be going," Yelka interrupted.

"What? Why not?" Cindy's snooty mood towards Sky gave way to a pout. "I want to go."

"I don't think I can send you without your parents' permission. Last year Joseph sent you because Max needed help. Your parents didn't know anything about the war. This year they do, so I can't let you go."

"If I get their permission, can I go?"

"Yes, but but…" Yelka tried to get in another word as Cindy dashed out of the room and headed for home.

"She's not going to wake her parents in the middle of the night is she?" Sky asked.

"You obviously don't know Cindy," Max chuckled.

"Did you get the key?" Yelka asked.

"Yes."

"What about your pack, do you have supplies?" Sky asked.

"I'll be right back," Max said as he, too, dashed out of the room.

Max returned with his pack loaded with food, water, a compass and various other supplies for survival in the wild. Cindy hadn't returned, which indicated she hadn't won the argument with her mother. Yelka and Sky were busy discussing plans as Max approached.

"There's a forest about a mile south of where Joseph is being held. If we open the gateway there, you should be able to enter Sladkor without being detected by the Trogs," Yelka informed them.

"I'm sure there are more than Trogs we have to worry about," Sky said.

"Yes, but the Trogs don't know they have Grandpa," Max added, to their surprise. "So, it's not like we're going to bust a prisoner free." The words hit Max like a kick to the gut and it took everything he had to stop the tears he could feel forming. It wasn't Grandpa he was worried about, it was his mother. The words "bust a prisoner free" had triggered the emotions building up inside him.

"Max, are you okay?" Yelka asked. "You look rather pale."

Max took out his water skin. "I just need a drink," he said, and swallowed some water.

"Are you sure?"

"Yes."

"The last thing I need on a dangerous mission is a sick companion," Sky added, her eyebrows raised.

"I'm not sick!"

The sudden arrival of Cindy and her mother spared Max any more interrogation about his well-being. Surprise replaced the feelings of dread for his mother. Cindy and her mother wore backpacks and traveling cloaks.

"Yelka," Mrs. Carlson began, as she drew near. "Cindy has my permission to go on this rescue mission as long as I accompany her."

"Wait one moment." Sky held out her hands as if to stop oncoming traffic. "I agreed to take Max so we could be in and out quickly. The more people we have, the more dangerous it is. I mean, I understand Max and Cindy have some experience, but you don't have any." Sky met Mrs. Carlson's gaze, which looked like Cindy's had fifteen minutes earlier.

"I have plenty of experience," Mrs. Carlson snapped, with her arms folded across her chest. "How old are you, anyway?"

"In Earth years, I am eighty-four, but in my world I am twenty-six. I have been in fifty-seven battles. How many have you been in?"

What happened next shocked Max: one minute Mrs. Carlson was a block of ice and the next she was soft like new-fallen snow. "Please, I want to have the experience. We're all at war and need to learn to fight."

Sky's expression was no less astonishing. She looked at Mrs. Carlson with admiration. "The courage and desire to fight are necessary, and you have proven to me that you have both. I am Sky, welcome aboard." She held out her hand, and Mrs. Carlson smiled as she accepted it.

"So, everyone's going?" Yelka asked.

"Yes," Sky smiled. "As long as everyone is willing to follow my orders."

"We are," Mrs. Carlson agreed, and shot a look at Cindy and Max, who both nodded.

"Does everyone have what they need?" Sky asked.

Everyone said they did, and Yelka fired up the gateway. The force field spread from the five pillars and formed a dome, which almost filled the entire room. The familiar hum vibrated through the house as the antique mirror started to revolve. Soon the ball of light that joined their world to others replaced the spinning mirror.

"Everyone, watch each other's back and be safe," Yelka ordered. "I'll wait for your signal, and Godspeed."

"Stay close to me and do exactly what I tell you," Sky repeated, as she entered the gateway.

###

They stepped out of the gateway into the middle of a strange pine forest. The needles on the trees were almost a foot in length, the weight causing them to droop towards the ground. The trees were not so thick to stop the light of the full moon from penetrating to the grass-covered forest floor. Max and Cindy caught Cindy's mother and supported her until she regained her balance as she walked through the gateway. They had forgotten to tell her to step down.

Sky examined a compass on a chain hanging around her neck. "The camp should be about a mile that way," she whispered, as she pointed north. "Stay low and follow me."

She led them north, scampering in a hunched position, and always staying in the shadows of the trees. The light of the full moon made it easy for them to make their way quickly through the sparse trees and other plant life. After they had advanced over a half mile, Sky brought them to a halt behind a group of tall shrubs with massive heart-shaped leaves. "Wait here," she whispered and then disappeared before their eyes.

"Did she cast a spell?" Mrs. Carlson asked in a hushed, confused voice.

"I think so," Cindy answered.

"If she did, she didn't say it out loud," Max added, as he peered around the bush in an attempt to see the Trogs. Through the trees, Max spied the occasional flicker of firelight, but not enough to make anything out.

"Do you see anything?" Cindy asked, as she put her hands on his back and looked over his shoulder.

"Some lights beyond the trees, but nothing else. My guess is that it's the Trogs' camp."

"Do you think she'll just get your grandfather and bring him back?" Mrs. Carlson asked.

"She doesn't have the skeleton key. She must be checking things out," Max responded.

After what seemed like hours of waiting, Sky appeared right in front of them. Her sudden presence startled Max, Cindy, and Mrs. Carlson. Mrs. Carlson covered her mouth to stifle a sharp cry.

"I found him," she whispered.

"Did you talk to him?" Max asked, as they huddled together.

A loud animal cry nearby caused them all to whirl around in its direction. After a brief pause to make sure it was not a scout, they went back to their conversation.

"He is on the other side of the camp where cover will be sparse," Sky continued. "I found a good spot to hide, but it is nearly a quarter mile away from the camp. After that, I think Max and I should go in to get him."

Cindy tried to object, but Sky held up a hand to silence her. "Can you perform the invisibility spell?"

"No." Cindy hung her head.

"We will not be gone long." Sky sounded like she wanted to lift Cindy's spirits. "In quick and out quick. Not more than ten minutes. Now, follow me and keep quiet."

It took them a long time to circle the Trog army and reach the spot Sky had mentioned. Trees were few and spread out, but just as Sky had said, about a quarter mile from the camp was a large boulder, which hid them from the enemy's view.

"Wait here," Sky whispered to Mrs. Carlson and Cindy. She turned to Max and pulled out a thin cord that seemed to change colors as it moved over objects, like a chameleon. She fastened one end through one of Max's belt loops and then tied the other end around her waist. "Do not let anything break your concentration. Pay close attention to the slack on the cord. Keep it firm but not tight. I will whisper commands when I can. *Izginim se.*"

"*Izginim se,*" Max muttered, and disappeared.

Max kept one hand on the cord and found it easy to follow Sky's invisible lead. The ground was smooth and even. Sky avoided the few obstacles in their way and advanced at a steady pace.

Once again, Max could feel his heart beat like a base drum in his chest—thud-thud-thudding—as Sky headed straight for the Trog on watch. *What's she doing?*

The guard sat on a rock, watching the open ground which Max and Sky had just crossed. His hand held onto a spear with its tip pointing skyward and the other end stuck in the dirt.

Max's anxiety increased as the soft thumping of his own footfalls reached his ears. He tried, but was unsuccessful at detecting Sky's footsteps. When they were within ten yards of the guard, Max held his breath.

The Trog's head snapped in their direction as Max's shoe snapped a loose twig. Before he could get to his feet, a crack filled the air, and the Trog fell face down in the dirt.

The cord took a sharp angle to Max's right as Sky changed direction. They moved through the army of sleeping Trogs, towards a group of slaves huddled around a catapult. All but one of them slept as they approached. *Grandpa.*

"We are here," Sky whispered, once they reached Grandpa's side.

"Good," he replied, and lifted his robe to reveal the shackle around his ankle.

Max took the key out of his pocket and knelt down beside his grandfather. "How does it work?"

"Just put it in the lock and turn it." Grandpa answered.

"Hurry! Some guards are approaching," Sky warned.

Max put the key in the lock and a strange vibration shook his fingers. He twisted the key and a soft click told him Grandpa was free.

The deep raspy speech of the Trogs indicated they were close.

"Take this," Sky whispered to Grandpa. Max assumed she handed him another end of the strange cord.

"*Izginim se*," Grandpa whispered, and disappeared.

The slack of the cord disappeared, moving Max in the direction of the pull. They went back the same way they came, except Sky had them turn before they reached the unconscious guard.

"A SLAVE IS GONE! SLAVE ESCAPE!" Echoed across the entire camp.

"Run!" Sky whispered, almost yanking Max off his feet.

Her strength shocked Max as he hastily untied the rope to keep her from dragging him. They sprinted towards the rock and found Cindy and Mrs. Carlson ready to leave.

From the roar that filled the valley, Max guessed the entire army was awake and in pursuit.

"Come on," Sky urged, as they raced past the rock.

"Where are you?" Mrs. Carlson asked, as her head moved around like a spectator watching a basketball game.

"*Prikazim se*," Grandpa whispered, and appeared in front of Cindy, causing her to flinch. "Sorry, I just realized that you couldn't see us."

Max and Sky also cast spells to reveal themselves.

"Let's move," Sky stressed, waving her arm for them to follow.

They sprinted across the open ground towards the trees of the forest.

"THERE!" the rough voice of a Trog bellowed. "HEADING FOR THE TREES."

"CIVUS, LOOSE THE DIDOCS!"

Several high-pitched screams caused the hairs on the back of Max's neck to stand up like cactus needles.

"What made that noise?" Mrs. Carlson asked, her voice full of fright.

"You do not want to know. Just keep running," Sky answered calmly.

Another terrifying cry caused Max to jump. It took all his effort to keep from tripping over his own feet after hearing such a thing.

"They've spotted us," Grandpa announced, bringing up the rear.

"Should I have Yelka open the Gateway?" Max asked between gulps of air. Sweat formed across his brow and down his back, and his heart pounded in his ears.

"NO!" Grandpa warned.

"But they're gaining on us," Max yelled, as another hair-raising-scream caused him to look over his shoulder.

At least a dozen small animals the size of wolverines bounded after them. Long sharp spikes that looked like thin knives grew out of their backs and flashed a silvery color in the moonlight as they raced along the ground. One of them screamed a piercing cry as a blast of fire jetted from its jaws.

"These animals are called Didocs and if we teleport after being spotted by them, they will follow us home," Grandpa said, breathing hard. "They're ferocious trackers."

"Get in front of me!" Sky ordered, as she fell to the rear of the pack. She drew her swords from across her back without breaking stride.

"Don't let them touch you. Their scratch is poisonous," Grandpa said over his shoulder.

"What?" Mrs. Carlson shrieked.

"Just keep running," Cindy ordered her mother.

"They are not alone," Sky informed them, as they approached the forest.

Sweat ran down Max's back, and his legs screamed for him to quit. The cramp in his side added to his desire to stop. He had to focus on his footing so as not to fall down as he risked another glance over his shoulder. In that instant he saw a robed figure that was moving among the group of Didocs, keeping pace with their advance.

"That would be Civus," Grandpa puffed.

Civus moved into the moonlight. A white skull-like head floated above his robe. He raised his arms, and a huge gust of wind slammed into Max and the others, knocking all but Sky to the ground.

"Get up!" Sky ordered, as she turned to face their pursuers.

A short distance behind Civus and the Didocs, the Trogs' torches danced around like fireflies. It gave the sense that a small city was following them from the valley behind.

Screams from Cindy and Mrs. Carlson caused everyone to turn. In front of them was another Civus, approaching fast.

"That Civus is only an illusion! Run for the trees," Grandpa yelled, and the small group resumed their attempt to escape.

Once, twice, three times the paralyzing screams of Didocs sounded. It was like they were right on top of the small group, but had changed their cries to howls of pain, as Sky's blades flashed downward like lightning in the pale light of the moon. Sky's swift speed kept the remaining Didocs at bay, as Max and the others entered the forest. The Didocs, roaring with fury, held their distance from Sky.

"Watch out," Sky called, as the cries of the Didocs disappeared. "They went underground."

"What?" Cindy shrieked in a high-pitched voice.

"Keep running," Grandpa yelled, as a flash of lighting zipped across the sky. A strong wind slammed their faces slowing their progress to a crawl.

Max jerked his forearm up in front of his face to shield his eyes from flying debris. As he leaned forward into the wind, a Didoc sprang from the ground just ahead of Mrs. Carlson, who screamed out. Max yelled into the wind thrusting his hands forward, "*Premakni.*" The spell flung the Didoc into a tree, knocking it senseless.

"We need help," Cindy called over the howling wind.

"I can't argue with that," Grandpa said, as he pulled his communicator out of his robe.

Another pained wail told Max that Sky had encountered another Didoc. Suddenly Sky was everywhere in front of the group slashing down Didocs as they exploded from the dirt. As she passed Cindy, Sky handed her a sword and then did the same to Max. "I understand you know how to use it."

"A little," Max replied.

"Keep moving. Help is coming," Grandpa said.

Cindy thrust her blade forward as a Didoc sprang up in front of her. Her quick motion was just in time to keep the vile creature at a safe distance. The Didoc screamed in pain as it tried to free itself from Cindy's sharp sting. The Didoc's strength wrenched the sword from her grip.

"*Vrtinchim se,*" Sky said. Suddenly Sky began to rotate like a top, spinning so fast she was a blur. As she whirled about, she circled the group like a tornado, with her blades cutting up any Didoc that dared to get too close.

A deep, gravelly voice uttered a word that echoed like thunder through the forest. The spell hammered into Sky like a runaway freight train, driving her to the ground. The way the air escaped Sky's body as she hit the forest floor terrified Max.

"She's dead!" Cindy screamed, running towards Sky's limp body.

"Max, Cindy, send fire everywhere," Grandpa ordered. "*Prizgaj, Prizgaj, Prizgaj,*" he yelled, sending fireballs in all directions.

Max, and then Cindy, joined in the volley, launching fire all around the area. Suddenly the forest looked like a fireworks display. Fireballs exploded in the air and off the trees. A horrible cry filled the forest, and the shape of a retreating robed figure flashed through the trees.

"Keep sending!" Grandpa ordered, and Max and Cindy obeyed. Grandpa ran to Sky's aid, along with Mrs. Carlson.

Mrs. Carlson took Sky's arm gently in her hand. "She has a pulse."

"Help me get her up," Grandpa said, as he reached under her arm, and Mrs. Carlson did the same to the other.

Sky's eyes were open but her body was limp. She moaned as Grandpa and Mrs. Carlson lifted her to her feet.

"Sorry," Mrs. Carlson apologized.

As Grandpa supported Sky with one arm, he placed his other hand on Sky's forehead and closed his eyes. "*Zdravi.*"

Sky's eyes seemed to gain a little focus, and the lines of pain in her face eased some.

"We need to get you out of here," Grandpa said, looking into Sky's eyes.

She gave a slight nod.

"Max, Cindy, let's go. Keep your eyes open for Civus and Didocs. They're still out there and won't stay away for long," Grandpa said, as he and Mrs. Carlson helped Sky deeper into the forest.

"Don't forget the entire Trog army," Max added, and continued to glance over his shoulder for any signs of pursuit.

Another massive gust of wind hit them from the rear, scattering them like sand in the desert.

"How do we to get out of here with this wind?" Cindy asked, as she sprang to her feet.

"Cast more fireballs!" Grandpa ordered. Once again, he and Mrs. Carlson helped a weakened Sky to her feet.

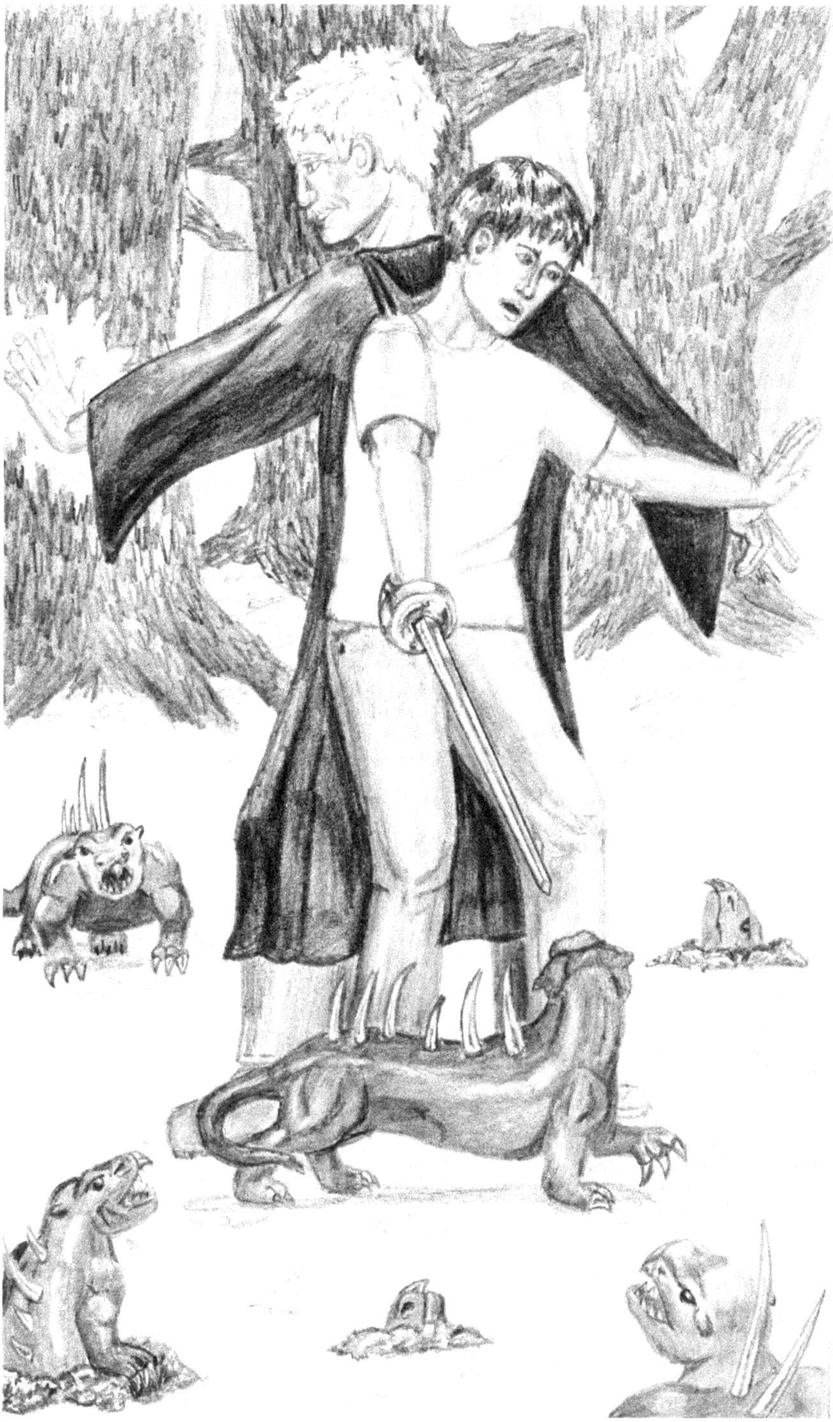

Max and Cindy did as Grandpa ordered, and sent blasts of fire in every direction. Civus let out a tortured cry and retreated out of the light.

"Cindy, to your left," Max called, and sent fireball after fireball in the direction of the retreating figure, and Cindy joined in. "He hates the light."

The group continued to move deeper into the forest, with Cindy up front and Max bringing up the rear. They had to send fire after the attacking Civus multiple times, but the Didocs had disappeared. Max knew they were still out there.

No sooner had Max finished this last thought when several Didocs emerged from the ground from every direction. Cindy launched several fireballs at the Didocs closest to her, scattering them into the forest. Grandpa had to leave Mrs. Carlson and Sky to join in the fight.

Max used his sword to slash a deep wound in the closest Didoc, which frightened the others into keeping their distance. As Max held three at bay with the point of his sword, another Didoc wailed wildly as an arrow pierced its side. Then several other Didocs went down with arrows buried in their bodies.

The screams of the wounded Didocs distracted the remaining creatures. Max was as confused by the arrows as the Didocs appeared to be, but kept his attention on his surroundings. He seized the opportunity and cast fire at more Didocs, who made easy targets. The blasts hit their marks, igniting the Didocs' fur like dry kindling. The Didocs thrashed and rolled on the ground, trying to extinguish the flames.

"Max!" Cindy screamed, when several people emerged from the trees with bows and arrows and began to destroy the Didocs.

"They're here to help us," Grandpa said, before Max or Cindy started to attack the new arrivals.

Another flash of lightning illuminated the night sky and a heavy rain followed. The storm's arrival gave the remaining Didocs the opportunity they needed to escape from their new attackers.

The new soldiers pursued the Didocs into the woods. Max looked at the others as the sudden, heavy rain soaked them.

Several spine-tingling cries rose above the storm, as three of the new soldiers appeared from the direction of the fleeing Didocs.

"Joseph," one of them said as he approached.

"Yes?"

"Something besides the Didocs is out there…"

Before he could finish his sentence, another cry, more horrible than Max had ever heard, drowned out all other sounds.

"It's Civus. He's devouring his victims, your friends. He grinds them to dust," Grandpa said.

"Follow us," the man said, his eyes wide and voice cracking. "We're under orders to escort you back to our camp.

The figure that spoke took the lead of the little party, and the other two watched the rear as they continued their escape. Max and Cindy took turns with Grandpa and Mrs. Carlson to support Sky, who was conscious but not alert. She gave an occasional grunt or groan as they helped her over fallen logs and small streams.

As they followed their escorts, it seemed that the forest had come alive, continuing the attack Civus and the Didocs had started. Not only did the rain penetrate their clothing, but it crept into their minds. Tree branches and shrubs scratched and pulled at their skin and clothing.

"This rain, it feels like it's crawling on my skin. I wish it would stop," Mrs. Carlson said, as she let Cindy take her turn supporting Sky.

"It isn't a regular storm," Grandpa said. "Civus has the ability to control the weather in this world. Quite remarkable."

Max had the feeling Grandpa actually admired Civus for this power.

They struggled through the storm the rest of the night until they reached a small camp of a hundred troops. Their guide led them through the busy camp of several green tents surrounding a larger tent in the center. Everyone seemed on edge as if awaiting an inevitable battle. Two guards parted to let the group pass. Four men huddled around a folding table, in deep discussion.

"Sir, we've brought Joseph, like you asked. Mico and Franz. . . they didn't make it," the man informed the others.

Max's blood froze and Cindy let out a scream as Marko, the traitor, the devil who had tried to kill them last summer, turned from the table. "That's grave news," he said.

12

The War Begins

"Max, Cindy," Grandpa stepped between them and Marko, while supporting Sky at the same time.

Cindy looked like she was going to cast a spell and Max pointed his sword at Marko.

"This isn't Marko! This isn't Marko." Grandpa kept repeating.

"Then who is he?" Max asked, not willing to back down.

All the men with Marko had also drawn their weapons and were aiming them at Max and Cindy.

"He's Marko's brother," Grandpa said. "He's on our side. I think we need to get Sky some medical attention before we deal with this."

"Marko's brother is on our side?" Cindy said in such a sarcastic tone that Max nodded his agreement.

How could Marko, the traitor—Marko, the one who tried to kill them and set Hudich free—have a brother who wasn't evil? Max felt ill; his insides squirmed like a can of worms. All the pain of Marko's betrayal came bubbling to the surface. Max remembered how much he had liked Marko, and how he thought he was his friend, only to have Marko attempt to murder them.

"Please, Please." Marko's brother put up his hands. "Put down your weapons and carry Sky to the medical tent," he ordered his men. They followed his command and took Sky from Grandpa and Mrs. Carlson.

"Max, Cindy, take it easy," Grandpa said. "Yes, he *is* Marko's brother. His name is Jax. After our incident with Marko last year, I had him checked out."

"What does that mean?" Cindy asked with raised eyebrows.

"Max, you learned the spell to reveal someone who practices good or evil magic, didn't you?" Grandpa asked.

"Yes."

"Well, cast the spell that reveals good magic at Jax."

Max didn't believe a simple spell, even if it showed Jax was good, could change how he was feeling. How could he trust a spell? Could there be a spell or a charm that repelled his spell to make him appear the opposite of what he wanted?

"He could use magic to make us see what he wants us to," Cindy voiced, confirming Max's doubts.

"Just cast the spell," Grandpa said with a smile. "We'll deal with tricks or counter-spells later."

Max still felt like it wouldn't work. "*Razkrim zlo*," he said pointing his finger at Jax while keeping one hand on the hilt of his sword. Nothing happened. The red light did not appear around Jax to indicate that he was evil.

"I thought you were going to cast the spell to show good?" Grandpa inquired.

"Very smart," Jax smiled, "you need always to keep the enemy on their toes. I like..."

"*Razkrim dobro*," Max cast the second version of the spell and a soft blue glow appeared all over Jax's body. "I guess we'll have to trust the results." Max reluctantly lowered his sword, still not trusting Jax.

"What Marko did was despicable. We were not close. I'd wager he never even mentioned me." Jax stated.

"No, he didn't," Max said. "Hey, wait a minute. Marko wasn't human but looked human. How come you look human?" Max thought he had Jax trapped. Marko only pretended to be human so Grandpa would trust him.

"We are half-human and can change between our two races. One race is Hudich's race but I choose not to wear that skin. Not all that belong in my race are evil, but many are. I do not blame you for not trusting me, but hopefully I can prove that I am on your side."

"Humph," Cindy grunted, and folded her arms as if she wasn't going to be convinced so easily.

"Why don't you have your men get them something to eat, and I can tell you what's been happening," Grandpa said to Jax.

"Why don't we just go home?" Max asked, trying to sound casual. He didn't want to spend a minute longer in a world with Jax.

"We may not be able to leave for a while. They will need our help to defeat the Trog army," Grandpa said.

"What can we do?" asked Mrs. Carlson. "How can we help?"

"You'll be able to help. Now, go get something to eat and get a little rest."

With that, Jax called for a guard to take Max, Cindy, and Mrs. Carlson to the mess tent.

After they ate what tasted like gooey oatmeal, the soldier showed them to a tent where there were cloth cots for them to sleep on. Max couldn't sleep; he needed to get out of Sladkor and work on a plan to help his mother and uncle. He knew where the key was now, he just needed a scheme. *Time's a wasting.*

"Max," Cindy called in a hushed voice. "Are you asleep?"

"No, but it sounds like your mom is," Max whispered back.

"Let's go for a walk so we can talk," Cindy suggested, easing herself up from her cot.

Max got up quietly and followed Cindy outside the tent. They headed for a group of trees a short distance from the camp where a guard appeared out of nowhere.

"Where do you think you're going?" the guard asked.

"Ahh, we just wanted a private place to talk," Cindy offered.

He peered at them, eyes squinted, and then relented. "I'll let you go about thirty yards that way," pointing to his right, "but stay where I can see you."

"Okay," Max agreed, and put his arm through Cindy's and led her in the direction indicated by the guard.

"I don't know about you, but I don't trust Jax one little bit," Cindy whispered in a sharp tone.

"Forget about Jax. We need to get out of here," Max said, looking in all directions to make sure they were alone before proceeding.

"What do you mean: 'Forget about Jax'?" Cindy's agitated voice rose, drawing the guard's attention. She stared at Max with her hands on her hips, and for the first time this summer Max remembered how pretty her blue eyes were.

"Shh," Max stressed. "I found the key."

"You found the key to Hudich's collar?" Cindy regained her composure and leaned closer so only Max could hear. "Where is it?"

"It's in a safe in Grandpa's den." Max double checked to see if anyone was around. He was about to tell Cindy about the book when a "psst" from a bush behind Cindy drew his attention.

"What?" Cindy asked, and started to turn around.

"Stay still, punks!" a hushed voice ordered, causing Cindy and Max to freeze.

"Larry?" Max asked. Panic rushed through Max's veins like ice water. "What are you doing here?"

"If I were you, I'd shut my mouth and listen, especially since you were given orders to not tell anyone about your mission. I could have sworn I just heard you tell Cindy something about a key."

The sinking sensation returned. Max felt dizzy, like being trapped in a whirlpool spinning faster and faster, about to go under.

"What mission?" Cindy pretended innocence.

"Don't play me for a fool. Your boyfriend's pale face tells me I'm right."

A whistle and a nod from the guard told them they needed to hurry.

Max flashed the guard five fingers, hoping the guard from this world would understand what he meant. "What do you want, Larry?"

"I'm here to check on your progress. And since I know you have the key there's only one snag."

"What's that?" Max asked, the weight of the world pressing on his shoulders, driving him deeper into an inescapable pit.

"What am I going to tell my dad about your betrayal?"

"If you touch my…"

"Don't threaten me," Larry interrupted, "or your mother will pay severely. But I'm willing to make a deal."

"What kind of deal?" Cindy asked over her shoulder.

"Oh, I don't know," Larry pondered, in a way that indicated he did indeed know, and had something nasty in mind.

"What do you want?" Max gritted his teeth.

"A little trade."

Another whistle from the guard told Max they were out of time.

"Make it quick," Max urged.

"Oh, I'll be in touch. This sort of thing takes time to think through. But if you know what's good for you and your mother, you won't tell anyone else about your mission. I'll see you soon."

Max was more desperate than ever as they headed back to camp. He trusted Larry less than Jax. Knowing Larry, he would have Max suffer something terrible and then still rat him out to his father, Alan. Fear crept up Max's spine like a huge, hairy tarantula. All he wanted to do was call Yelka and have her open the gateway.

They passed the guard and went back to their tent.

"What are we going to do?" Cindy asked, her face pale with worry.

Tears began forming in Max's eyes and he had to swallow the lump in his throat to keep from breaking down completely. "I don't know," he said, in the calmest voice he could muster.

They went back to the cots and tried to sleep. Max couldn't stop worrying about what might happen to his mother if Larry told Alan what he had heard. They removed his mother's hair last time. He was sure it was going to be something dreadful, something unthinkable!

A soft shake brought Max back to the world of Sladkor.

Grandpa stood over him. "We need to get going. The war is coming."

"Are we going home?" Max asked. "I thought I was training my replacement." Grandpa frowned.

"Wha. . . what do you mean?"

Grandpa smiled grimly. "We don't run and hide in the face of danger. We stand and fight! Besides, the inhabitants of Sladkor need our help."

"How can we help?" Max sat up in the cot. Cindy and her mother were already awake and joined them.

"Yeah, what can we do?" Cindy asked, with a doubtful look.

"Well, we have one big advantage over the Trogs. We know magic and they don't," Grandpa said.

"Yes, but I'm sure whoever brought them here has magic and will use it. That Civus," Mrs. Carlson piped up, shivering.

"What about those who live here? Don't they know magic?" Max queried.

"No, not really. Jax and his troops know a little, but they weren't brought here for their magical abilities."

"I'm sure Jax knows more than he says." Cindy tapped her foot on the ground.

"Actually, he doesn't. I know you and Max don't trust him, and I don't blame you. But Marko learned his magic from Hudich. Jax hasn't studied under him, and Yelka has only taught him a little. I think the lack of magical talent here in Sladkor is what made it an obvious choice for invasion by an army also without magical skills."

"Yes, but they're armed with some top-notch weapons," Max responded.

"That's true, and that's why Olik is on his way, to help even out the playing field. He's also bringing something extra, and that's where we come in."

"What's he bringing?" Mrs. Carlson asked. "I don't want Cindy taking any unnecessary risks."

"Mom!" Cindy glared at her mother, as her voice hit an octave Max had never heard before.

"Mrs. Carlson, I won't have Cindy do anything you don't approve of. But the way I see it, you can let her fight in other worlds so she doesn't have to fight in ours," Grandpa said.

Mrs. Carlson didn't look too happy with Grandpa's comment. Max wanted to put an end to an argument before it began. "How's Sky?" he interrupted.

"She's bruised like she's been run over by a semi-truck, but she'll recover. She's a lot tougher than you think."

"Can we go and see her?" Max asked.

"I think that's a good idea, since she's your self-defense instructor." Grandpa said, and extended his hand to help Max to his feet.

They followed Grandpa to a large field tent, passing two guards as they entered. Rows of empty cots lined both walls like a bunkhouse. At the far left end of the tent stood Olik, with large round black eyes that appeared glossy from the limited light, and his pale green skin. He gave credence to all the UFO chasers as to what aliens look like. Olik wore a silver jumpsuit which looked like it was made from tinfoil. He also had a gun hanging from his hip, giving him the appearance of a space cowboy.

Sky stood on wobbly legs.

"You really should rest a while," Olik said.

"We have no time to rest," Sky replied.

"How's she doing, Olik?" Grandpa asked.

"In case you had not noticed, Joseph, I am right here," Sky objected, pointing to her chest with her thumb.

"Yes, but I trust Olik to tell me how injured you really are," Grandpa chuckled.

"You know me." A smile crossed her beautiful face.

"Well, using her magic to help herself heal, she should be all right. It's just that I'm used to normal patients," Olik said.

"Yes, my genie has the ability to heal quickly. Did you bring the other things we need?" Grandpa asked.

"Of course."

The tent door flew open and in marched Jax, followed by two of his men. "Joseph, we need to go. The Trogs are on the move, and they are not alone. The cloaked skeleton and others are traveling with them. They are heading for the city of Putooee."

"Max, Cindy, Mrs. Carlson: get your stuff," Grandpa ordered, then turned to Jax. "Has Putooee been notified of the danger?"

"I sent a message, but you know how they feel about humans," Jax said, as Max, Cindy, and Mrs. Carlson rushed out of the tent to collect their belongings.

"What did he mean about 'how they feel about humans'?" Mrs. Carlson asked as they gathered up their supplies.

"It sounded like the inhabitants here don't like humans," Cindy offered.

"That's what I thought," Mrs. Carlson said, somewhat disheartened. Lines of worry wrinkled her forehead as she slung her pack over her shoulder.

They heard a rustling outside and one side of the tent collapsed. Obviously the troops wanted to move the camp quickly and had already begun disassembling it. In no time at all the entire area looked like the rest of the forest. No sign of a camp remained, and the soldiers had disappeared into the trees. Max, Cindy, Mrs. Carlson, Grandpa, Olik, and Sky stayed together and marched in a northeasterly direction.

Every now and then, a glimpse of a troop flashed through the trees. Jax showed up every so often to give reports to Grandpa. Jax informed them that his men had warned Putooee, and they were preparing for war.

In the light of day the dazzling shapes and colors of the forest and flowers were so rich it made everything look surreal. The long pine needles looked like green strands of rope licorice, while transparent petals of wild flowers appeared to be thin pieces of rock candy. Max felt as if he was walking through a candy land.

"Grandpa, what did Jax mean exactly when he said, 'You know how they feel about humans.' Do the people in Putooee hate humans?" Mrs. Carlson asked, as they stopped for a short breather.

Grandpa handed a water skin to Mrs. Carlson. "No, they don't hate humans, they fear them. There are humans living in this world, but most of them are evil. The peaceful inhabitants of this world are called Ljudje. They are human in form, but their bodies are crooked and bent severely. They'll make easy targets for the Trogs to conquer."

"How far is Putooee?" Cindy asked.

"About six hours if we don't stop for too many breaks," Sky replied through gritted teeth.

"Are you in a lot of pain?" Mrs. Carlson asked.

"Nothing I can't handle," Sky answered.

They resumed their march towards the city of Putooee. Several times they had to find an alternate route to avoid wide rivers and steep canyons.

Max fought the urge to run. To scream. He wanted to help these people, but he needed to rescue his mother. The fear that Larry wouldn't keep his word loomed ever present in the front of his mind. *Larry! That idiot couldn't track us down out here all by himself. Something else is out there, following us. Watching us. How? The air or trees?*

Everything around them seemed normal, with the occasional soldier appearing between the trees and bushes.

Sweat ran down Max's face, and dripped off his nose and chin, as they climbed a steep hill. As he wiped his forehead on his sleeve, out of the corner of his eye, a blur of some kind leapt from one tree to another. Max expected to hear branches cracking as the object landed, but only the breeze blowing through the trees reached his ears. Whatever he saw had vanished, and he wondered if he had imagined it.

Max pretended to watch Sky as she walked ahead of him. Her steady, smooth glide from the day before was replaced by a labored stride, the result of last night's injury. As Max kept his eyes in this forward yet unfixed position, the blur appeared again. At first there were only momentary glimpses of it, but once Max knew where to look, he could follow its movements.

Quickening his pace, Max caught up to Grandpa and Sky. "We're not alone," he whispered.

"You've noticed," Sky said under her breath, giving Max a sly wink. "He's been following us since we broke camp."

"He?"

Sky nodded. "Don't worry. It's under control. Just fall back and act like nothing's wrong."

Max slowed again and fell in line with Cindy. "What do you think?" he asked, covering his mouth to muffle the sound.

"I think we're walking into a trap." Cindy replied out of the corner of her mouth.

"Larry's involved somehow," Max said.

"Larry! Larry couldn't have found us by himself. No, Larry's so dumb his mother had to write TIF on his shoes."

"TIF?" Max questioned.

"Toes in first!" Cindy smirked.

"Oh." Max smiled. "Anyway, Sky and Grandpa know we're being followed. I didn't tell them about Larry, but I noticed something moving in the tree tops."

"In the trees? Where?"

"Above my right shoulder, at two o'clock. You will only see a blur move from tree to tree."

"Well, that's a different tracker than I've seen. I think the one I've noticed has been picking off Jax's men." Cindy said.

"What?" Max shouted, bringing the entire company to a halt.

Before anyone could ask what's wrong, Night Shades sprang out of the trees from every direction, followed by a volley of spells. Sparks, fire, and debris exploded everywhere, creating dust and smoke, making it difficult to see and breathe.

Max couldn't tell where anyone was. The only thing to indicate he wasn't alone was the familiar spells being cast by Grandpa, Sky, and the others.

The unrecognizable words of the enemy gave away their location. Max shot several fireballs in the direction of these foul enchantments, hoping he would make contact. A shriek of pain told him that at least one of his spells had hit the mark.

"*Prizgaj*," Cindy called, sending her own fireball after an unseen attacker. Even Mrs. Carlson engaged the enemy with her own assault of spells.

Max spun around and launched another strike. He used the *premakni* spell to keep two Night Shades, who had materialized from the dust and smoke, from grasping him with their clawed fingers.

A blast propelled Max to the ground stirring up wood chips, rocks, and dirt that rained down upon him. Visibility went from poor to almost nonexistent.

Screams from Cindy and Mrs. Carlson came from somewhere off to his right. The congested air made it impossible to see, as Max rubbed his burning eyes and coughed multiple times in an effort to expel the polluted air from his lungs.

"MAX," Grandpa called, from what sounded like a considerable distance, but the noise of the battle distorted everything.

Max tried to reply, but the lack of breathable air constricted his throat. He managed a weak, "Grandpa," that didn't even reach his own ears.

Suddenly, a tremendous force launched Max through the air like a jet pilot using his ejector seat. The impact of his landing knocked from his body what little wind he had left.

Grandpa shouted again, indicating he was even farther away than before. At the sound of footsteps running close by, Max rolled under a group of shrubs for shelter. The thick layer of dust and smoke concealed him as the enemy rushed by.

"Mom! Mom!" Cindy's call came from the opposite direction of Grandpa's.

Another blast echoed from Grandpa's direction, then the sound of more spells being cast.

Max wiped his eyes again as the shapes of trees and shrubs came into focus. *What's happening?*

Three Night Shades sprinted past him. Max waited until their backs were to him, and then he leapt from his hiding place. "*Premakni*," he screamed, and the force of his spell scattered them like dry leaves.

Still farther away, swords clashed and clanked. Sky cast several spells in a row and the battle of blades stopped.

Max picked his way through the hazy forest, moving in Sky's direction, because all other recognizable sounds had stopped. As soon as he thought he must be in Sky's last known position, several more explosions all around him left him as blind as a mole rat.

Grandpa cast more spells, closer to where Max stood.

"Grand..." The searing heat of fire pulled the air from Max's mouth and scorched his exposed skin. He dropped to the ground and began rolling over and over. As he came to a stop, a Night Shade was almost on top of him. Instead of screaming from the pain caused by the burns, he focused energy on unleashing a violent spell. "*PREMAKNI.*"

A wail of terror, like a tortured soul, filled the air where the Night Shade had been, then silence. The congested air clouded Max's vision, preventing him from seeing what happened to the Night Shade. Deep down he knew he had destroyed another life. The rush that surged through his body was exhilarating and frightening at the same time.

Max rose carefully, gently probing his face, finding severe burns on the left side and a large section of his hair missing. There were burns on both arms, which had blistered, but his hands were fine. Large black patches and singed holes covered his clothes. His burns screamed as if they had a voice of their own, but Max could only hear the shrieking pain in his head.

Gritting his teeth, Max struggled through the tears in his eyes and the thick air, trying to find anyone from his group. Spells were now few and far away. Max caught his foot on something and went down face first. He wanted to scream from the excruciating pain that flooded through him. It felt as if his arms had been dipped in boiling water.

A soft moan pulled Max back to his senses. Max's mouth went dry, and there was a ringing in his ears as he tried to listen. The groan came again; it was so close this time it caused Max to jump. He peered around. The lump he had tripped over was a body. His hands shook as Max rolled the limp person over.

He gasped as he looked down on Mrs. Carlson's face. Taking her wrist in his hand, he found a faint pulse. Another moan told him she was just unconscious and not dead. He hoped her injuries weren't serious.

Max cautiously moved his hands over Mrs. Carlson's body in an effort to find any obvious wounds. He found a large gash on the outer thigh of her right leg. Taking his jacket out of his backpack, he tied it around her leg to stop the bleeding. He took his water skin out of his pack and poured a couple of drops onto Mrs. Carlson's lips.

She moaned again as her tongue flicked out across her moistened lips.

"Max," a voiced called from behind him.

Max turned as three figures emerged from the haze. As they came into focus, Max's blood turned cold as if his heart was pumping ice water through his veins.

There in front of him stood Jax, followed by two Night Shades.

13

Max Disappears

Max gritted his teeth. Rage burned through him like boiling lava at the sight of Jax and the Night Shades. *How could Grandpa have trusted Marko's brother?* Max clenched his fists. "I knew you were a traitor," Max spat. The memory of Marko's betrayal returned as if it had happened yesterday. Not only did Jax look like Marko, but he had duped everyone as well. "You're just like your brother."

"In some ways," Jax smirked.

"Shutss ups yo…" The Night Shade never finished his sentence.

Jax whipped around slamming each Night Shade in the face with his fists. While kicking his leg out, he spun around again sending them to the forest floor. He then proceeded to pick up a broken tree branch.

His attack was so quick, the Night Shades only managed to gasp before the tree branch crashed on their heads knocking them unconscious.

Max stared at the scene with his mouth agape. *Was this a trick? Was he only trying to build trust just like Marko had done?*

Jax kicked each of the unconscious Night Shades, verifying their condition. He then walked over to Max. "How is Mrs. Carlson?"

"I'm not sure. She has a large gash in her right thigh and she's barely conscious."

"And your arms, your face?"

Jax's question brought back the invisible fire that danced up and down Max's arms. "I'm all right," Max said, with a slight wince.

"You certainly look fine," Jax chuckled. "I admire your courage, but your ability to lie is somewhat lacking."

Jax opened his pack and took out a tube of green gel. "Spread this gently on your burns. I'll take a look at Mrs. Carlson."

Max held the tube and glared at it. *Another substance to take away pain. Just like Marko.* "What's this supposed to do?" Max eyed it suspiciously.

"It will relieve the pain a little and help with the healing process," Jax said, as he checked Mrs. Carlson for other wounds besides the cut in her leg.

"And where did you get it?" Max asked, not even trying to hide his accusing tone.

"From your world. I think you call it aloe vera. Yelka gave it to me. She said it had healing properties."

Max wanted to retort, but decided he needed to stop the pain that was about to overpower him. He unscrewed the cap and squeezed the gel into the palm of his hand. As the aloe vera made contact with his burns, the pain subsided. The cooling effect felt like diving into a lake on a hot summer day.

"Wha, whaat happ…" Mrs. Carlson muttered, as she regained consciousness.

"I think she has a slight concussion along with the injured leg," Jax said, with one hand on her forehead, pulling her eyes open. "Her pupils are dilated and not very responsive."

"What does that mean?" Max moved in for a closer look.

"It means we need to keep her awake." Jax took off his cloak and covered Mrs. Carlson with it.

"Where…where's Cindy?" Mrs. Carlson asked, as she tried to sit up. Her face went as white as a sheet and her eyes rolled back in her head in her effort.

Jax caught her to keep her from falling backward and helped her lie back on the forest floor. "Easy, Mrs. Carlson, you need to stay still."

"Where's my daughter?"

"We're not sure," Max offered. "I'm sure she's okay."

"You'll have to stay with her, while I go search for the others," Jax said looking at Max.

Max nodded his agreement, but he still didn't trust Jax, and the sooner he wasn't around him, the better.

"Elevate her feet and give her some water. Make sure she doesn't go to sleep until Olik can take a look at her," Jax said, as he stood and turned to leave.

"How long were they following us? Before they attacked?" Max queried.

"From the moment we left camp," Jax answered, and then disappeared into the forest.

Max propped up Mrs. Carlson's feet. He poured a little water into the palm of his hand and wiped her forehead. "I'm sure Cindy is fine," Max offered, not knowing what else to say.

"I didn't do very well," Mrs. Carlson's voice cracked, and tears welled up in her eyes.

"You did great. Anyway, you did a lot more than Cindy and I did our first time. You were able to fight back. All we could do was run, while Grandpa got stabbed by a poisonous dagger and almost died."

Mrs. Carlson managed a weak smile. "Thanks, Max," she sniffled. "I'm so tired." She closed her eyes.

"NO!" Max shouted, looking in every direction, fearing someone might have heard him. He returned his gaze to Mrs. Carlson, her eyes were wide open. The forcefulness of his shout obviously startled her. "Sorry, but you need to stay awake."

The burns on Max's arms started to tingle, indicating the effect of the aloe vera was wearing off. He kept his concentration on Mrs. Carlson, though, not wanting her to doze off. Her injury was much worse than his at this moment.

"Max!" a hushed whisper came from behind him. "Max, is that you?"

"Yes," Max replied in a soft but hoarse voice. He turned as Cindy crept out of the haze towards him.

"Cindy." A flood of relief ran through Max.

As Cindy reached him, her eyes fell on her mother. The sight of her mother lying on the ground instantly drained the color from her face. "Mom," she exhaled, as she dropped to her knees and took her mother's hand.

"She's got a concussion and a deep cut on her leg," Max wheezed, trying to keep Cindy from worrying too much.

"Mom, are you okay?" Cindy asked, as if she hadn't heard a word Max had said.

"Cindy," Mrs. Carlson smiled. "I'm fine."

"We need to get her out of here." Cindy turned to Max. "Where is everyone?"

Max explained what had happened to him. He told Cindy that Jax was out trying to find the rest of the group. Cindy wrinkled her nose with distaste at the mention of Jax, and Max felt the same. "He told me to make sure I kept your mother awake."

"I've heard that people who have concussions can sometimes slip into comas." Cindy double-checked her mother to make sure she was awake.

Dissipating smoke and settling dust indicated the battle was over. The forest around them seemed quiet and still. Suddenly a strange blur leapt from a tree directly above them to another about thirty feet away.

Max leaned in close to Cindy. "We're not alone," he whispered, his heart doing jumping jacks in his chest.

Cindy stared at him with her eyes opened wide.

"Trade me places," Max spoke in a rather loud voice. "I need to put more lotion on my arms."

"Max." Cindy eyed the burns on his arms. "Does it hurt?"

"Yes."

Max stood and stretched his legs, which were beginning to cramp from kneeling. Once again, he opened the tube Jax had given him and applied another layer of the soothing plant extract. Taking a deep breath, he dropped the tube and spun on his heel. *"Premakni,"* he shouted, extending his hands towards the spot where the blur had landed.

There was a high-pitched scream as the spell thrust a young man from the top of the tree. His arms thrashed through the air before he slammed to the ground.

Max rushed to the area where the young man lay on the ground. The only sign of life was the sporadic rise and fall of his chest as he inhaled and exhaled. A thin stream of blood ran from the corner of his mouth down the side of his face. He appeared to be in his late teens, with tons of freckles and an unruly mop of red hair. He wasn't wearing any shoes, and he wore a pair of baggy overalls and a white t-shirt.

Max tried to wet his cracked lips with his tongue but his mouth was dry. The racing of his heart made his burns throb as he leaned over the man.

"AAAAWWWWWWW," the man groaned, and his legs thrashed around.

Max almost jumped out of his pants as he stumbled backward and fell to the ground in his effort to get away. Max remained frozen until he didn't see the man move again.

Max couldn't decide what to do. He wanted to take the man back to where Cindy and her mother were, but he didn't know how to do it. *I have it.* He snapped his fingers and hurried back to Cindy.

"What happened?" Cindy anxiously watched Max approach.

"I got him. Hang on and you'll see." Max turned towards the man. He extended his arms and slowly drew them in. *"Pridi."*

The spell lifted the man off the forest floor. He floated through the trees and landed gently on the ground close by.

"How is he?" Cindy asked, as she offered her mother some water from a skin.

"He's been following us from the time we left camp this morning. I could only see a blur when he moved. Otherwise, I don't have a clue about him."

"What are you going to do with him?" Cindy asked.

"I don't know, but I hope the others show up soon. He's injured so I don't think he's a threat at the moment."

"Are you sure?"

"Is he sure about what?" Mrs. Carlson asked, looking from Cindy to Max.

"It's nothing." Cindy patted her mother's hand reassuringly.

"Someone's coming," Max whispered, as the outlines of several people appeared through the trees.

Cindy looked up from her mother. "I don't think they're with us." She grabbed the bottom of Max's shirt and pulled him down.

"What makes…"

"Hey, punk, you surprise me," Larry sneered, as he, his father, and Grd strolled right up to them.

The ever-present weight of everything that had gone wrong this summer, and what the enemy required of him, pressed down on him once again. He didn't know what to do. He didn't know where Grandpa or the others were; Cindy's mother was injured; and now his two least favorite people in the world stood before him. To make things even worse, they wore grins that suggested they were enjoying the moment.

"Who's here?" Mrs. Carlson tried to see who had arrived.

"Don't worry, Mrs. Carlson, we won't be long," Alan said, in his usual smug tone.

Max was sure Alan hadn't been involved in the battle because his light gray suit was spotless and neatly pressed, as if he had just picked it up from the cleaners.

"We're here to collect our friend, for one thing," Alan said, nodding towards Grd.

Grd picked up the young man and flung him over his shoulder like a sack of potatoes. None of them seemed concerned about the man's injuries. Cindy's mouth hung open, and it seemed as if she wanted to say something.

"Oh, don't worry about Billy Bob," Alan gestured towards the man hanging from Grd's shoulder. "He is very resilient and will be as good as new in just a few hours."

"You have what you want, so get out of here," Cindy snapped.

"Who said we have everything we came for?" Alan's voice flared with anger.

"Yeah, so why don't you just shut your hole, Cindy," Larry ordered, as he started advancing towards her. His father's outstretched hand stopped Larry from reaching her.

"We have some business with Max," Alan said in a calming voice. "You do remember that his mother has, unfortunately, disappeared." A huge smile crossed Alan's face, suggesting he had everything to do with Max's mother vanishing. "So, Max, this way." Alan waved for Max to join them in the forest.

"Max, don't go," Cindy pleaded.

"It'll be all right." Max managed a weak smile. "I'll be right back. Stay with your mother and wait for the others."

Max followed Alan and the others into the trees, away from Cindy and her mother. They went far enough to be out of sight and sound from anyone else.

"I've been informed that you know where the key is." Alan stated with his back to Max.

"Uh, yes." Max glanced at Larry, who had a wicked smile. "But I don't have it with me," he added.

"When can we count on you having it *with you*?" Alan asked, with an icy tone as he faced Max. "I hope it will be soon. Your poor mother asked me to tell you to hurry. I hate to see her suffer so. She is rather a pretty woman, and there are many creatures that love human women." He shot a smile in Grd's direction.

Grd's reptilian tongue flicked out as if tasting the air for something he desired. His scaly face drew back into an evil grin, revealing his hooked teeth.

Max wanted to retort, attack, do something to this vile excuse for a man standing in front of him. Max knew that giving in to taunts was what Alan wanted, so he kept quiet.

"Well?" Alan asked.

"I was hoping to get it as soon as we get back," Max nodded in Cindy's direction. "As you can see, I've been a little busy with this war you started."

"Yes." Alan rubbed his chin in thought. "How did you discover the Trogs were here?"

"It was just luck. Some troops are being trained here," Max offered, hoping Alan wouldn't want to know more. Although what he said was the truth, he didn't want Alan to know they had figured out the source of their gateway.

"Luck. It figures." Alan shook his head, preoccupied with his own thoughts. Alan stared hard at Max. "We want that key and we want it soon. Do it quickly, or your mother and uncle will have flare worms placed on their legs." Alan smiled.

Max held up his hand as the painful memory passed through his mind. The blisters on his arms caused by the fire enhanced his flashback with the flare worms. Max tried to stay calm so he wouldn't provoke Alan into harming his mother or uncle.

"So, if I were you, I'd finish this job quickly. You can tell your foolish Grandfather this war can't be won. Not here. Not anywhere. Granted, the Trogs aren't the brightest race in the universe, but they serve their purpose. In any case, you will be hearing from us very soon." Alan turned. "Go back to your friends," he ordered, and walked away, with Grd following.

Larry, who still had a huge sneer on his face, advanced on Max. "You see, I didn't tell him about our entire conversation, but I will if you don't do whatever it is I've decided for you," Larry whispered. He raised his hand and slapped Max's burned arms.

"Ahh," Max cried out, and fell to his knees as pain exploded through his arms, causing his vision to go black momentarily.

"See ya, twerp," Larry yelled over his shoulder. He ran to catch up with his father.

Max's head swam and tears formed in his eyes as his vision returned. He fought back the urge to vomit as the blurry forms of Alan, Grd, and Larry navigated the forest.

"Now, Larry, that wasn't nice." Alan's sarcastic remark drifted back to Max as they slipped from view.

Rage spread through Max's brain like fire, his anger replacing the pain. *Focus! I have to find my mother!* He took a couple of deep breaths to gain his concentration. He knew what he needed to do, and that was to master the transportation spell. He crawled over to the nearest tree and got into the most comfortable position he could find.

Closing his eyes, Max tried to remember the coordinates to Sladkor. *If I just reverse them, I should get home.* "*Preselim se* Earth," he muttered several times under his breath.

Once again, Max felt a biting wind hit his body. The effect was so real it soothed his burns. It passed through his skin and muscles and the forest turned black. Air raced past him, through him. His hair and clothes danced and waved with the force of it. Little streamers of light shone in the darkness. They reminded Max of long-exposure photographs of cars with their headlights on, traveling at night. Max gasped as the Earth appeared in front of him. He zoomed towards it at an incredible speed. At first it was only a tiny dot, but it rapidly grew, Max stretched out his hand as if to touch the approaching globe and noticed his arm was transparent.

When he turned his attention back to the Earth, it was receding from him as quickly as it had been approaching. "Max. Max," someone called, from what seemed like a great distance. The white streamers zipped past him in the opposite direction.

Max recognized his grandfather's voice. Then another voice joined in the chorus, it was Cindy's. Everything went black for a couple of seconds and then several people came into focus. It looked as if they were searching for something.

"Max," Grandpa called.

Max tried to answer but his voice was just a whisper. He attempted to get up but his muscles wouldn't obey. His legs and arms acted as if they didn't belong to him. He couldn't do anything but remain slumped down against the tree. Max couldn't recall ever having felt so exhausted.

"Grandpa," Cindy called. "He's here."

The thud of approaching footsteps told Max that Cindy had found him. Max lifted his head, which took every ounce of his energy. Cindy knelt at his side, and Grandpa soon joined her.

"Max, what happened?" Cindy asked, looking him in the eyes.

"Are you okay? Where are you hurt?" Grandpa asked.

"I-I'm," Max voice was a weak mumble, and he wondered if anyone but himself could hear it.

"Let's get him back to the others," Grandpa said to Cindy, as he placed his hand under Max's armpit.

Cindy stood on Max's other side and lifted. She and Grandpa proceeded to help Max back to where Mrs. Carlson and the others were waiting.

As Grandpa and Cindy carried him towards the others, the effects of the spell started to wear off. Ahead of them, Olik tended to Mrs. Carlson, who was now sitting up on her own. Sky was there as well, along with Jax, and several others from his squad.

"What happened to him?" Jax asked as they approached.

"Set him down here," Olik motioned to a spot on the ground next to Mrs. Carlson.

Jax helped Grandpa and Cindy lay Max gently on the ground.

"I'm fine," Max managed, with a lot more volume than before.

"Where are you injured?" Olik asked, examining the burns on his arms and forehead.

"I just have the burns." Max answered, now with enough energy to sit up.

"Cindy said that Alan, Larry, and something named Grd took you into the forest. What did they want?" Grandpa asked. "How did they know you were here?"

Max told them about the young man named Billy Bob and how he was the blur that had been following them in the treetops. He continued, saying that Alan wanted to know how they had discovered the movement of the Trogs. He said he used Max's mother as leverage to obtain information from him. "I told them that it was just pure luck that we found out about them. I said Jax's squad was using the area as a training ground and found the Trogs accidentally." A terrifying chill crawled up Max's spine as he scanned the trees. He motioned Grandpa to move in a little closer. "I didn't tell them we were researching their gateway," he whispered. Max didn't tell Grandpa about the key, for the safety of his mother.

"Good boy," Grandpa whispered back, and he too looked in every direction. "Did they cause these burns?"

"I got these in the battle," Max said, holding up his arms, which felt a lot better because Olik had wrapped them in a cloth which had been dipped in some sort of ointment.

"Then why were you slumped against that tree?" Cindy asked, folding her arms across her chest, causing Max to smile. "What's so funny?"

"You kind of reminded me of my mother just now. The way you crossed your arms and demanded an answer."

"I think it was a combination of being so tired and my injuries," Max lied. "Alan, Larry, and Grd must have heard you coming because they seemed spooked. Anyway, I didn't want to give them another hostage, so I used the invisibility spell to get away. They tried to find me for a little while by casting spells. I had to run, and I used the spell so long that it zapped my strength."

Everyone but Cindy seemed satisfied with his answer. He gave Cindy a sly nod, and she backed off her interrogation.

"We need to get moving," Sky urged, as she surveyed the surrounding forest.

"Olik, is Mrs. Carlson ready to move?" Grandpa asked, turning from Max.

"Yes, I gave her some medicine. She might have a headache for a couple of hours but then she will be back to herself," Olik said, as he helped Mrs. Carlson to her feet.

Grandpa looked at Jax. "How many did you lose?"

Seven out of twenty," Jax answered.

Sky joined them, her head swiveling around like a bobble-head doll. "We should leave this place before the Night Shades have a chance to regroup."

"We're safe for the moment," Jax said to Sky.

"You thought we were safe thirty minutes ago. Did you even notice that something had been following us from the trees?"

"As a matter of fact I did, but we were busy protecting the perimeter."

"Yes, well, good job," Sky said, glancing at Mrs. Carlson and Max.

Sky and Jax eyed one another as if they were about to attack each other. Max wondered if there was bad blood between the two of them. He trusted Jax as much as he trusted Alan. He wondered if Sky could take him in a fight. She didn't seem like she would back down from anyone.

"Let's not wait around to be attacked again," Cindy interrupted.

"I agree," Mrs. Carlson added, appearing a little battered but ready to move.

Jax put his fingers to his lips, gave a loud, quick whistle, and then headed in the direction of what Max assumed was Putooee.

Sky leaned in close to Grandpa. "I'm going to take a look around myself."

"Be careful," Grandpa responded.

Sky disappeared into the woods before Max could blink an eye. Her movements were smooth and graceful again. She had an edge about her that suggested she could handle anything. There was a flash of steel as she drew forth a sword before she completely disappeared.

Max continued to study the trees for the blur that was the strange Billy Bob. *What kind of creature was he?* Grd had treated him as if his injuries weren't very serious.

They had been traveling for about an hour when they paused for a short break. Olik examined Mrs. Carlson and Max again. He changed the bandages on Mrs. Carlson's leg and on Max's arms. Their wounds had almost completely healed. The group was sharing some water and granola bars when Jax joined them.

"Where's Sky?"

"She's out doing her thing," Grandpa responded, in a disarming tone.

"I see," Jax said, crinkling his nose and spitting on the ground. "We should reach Putooee in about an hour," he added, wiping his face with his sleeve.

One of Jax's men approached from the trees behind them. He marched up to Jax and whispered something in his ear.

"Someone's coming," Jax informed the group in a hardened tone and signaled for everyone to hide. Jax and his soldier ducked behind a small rock ledge while the others melted into the trees.

Max's fear caused him to see movement where there wasn't any. Time seemed to have stopped; not even a bird chirped. Cindy trembled as she crouched beside him.

A few tense moments passed as Max held his breath, trying to hear something, anything. Abruptly, something thrashing about in the brush reached Max's ears. The snapping of small branches and the crushing of leaves mixed with the thuds of something running grew in volume.

Suddenly, a man dressed in black emerged from the trees. Jax immediately pounced on him. They rolled over and over before Jax pinned the man to the forest floor. "Wise? What are you doing?" Jax questioned the man, who happened to be one of his soldiers, as everyone emerged from their hiding places.

Wise gulped down several large breaths of air. "We need to get out of here," he gasped, sweat streaming down his face. "The Putooeeians are coming and they're armed for war. I tried to deliver the warning to them, but they didn't even let me speak. I had to make a break for it.

They captured Villi and Ongo. I don't know what has happened to them."

Jax shot Grandpa a worried look. "Something else is going on here."

"Yes," Grandpa agreed, rubbing his chin. "The Putooeeians don't trust humans, but they aren't usually hostile."

"We need to go. Now!" Wise said. "I don't think they're far behind."

"Where's Sky?" Cindy asked, looking around the group.

"I don't know," Jax said with a frown, as he got up and helped Wise to his feet. "She can take care of herself."

"This has Alan's signature all over it." Grandpa scowled. "We need to find a way to speak with the Putooeeians before the Trogs attack them."

"We can figure that out later," Jax stressed. "Right now we must move." Jax put his fingers to his lips again and gave another sharp whistle. With that, everyone gathered up their things and began marching back the direction they had come.

They had just entered the trees when they found themselves surrounded by an army of the most twisted, crooked, human-like creatures Max had ever seen.

The Putooeeian soldiers' stealth was so complete that their weapons were only inches from everyone's hearts and necks. Max stumbled right into the tip of an arrow still in its bow. "Ouch."

14

Battle for Putooee

"If I were you, I would remain still," one of the crooked-looking men called in a high-pitched voice.

The octave of the man's voice shocked Max so much his focus went from the arrow pointed at his chest to the creature standing in front of him. The human-like man's chirpy voice sounded like a bald eagle's call; almost a screech. Not only was his voice weird but he, like all the other creatures with him, had the most crooked bodies Max had ever seen. Their arms and legs were longer than humans' but they couldn't straighten them. If they could stand erect they would have been seven feet tall. With their curved spines and bent legs, they were the height of an average man. Even their faces were long and twisted and looked like they had been crushed, with their noses bent in all directions and their jaws misaligned.

"We've warned you about coming into our territory," spoke the one in front of him, who was obviously their leader. He limped back and forth in front of Max and his companions. The hitch in his walk didn't seem to be the result of some injury, but rather to the natural contortion of his body. "Now you must pay the consequence for your actions."

"Wait! Sir! Please!" Grandpa pleaded while a Putooeeian held a sword to his throat. "We came to help you. To warn you."

"Since when have humans in this world ever wanted to help us?" the leader snapped.

"We're not from this world," Grandpa said. "We came here to warn you that you're about to be invaded!"

"Silence! I'll have no more of your lies or you will die where you stand," the leader stopped pacing to glare at Grandpa.

There was a flash of movement that streaked from the trees to the Putooeeian leader. In a blink of an eye, the leader was on his back with Sky's knee on his chest and her sword at his neck.

"If anyone dies, you will be the first," Sky said, holding the Putooeeian leader in his place. "Now, tell your men to back away slowly."

Before the leader could open his mouth, Sky pushed her sword tighter against his throat. "Do not do anything foolish."

The man tried to swallow, but Sky's blade interfered with his Adam's apple. "Back up," he said, in an even higher pitch than before, as his eyes jumped to each of his men.

Max exhaled in relief, and he saw the others do the same. The Putooeeians retreated, keeping their weapons pointed at Max and the others. They continued to hold their swords and bows at the ready.

In one fluid movement, Sky lifted the leader off the ground, spun him around, and returned her sword to his throat. "Tell your men to move over there where I can see them," she ordered, and nodded to an area left of Max and the others.

The Putooeeian troops backed away. Max and the others joined Sky, never taking their eyes off the Putooeeians. Jax and his troops kept their hands on their weapons but didn't draw them.

Grandpa hurried to Sky, his hands extended as if he wanted to diffuse the situation. "Let's everyone calm down," Grandpa appealed. "We did come to warn you and help you."

The leader's eyes were wide and his face drawn and full of fear. He looked at Grandpa as if he were a monster from a horror picture.

"Please, please," Grandpa sounded desperate. "Your city is about to be attacked. Sky, release him."

Sky let the leader go but continued to point her sword at him.

The leader stepped a few feet away and then turned towards Grandpa and the others. "We already know our city is about to be attacked. By you," he coughed, rubbing his throat.

"You've been lied to. Do you think our little band could actually pose a threat to your city? We're here to warn you that there is a huge army approaching your city, an army that is not from this world."

"What are you talking about? How could an army from another world get here?"

"We don't have time to explain," Grandpa said, walking towards the man. "I hope that you at least listen to what I have to say."

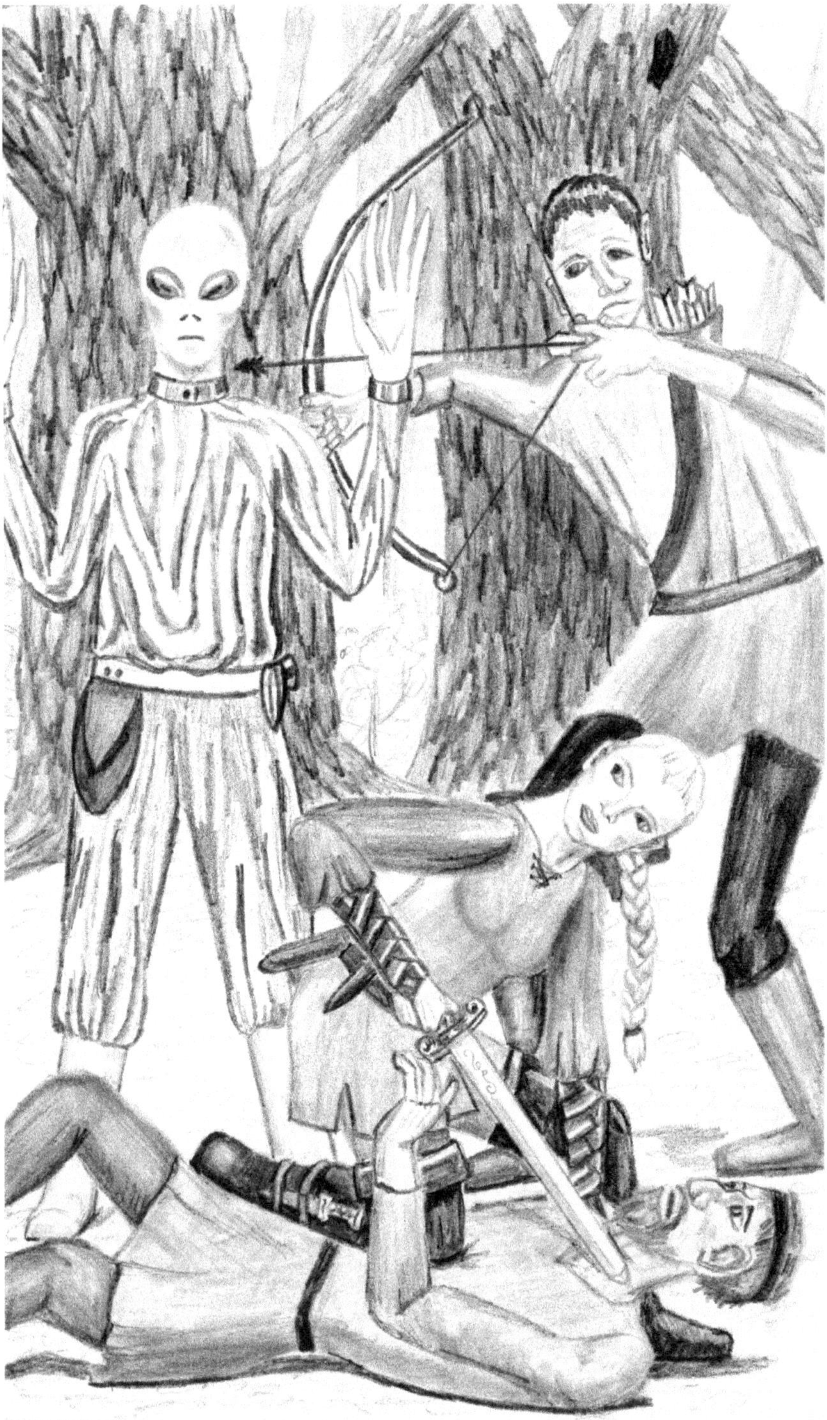

The man stood before Grandpa, eyeing him with an air of suspicion. "You're right—the size of your group isn't really a threat."

"Before it's too late, let me explain what's going on."

The man shot a glance to his troops, who nodded their agreement.

"Okay, we shall give you a chance to speak," the leader said, extending his hand. "My name is Skeet."

"And I'm Joseph," Grandpa said, taking his hand and giving it a shake. "I'll introduce the others later. Right now we must move." Grandpa placed his arm around the leader's shoulders and started leading him towards the Putooeeians' city.

Skeet waved for everyone to follow. The Putooeeian troops trailed behind for a short distance and then spread out into the forest.

"The attack will probably come from the south. You should send scouts there immediately," Sky advised, as she moved in behind Grandpa and Skeet.

Skeet glanced at Grandpa, who agreed. Skeet gave a call that sounded like a bird chirping, and two Putooeeian soldiers appeared out of nowhere, limping along in their peculiar manner. Even with their crooked limbs, they covered a lot of ground quickly.

"Go and organize all troops to the south side of the city and then send a squad to the pass of Celje to set a trap," Skeet ordered.

"Sir, you trust these... humans?"

"Yes, for some reason, I do. I have never believed a word Billy Bob has said, and I do not know what prompted me to do so this time. When he told us about these people and their intentions, I had my suspicions. Now I think my suspicions were correct. I was right to be skeptical of Billy Bob in the past, and we should be so now."

"Very well," the soldiers gave a jerky salute and scuttled away.

"How far is the pass of Celje?" Sky asked, still walking a pace behind Grandpa and Skeet.

"It is approximately an hour's march from the south of Putooee," Skeet said over his shoulder.

"I think we should head to the pass," Jax said, as he stepped in with Sky. The two of them sneered at each other.

"What are you thinking?" Grandpa asked, turning around and eyeing the two of them.

"We came here to stop the Trogs from attacking Putooee, not to break up a siege," Jax said.

"For once, I agree with Jax," Sky added. "I think we need to go now and help set a trap for the Trogs."

"Hopefully the Trogs think we were killed or captured by the Putooeeians. We might be able to surprise them," Jax suggested.

"You have a point," Grandpa agreed. "Skeet, I don't want to tell you what to do, but we need to get to that pass as fast as we can. Can you give us one of your men as a guide? I think having one of your men with us would be a way for your people not to confuse us with the real enemy."

Skeet gave a different high-pitched signal, and his entire squad came out of the trees. He signaled to one of his men to follow him a couple of paces away from everyone else. Several chirps from their squeaky voices rose from their little huddle, but nothing else. After a few minutes, they rejoined everyone.

"Reese, here," Skeet nodded towards the Putooeeian to whom he had been speaking, "is heading back to the city to make sure it's secured. The others and I will lead you to the pass."

With that, Reese gave a crooked bow in their direction, saluted Skeet, and departed in the direction of the city.

"This way," Skeet said, beckoning with his bent arm. "If the threat is as great as you say it is, then we need to hurry." He immediately broke into a jog.

"I'm getting too old for this." Grandpa looked at everyone before he followed.

The speed at which the Putooeeians scampered surprised Max. He had to sprint to keep up. It appeared that Grandpa, Cindy, and Mrs. Carlson were having a difficult time sustaining the pace too. On the other hand, Sky, Olik, Jax, and his troops handled this dash for the pass of Celje with ease.

They emerged from the edge of the forest and entered upon an area of rolling hills which had dense, towering grasses. The group had to rely on Skeet and his men to lead the way through the massive, green maze. Due to the sharp edges of the grass blades, Max and the others placed their arms over their faces to prevent cuts and scratches. With his hands raised protectively over his head, Max lost his balance and almost fell several times. Mrs. Carlson wasn't as lucky. Olik was there to help her to her feet, and he gave her an orange liquid to drink. Max wondered if it was to take away the lingering effects of her concussion.

"How much farther?" Cindy took her mother's arm to help her along the way.

"Not far. Not far. After these fields we will reach a rocky area and then Celje Hill. At that point we'll climb to the top which will take us above the pass," Skeet said.

"How high's the hill?" Mrs. Carlson asked, her face pale and blotchy.

"Not high," Skeet said with a crooked smile.

Max wondered if Skeet played down the size of the hill to keep Mrs. Carlson going. He hoped it really was an easy climb, because he was starting to feel light-headed himself. Jogging, sleep-deprivation, and injuries, completely sapped his energy. Sweat rolled down his forehead, and he wiped the back of his hand across his brow to keep the salty beads from stinging his eyes.

He managed to get in behind Sky as she tailed Grandpa and Skeet. "How close do you think the Trogs are?" Max asked her.

"I am uncertain. If Skeet's troops are ahead of us, they may have already encountered the Trogs. We may be marching into a battle," she shot over her shoulder.

"That's what I'm afraid of," Max responded.

"Are you afraid of battle?" Sky turned her head to look at him with one raised eyebrow.

"NO! That's not it at all. I'm exhausted and would like some sleep before we fight."

"Smart and brave. Joseph didn't lie. I told him I wouldn't teach a coward." She gave him a smile then focused on the trail in front of her.

The hill turned out to be a small mountain and the climb was anything but easy. They navigated a couple of steep cliff faces that resembled the sides of skyscrapers, but Skeet led them safely to the top. At the summit, Skeet gathered everyone close together.

"We need to be very quiet from here on. The trail is narrow so we will need to walk in a single file. The trail will keep us hidden from the valley below. I will go first and the rest of my men will bring up the rear," Skeet said as they huddled together. "Darkness does not fall for about two hours. That gives us enough traveling time to get to the pass. We can take a short break, so if you need some food or water, take it now."

Skeet and his men formed their own little group and only an occasional squeak or chirp indicated they were discussing something.

Max and the others rested on some large boulders. Max opened his water jug and drank most of its contents. He was thirstier than he'd realized.

Grandpa sat next to him. Grandpa's face had more lines and wrinkles around his eyes, and he looked older than ever before. "Not the man I use to be," he said, with a weak smile.

"Don't worry. It was a tough hike for everyone," Mrs. Carlson added.

As Max ate a banana, two of the Putooeeians broke away from the group and disappeared down the hill. "How are we going to help?" Max asked Grandpa.

"Olik and I have a surprise for the Trogs and their friends." Grandpa winked at Olik, who gave a thin smile. "It will require everyone's magical capabilities to pull it off."

"What is it?" Cindy asked with raised eyebrows, as she munched on a granola bar.

All eyes were on Grandpa as he seemed to be savoring the moment of suspense. He took out his canteen, screwed off the cap and poured some water into his mouth. "You will see soon enough."

Olik continued to smile but didn't offer any clues as to what they had planned for the Trogs. Max looked into Olik's large black eyes but couldn't read what he was thinking.

Max opened his mouth to ask a question, but Grandpa shook his head. Instead, he filled his gaping jaw with the rest of a banana.

"How are your arms feeling?" Olik asked.

"They itch a little but otherwise they feel fine," Max responded, thinking about his wounds for the first time since Olik had changed the dressing earlier. The way Olik could heal severe injuries in such a short amount of time astonished Max.

"Let me take a look," Olik said, as he unwrapped Max's arms to reveal what looked like a slight sunburn. "I think they should be fine by morning," he added, reapplying the ointment and bandages.

After Olik finished with Max, he went to see Mrs. Carlson. While Olik examined Mrs. Carlson, Cindy sat down next to Max.

"What do you think Grandpa's plan is?" She asked out of the side of her mouth.

"Not a clue," Max answered. "But knowing Grandpa and Olik, it's going to be big."

Everyone had refreshed themselves with a little food and water when Skeet joined their group. "Are we ready to go? We need to travel now, do not deviate from the trail in any degree. The results could be disastrous."

"Let us depart," Sky said, getting to her feet.

Even though everyone was exhausted, they prepared to leave. Cindy went back to her mother's side and offered to carry her mother's pack. Before her mother could protest, Cindy grabbed it and slung it over her shoulder. Mrs. Carlson smiled and patted Cindy's arm in appreciation.

Skeet moved over to his men and spoke in his high chirping tone. In a few seconds, Putooeeian troops scampered along the trail. Skeet nodded for Grandpa and the others to join him. When everyone gathered around Skeet, he reminded them of the formation down the trail. "I shall go first, you follow. My remaining troops will bring up the rear." Skeet turned and stepped onto the narrow precarious trail that led through the mountain pass.

They traveled across the rocky mountaintop before they turned down a narrow path between huge monster-like rocks. Soon the rocks disappeared on their right to reveal the gapping mouth of a deep gorge below. The trail became extremely narrow with a plunge to the right and a steep mountainside to the left. The fact that the Putooeeians, with their crooked bodies, could navigate the path without falling off amazed Max. He and the others walked sideways, their backs to the drop-off, grasping at scrub grasses or whatever they could find to keep from tumbling over the edge.

Just when Max thought the trail couldn't get any worse, it started to descend at a sharp angle. The steepness of the grade made it necessary for them to use their hands and arms for balance. It was as if they were walking a tightrope at a circus, but without a net at the bottom.

To add to his discomfort, he could hear eerie moaning sounds from the breeze blowing up from the gorge. It was a sinister hum that suggested pain, horror, and anger. They finally reached an area of the trail that was wider, and the angle was less severe. Max's relief soon disappeared as he realized the cries were coming from somewhere ahead.

The trail started to decline after a few hundred yards, then opened onto a spacious rock-shelf the size of a basketball court. The platform rested hundreds of feet above the pass and had a rock wall built along its edge. A squad of Putooeeians scrambled about its smooth surface, firing weapons, loading catapults and restocking archers with arrows. As they traveled the last portion of the trail, Max noticed another shelf on the other side of the canyon, where more Putooeeians rained arrows and boulders down on the advancing Trogs.

As soon as Skeet reached the platform, a Putooeeian rushed towards him. They began chirping at each other at a frantic pace. Skeet turned towards them. He screeched above the smashing of boulders against the mountainside, "You were right, Joseph. If I hadn't listened to you, the army below would have made it to our city."

The group followed Skeet to an open section of the wall and gazed upon the angry hornets' nest raging beneath. The Trogs occupied the large bowl-like valley below the entrance to the pass. Because of the mountains surrounding the valley, the Trogs' only exits were through the pass or back the direction they had come. Trogs scurried around like ants after someone had destroyed their mound.

"Something's wrong here," Grandpa said.

"What do you mean?" Skeet asked.

"The Trogs are using catapults and other crude weapons. When I was at the Trogs' camp, I helped load a stockpile of modern weapons. Why haven't they started using them?"

"What kinds of weapons are you talking about?" Skeet asked.

"Weapons that can wipe out your city in less than a day. I think we need to hurry," Grandpa said, as he stared over the edge. "Olik, we don't have much time. Let's get to work."

Olik smiled and took his pack off his back. Kneeling on one knee, he pulled several items out of the pack and laid them across the ground. "Mrs. Carlson, have you ever fired a gun before?" he asked, as he started assembling several metallic objects.

"Um, yes," she replied, edging closer for a better look at what he was doing.

In a matter of seconds, Olik assembled a weapon that resembled a bazooka. It was long with a stock, barrel, scope, handle and trigger. "I want you to stay here. Use this weapon to protect yourself and the Putooeeians from the Trogs. This weapon, along with those Jax and his men have, should be able to keep the Trogs in the valley." He handed the device to Mrs. Carlson. "Whatever you spot in the scope will be destroyed."

"And where is everyone else going?" She asked, taking the gun from Olik.

Olik stood and shot Grandpa a sideways glance.

Grandpa met Mrs. Carlson's stare. "We have a plan that will enable us to send the Trogs back to Pekel," Grandpa said. "We're going to need Cindy's help."

"You're going down there, aren't you?" Mrs. Carlson said, pointing towards the valley.

"Yes."

"Well, then I'm going with you," she demanded. "I'm not going to stay behind and let my daughter go into the lion's den."

"We aren't actually going into the valley. Most of us will be on the backside of it keeping the Trogs in the valley so they can't escape the way they came," Grandpa said.

"But why do I have to stay behind?"

"Because, you still haven't fully recovered from your concussion," Olik piped up.

"Mom," Cindy said, taking her mother by the hand. "I'll be all right. And-and this is war. If we don't stop it here, it will be in our world someday soon."

"It's not that," Mrs. Carlson swallowed, looking into her daughter's eyes, "it's not just you I'm worried about. I'm worried about all of you, and I don't want to be left behind," she glanced at all of them.

"Don't look at it like that," Grandpa said. "The Putooeeians don't know how to use guns. You're going to protect them, and we may need a diversion."

"Joseph," Olik interrupted. "Are you sure that's a wise move? If she uses the gun first, it might cause the Trogs to use theirs. It could turn into a very ugly battle in a hurry."

Grandpa stood rubbing his chin as if in thought. "She'll only fire on our signal. Is that clear, Mrs. Carlson?" he said, turning back to Cindy's mother.

"What's the signal?" Mrs. Carlson asked, holding the gun with one hand, and the other hand on her hip.

"Olik has a communicator for you and we'll call you on that," Grandpa said.

"Does he have one for Cindy?"

"Of course," Grandpa replied. "Olik will show you and Cindy how to use them."

Grandpa waved Max over as Olik nodded and proceeded to show Cindy and her mother how to use their communicators.

"What are we going to do?" Max asked, keeping his voice low. It was clear Grandpa didn't want to reveal too much to Mrs. Carlson.

"Well," Grandpa ran his hand through his thick, white hair, "first off, there won't be a signal. My plan should avoid any need of Mrs. Carlson's shooting skills. What I'm going to tell you will sound unbelievable."

"Just tell me," Max sighed. "I've learned that almost nothing is impossible."

Grandpa chuckled. "We're going to place the Trog army in a dimensional prison. It's a device Olik invented. We've used it to transport groups or larger objects through the gateway."

"So, what's the problem?"

"We've never transported something as big as an army. We're not sure it's going to work. If it doesn't, we're facing a real war, and we won't be able to get enough help here in time to save the Putooeeians and others in this world."

"So, how does this machine work? I mean, I think I understand what it's supposed to do, but what do we have to do?"

"We will need to place some sensors all the way around the Trogs. Once in place, we can activate the machine. Hopefully, it will move them into a temporary dimension created by the device, which is actually the size of a shoebox. Then we can transport them back to Pekel."

"There's a problem with this plan. Alan and Hudich can move them right back through their gateway. Or to some other world."

"I know. Hopefully the book we brought back from Pekel will help us figure out how to destroy their gateway and get your mother back," Grandpa said.

"I understand."

Grandpa put his arm around Max's shoulder as they joined Olik in his demonstration of the communicators.

"Are we ready?" Sky asked over Grandpa's shoulder.

"I guess so," Mrs. Carlson acknowledged with a disappointed tone. "You promise you'll signal me if you need help." She looked into Grandpa's eyes.

"I promise." Grandpa gave her a sincere smile.

"We should go," Sky urged. "It is getting dark. We need to be in position before the sun rises, and that means some of us will be traveling most of the night."

"Wait," Mrs. Carlson grabbed Grandpa's arm. "I want to know the plan. I want to know what you're going to do."

"Olik has a device that will place the Trogs in a dimensional prison. Once we have them there, we can ship them back to Pekel. We need people in certain positions to use the *premakni* spell to keep them in the valley in case they try to run once the machine has been activated," Grandpa informed her. "Now, we really need to get going. We have a long hike to get into our positions."

"Promise me you will call if you need help," Mrs. Carlson cautioned Cindy.

"We promise, Mom." Cindy gave her mom a hug. "I'll be careful."

"I love you so much, my brave girl," Mrs. Carlson said, as she returned Cindy's hug.

"You too, mom," Cindy added. "Keep an eye on Jax. Neither Max nor I trust him," she whispered in her mother's ear before they released each other.

"Let's get going," Sky said, with an impatient tone.

It was night by the time the small group reached the top of the mountain above the platform. Max thought the trip to the platform was bad, but it was nothing compared to the climb out in the growing darkness. Max found it nerve-racking when he couldn't see where to put his feet down or where to grab on the steep ledges.

They stopped for a short break at the same spot where they had rested earlier to drink some water. Olik gave each of them a pair of goggles. When Max put them on, the landscape went from dark to light as if it were the middle of the day. They were the best night vision devices Max had ever seen. Usually, night vision glasses made everything look a reddish or greenish color, but these made everything look like the sun was high in the sky.

After everyone had their goggles on, Olik handed all but Cindy a small device that fit in the palm of their hands. It was gray and about the size of a silver dollar. It was perfectly round except for a tiny extendable antenna on one side. A single button sat in the center of the device.

"How come I didn't get one?" Cindy protested.

"You and Max are going together," Grandpa said as he kneeled in the center of the group. He drew a crude map of the surrounding areas in the dirt with a stick. In a matter of seconds, Grandpa had a sketch laid out before them that everyone could read. He pointed to the valley where the Trog army now waited. "Sky, you have the toughest job. You need to get down into the mouth of the pass to place your control."

"How much time do I have?" She asked, eyeing the spot Grandpa was pointing to.

Grandpa checked his watch. "It's 10:15 right now. I'm thinking we all need to be in position by 3:30."

"Where do you want me and Cindy?" Max asked.

Grandpa pointed to the side of the valley that sat diagonally from the platform they had been on earlier. "You'll need to move fast to get there. I'm going to the other valley. You and Cindy will travel with me that far and then continue on to your area. Olik, you get the side opposite Max and Cindy. You should get there first and have plenty of time to set up."

Olik nodded.

"Do we need to turn the controls on at the same time or...?" Sky started to ask.

"No, you just need to get it in position and have it on before 3:30," Olik said.

"Do we all know what to do? To make sure we all understand, I'll go over the plan one more time. Take the control you were given and place it in your designated area. Turn it on by extending the antenna and pressing the button in the center. After that, find a good hiding place and wait. What I told Mrs. Carlson is true. Once Olik activates the device, the Trogs and the others will try to escape. Use the *premakni* spell to send them back into the valley."

"So, where exactly do you want us?" Cindy asked.

"As close to the opposite side of the valley as possible," Olik said.

"Let's get on with this before the Trogs decide to leave this valley. I do not know what they are waiting for, but we had better go while we still have time," Sky said.

"Sky's right, we should get going," Grandpa agreed.

"Well everyone, be careful," Sky said, slinging her pack over her back. "See you in the morning." She waved goodbye and departed to the north.

"We need to go south. Come on. Let's go." Grandpa steered them towards the side of the mountain, with Olik in the lead.

They descended the mountain and traveled through the forest in a southward direction. Travel was easy with the aid of the night vision goggles. They had to swim across one river and go around a deep ravine, but otherwise they made good time. They followed an existing path south, with the mountains between them and the valley with the Trog army. It was about 11:30 p.m. when Olik left the group, turning right on a trail that led to the mountains.

Shortly after Olik departed, the terrain changed into rolling hills filled with locust trees and wheat grasses. The air, which had been cool, switched to a warm breeze carrying the sweet smell of wild flowers. Max pulled his t-shirt away from his skin to let the breeze cool the sweat along his back and stomach. Grandpa set a good pace which kept Max jogging to keep up. "Grandpa, can we take...?"

"NO!" Grandpa answered before Max could finish the question. "It's almost midnight and you need to be in position by at least 2:45."

"Yeah, Max, don't be such a wimp," Cindy teased, as she passed him to take up the position behind Grandpa.

Max just smiled and hustled to keep up.

"In fact, to meet the 2:45 timeline, you two are going to have to move even faster than we are right now," Grandpa said, as he veered right and quickened his pace.

Every few yards the trees became more sparse. Once in a while Max removed his goggles and noted a soft orange glow in the sky ahead and to the right. It continued to grow.

Grandpa brought them to a halt. "I'm going to move into position from here," Grandpa whispered. "You need to head straight from here and turn right along the mountains."

"How will we know when to turn into the mountains?" Cindy asked in a hushed voice.

"You'll just have to make a good guess. Hopefully, you'll find a trail. If not, you're going to have to climb over the mountains."

"We better get going," Cindy urged. She gave Grandpa a quick hug. "Be careful."

"You too." Grandpa squeezed her back, and as soon as he released her, Max embraced him. "Don't be late."

"We won't." Max and Cindy stared after him a moment, and then took off at a brisk walk.

Soon they reached the area the Trogs had crossed. It was easy to spot by the way the grass had flattened in a hundred yard swath running south to north. After checking for any stragglers, they bolted across the path towards a rolling meadow on the other side.

They jogged longer than Max had ever wanted to or thought possible. When they reached the mountains they began skirting the edges. They had to wade across two small creeks, but otherwise traveled without any problems. They stopped once in some bushes to listen as a large unseen animal passed them by.

"I think we need to start looking for a trail over the mountains," Max suggested.

"What if we don't find one?" Cindy asked.

"Well, if we don't find one after we go around the next two hills, then we'll just start climbing," Max said.

"Okay," Cindy agreed.

Their search for a trail was not long. They soon came upon what looked like an old animal trail winding up the slope of the hill. The climb was a lot steeper than they had expected.

Sweat flowed freely down Max's forehead and back. His calves ached and his breathing came in large gulps. Max worried the Trogs would hear his breathing from miles away.

"We're never going to make it," Cindy gasped, as they reached the top of the slope.

"Yes, we are." Max pointed to a narrow gully running between two mountains. He extended his hand to help Cindy to the top.

They raced through the canyon and were relieved to find it descended all the way to the base of the valley. It appeared to be a wash of some kind and was deep enough for them to proceed unseen by the Trog army. When they reached the edge of the camp, the Trogs in the immediate area seemed to be sleeping. In the distance they could hear the sounds of battle and gut-wrenching screams.

Max drew Cindy down behind some shrubs and pointed to a massive boulder to their left as he held up the small device.

Cindy nodded her approval, and they moved into position behind the rock. Max slithered out of the wash and got behind the huge formation. Max turned to Cindy, who kept watch from the edge of the ditch. He extended the small antenna and pressed the "on" button. When Cindy gave him the thumbs up, he sprang up the rock and placed the device in a secure spot. He looked up to make sure he hadn't been seen and then jumped off. He rushed to rejoin Cindy.

He pulled her ear close to his lips. "Let's move away from this rock. I don't want to be caught in Olik's contraption."

They crept back up the wash and found a good place where they could keep an eye on the camp.

"Don't fall asleep," Cindy warned. "We can't let any Trogs escape."

Max nodded and focused his attention to the army before him. Max's eyelids felt like they weighed a thousand pounds as they waited in silence. Out of the corner of his vision, Cindy's head bobbed. Max reached out to give her a gentle shake when the ground started to vibrate. Then a sound like a foghorn echoed across the valley and began increasing in pitch.

Trogs sprang from the ground and from inside their tents, covering their ears. As Grandpa had predicted, Trogs began racing towards the mountains. Max and Cindy leapt from their hiding place and cast the *premakni* spell over and over, casting the Trogs back into the valley as they attempted to escape.

The air around the Trogs began to thicken and looked like smoked glass as Max and Cindy continued throwing Trogs back into their camp.

Just before Max and Cindy could no longer see the Trogs behind the smoky layer, Max noticed a Night Shade moving towards them.

Suddenly, a spell caught Max and Cindy, yanking them into the camp and the prison solidified around them.

15

Out of the Frying Pan into the Fire

Max and Cindy crashed to the ground, tumbling over each other before smashing into a cart full of food and cooking utensils. They tried to stand but found themselves being shifted to the center of the valley. Instead of the entire army being spread out across a large valley, it now rested in an area a fraction of the size. Everything was a heap of bodies, weapons, carts, and tents.

Max and Cindy lay covered in foodstuffs under an overturned wagon.

"Are you..."

Max clamped his hand over Cindy's mouth to stop her from finishing her question. "Shh," he whispered in her ear.

The guttural sounds of Trogs yelling and arguing paraded nonstop through the air.

"GE OFF ME!"

"MOVE YER KNEE!"

"I'LL KILL YA IF YA DON' MOVE."

"We're in the dimensional prison," Max whispered. "We're right in the middle of the army of Trogs and who knows what other evil creatures. The Night Shade pulled us in here."

"What are we going to do?" Cindy stared at Max with wide eyes and a fearful expression. "We need to get out of here."

"I need to contact Grandpa on my communicator and tell him where we are," Max continued in his hushed tone.

Cindy nodded.

Max started to take the communicator out of his pocket when the cart slid, moving them with it, freezing him instantly.

"DON' SHOVE ME!"

"I'LL SHOVE YA IF I WANT," A deep voice said, followed by a loud thud.

"OUCH!"

"THAT'LL TEACH YA."

"WE CAN'T MOVE IN THIS PLACE."

"WHAT HAPPENED?"

Max's fingers punched in a message to Grandpa, and he and Cindy waited for a reply. After watching the device for several minutes with no answer, Max resent the message.

"Why isn't he answering?" Cindy asked with alarm. She took out her communicator and entered her own information.

"Something's wrong," Max said. He tried to keep his voice from shaking so as not to worry Cindy any more than she already was.

Joe walked through the southern entrance to the valley and headed towards the center. He took out his communicator and told everyone to meet at the center of the valley. Sky and Olik responded instantly but there was no answer from Max or Cindy. He couldn't help staring at the device as he continued his march forward. He sent the message again. No reply. Again. Nothing.

"What's happened to them?" He muttered to himself, an uneasy feeling spreading over his body.

He glanced up and saw Olik gliding with his long skinny legs towards the rendezvous point. After a couple of minutes, he could see Sky advancing in his direction, but his gaze kept turning to the left where Max and Cindy should have been.

A gnawing sensation started in his stomach and crept up his throat, turning his mouth into a desert. *What could have happened?* He checked the communicator. No reply.

He went into a jog in an effort to find Max and Cindy.

"Olik," Joe called, waving his arm as he drew closer.

Sky started sprinting towards them. "Where are Max and Cindy?"

"What?" Olik asked as he, too, ran to the center of the valley.

They arrived at the same time to see the box-sized prison resting in the grass.

"What happened to Max and Cindy?" Olik asked, looking towards the western mountains.

"I don't know, they're not answering their communicators," Joe said, a sinking feeling starting to press down upon him.

"Let's see if we can find out what's happened to them," Joe said as Olik gathered up the prison.

They hustled towards the mountains at a brisk pace.

"They put the sensor in place. If they hadn't, there would be a lot of Trogs still left on this side of the valley," Olik said.

"Well, they were definitely in position," Sky offered over her shoulder, as she strode out in front of them.

Joe's heart raced as his communicator flashed an incoming message. He almost dropped the device in his excitement to answer it.

"Is it them?" Olik watched Joe's effort to answer the call.

Sky spun and began walking backwards, her eyes on Joe.

That excitement changed to a drowning sensation. He struggled for breath, and staggered to a halt. "It's Mrs. Carlson. What am I going to tell her?"

"Tell her the truth," Olik advised.

Joe glanced from Olik to Sky, who nodded her agreement. His fingers shook as he told Cindy's mother about losing contact with Cindy and Max. When he saw her reply, Joe flinched as if he could hear the tone in her voice. The words "YOU TOLD ME YOU WOULD WATCH OUT FOR HER" stung his conscience.

"She wants to come down here," Joe said.

"Tell her to stay put. We don't want more missing people," Sky stated, and rotated on her heels as she left Grandpa and Olik to answer Mrs. Carlson's page.

"She didn't like that," Grandpa told Olik, as the two of them hurried to catch up with Sky.

After they reached the mountains they looked for any sign of what might have happened to Max and Cindy.

"They could have come down any number of gullies to plant the sensor," Olik said as they searched the edge of the mountains.

"They could be injured or…" Joe couldn't finish the sentence.

###

Max and Cindy remained under the overturned cart listening to the bickering and fighting of the Trogs outside.

"I knowss you're here ssomewheresss," the familiar hiss of a Night Shade called, sending goose pimples down Max's spine.

Max and Cindy exchanged frightened looks.

"Why doesn't the communicator work?" Cindy whispered.

Max could feel her shaking as she huddled next to him. "It must have something to do with the prison. The communicators use the gateway to send their signal. This prison must block the signal to the gateway."

"So, how do we get out of here? I don't want to be trapped in a prison at all, let alone with the Trogs."

The word prison added to Max's growing despair. Mother. *Time's wasting. I can't help her from here. I need to find her...*

"What are you thinking?" Cindy stared directly into Max's eyes.

Max regained his focus and cracked a wry smile. "Magic."

"Magic? What are you talking about?"

"Maybe I can use the *preselim se* spell and get out of here," Max offered.

"What? There's no way you can get out of here with that," Cindy stated. "You haven't even practiced that spell. What makes you think you can do it now?"

"I have practiced it. In fact, I almost performed it the other night in the forest."

"What? When?"

"When you found me all weak by that tree. I had just met with Alan, and I wanted to find my mother so badly that I attempted the spell," Max said, breaking Cindy's gaze to look down at his hands. "I had almost made it back to our world when you and Grandpa called me back."

"Are you serious?"

"Yes, but if our communicators don't work, I'm not sure the spell will. And there's one more thing."

"What's that?"

"I'll finds yousss," the Night Shade taunt's interrupted their conversation.

"You'll be alone for a little bit if the spell works."

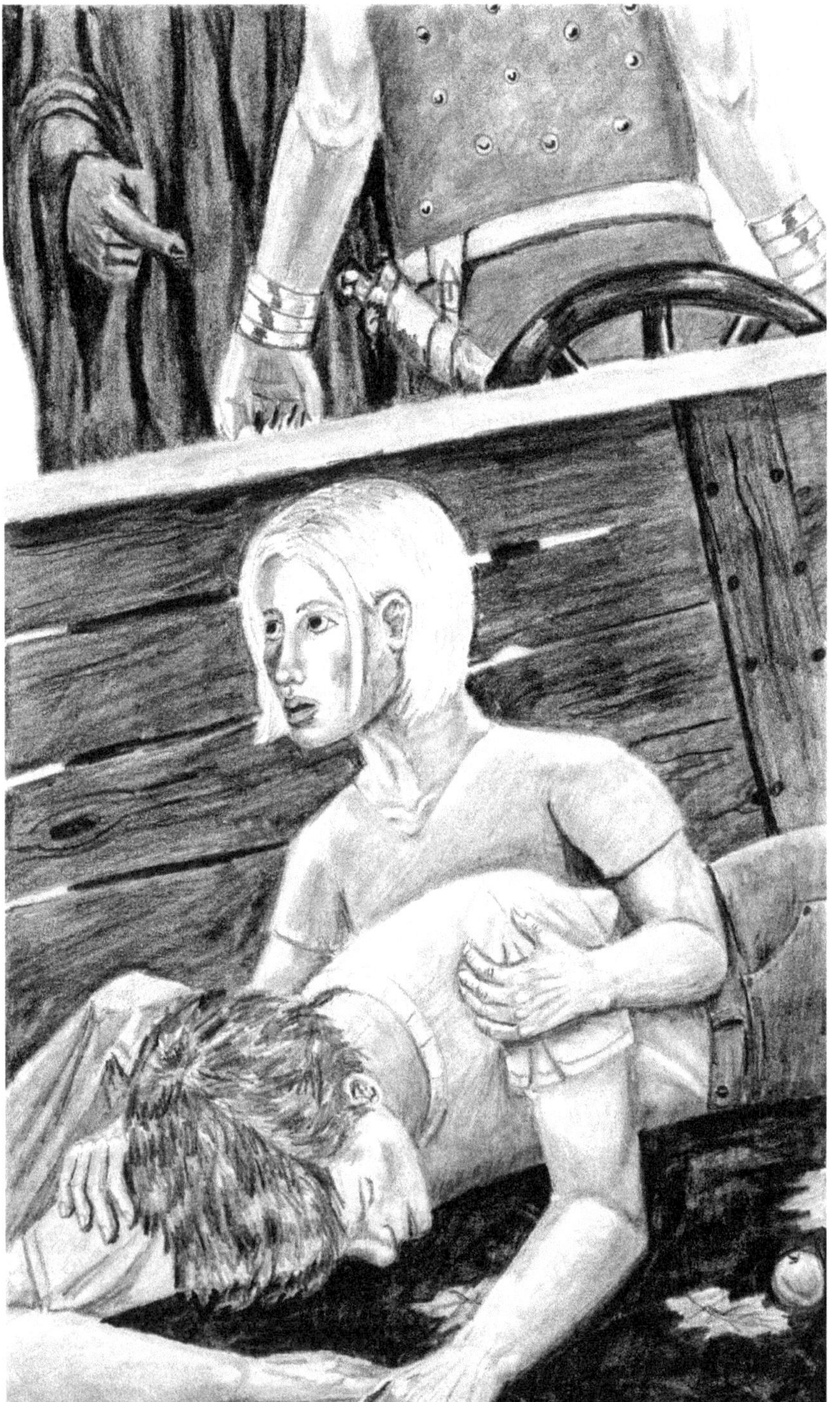

"If you don't try, neither of us is going to survive," Cindy said, taking Max by the hand.

Max's heart fluttered in his throat. For the first time this summer, he remembered how much Cindy meant to him. He tried to speak but no words would come.

"Just hurry," she said.

"I will," he stammered, and brushed his lips on her cheek.

She smiled, and even in the dim light under the cart, her bruised face turned a shade of red.

Max held her gaze for a second and then tried to find the most comfortable position he could without giving them away. He took a couple of deep breaths to relax and clear his mind. He remembered where Earth was from his last attempt and figured that was the best place to start.

"*Preselim se*," he muttered, and immediately his vision became blurry.

"I think I found the canyon they came down," Sky called, waving her hand towards Joe and Olik who were farther down in the valley. As they started to climb towards Sky, she descended the wash, following Max and Cindy's footprints in the sand of the dry riverbed. "They came down this gully."

"I've found their tracks down here as well," Grandpa said.

"They placed the prison sensor on this rock. There are obvious signs of the reaction from when I turned it on," Olik said, as he stood on the rock Max and Cindy had used.

Suddenly, there was a white flash that caught Max's attention, and then darkness. Before the white streamers began, Max tried to discern what the white flash had been and turned around to see the world of Sladkor before him. Sladkor started growing faster and faster. Everything went blurry and then the white flash and Cindy's worried face came into focus.

"What happened?" She asked.

Max's head fell forward, and he struggled to hold himself up on his elbows.

Cindy's voice went from curiosity to concern. "What's wrong?" She reached out to help support him.

"I'm exhausted. It takes a lot of energy to perform that spell. The enemy must be very powerful to be able to stay in another world for even a few minutes, not to mention an entire day."

"What happened?"

"I was heading for our world when I noticed I had left Sladkor. I think getting out of this prison will be easier than traveling back to Earth. I just didn't realize it until it was too late. I couldn't control it and returned here."

"Maxssss, Cindyssss, where are youssss?" the Night Shade's voice was closer than before.

"I need to try it again," Max whispered. His muscles started to prick with needles as their feeling returned.

"You barely have enough energy to talk let alone use that spell again."

"Yes, but if we don't get out of here, we're dead."

Being careful not to give away their position, Cindy took out her water bottle and passed it to Max.

Max swallowed a couple of mouthfuls and felt better. He tried to block out the arguing Trogs and the calls of the Night Shade. Taking a deep breath, he pictured the other side of the barrier that held them captive. *"Preselim se."*

"So, it looks like this is their last known position," Sky said as she kneeled over the spot where Max and Cindy had stood to keep the Trogs in the valley. "But I haven't got a clue what happened to them."

"They were far enough behind the sensor," Olik commented, looking back at the rock.

"What are you thinking?" Sky eyed Joe as he stood rubbing his chin while staring out towards the field.

"You don't think they...somehow, something pulled them into the prison?" Joe asked aloud.

"Nothing outside the sensors has ever been drawn into the trap before," Olik stated.

"Maybe it wasn't the trap that pulled them in?" Joe said.

"Night Shades and others attacked us earlier," Sky offered.

Suddenly, Max dropped down next to Olik. He struggled to his knees. "Grandpa."

"Max," Joe called, and raced to his side. "Where have you been? Where's Cindy?"

Sky and Olik knelt around him as Joe tried to help him up.

"We're in the prison." Max lifted his head to look Joe in the eyes.

"What? How?" they all asked.

"How did you get here?" Joe asked.

"Magic…" Max's body started to fade as if he were a ghost. A bright light flashed around Max and he disappeared.

Sky and Olik stared open mouthed where Max had vanished. Max's words hit Joe in the stomach like a punch and fear slithered over every inch of his body like a snake. He took out his communicator and entered a message.

"Who are you calling?" Olik asked.

"Yelka, I'm telling her to open the gateway immediately. Then Mrs. Carlson. I'm going to tell her we're leaving, and that Yelka will open the gateway for her later." Grandpa waited for Yelka to respond before sending the second message to Mrs. Carlson.

"Are we heading to Pekel to let them out?" Sky asked.

"No, we need to pick a world where we can use magic. Max and Cindy are in the middle of the Trog army. This is going to be a rescue mission. We'll need every advantage we can get, especially since the Trogs have modern weapons."

"The world needs to be a place where the Trogs won't be the dominant species," Olik interjected.

Grandpa took out his crystal and waved it through the air towards the center of the valley. The response was quick as the crystal flashed in front of the gateway. Joe sprinted towards the gateway with Olik and Sky on his heels.

Max returned to Cindy motionless, and fighting the urge to vomit as the spell had sapped every ounce of strength.

Cindy pulled him close and wrapped her arms around him. "Just rest," she said, gently rubbing his back and arms.

"They know." His body shook with the effort to speak. "I found them."

"I knew you would," she said. "Do you know how they'll get us out?"

Max didn't answer. He didn't have the strength to open his mouth. He didn't want to move and he felt numb in a strange, comfortable way. He didn't hear the Trogs or the Night Shade as they rustled nearby. At this moment all his thoughts turned to his mother and how he would help her. He had performed the *preselim se* spell and now he just needed to get stronger at it. The thought of giving into Alan and Hudich's demands sickened him, but he would do it to save his mother. A weak smile turned the corners of his lips as the formation of a plan entered his mind.

Joe, Sky and Olik stepped out of the gateway and onto the third floor of Joe's house to find Yelka waiting for them.

"Turn off the gateway," Joe ordered moving to the edge of the force field. "Change the gateway to the Velik Valley in the world of Zeeval and get your things. You're coming with us!"

Yelka almost jumped at the forcefulness of Joe's words. "Joseph, what's wrong?" she asked, but by then the force field was off and Joe had bolted from the room.

"We don't know how, but Max and Cindy are in the prison with the Trogs," Olik stated.

"What? What are we going to do?" Yelka asked, as she picked up her pack sitting by the control panel.

"We're going to take the prison into Zeeval and open it there to get them out," Sky replied, as she looked at Olik.

"We decided if we did it in Pekel, we wouldn't have the advantage of magic," Olik said.

"The Trogs are carrying advanced weapons, we need magic to improve the odds of a rescue," Sky finished.

Joe re-entered the room, his arms loaded with some silver futuristic-looking guns. He handed a gun to each of them. "According to our good friend Olik here, these are the most powerful guns in the universe. Yelka, turn on the gateway."

"I guess we'll find out if my theories are correct," Olik said, as the old revolving mirror spun faster until it became the light of the gateway.

"Be ready. There are more terrible things than Trogs in Zeeval." Joe took a deep breath as he entered the gateway.

As Joe exited the gateway into the Velik Valley, he startled a herd of grass-eating dinosaur-like beasts. Even though they were three times his size, they ran from his presence. Olik, Sky and Yelka arrived in time to see the creatures flee into the broad-leaved, skyscraper-tall trees that surrounded the widespread valley.

"How far away from the gateway does the prison need to be?" Joe asked.

"I would say at least a half a mile," Olik answered.

"We need to hurry. Some predatory reptiles have spotted us. At this moment it appears they are unsure if we are prey. I do not think we should wait around until they decide that we are." Sky stared out into the field as if watching something out in the distance.

"There." Joe pointed with his gun to a section of the field where the grass was short and there wasn't any wildlife. "Keep your guns ready. I can guarantee that we'll need them, for either the Trogs or the animals."

They moved in a tight group towards the spot Joe had designated for the prison. Sky led, followed by Olik and Yelka. Joe brought up the rear, swiveling his head, watching for what hunted them.

They arrived at the spot. Olik placed the prison in the grass, while the other three kept watch. Olik adjusted a dial and pressed a red button on the top of the prison.

"Okay, we have ten minutes to get out of range or we'll be in the middle of the Trog army."

"Let's head back towards the gateway," Yelka suggested.

"We cannot," Sky warned. "The beasts are behind us now, following our scent. We need to go in the opposite direction."

"With any luck, the creatures won't attack until after the prison opens. There will be so much confusion it might scare them off," Grandpa said.

"Hurry," Sky snapped, as they dashed away from the prison.

Joe struggled to keep up. His aging body didn't respond the way it used to. A stitch pained his side, and his lungs burned.

"They are circling us," Sky called out to the group.

###

The pins and needles in Max's limbs slowly disappeared as his strength came back.

"Well, at least you're looking better. You don't look like a ghost anymore," Cindy whispered with a smile.

"I can sssmell youssss. I'm gettingssss clossssser," the Night Shade's voice came from somewhere nearby. "I knowssss you are hidingsssss."

Cindy held Max down as he tried to sit up.

"He's going to find us," Max whispered.

"I know, but you don't have enough energy. If we're going to have to fight a Night Shade and the entire Trog army, I want to at least leave a mark they won't forget."

An ironic smile spread across Max's face. "I love the way you think. And by the sound of him we don't have to wait long."

"Movesss awayss from that cartssss," the Night Shade ordered.

"You don't tell us what to do," a Trog objected.

A loud bang and then a sharp cry preceded the creaking of the cart as if several Trogs had removed themselves from the overturned wagon.

The Night Shade lifted the cart and his eyes met Max's. The Night Shade stood like a statue with his arms over his head supporting the cart.

"*Premakni*," Max and Cindy called and the spell threw the Night Shade backwards into a group of arguing Trogs.

The power of the spell also flipped the cart off Max and Cindy, exposing them to the eyes of hundreds of Trogs in the prison. A wave of excitement rolled around Max and Cindy, as Trogs grabbed their weapons.

A bright flash of light temporarily blinded everyone, and then a tremendous force tossed everything around like a tornado had crossed their path. Trogs, carts, weapons, slaves, supplies and even Max and Cindy, flew in every direction. Max and Cindy held tight to each other to keep the energy of the opening prison from separating them.

The impact from their landing knocked the wind out of both of them. Struggling for air, Max staggered to his feet, pulling Cindy with him. The Trogs appeared dazed and confused by the force that just hit them. Max took advantage of the situation. He led Cindy by the hand as they dashed for the nearest edge outside the Trog army.

###

Joe caught up to the others and they formed a circle to protect themselves from the advancing predators. "How much time until the prison opens?" Joe asked.

"Two minutes," Olik answered.

"They're going to attack before that," Sky announced.

"Wha…"

The attack came so swiftly, Yelka didn't have time to finish her question. A dozen or so raptor-like dinosaurs exploded out of the tall grass from almost every direction. Grandpa fired his gun at one of the reptiles and the laser hit its mark. The wounded raptor skidded towards them throwing grass and dirt as it kicked and screamed in agony.

"*Unichi*," Yelka called, and another raptor let out a wail before it turned to ash.

Olik and Sky fired several shots, killing one and wounding two others. The remaining raptors fled into the valley in the direction of the prison as it opened. The expanding prison threw the raptors backwards into Joe and the others.

"Joe," Olik screamed, as a panicked raptor attacked him.

Joe blasted the beast in the head, killing it. The remaining raptors fled into the surrounding forests.

Sky bounded into the thick of the Trog army. She advanced so quickly, the bewildered Trogs didn't have time to defend themselves against her. With a sword in one hand and the gun in the other, she cut a path right into the heart of the Trog camp.

Joe rushed to a moaning Olik and rolled the dead raptor off him. Olik's silver suit was torn across the stomach and on his right leg. A dark green blood oozed from the tears in his flesh.

"Where's…?"

"I'm here," Yelka answered, before Joe could finish his question. She had already started applying pressure to the wound on Olik's leg as it seemed to be bleeding the most.

"I'll be all right," Olik said, looking a paler shade of green than usual. "I have Yelka to help me. Go find Max and Cindy, or at least stop Sky from killing the entire Trog army." He flashed his thin line smile.

Joe patted him on the shoulder. He picked up Olik's gun and placed it in his hand. "You may need this. This noise is liable to attract worse things. As soon as he can move, find cover."

Yelka nodded.

Joe turned towards the Trogs to see if he could locate Max and Cindy. They were nowhere to be seen, but the destruction left by Sky could not be missed. The thought of calling Max and Cindy crossed Joe's mind but the gun blasts, clanging of swords, howls and general confusion would have made it impossible to be heard.

Joe jogged around the perimeter of the Trog army, looking for Max and Cindy. Sky was deep into the center of the camp. At first, Trogs tried to overpower her but now they fled from her fury. She looked like a cat in the middle of a field of mice. Trogs and others scattered like dandelion seeds in the wind as she advanced.

Suddenly, Joe spotted Max and Cindy ahead of him. They were fighting their way out of the camp.

As Max and Cindy fled to escape the Trog army, shouts of excitement spread around them.

"*Premakni*," Max called.

"*Premakni*," Cindy screamed.

Every time they tossed a Trog from their path, another replaced him. As more and more Trogs entered the chase, Max and Cindy's escape slowed to a crawl.

"We're not going to make it," Cindy yelled, as the circle of Trogs around them began to tighten.

Exhaustion was building up and Max was losing hope. He concluded that things couldn't get worse when a deafening roar filled the entire valley, bringing a halt to all the commotion. A nervous silence fell across the battlefield, followed by a second roar and then another.

16

Monsters and Rivals

The atmosphere tingled as if a giant vacuum had sucked all the air out of the valley. Another roar and the thrumming vibration of enormous footsteps filled the space, gripping everyone with horror and panic. The confusion caused by the prison opening didn't equal the mass hysteria that was now taking place. Everyone in the valley broke for the cover of the trees surrounding the area. More roars, closer, and from different directions, quickened the flight of all.

Max didn't know what to do. He and Cindy wanted to escape the Trogs, but whatever was approaching seemed far worse.

Max jumped when he felt a hand on his back. He spun on his heels, and his fright melted into delight at the sight of his grandfather.

"Max, Cindy, we need to get out of here," Grandpa urged, as Sky ran up and joined them.

Suddenly, two dragons the size of jumbo jets burst from the trees, their scaly red and yellow bodies spraying leaves and branches everywhere, while a third swooped down from the sky belching fire ahead of the fleeing Trogs. Their razor sharp claws ripped apart anything in their path, and the wind from their beating wings made it difficult to stand. The stench of rotting flesh rose from their bodies, choking their lungs and making their eyes water. The vicious dragons devoured everything in their path, clearing swaths of Trogs from the valley, gulping them down in huge mouthfuls. Trogs shot their weapons in an effort to deflect the snatching jaws of the great scaly beasts. Fire erupted from the dragons' lips, cutting off all paths of retreat.

"What do we do?" Cindy wailed, her voice full of fear.

"We don't panic. And we concentrate," Grandpa emphasized.
"Concentrate on what?" Max screamed.
"The spell *izginim se*," Grandpa yelled. "We need to vanish."
"I've never mastered that spell!" Cindy shrieked.
"Today, you will! Now!" Grandpa ordered.

Everyone, including Cindy, cast the spell and disappeared, just as the flying dragon swooped over them, his red and yellow scales glinting in the sunlight. A wave of heat and the sickly sweet smell of decaying carcasses accompanied its pass. Fire burst from its gaping maw, tightening the noose around the fleeing Trogs.

Several Night Shades grouped together and dispersed their own fire into the head of a dragon blocking their path. Their evil fire burned the face of the dragon, scorching the flesh beneath its protective scales. It howled in pain and made way for the Night Shades. The Trogs followed the Night Shades in an effort to reach the woods and the protection the trees would provide.

Max and the others managed to escape the fiery nets of the dragons and proceeded towards Yelka and Olik's last known position. Grandpa led the way, and they stayed in a group by holding hands.

"Shouldn't Yelka have left by now?" Sky yelled above the constant roaring of the dragons and the screeches and screams of the Trogs.

"Perhaps, but she wasn't in the path of the fleeing Trogs or the dragons, so she might have remained where she was," Grandpa shouted in reply. "Keep concentrating, Cindy! You're doing great!"

Once they found the spot Yelka and Olik had vacated, the battle between the Trogs and the dragons moved off into the woods on the opposite side of the valley. Everyone released hands and began searching for signs of Yelka and Olik.

"Their trail leads away from the battle," Sky announced, as Cindy reappeared suddenly next to Max.

"Cindy, get down," Grandpa ordered.

She looked as if she was about to faint and collapsed to the ground. Max stood watch over her as Grandpa knelt next to her, his canteen in his hand.

"You did great, Cindy. Here, drink some of this. You need it." He held the open end of a canteen to her lips. "To hold the spell that long under this kind of pressure was amazing."

"Max, help me pull her back into this taller grass," Grandpa ordered.

Max took Cindy under one arm while Grandpa seized the other. With Cindy in such a weakened state, they needed to help her away from

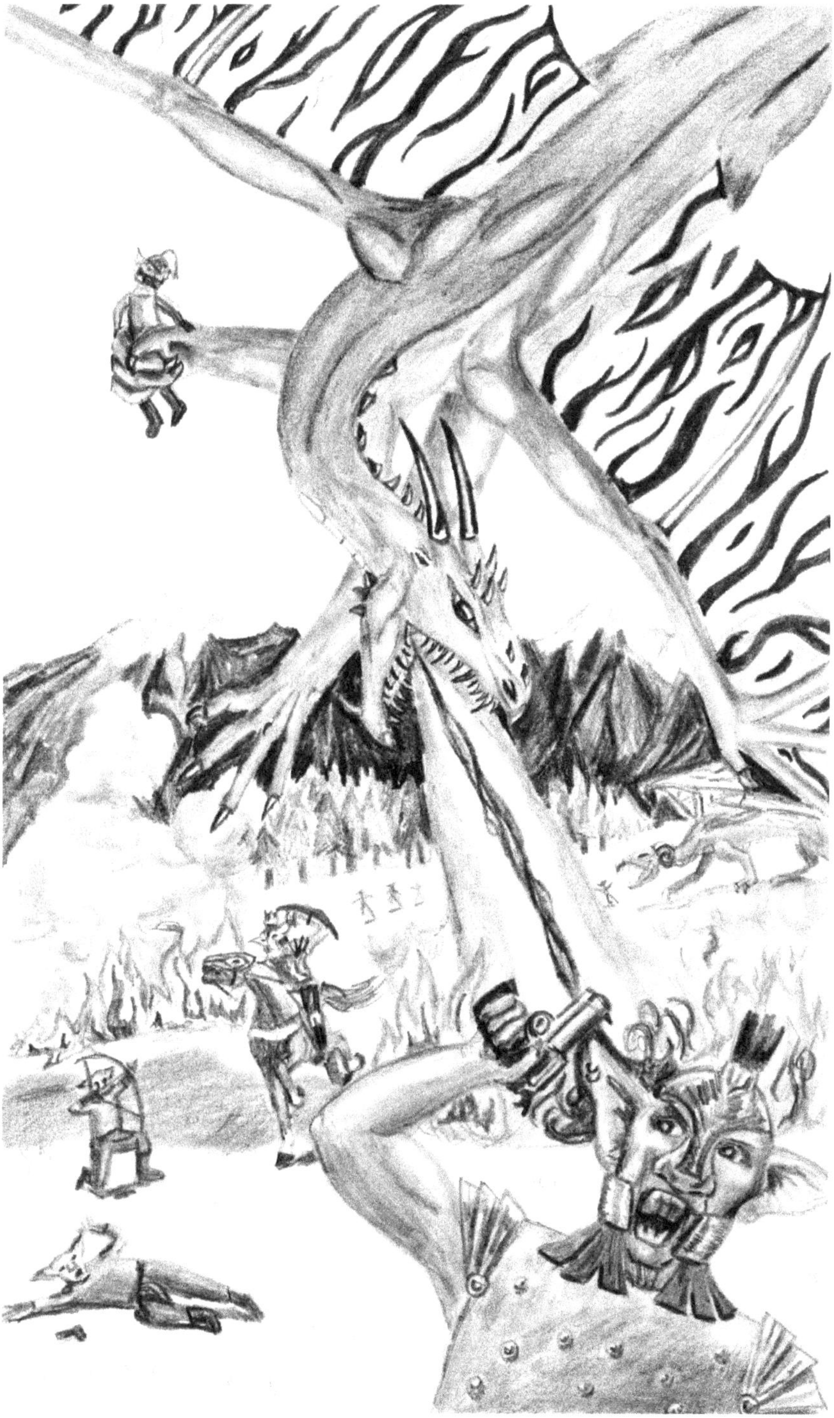

the living, breathing volcanoes and their prey, and into the concealment of the high grass.

Finding a small depression in the taller grass, Max and Grandpa laid Cindy down where she had adequate cover. Cindy's pale face slowly regained some color, and she began to eat some dried fruit Grandpa gave her.

Sky returned after a short absence. "I have found them. There is a deeper hole about twenty yards farther away from the action."

"I think I can move on my own," Cindy said, after sipping some water. She tried to stand but after taking a step toppled over.

Once again, Max and Grandpa hauled her to her feet, but this time they didn't have to drag her. She managed a quick scamper with their aid. They hurried along, staying as low to the ground as possible. With Sky leading the way, they reached the spot where Yelka and Olik waited.

Yelka sat by Olik's side. Olik lay in the grass with his eyes closed. He had bandages wrapped around his stomach and right leg.

"How is he?" Grandpa asked, as Sky took off once more.

"He'll be all right. I finally had to use the *zaspi* spell on him because he refused to relax. I couldn't stitch him up because he kept flinching."

"We may need to wake him," Sky said as she rejoined them. "The fight is heading this way. We must seek shelter in the trees."

"*Zbudi*," Yelka said, just as a deafening dragon roar thundered across the valley, followed by a wave of blistering heat as the dragon sent fire ahead of some fleeing Trogs.

"What happened?" Olik asked, as Sky and Yelka lifted him to his feet.

"Hurry!" Max assisted Cindy, who had recovered.

They raced across the open ground, trying to avoid being spotted by the dragons and the Trogs. The edge of the forest loomed in front of them. Another dragon roar, closer than before, propelled them forward at a faster pace. Sky left Olik in Yelka's hands and took up a position at the rear of the pack.

"Joseph," Olik yelled over his shoulder, "you do realize the forest we're running towards?"

"Yes, but keep going," Grandpa replied, between gasps for air. "We'll worry about that later."

Max noticed Cindy staring at him. He shrugged his shoulders as if to answer the same question she was thinking. *Can whatever lives in that forest be worse than three dragons and an army of Trogs?* At the moment, Max couldn't care less. He needed to rest and didn't know how much longer he could run. He imagined Cindy felt worse than he did. They hadn't slept in over twenty-four hours and had been using advanced magic which rapidly consumed their energy.

"On the ground! Now!" Sky called, and everyone dropped to the valley floor, adding more scrapes and bruises to their already exhausted and battered bodies.

A dragon soared over them and blasted a line of searing fire directly in front of them, effectively blocking their escape.

As the winged beast circled the sky for another pass, Yelka sprang to her feet and extended her short arms. "*Ugasni*," she called, and the spell extinguished the burning grass.

"Everybody, get ready to fire!" Grandpa stood, pointing his gun at the approaching dragon. "Aim for the mouth when it gets in range."

Max and Cindy watched the others prepare to battle the ferocious beast.

"What do we do?" Cindy looked to Max for answers.

"Use *prizgaj*," Max told her and got ready to cast the spell.

The dragon turned and flapped its giant bat-like wings, picking up speed as it dove towards them. Its vicious, spiked tail whistled through the air as the dragon zoomed in on them like a heat seeking missile.

"Ready!" Grandpa shouted.

Time crawled as the gargantuan animal approached with its deadly intent. Its jaws open wide to snatch up its meal.

"Now!" Grandpa screamed at the top of his lungs, and they all fired their weapons. Max and Cindy cast their spells.

Almost everyone hit the mark, striking the dragon in its most vulnerable spot, the soft tissue of its mouth. The dragon spun out of control, slamming into the valley only a few yards from where they stood, gasping. Its wings and legs thrashed about violently, throwing dirt, rocks and grass everywhere.

"Uh, Grandpa. We need to go," Max said.

With one of the dragons down, a route of escape had opened for the Trogs, who raced towards the spot Max and the others now occupied.

Sky spun toward the advancing Trogs and fired her weapon several times causing the approaching army to hesitate. A barrage of return fire erupted all around as the Trogs sent their own volley. The lack of controlled aim from the Trogs indicated their unfamiliarity with guns and enabled Max and the others to flee unharmed into the forest.

"Everyone, stay close together," Olik advised. "There are worse things in this forest than dragons, Trogs, or Night Shades."

"Then why did we come this way?" Cindy asked, her voice leaning towards hysteria.

"Because, nothing but the inhabitants of this forest can track us," Grandpa stated. "When Olik said stay close together, he meant it. If you get lost in here, we'll probably never find you again."

"Magical creatures called Death Mists live here and they control this forest," Olik added.

"What are we going to do?" Yelka asked.

"We need to circle around and get as close to the gateway as possible. Everyone speak as little as possible, and if you have to say something, whisper," Grandpa said, wiping his brow on his sleeve with obvious weariness. "Let's move back far enough so that we can see the valley but not close enough to be seen by anything in it. We'll go a little way, take a rest, and assess the happenings in the valley."

Sky took the lead and they proceeded through the forest, keeping as close as possible without knocking into one another. The trees were dense but not so thick that it hindered their progress. The forest had an eerie feeling, as if some unknown, unwelcoming presence watched them. Despite the shade from the large leafy trees, the air temperature increased. A damp, musty smell hovered over them, and no wind or air currents penetrated the thick canopy above. Even the sounds of battle in the valley they'd just left seemed as if it were coming from a great distance.

"There," Grandpa whispered to Sky, pointing out a little patch of ground where the sun filtered through the leaves.

Everyone but Sky found a comfortable spot in the sun and took a seat. Max and Cindy sat together against a large tree trunk. Yelka stayed close to Olik and pestered him like an old nurse, attempting to check his injuries. Grandpa rested on an old log, chuckling as he watched Olik trying to fend off Yelka's inspection. Sky watched for any Trogs that might have followed them into the forest.

Max wondered if they could speak now and wanted to ask what sort of creatures the Death Mists were.

"You would've been proud of your students today," Grandpa said in a quiet voice to Yelka.

"Oh?" Yelka looked up from Olik.

"Cindy mastered the invisibility spell, while Max was able to travel from one place to another magically." Grandpa winked at Max and Cindy, whose faces flushed with embarrassment.

Yelka didn't say anything, but the smile she wore said it all. She visibly relaxed and, to Olik's great relief, she quit tending to him like a mother hen.

"You can rest, Sky. The Trogs won't be able to find us in this forest," Grandpa said.

"Why's that?" Cindy blurted out rather loudly. She quickly covered her mouth with her hand. "Sorry," she added with a whisper.

"This territory belongs to the Death Mists. They are very magical creatures, in the forms of spirits or ghosts, whatever you want to call them," Grandpa said.

"Ghosts," Max muttered under his breath, unable to resist taking a quick glance around. Cindy did the same.

"All who walk through the forest are not welcomed by the Death Mists. Their tracks vanish as soon as they're made and the trees move to block their way back," Olik added.

"Then how will we find the valley?" Sky asked.

"With a compass. They can't change directions." Grandpa held his compass up for all to see. "Olik and I have traveled in and out of this forest before."

"Only just," Olik commented, causing Grandpa to frown as if he didn't want the circumstances of their previous adventure mentioned.

Max listened, but he was completely spent, and the longer he remained still the more he struggled to keep his eyes open. The warm sunshine added to his comfort, and his head swam with thoughts of a good slumber. The figures of Grandpa and the others became a blurry array of colors through the slits between his eyelids. Soon he saw only the sleepy, orange glow of the sun behind his closed eyes.

Max awoke to Grandpa shaking his shoulder. His heart jumped into high gear with the shock of being disturbed from a deep sleep. The sun was far in the west and no longer warmed the forest where they were sitting. The tall trees now blotted out the sun.

"We need to get going. The Death Mists come out when the sun goes down," Grandpa whispered, and then he nudged Cindy, who had fallen asleep next to Max.

"Cindy, I just thought you ought to know, I radioed your mother. She's okay. I told her our situation, and that we'll get to her as soon as we can."

"Oh, thanks. That's a relief. She must be really freaking out about now!" Cindy yawned and stretched her arms over her head.

"She wasn't happy to say the least." Grandpa patted her shoulder.

Max stood and walked around their little resting place to get the strength back in his legs. Even though he had slept, he still didn't feel refreshed. He wished he could be back in his warm bed at home. *Home! Mom! I'll start my search soon. I'm coming for you.*

The forest seemed different now than before Max had fallen asleep. He could no longer see the valley like he could when they had stopped earlier.

"It's the magic of the Death Mist's forest," Olik said from behind him.

"We need to hurry," Yelka said. "I have a growing sense of uneasiness here."

Yelka's tone of voice gave Max a shiver, and he wrapped his arms around himself as if fighting a chill. Cindy, standing next to him, did the same.

"Sky, we need to head that way," Grandpa said, holding his compass in one hand and pointing with the other toward what looked like endless forest.

"I know the way." Sky smiled, and led them from their resting place.

The way back to the valley took a lot more effort and time than the trip in. Trees had sprung up where nothing had previously been and blocked the path everywhere they went. The little group did not see the valley until they almost walked out into it. The sun dipped below the horizon as they reached the end of the trees. Sky kept them behind the trees to prevent them from venturing out and being spotted.

Campfires dotted the valley only twenty yards ahead of them.

"What happened to the dragons?" Cindy asked.

"I believe the Trogs and the Night Shades were more difficult prey than the dragons had anticipated," Olik said.

"Where is the gateway?" Sky asked, looking at Grandpa.

He took out his crystal, held it before him and floated it across the valley. The crystal gave a flash on the right edge of the Trog camp. "Just to the right of the camp. How do you want to proceed?"

"You wait here. I will go investigate the guard situation," Sky said and then snuck out into the valley. She ran like a black apparition with the occasional flash of blond hair. Her movements were smooth and light as she proceeded through the grass with silent ease.

Max watched with open mouth as a Trog guard noticed her too late to raise the alarm. The hilt of a knife slammed into the side of his head, knocking him out cold. Even with the Trog's large bulky frame, Sky caught his fall and gently laid him in the shadows behind a tent. She continued to do the same to the other guards all along the right edge of the camp.

"Joseph, we need to get out of the trees. Now!" Olik whispered.

"I can sense something coming," Yelka added, as she turned her head to watch the trees behind them.

"We'll just have to chance it," Grandpa glanced into their eyes. "Follow me and stay low. If I raise my hand, use the invisibility spell. Does everyone have their crystals?"

"I don't have one," Cindy whispered.

"Stick with Max. If we get separated, just make for the gateway."

Max reached into his pack and took out his crystal. He found it strange that he hadn't used it yet this summer, considering all the worlds he had already visited. With a wave of his hand, he located the gateway's precise position.

Grandpa led them into the valley and along the tree line, away from the enemy. They hurried through the grass, staying low to the ground. The light from the Trog campfires danced in and out of sight as the gaps between the tents revealed the shapes of the Trogs huddling close to the flames.

Grandpa stopped so suddenly that Max and Cindy collided into his back. The sound of ripping flesh and the smell of burnt, rotting meat assaulted their senses, sparking instant terror. Grandpa started moving sideways, not turning to worry about the Trogs or the Night Shades.

Grandpa slid cautiously out of the way to expose the corpse of one of the dragons, with all manner of beasts feasting upon it. The abundance of meat allowed all to eat without skirmishes and with plenty of space to gorge themselves.

Even though the gluttonous feeders seemed preoccupied with their meal, the tension caused by their close proximity crept up Max's spine like a tarantula. He couldn't remove his eyes from the gruesome scene in front of him. It was ten times more graphic than anything he had ever watched on nature shows.

Cindy took him by the hand and pulled him after Grandpa. Olik, at the back of the line, proceeded to back away from the disgusting feast until they were a safe distance from it.

As Grandpa waved his crystal once again through the air, it flashed in front of them at the edge of the Trog camp.

One minute there was nothing but grass between them and the Trogs' camp, then suddenly, Sky was there.

"The way's clear. Follow me," She whispered, and turned back towards the camp. As the group drew near the gateway, the Trogs guttural voices rang through the air.

"Hey!" A Trog shouted, pointing in Max and the others' direction from inside the camp. Conversations stopped as Trogs throughout the camp turned to see them.

"Run," Grandpa yelled, and they bolted for the gateway. Before the Trogs had time to react, they all dashed into the gateway and arrived in the comparatively warm and inviting third floor of Grandpa's house.

"Are you going to leave the Trogs there?" Yelka asked.

"I don't think we'll have to worry about them," Grandpa said. "If they're really an important part of the enemy invasion, the Night Shades will inform everyone where they are. I think we can plan on seeing them somewhere else very soon. If I can figure out how to destroy the enemy gateway from the book Max brought back from Pekel before they move the Trogs, I'll move them later."

"What about my mother?" Cindy asked.

"Oh yes." Grandpa took out his communicator and typed in a message. The response was almost immediate. He then went to the control panel and started entering new coordinates. In just minutes, Mrs. Carlson was back from Sladkor, hugging and kissing Cindy.

Grandpa and Max went downstairs, and with the help of Martin and Aunt Donna, they fixed everyone a nutritious hot meal. As they ate, they told Martin and Aunt Donna all that had happened since they left. Martin and Aunt Donna relayed some distressing news. The Verrellis had been taken into custody after another body had shown up in their yard. As of now, the two victims remained unidentified.

Everyone seemed to lose their appetite after that bit of news and went to the front room where Olik and Yelka inspected everyone's wounds. Thanks to Olik's advanced medical techniques, everyone's injuries had almost completely healed, including his own.

Max's arms only seemed mildly sunburned, though what little hair they'd had before was gone. When Olik finished with him, Max went outside and sat heavily on the porch swing, rocking gently in the cool, night air. He peered up at the sky and noticed the big dipper between the house and the treetops, while crickets chirped loudly out of the darkness.

His mind drifted to his mother and how he might find her, when Cindy joined him on the swing. She sat so close to him that Max could feel her arm touching his, and he didn't move away.

"You're going to search for her, aren't you?" She asked, after a short period of silence.

Max could sense her eyes on him. "Yes." He gazed up at the stars, feeling her arm on his, almost holding his breath. He hoped the moment would go on. He wished his mother was safe at home and that he didn't have to do what he was planning.

"I want to come with you."

Max turned his gaze to those blue eyes of Cindy's; they were so deep he could almost fall into them. Though the light of the stars was not bright, he could see from the expression on her face that she was serious. "How? I'm going to use the transportation spell. You haven't mastered it yet. Even I haven't really mastered it."

"Then help me. I'll learn the spell, or maybe we could travel together." Cindy didn't break her stare. "Help me practice."

"How can we travel together?"

Cindy's hand slid forward and took hold of Max's. "We could hold hands," she said softly.

Blood rushed to his face and he was glad for the relative darkness of the night sky that hid his flushed cheeks.

"Please. Let's try."

Maybe it will work. Calm filled Max from the inside out. He felt better than he had all summer. For one small moment, he thought everything would turn out right. "Okay, but first we need to rest and get our strength back."

Cindy smiled and leaned back in the swing.

They spent the next three weeks working on their spells together. They had plenty of undisturbed time while Grandpa and Yelka translated the book from Pekel, and Martin and Aunt Donna attended magic lessons at the school. Cindy had fully recovered from her fight and Max from his burns.

Late one evening they sat once again on the porch swing, enjoying the evening air.

"I think we should attempt to travel to another world tonight," Max said. "We need to hurry. I'm surprised I haven't heard from Alan or Larry about the key."

"Okay." Cindy nodded her agreement. "When do you want to do it?"

"Meet me here tomorrow morning at 5:00 a.m."

"I'll be here. Now, I'd better get home." Cindy stood and stretched her back.

"Cindy, be careful tonight. Something is out there," Max said, looking down the street.

"What do you mean? What's out there? Oh, the murderer. I almost forgot."

"I think I know what's behind it. Remember the creature that impersonated my uncle? I have a feeling he's here and he needs to feed."

"You think it feeds on humans?" Cindy gasped.

"Yes, and more." Max continued to watch the street.

The alarm clock jump-started Max's heart and blasted open his eyes as he tried to figure out where he was. When he realized what was happening, he switched off the buzzer and climbed out of bed. He was about to get dressed when he noticed he had fallen asleep in his clothes. Not wanting anyone to know he was up, he crept to the door. He slowly turned the knob and opened the door. The darkened hallway meant that everyone was still asleep, so he slipped out of his room.

He had only taken a few steps when a slight cough froze him like a statue.

"Max, where're you going?" Martin whispered, his head poking out through the crack of the bedroom door.

"Nowhere! Go back to bed!" Max said in a hushed voice.

"Yes, you are. I don't think you should go out. You know, with that murderer on the loose."

"I'm not going to leave the yard. I promise. Now, go back to bed, and I'll tell you about it in the morning."

"You promise? You won't leave the yard?"

"I promise."

Max waited for Martin to close the door before he hurried outside to wait for Cindy. As he shut the front door behind him, Cindy tapped him on the shoulder, which almost made him yell out. "You almost scared me to death," Max snapped.

Cindy's quiet giggle and the glee written in her smile reminded him of the Cindy he had missed all winter.

"So, where do you want to do this?" she asked, taking on a more serious tone.

"Let's sit in the swing." Max motioned for her to take a seat.

Cindy dropped into the swing and Max sat next to her. "How do we begin?"

"You remember the spell?"

"*Preselim se*"

"Yes," Max answered, then explained to her what had happened to him on his previous tries. He told her about the blackness, the streamers, and seeing Earth.

"How can we do it together?"

"Well, I think we should hold hands. And…"

Cindy took Max by the hand. "Any excuse to hold my hand; I know how you are." She batted her eyelashes at him and smiled.

Max was grateful no one could see him blushing or the huge pathetic grin plastered on his face. "Okay, I want to try for Mir. Do you remember the coordinates on the control panel?"

"I think so."

Max told her how he had figured out the gateway coordinates and explained where Mir should be. "Now, concentrate on the spell and the direction of Mir."

"How is Mir going to help us find your mother?"

"Remember how tired you were after performing the disappearing spell in that world with the Trogs? The transportation spell is ten times worse. We need to build up our strength and master the spell at the same time. I figure a couple of trips to Mir, a safe place, might help."

Cindy muttered the spell under her breath. Max listened to the words of the spell but somehow they seemed wrong. It sounded like she was saying the wrong spell. *No. That's not it.* "*Preseliva se* Mir," Max muttered and the night grew darker as if there were no streetlights or moonlight.

The streamers appeared and zipped by more quickly than before. A different world appeared ahead of them, growing at an exponential rate. Then everything went black for a second and Max and Cindy landed on the forest floor in the early morning light. Their legs gave out with the force of the impact, and they fell forward onto the ground.

"Wow!" Cindy slowly sat up.

"I know," Max got up and brushed himself off. "Incredible isn't it?" They were in the forest where they had started their self-defense training a year ago. There was the trail and the blind, the hiding place Marko had constructed. *The blind is still there.*

"Max," Cindy's voice sounded strange. "Something's wrong."

"What."

"I can't stand and I feel sick."

"It's the spell. It's stealing your energy."

"What do I do?"

"Think of home and say the words, *vrnim se* Earth," He said, kneeling down and helping her remain upright.

"But I don't want to leave you here alone. I want to stay," she whined with lips pouting.

"I'll be right behind you. I just need to build up my strength."

"I think I'm going to be sick."

"You need to go. Concentrate on Earth and say the spell."

Cindy did as he suggested and instantly vanished.

Max felt a little weak himself. It reminded him of the first day of baseball practice when the coach had made the team sprint around the outfield several times. He strolled towards the blind. It appeared to be a normal cluster of trees and if he hadn't known what it was, he would have missed it.

His mouth was so dry he wished he had brought some water. He crossed the path and headed for the blind.

Suddenly, there was a strange looking man blocking his path. He wore bright, forest-green clothes and a hat with a feather in it. His outfit reminded Max of the old Robin Hood movies. The man's nose was very long and pointed.

"Who are you and what is your business here?" he asked in a stern tone.

"What concern is it of yours?" Max answered back sharply. He was tired and feeling grumpy. The urge to sit and rest occupied his thoughts like never before.

"I work for Helaina. She's cracking down on all the mischief going on in her kingdom. All visitors are required to check in or leave immediately," the man stated, with his hand on the hilt of a sword.

Max's need for rest overrode his desire to stay and inform the man who he was. "Fine! *Vrnim se* Earth." Mir zoomed away from under his feet and the streamers zipped by. Max's head spun with drowsiness, and he didn't know if he could remain awake long enough to reach home.

Suddenly, he jerked and fell off Grandpa's front porch swing. He struggled to push his face up off the porch, while Cindy lay on the swing, eyes open but looking extremely unwell.

"I feel terrible," Cindy said. "You were right about how bad the effects are."

Max managed to use the swing to pull himself to his feet. His legs shook as he gulped the cool air, fighting the desire to throw up. When his head stopped spinning, he sat down next to Cindy to rest.

"It was worth it though." Cindy looked at him with a twinkle in her eye.

"Yes, I'm getting better at it."

They remained on the swing for over an hour, just trying to recuperate. The morning sun rose farther into the sky.

"Hey, punk," Larry called from the sidewalk in front of the fence. He stood a few feet ahead of Jo and his friends. His lips drew back to reveal his usual, evil grin. "I'm here to call in my favor."

17

Larry's Trap

Max thought he couldn't possibly feel any worse after his trip to Mir, but now in his weakened state, Larry and his crew of misfits wanted him to do who knows what. *Will this never end?* Max sighed.

Cindy stared at him, still unmoving in the porch swing. "I can't budge."

"I'll be all right." Max took a couple of deep breaths.

"Come on, let's go, I haven't got all day," Larry barked at him from the other side of the iron fence.

"Yeah, hurry up," Jo taunted, and the others joined in with their taunts and jeers.

"Don't force me to have a little chat with my dad," Larry threatened, and the smug grin on his face widened even more.

I'd love to break that ugly nose again. "I'm coming," Max said. He staggered to the porch steps and held onto the rail to keep from falling. His legs felt like jelly, but he forced them to continue down the steps where once again he had to pause to steady himself.

"What the heck's taking so freakin' long?" Larry called, a scowl replaced his grin. "Get out here before I call the whole thing off and go find my dad."

"Sorry," Max answered grumpily. Having to apologize to Larry went so completely against the grain it almost hurt. "I'm not feeling well."

"Like we care," Jo snapped over Larry's shoulder, and the others added their agreement.

Pins and needles tingled and stabbed every inch of Max's body, sending signals that his strength was returning. He licked his parched lips and lumbered off the walkway toward the spigot where the garden hose was connected. This maneuver brought more shouts of disapproval and annoyance from Larry and his gang.

Max turned on the nozzle, picked up the end of the hose and gulped down several large mouthfuls of water. The cool liquid rushed through his body, reviving and refreshing at the same time.

"Oh, come on," Larry growled in irritation. "You want me to go tell my dad what I know, don't you? Get a move on!"

He's not going to tell. At least, not yet. He wants something. But what? Max shut off the water and slowly wiped his mouth on his sleeve. He could tell Larry wanted him to hurry but Max had already decided not to give in to Larry's demand. He was going to get as much pleasure out of this bad situation as he could. Max reached his arms high over his head and stretched his back and sides. Moving as slowly as he could, he shuffled back to the main walk, still near the porch.

Cindy had managed to sit up but it was clear that she wasn't going to be able to come. "Be careful."

"Don't worry. I'll be back."

"Are you sure?" Cindy frowned.

"I figure they can't do any serious damage. I don't think Larry would really dare to interfere with his father's plans. That means Alan needs me around," Max answered quietly, so only Cindy could hear. He gave a short wave and then headed to the gate at a leisurely pace.

Jo stepped forward. "What? Cindy too afraid to come along?" She taunted in a babyish voice.

"Just me. That's all that was agreed to," Max said, as he reached the gate.

"You're not in a position to decide anything." Larry puffed himself up. "I'm in charge here."

"Yeah, yeah," Max smirked, and shook his head. Larry's death-ray glare was so full of fury that Max could practically feel the heat on his skin. Larry didn't like being mocked so Max couldn't resist relishing this rare chance to do it. "You're the big man," he added, while rolling his eyes so everyone could see.

"Max," Grandpa suddenly called, emerging from the front door. "Where are you going?" He didn't look pleased to see Larry and his gang standing outside the fence and Max with his hand on the gate latch.

"I've got something to take care of," Max said.

"With...Larry?"

"Yes."

"Don't worry, you crazy old man. He'll be back in time for lunch," Larry yelled.

Grandpa didn't even look at Larry. "Max, are you sure you know what you're doing?" Grandpa's eyebrows were knit together as if questioning Max's logic.

"I have to do something *important*. Don't worry, I'll be back." Max unlatched the gate and stepped out onto the sidewalk.

Grandpa moved to the edge of the porch as if expecting a fight to erupt at any moment. He twirled the end of his beard nervously with his finger.

Max glanced at him over his shoulder as he weaved through Larry's friends. He did not want to show any fear even though his stomach felt bunched in a painful knot. He marched up the street away from Grandpa's house as if he knew their destination.

Larry had to hustle to keep up with Max's pace. "What are you doing? You don't even know where we're going!"

"I know that, but I don't want my grandfather to follow us. And neither do you." Max didn't look at Larry, but continued to stare straight ahead. "So, where are we heading?"

This question brought Larry's smug, sinister grin back. "To a cave near my house. With our gateway, we managed to bring in a new pet that I want you to meet."

Max held back a snide remark about the way Larry had used the term, "our gateway." Larry wasn't smart enough to solve a puzzle designed for toddlers, let alone master the science to travel between worlds in the universe. He decided against saying it, though. It was probably best to watch his tongue while surrounded by the enemy, especially considering he was still in a weakened state after his trip to Mir.

"So, Max, have you heard about the murders out at the Verrellis' house?"

"Uh, yes." Max was confused. He thought he knew who the murderer was, but Larry's question both surprised and shocked him. *Had they turned something loose in our world? And the Verrelis were in prison for nothing?* When Max finally met Larry's stare, the expanse of Larry's wicked smile had reached new dimensions.

"Good. Turn right on the next side street," Larry ordered.

"So, what about these murders?" Max tried to keep his tone disinterested. He didn't want to give Larry any more gratification than he was obviously getting at the moment just by having Max somewhat under his control.

"A little scary, don't you think?" Jo asked, but the delight in her voice and her amused expression indicated she was anything but frightened.

Max stopped and faced Larry. "What is it you really want? Why am I here?"

"I want to show you something," Larry sneered. "Something that can put an end to these murders."

"You think *you* can stop the killer?"

"Well, I don't really know who the murderer is, but my dad does."

"So why doesn't he tell the police? We all know it isn't the Verrellis," Max stated.

"Oh, the police know that too," Jo laughed. "But it's so much fun with the Verrellis in prison, thinking their lives are destroyed."

"Anyway," Larry said, getting back to his point, "I guess you've heard that the victims are still unidentified. My old man and the others are a little on edge about these deaths. They seem to think that someone in this town might be one of the next victims. They also believe that the murderer might not care who that someone is. What I mean is, my dad's afraid that the next victim could even be someone on our side." Larry turned sharply and proceeded up the street.

This time, Max had to quicken his gait to catch up to Larry. He knew he was giving Larry back the control he desired but this little divulgence piqued Max's interest. Max wanted Larry to spill his guts. *What are Alan and the Sherriff afraid of?* "So, your dad's worried?"

"Yeah, I guess so. That's why they have a plan in case things go wrong," Larry continued.

"What kind of plan? And what's it have to do with me?" Max asked.

"I have a scheme of my own." Larry peered at him again in pernicious delight as Larry's entire gang snickered and chuckled to each other.

Max hadn't really been that concerned when Larry showed up at his gate because he knew Larry wouldn't dare mess up his father's plans. Aside from the fact that he was exhausted from the transportation spell, he had felt almost at ease. Now, however, an ominous sensation oozed its way over his body like sliding into quick sand. It slowly began to press in on him, and at any minute he felt he wouldn't be able to get air.

They continued on in silence, down several streets and into a neighborhood Max had never visited. By the size of the houses, Max assumed wealthy families lived in this area. Otherwise it seemed to be like a regular street in any town, until Max took a closer look. Many of the houses had strange decorations. Max began to realize that this wasn't an ordinary street at all.

Several of the yards contained grotesque statues of horrible beasts fighting each other. Some houses had winged monsters on the roofs the way old cathedrals were decorated with gargoyles, only these certainly didn't seem to be for the purpose of carrying rainwater away from the building. They approached a house that stood out like a horse among zebras. Not for the fact that it was the largest and most ornate, but for the large statue of Hudich in the front yard. *That has to be Larry's house.*

Just before they reached the house Max assumed was Larry's, the group led him down an alley. Based on the width of the walkway and the look of the gravel on the ground, it was obvious that the alley was frequently used. Rows of scrub oak on either side formed a natural barrier to shield the path from outside eyes. Larry's neighborhood sat in close proximity to the surrounding hills, which loomed above the path. As they approached the nearest hill, the trail led them to the mouth of a large cave.

"Look on the bright side, Max, you're going to get to see something no one on your side has ever seen...and lived to tell about it." Larry laughed, and the others joined in.

"Well, if I get to see it, what is it?" Max asked, fearful but curious to find out more.

"It's like a training, storage, prepping area," Jo said. "But don't worry. You'll never want to return to this place after today's little lesson."

As they entered the cave, Max's eyes took a moment to adjust to the torchlight, which paled in comparison to the bright morning sunlight. The cave was much larger than the opening indicated, and it appeared to be manmade. Huge wooden support posts and beams held up the ceiling in several spots. The first chamber was for storage. Crates were stacked to the ceiling and other supplies were piled on top of each other so that the walls were completely lined on both sides by large boxes and containers of various sizes.

The group passed through a short hallway with torches dimly lighting the way forward. There was a wooden door on either side of the hall, but these were closed, keeping their contents hidden.

The next chamber opened up on their right and the sight of its furnishings sent a chill up Max's spine. There was a metal table with wrist and ankle bindings. One section of the wall had harsh-looking, steel shackles while the other had an array of bloodcurdling torture devices. Three fireplaces were distributed around the room, each with immense, black caldrons supported in their wide mouths and a number of frightening, wrought iron fire pokers lined up on the hearth.

This led to another hall and yet another room, which appeared to be some sort of science laboratory. Rows of tables lined the room, their surfaces littered with pots, beakers, measuring instruments, books, and foul-colored liquids in glass jars.

Larry stopped them before they entered the next hallway, and his gang formed a circle around Max. Larry faced Max and crowded his space. Rank breath stung Max's nose, and he automatically took a step back, but Fred shoved him forward.

"Now for the reason we're here," Larry said, with his sinister smile. "My dad seems to know who or what the murderer is. I'm guessing it's more of a what by the way it's eating its victims, which is why the contingency plan is a pretty drastic one."

"Well, I can tell you that the killer is both a who and a what," Max said, with his own triumphant grin.

Larry and the others' mouths dropped open and no one seemed to know how to react.

"Yeah, right." Jo recovered quickly, and sneered at him. "Like you know anything."

"You're so full of crap your breath stinks," Larry said, his nose almost touching Max's

"Oh, I can even tell you who it is. I know his name and I've seen what he can become," Max said, bumping the end of Larry's nose with his own.

"Prove it," Larry challenged, and the others echoed the same chorus.

"Tell me why I'm here, and then I'll decide whether or not to tell you," Max responded, casually puffing out his chest after having stolen some of Larry's thunder.

It took Larry a moment to collect his thoughts. "Whatever. Anyway, back to this contingency plan. My dad seems to think this murdering creature could be a threat to our plans. He, or it, could reveal things we would rather keep secret at this time."

"Like, the fact that other worlds exist and that you're trying to take them over?"

"Maybe," Larry said, again looking a little confused.

I knew he wasn't very bright! His father hasn't confided in him either!

"So, to keep our secrets safe, we imported something we can control. Now, we'll only use this thing if we need to, to get rid of the other threat."

"And...? I'm still wondering what all this has to do with me!"

"I figured there's no point in having something imported and then never use it. I need you so I can make sure that the talents of this thing aren't wasted," Larry said.

As if you had a say in bringing whatever it is here. Max rolled his eyes, much to Larry's displeasure.

"You won't think this is such a load of crap in a few minutes," Larry hissed. "Let's go!" He turned into the tunnel, which ended in a prison similar to the one where his mother and uncle were captives. This appeared to be the final room in the underground complex. Five cells stood along the back wall, all empty save one.

All the torches around the prisoner were extinguished, leaving the person or thing within hidden from sight. A rough, gurgly breathing filled the cavern, vibrating off the walls. Bang! Something large smashed into the side of the cage and started pacing back and forth with low grunts.

"That, my friend, is a Zbal," Larry said, not venturing too close to the cage, with the rest of his gang standing well behind Max. "We brought it here to hunt down and destroy the other threat, if need be. Once a Zbal is after you, it will never quit. And they aren't at all easy to kill. All you have to do is give it a taste of its prey's blood, and it will drive itself insane trying to catch and devour it. The best part is that it can hunger for more than one prey."

The relaxed feeling Max had in his grandfather's yard this morning now completely evaporated. A sense of what Larry had in mind crept over Max, making it difficult to stop his knees from shaking.

"Remember our deal, Max. You have to do what I say or I spill my guts to my dad."

"I remember." Max tried to keep his voice from quivering.

"Get him," Larry barked.

Everyone behind Max seized him from all sides, holding him fast. Larry slid a long knife out of a sheath he'd had tucked in the back of his pants. The blade flashed in the torchlight as Larry held it up for Max to see.

Max wanted to struggle. Wanted to fight but knew the consequences could be severe for his mother. He took a couple of deep breaths and remained calm.

"Bring him closer and hold out his hand," Larry ordered, and his gang pushed Max forward, forcing him to obey Larry's command.

Larry grabbed Max's hand and turned it palm up.

"What's with you and your people's obsession with my hands?" Max asked, anger and fear racing through him like electricity.

Larry's evil grin flashed across his face as he sliced Max's palm right through the middle of his scar. Warm blood formed a pool in the center and then ran over the sides and through his fingers to splatter on the floor. Bang! Clang! Bang! The creature struggled against the confines of its prison.

"It smells your blood," Larry announced, as he went and found an old rag in one of the empty cells and thoroughly cleaned the knife before putting it back in its sheath.

He rejoined Max in front of the Zbal's cage. "Now, I want you to go and stick your hand in front of the bars of the cell."

"WHAT!"

"It's either that or your mother will receive some horrible punishment," Larry threatened.

Larry's gang released their grip on him. It seemed they didn't want to get any closer to the cage than he did. He fought to make his feet move but his steps were slow and hesitant. He hardly dared to breathe.

BANG! BANG! The creature slammed into the bars multiple times, but in the poor light, it was only a dark shadow.

Max's heart jerked higher into his throat every time the creature smashed into the cage. Its grunts and gurgling breath made Max's skin crawl.

Hot blood continued to spill out of Max's lacerated hand onto the concrete floor and each jarring step seemed to cause more to fall.

"Oh, hurry up," Larry ordered.

Max reached the bars and stood motionless, staring into the darkness.

SLAM! The creature's hideous face appeared sideways as it tried to squeeze itself through the vertical bars holding it inside. The creature's

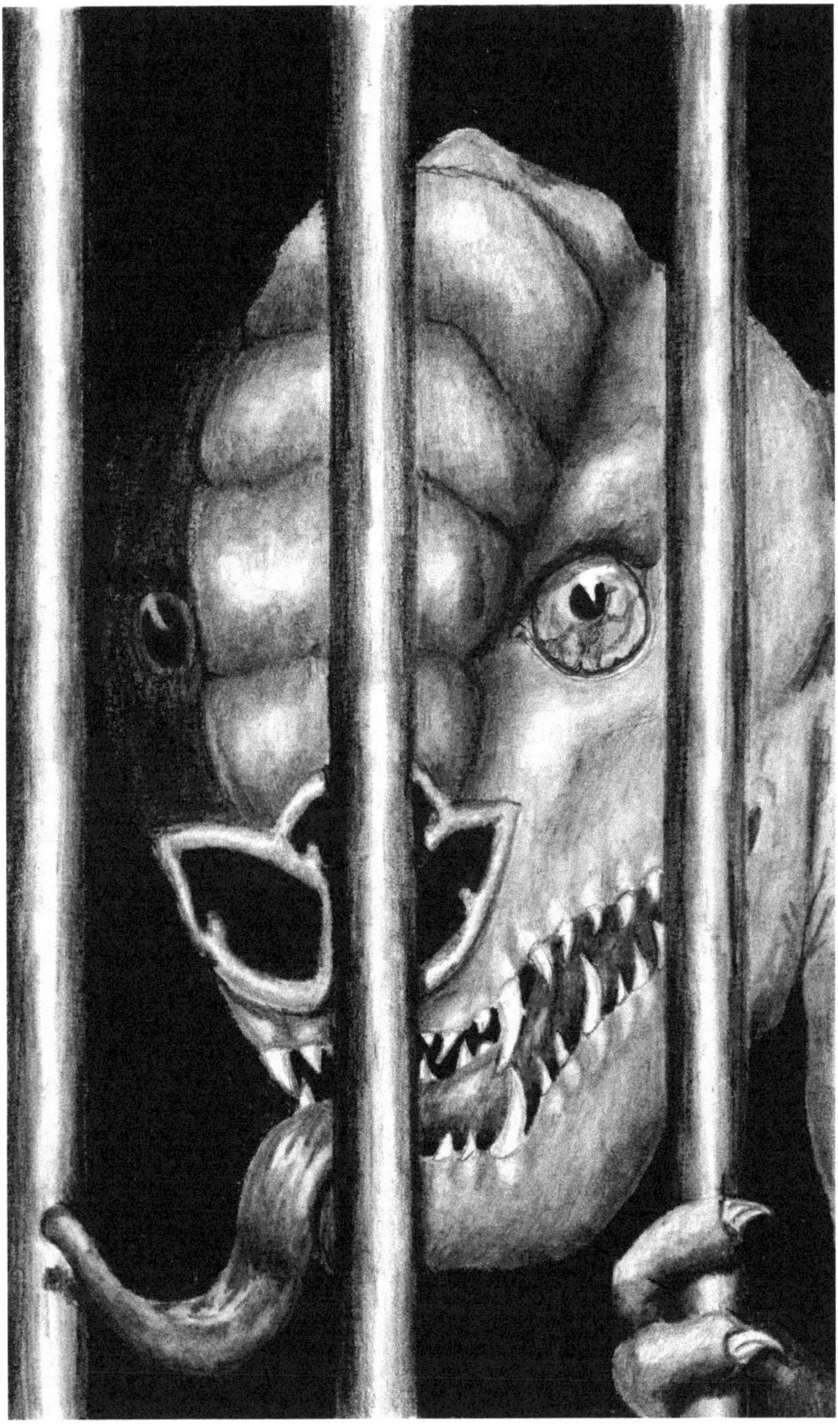

reddish bald skin stretched back to reveal enormous white teeth, resembling those of a tiger. Its nose was a dark maroon color and its nostrils flared wildly as it struggled to breathe with its face crammed into such a tight space.

Max lowered his shaking hand towards the beast's nose, which only excited the thing more. It jammed its face forcefully into the bars several times, trying to get at the blood only inches away.

Max flinched every time its face reappeared. Summoning up his courage, he turned his hand so that his bleeding palm faced the creature's mouth. A long, thick tongue licked out from between its clenched jaws and lapped at the blood oozing from Max's hand.

Max gritted his teeth and fought the urge to ignite the beast into a ball of flame. The hairs on his neck and back stood on end as the scouring-pad tongue continued to wipe across his agonized hand so as to get all the blood possible. Max closed his fingers into a fist to keep the animal's tongue from actually entering the open wound.

"That's enough," Larry said, after what felt like ages.

The instant Max withdrew his hand a fury erupted from the creature, prompting several members of Larry's gang to flee from the chamber.

Max whirled around as the Zbal crashed its body into the bars so many times and with such force, Max thought the cage was going to give way. The Zbal thrashed and ranted with a frenzied cry that reminded Max of a spoiled two-year-old whose mother had taken away a prized toy.

Larry and his remaining gang members ran for the other chamber with Max tailing right behind. The Zbal's shrieks rang through the entire structure. Its sound struck fear into the heart of everyone who heard it.

"Are you finished with me?" Max asked, as they reached the exit to the cave.

Max stepped into the sunlight. He squinted against the intensity of its rays when, SMACK, Larry's fist slammed into the side of his head. The blow staggered Max but he managed to keep his footing. THWUMP! Another blow caught Max in the stomach. He dropped to his knees as he recognized Fred as the one who delivered it.

A sudden rush of adrenaline brought Max back to his feet and he slammed his fist into Fred's chin casting a spell at the same time. "*Premakni.*" The force of the spell-punch laid Fred out cold. Max spun to face the others, his fists raised. "My deal was with Larry! Not anyone else!"

The rest of Larry's posse parted, clearing the way for Max to leave.

"Can I go, now?"

"Go. We're done here," Larry laughed, but didn't look completely unfazed by Max's sudden anger. "Just remember. That thing, once loose, will never stop hunting you."

As Max left Larry's neighborhood, his adrenaline level returned to normal. The punch he threw at Fred had aggravated the cut on his hand causing blood to run more freely down his fingers. He could also feel his left cheek and eye swelling painfully where Larry had hit him. Now that his heart had quit racing, exhaustion once again flooded through his body. He still hadn't recovered from this morning's jaunt to Mir, and the lack of food made him a little nauseated. Now well past noon, the heat from the summer sunshine only added to his discomfort. Max walked under the trees so that he could stay in their cool, protective shade.

In Max's fatigued state, the trip back to Grandpa's lasted much longer than it should have. His hand and head throbbed, and his empty stomach complained frequently. *Better get some peroxide on this. Who knows what kind of diseases that thing has?* To his surprise, no one was waiting for him on the porch. Cindy had apparently recovered and gone home or perhaps she was inside. And the look Grandpa had given him when he left had made Max think that he would be anxious for his return.

His energy ebbed even more as he climbed the steps to the front door. He found the same thing in the house as he had in the yard, emptiness. Max went to the kitchen and turned on the faucet. He put his injured hand under the hot water but jerked it away from the sharp stinging pressure the flowing stream caused. Gritting his teeth, he forced himself to hold his hand under the running water and clean the gash.

After he washed his hand, he went to the bathroom to get some peroxide and bandages out of the medicine cabinet. The mirror revealed a large swollen area on his left temple, with a little color starting to spread towards his left eye. He thought washing his hand was painful until he poured some peroxide in the wound. Tears formed in his eyes as he sucked air through his clenched teeth and pounded the wall with his good hand. Once the pain eased, Max wrapped his hand with some sterile gauze.

He headed back towards the kitchen to get something to eat when he heard the floorboards creak from the third floor. "So, that's where everyone is," he muttered to himself. He grabbed some orange juice and a slice of bread from the kitchen before heading upstairs.

It surprised Max to see Ell in the center of the room, with Grandpa, Cindy, and Yelka standing around him, their hands on his neck. Everyone turned to look at Max as he entered the room, and their expressions went from grim to concern.

"Max, what happened?" Yelka asked, rushing to meet him.

"Did Larry do this?" Grandpa asked.

Only Cindy remained beside Ell. Max figured she had expected this because of what Larry knew about Max. "I'm all right." Max tried to dismiss his injuries.

"What were you doing with Larry?" Grandpa asked, eyeing him suspiciously.

"It's nothing, really. Give me a second." Max walked up to Ell. He put his hand on Ell's neck. *I need your help!*

When Max had finished his conversation with Ell, Grandpa and Yelka started the interrogation again as he knew they would. Max managed to deflect all their queries by telling them it wasn't important and that it was something he just had to do, though they didn't look convinced. Max almost wished he had thought of a cover story to help stave off the questions, but then lying to his grandfather outright would feel worse than just not telling him everything. It was agony, but Max wanted to make sure nothing bad happened to his mother.

"And furthermore, I don't think you should be randomly searching worlds for your mother." Grandpa suddenly changed the topic.

"What?" Max shot Cindy a sharp look, but she appeared shocked by Grandpa's statement as well.

"Oh, I'm a little smarter than you give me credit for," Grandpa chuckled. "It doesn't take a rocket scientist to figure out why you wanted to learn that spell. I do have to give you kudos for mastering it, however. You're one up on me. I've never had the need for that spell before. The thing is, many worlds are extremely dangerous and not just because of the enemy."

"How are we going to find my mother then?" Max fought to contain the tears welling up in his eyes.

"We don't need to find her," Yelka said with her familiar singing voice.

"What?" Max frowned, his sorrow turning into anger. He assumed that they meant to abandon the search.

"We don't need to find her, because we already know where she is!" Grandpa smiled.

18

Max's Plan

"What do you mean, you know where she is?" Max's voice rose an octave in confusion.

"Just what I said. We know right where she is," Grandpa answered. A happy smile spread from ear to ear.

In the same way a snack helps relieve hunger pangs, this news helped Max to feel a small measure of relief from the pain and stress that had been eating away at him for several weeks. "Why haven't you told me before? Don't you know how worried I've been?"

"Yes, I know. And I'm sorry we didn't tell you before but I knew you would want to go to her immediately and attempt to get her out of that prison. We have been trying to work on a plan for rescuing her and your uncle without getting anyone killed."

"How do you know? How did you find her?"

"The moment Alan had you use your communicator after he took you to see her," Yelka answered. "Our communicators use the gateway to send their messages, so naturally, the gateway logs from which world this information is sent."

"Really?" Cindy said, with her hand still on Ell's neck.

"I didn't think of that," Max said. "I remember you telling me that last summer but I didn't put it together."

"Alan doesn't fully understand how our technology works, which is to our advantage. In any case, not only are we working on a rescue mission but we want to destroy their gateway and any materials that could aid them in building another one," Grandpa said. "And because of our trip into Pekel, I now know how to get rid of their gateway. From what

Ell has just told us about what he's learned while following the enemy, we need to hurry, too. It sounds like they are on the move and they are planning to relocate Hudich soon. Yelka, please turn on the gateway. We'll let Ell go home to get some rest."

After everyone said goodbye to Ell, and Grandpa had sent him back to Yelka's world, they went downstairs. Grandpa fixed a big breakfast and they sat around the table discussing everything they knew. Yelka worked her healing magic on Max's hand and she put some ice on his eye, which by now was red and swollen.

"So how does their gateway work? Is it like the one upstairs?" Cindy asked, leaning forward.

"Not quite. It's an entirely magical structure that doesn't involve any technology whatsoever. Unless you count an hourglass or a stone archway as a scientific piece of equipment. The archway does have a mechanical element to it, in that it's rotated to change worlds," Grandpa said.

"What's the spell they use to activate it? I mean, how can something like an hourglass be that crucial in opening a hole into another world?" Max asked with astonishment.

"You couldn't be more wrong, Max. The hourglass is the most instrumental cog in the wheel that is their gateway."

"But what can an hourglass do?" Cindy questioned. "Why is it so important?"

"Because it is an evil device. Max, do you remember the small multi-colored lights that made up the contents of the hourglass?"

"Yes." Max paused a moment, recollecting the magical swirling marbles inside the hourglass.

A grave expression blanketed Grandpa's face, and he seemed to age right before their eyes. "Those lights are the trapped souls of life forms imprisoned in that hourglass. The energy from their life forces is what generates enough power to tear a hole through space, creating their gateway."

Cindy gave a gasp, and Max's mouth fell open.

"An hourglass of souls," Cindy whispered, sitting back in her chair like a reprimanded child.

"Yes." Grandpa hesitated and took a deep breath. He looked to Yelka as if asking whether he should continue, and she gave a short nod. "Those poor individuals cannot continue on their journey until they are released. It's my theory that if we break the hourglass, it should free those prisoners and make their gateway inoperable. I don't think they understand the magic needed to create another hourglass or add anymore souls to it."

"What makes you think that?" Max asked.

"From what I've understood from the book we brought back from Pekel, some very evil wizards, more powerful even than Hudich, created the hourglass. They discovered the secrets to unlock this vile magic. These wizards were rumored to have a very cruel nature and desire for power. They confined their victims' souls in the hourglass. They learned that the more souls they captured, the better their gateway worked and the longer it stayed open. From what I can tell, their gateway can only stay open as long as souls continue to fall through the neck of the glass."

"What about the spell? The one Alan and the others are using." Max inquired.

"Well, it seems that the souls trapped in the hourglass aren't responsive to just anyone. While in the hourglass they belong to their jailers, the wizards who originally imprisoned them. Alan and the others are using a control spell to gain temporary mastery of these souls. The spell they use is a simple one, but it takes a lot of them casting it to generate enough might to overpower the captive souls. My biggest fear, and Ell's report has added to my anxiety regarding this, is that they will move Hudich. I think he might be able to unlock the secret to the souls and be able to reconstruct the device. If that happens, they will have the advantage. While we had the only gateway, we were in control, but now..."

"Why would they have the upper hand if they had a gateway?" Cindy asked.

"Because they are more organized than we are and have greater numbers. Most people don't even know the war exists except for the few on our side trying to keep all the worlds safe."

"What you're saying is there might be more books written by these other, more powerful wizards that could contain the magic necessary to duplicate their gateway?" Max asked.

"I think that is exactly what he's saying," Yelka said.

"How are we going to find them all?" Max asked.

"I think we're going to need a lot of luck on this one. I'm sure the gateway information was in the same world as their gateway at one time. The book briefly mentions some protectors the wizards used to guard their gateway and their secrets. I'm hoping that Alan and the others haven't found a way to appease these protectors, if they still exist. It appears that these wizards have been dead a very long time. Let's pray that Alan and the others are still looking for the secrets of the gateway or, if they have found that information, that they haven't already moved the information to some other world. Ell said it looked like they were getting ready to move Hudich soon, so I'm still hopeful it remains in Kleen," Grandpa said with a frown.

"What's Kleen?" Cindy and Max asked simultaneously.

"Kleen is the world where their gateway is," Yelka answered.

"And where my mother is," Max said, his voice trailing away as he sat back in his chair.

They all sat in silence until the sound of the front door opening and closing snapped them out of their contemplation.

Martin sprang into the kitchen, full of enthusiasm. "Guess what, everyone?"

This was the first time Martin had seemed happy all summer. He usually stuck by his mother's side wherever she went and acted like a whipped dog.

"What?" everyone asked in unison, as Aunt Donna entered the kitchen.

"I cast my first successful spell today!"

"Reeeaaally?" Yelka's voice sang.

"Good job," Max and the others added.

Aunt Donna, looking tired and worn, patted Martin on the head. The large dark circles under her eyes suggested she hadn't been sleeping, and lines of worry had set up camp across her forehead. Max suspected she had more gray hairs than when he had been sent to her house at the beginning of the summer.

"How are your spells coming along?" Yelka asked Aunt Donna.

"Oh, I managed a few," Donna responded casually, as if she didn't want to detract from Martin's happy accomplishments.

"I'm going to go out into the yard and practice," Martin announced, as he poured himself some of Grandpa's homemade lemonade from the refrigerator.

"I'm sure you will conquer them all," Yelka said with a smile, while Martin happily drained his glass and headed for the back door.

"So, what's going on?" Aunt Donna took a seat at the table. "Any news on my husband?"

Max was glad for the interruption, because now he didn't have to answer any more questions about his meeting with Larry. Pieces of his plan formed in his mind as Grandpa explained to Aunt Donna what he had discovered about the enemy's gateway. Max caught Cindy staring at him several times and knew she wanted to go somewhere to talk. He had just thought of an excuse to leave when Aunt Donna asked, "What about these murders?"

Grandpa frowned and rubbed his chin thoughtfully. "I don't think they're being done by a human. I think the enemy has brought something from another world."

"I think it's that creature who pretended to be Uncle Frank," Max exclaimed.

"What?" Aunt Donna gasped.

"I'm afraid I agree," Yelka said. "Remember that thing that impersonated your husband and attacked us when we tried to leave your house?"

Donna wiped tears away with the back of her hand and gave a sniffle. "Yes!"

"There are four things we must accomplish in order to get everything back to normal," Grandpa said.

Max wanted to tell them about the other creature held in the cave behind Larry's house, but that would mean exposing his mission. He needed to develop his own plan to achieve everything Grandpa had mentioned. Cindy could help, but she was the only one.

Max stood, stretched, and excused himself from the room. Cindy followed. As they left, Max could sense Grandpa eyeing him, and he had the strongest impression Grandpa knew everything.

"Where should we go?" Cindy whispered, as they entered the front room.

"I don't know. I was going to suggest a hike, but with the new subdivision there's no way we could reach the hills without anyone noticing."

"Let's go to my house. My parents are at work and we can be alone."

They went out the front door, down the steps, and towards the gate when Max spotted Grd in his uncle's likeness. He stood under the same tree where all last summer a Night Shade had maintained watch over of them. Grd leaned against the tree picking at his teeth with a toothpick.

Max felt sick to his stomach at the thought of that creature feeding on human flesh, and he paused in front of the gate.

"What? Oh!" Cindy said, as she followed Max's gaze.

Grd looked at them and gave them a wink and a smile. He continued to clean his teeth.

"Are you sure your house is safe?" Max hesitated by the gate.

"My mom and dad asked Yelka to add some more enchantments to protect our house before sending me to boarding school. We should be safe enough." Cindy pushed past him and opened the gate.

"Just hurry," Max urged as they stepped into the street. "I don't want to have anything to do with that thing."

They hustled over to Cindy's house and locked the front door behind them. They sat in the front room, Cindy on the sofa in the middle of the room and Max in a lounge chair positioned where he had a view out the window. He told Cindy about everything that had happened in the cave with Larry and the Zbal. During the entire narration he kept an eye on Grd, who remained under the tree down the street.

"So, even Alan doesn't want that thing running around in our world," Cindy stated, coming to her feet and pacing around the room.

"It's definitely Grd. Alan and the others clearly don't trust him and can't control him," Max said.

"I'm sure you're probably right. Even Yelka thinks so." Cindy continued walking back and forth, her arms flailing a bit, as she tended to do when deep in thought. Suddenly her arm jabbed out towards Max. "So, what's your plan?"

"First, we need to find Grandpa's coordinates book and see where Kleen is. Then, we need to go there and scout around."

Cindy stopped and looked dubiously at Max. "Don't you think Grandpa knows you will try that?"

"I suspect he does, but I still have to do it. I'm not here to tell you what to do, and if you want to come, I'll be glad to have you with me. I don't know how long you'll be able to stay before you have to come back, though."

"Oh, I'm definitely coming. But I think we should convince Yelka to give us some more of that plant that builds up our magic first."

Max finally turned from the window. Cindy stood smiling at him and Max's mouth split into a grin. "Cindy, that's brilliant! Why didn't I think of that? That could help build up our strength so that we might be able to stay longer and really snoop around."

Max, suddenly inspired, leapt out of the chair. "Let's hurry before she goes home. We could say we want to spend a little time with Ell and we need a break."

"Hey, maybe we don't even need to get it from Yelka."

"What do you mean?"

"Ell has been living on Svet for a year now. Maybe he knows where to find it."

"Cindy, that's two great ideas! Come on," Max bolted for the door.

"I'll have you know, I'm full of great ideas," Cindy said with a grin, and bounced after him.

Max hadn't been this excited about anything all summer. All the pieces were there before him: the key, the world where his mother and uncle were captives, and the formation of a plan to get them out.

As he jumped down the porch steps at Cindy's house, Grd now stood outside the white picket fence around her house. Max and Cindy stopped a few feet away from her porch. Max's heartbeat changed from excited to racing panic. He took Cindy by the hand and continued walking towards the sidewalk.

"Are you fulfilling your mission?" Grd asked in a mocking tone.

"Yes!" Max spat, shooting Grd an angry look as he opened the gate. He pulled Cindy through and shut the gate behind him. They hurried towards Grandpa's house.

"I don't think you quite understand the importance of your job," Grd sneered with an evil smile, while quickening his gait to catch up. "I think a little more motivation is in order." Grd's body flashed from human to the gray scaly monster and he tore after them.

"*Preseliva se* Svet," Max uttered, and he and Cindy exploded off the ground. Streamers zipped past faster than ever before. The rolling, green hills around Yelka's house on Svet appeared under their feet and they toppled to the ground on impact.

"I really need to get better at the landing," Max grumbled as he clambered to his feet and helped Cindy to hers.

"What did you do that for?"

"It was the only spell that popped into my head, and it got us out of there didn't it?" Max glanced around and spotted Ell running towards them.

"Max, I don't think I can stay very long," Cindy said, looking pale and half falling-half flopping down into the grass.

Max took out his communicator and entered a message as fast as he could.

"What are you doing?"

"Telling Grandpa that Grd is outside so he can help protect you when you get back."

"Me? Aren't you coming too?"

"Don't worry, I'll be right behind you. Right after I tell Ell what we want." Max gave her a wink as his communicator flashed Grandpa's response.

"Grandpa will be there. You can go," Max said, just as Ell trotted up to them.

Joe sat in his study poring over the pages of the book they had found in Pekel. He read and reread the parts about the hourglass to make sure he hadn't missed any details. Some particularly strange looking symbols on the top of one page had caught his eye when his communicator started vibrating in his pocket.

"Sky must be finished with her scouting mission," he muttered to himself, as he took out his communicator and read the message. "What?" He jumped to his feet knocking the book on the floor. "Yelka, meet me outside at once," he yelled, as he scrambled to the front door.

Yelka bounded down the stairs just as Joe threw open the front door to see Grd, the hideous beast, having a fit in the street. He thrashed about in a snarling outrage, clawing and sniffing at nothing. He pounced and vaulted about in one particular area as if he were looking for some prized possession he had lost.

The preoccupied beast didn't see Joe and Yelka until it was too late.

"*Premakni.*" Joe launched Grd away from the spot that tormented him. Grd crashed heavily into the ground and as he pulled himself up, Yelka cast a spell of her own.

A huge gust of wind knocked Grd completely off his feet and another rolled him turbulently down the street.

A sudden flash of light winked in the air at the spot in which Grd had been busily engrossed and Cindy appeared out of nowhere. She sat on the ground shaking, her skin a pasty white.

Grandpa rushed to her and scooped her up in his arms. "Where's Max?"

"He's coming," Cindy answered weakly, and a second flash of light announced Max's arrival.

Yelka still held her hands out in front of her, continuing her assault on the retreating Grd.

Max and Yelka followed Joe as he carried Cindy into the house.

###

Cindy recovered from the effects of the travel spell much faster this time. Max was doing better, too; only a little less tired and hungry. If it wasn't for the cut on his hand and the bruise around his eye and temple, he would have been in excellent condition. He wondered if some of the lingering effects were due to the lack of sleep because of getting up at 5:00 am.

"After seeing that thing in the street, I'm convinced that you're right, Max. That it's the one behind these murders. And after studying the book more, I'm also fairly certain that it's one of the guardians employed to guard the secrets of the ancient wizards. They are called Haireens," Grandpa asserted, while Yelka tended to Cindy on the front room couch.

"Are you sure that thing is one of the guardians?" Yelka asked, as she helped Cindy into a sitting position.

"Yes, I believe so. The book states the Haireens can change shapes but that their real skin is as strong as dragon scales. It also mentioned an incurable hunger for fresh meat and the only magic they possess: the extremely powerful aptitude for shape shifting, gives them their physical ability. It seems Haireens are unaware that it takes magic to change shape. They think of it more as a natural talent, which is why, I believe, the wizards used them in the first place. They weren't magic-seeking creatures because they didn't understand magic, and that pleased the wizards. I think the wizards just left them to do what they do best. Kill and feast."

"How do we get rid of it?" Yelka asked. "We can't simply let it run loose, murdering at will."

"No, we can't," Grandpa answered. "It seems our to-do list continues to grow by the minute."

"Will this nightmare never end? I just need a break," Max said, drawing everyone's attention. Now was the perfect time to implement his plan. "I mean, it's all just too much. I really need to get away from everything for a few hours."

"I agree. You've been under a lot of stress this summer. What did you have in mind?"

"Do you think Cindy and I could go visit Ell for a couple of hours?" Max asked hopefully, and his eyes flicked to Donna as she came into the room.

"That's a wonderful idea," Yelka sang with a smile. "You've only visited my home once this summer and I could fix you a nice lunch. Perhaps Martin and Donna will join us."

"I'll have to stay here. We're expecting Sky. She's on a little mission," Grandpa said. "But I think a trip to Svet would be a nice little getaway for the rest of you."

"Do you think you're strong enough to move?" Yelka asked Cindy.

"I think so." Cindy held out her hand for Yelka to help her up. Yelka pulled Cindy to her feet and escorted her up the stairs.

"Max, go get Martin and we'll meet you upstairs," Yelka said.

Max ran outside and told Martin where they were going. They joined everyone upstairs and Grandpa turned on the gateway. The force field sprang to life and the old mirror started to rotate.

"Now, Martin, Donna, don't panic at the site of Ell." Yelka described the enormous creature they were about to meet.

"Signal me when you're ready to come home," Grandpa said, as the gateway finished opening.

"We will," Yelka said. "Martin and Donna, your first trip to another world. How exciting."

"Remember to step down," Grandpa reminded them before they entered the gateway.

Once in Svet, Max, Cindy, and a reluctant Martin went off to spend time with Ell, while Aunt Donna followed Yelka to her house.

As Aunt Donna and Yelka strolled away, Cindy leaned into Max's ear. "Your Grandpa has the coordinates book in his back pocket."

"Are you sure?" Max asked Cindy out of the side of his mouth. Martin stood several yards away because of Ell, so Max didn't think he could hear their conversation.

"Yelka had it but gave it back to him while you were getting Martin. I saw him put it there."

Max smiled. "Come on, Martin, touch Ell," Max raised his voice cheerfully.

Martin shook his head. He utterly refused to touch or even get close to Ell. He kept Max and Cindy between him and Ell the entire time they were there.

To Max and Cindy's great delight, Ell knew right where to find the plant to strengthen their magical powers. Ell told them that Yelka had been feeding the root to him as well, in order to help him learn magic, too.

Max and Cindy each ate two of the roots and stuffed their pockets full with several more.

"Wow! I feel better already. That exhausted feeling is gone," Cindy said, as Martin eyed the root suspiciously.

"I'm telling you Martin, it will help you learn magic a lot faster than those kids back at school. It tastes bad but the effects are awesome."

Martin managed to eat one of the roots and then tried the *premakni* spell on a stack of stones and sent the pile flying. After which he, too, filled his pockets with a bunch of the roots.

"Just don't tell anyone that you have those or that we showed them to you." Max said.

Martin smiled and nodded his head.

"In fact, you should act like you're still struggling with your spells," Cindy added.

After a three-course lunch at Yelka's, with delicious foods the likes of which they had never tasted, everyone felt refreshed. Even Aunt Donna seemed more at ease than she had all summer. Everyone was complaining about how short their stay had been when they traveled back to Grandpa's house.

###

Later that afternoon, before Cindy went home for dinner, she managed to get Max alone. "What are you going to do?"

"I'm going to take the book. Tonight! After I get the coordinates I need, I'll put it back. From what I can tell he still has it in his pocket."

"When do you want to leave for Kleen?"

"As soon as I have its location."

"I'll sneak over as soon as I can," Cindy stated.

"Be careful. Grd is still out there somewhere," Max cautioned and accompanied her to the street. To Max's great relief, Grd wasn't anywhere to be seen.

"See you tonight," Cindy said as they parted.

The rest of the evening, Max kept an eye on Grandpa and the outline of the notebook in his back pocket. The idea of taking the notebook bothered Max. He didn't enjoy the thought of betraying his grandpa's trust, but the desperate need to help his mother was far greater. The excitement he had experienced at knowing his plan was taking shape, was replaced by thoughts of his mother. He missed her so much it pained him. His heart longed for her safe return, and his desire to see her made his whole body ache as if a great vice squeezed him.

Max stared down at his dinner, his appetite gone.

"Are you all right, Max?" Martin asked.

"Yes." Max stuffed his mouth full of mashed potatoes even though he wasn't really hungry. He wanted to answer questions even less.

After dinner, Max went up to his room and turned off the lights. He lay on his bed in the enveloping darkness, concentrating on the task at hand. *Grandpa must keep it close, like a set of keys.*

It was midnight when Max decided to get out of bed. He took out some of the roots he had hidden in his backpack and put them in his pockets before making his way to the bathroom, as if that were his intended destination all along. The house was dark, and only the sound of chirping crickets floated through the bathroom's open windows. The room was cool but comfortable, and Max wished he didn't have to do this, but he just couldn't think of a better option.

He didn't continue his bathroom charade for long. Taking a deep breath to settle his nerves, he quietly slipped out of the room. He snuck down the stairs, avoiding the steps he knew would creak. Still nothing stirred. He paused once or twice to listen, and when he was satisfied that no one had heard him, he continued forward. Down the hall and past the kitchen he went, until Grandpa's open doorway stood before him. Soft snoring sounds, mingled with the chirping of the crickets outside, told him Grandpa slept.

Tiptoeing through the open door, Max struggled to see. Grandpa had pulled his window blinds leaving the room in almost complete darkness. Max paused for a few minutes, allowing his eyes to adjust to the lack of light. The general shapes of Grandpa laying in his bed, the chest of drawers, and the nightstand beside the bed took form. He proceeded to the dresser against the far wall, not wanting to get too close to his sleeping grandfather.

As slowly as possible, Max slid his hand across the top of the dresser trying to feel for the notepad. The bedsprings creaked as Grandpa rolled over, causing Max to knock over a picture frame. He caught it in midair and placed it carefully back on the dresser. Without any success at the dresser, Max worked up his courage and sidled gingerly to the nightstand. Once again he brushed his hand delicately over the surface of the furniture. This time, however, it was Grandpa's communicator that he almost knocked onto the floor. But instead of falling, the communicator bumped into the notepad pushing it over the edge. SLAP!

The notepad hit the floor. Max held his breath as Grandpa stirred once more. He had to have heard the notepad and if not, then he must hear Max's heart thudding like a stampede of wild horses in his chest.

Max carefully picked up the object and scurried out of the room. As he looked over his shoulder to make sure his grandfather hadn't awakened, he collided with Cindy.

"Ouch," Cindy whispered.

"Shh! How did you get in?" Max whispered, glancing back again at Grandpa's room.

"Through a window. I removed the screen."

"Never mind, I've got the notebook." Max took Cindy by the arm and led her up to the third floor. He turned on the light and hurried over to the gateway's control panel. As he held up the notepad to begin his search for the page containing the coordinates for Kleen, he saw that the top page was the one he wanted.

"Hey, the notepad is already open to Kleen," Max continued to whisper.

"What do you think that means?" Cindy peered down at the writing on the paper.

"I don't know," Max answered, rubbing his head in confusion. Well, they had no time to waste wondering about it. He read the instructions and then double-checked it on the control panel. "Okay, I know where it is. I'll take the notepad back to Grandpa's room and meet you out on the porch. Did you bring some roots?"

Cindy nodded.

"Good. Let's each eat two before we go."

Returning the notebook was a lot smoother and less nerve-racking. Before Max knew it, he and Cindy sat on the porch swing, eating the puke-tasting plants.

"I think I want to try the transportation spell by myself this time," Cindy whispered.

"I believe you can do it, Cindy, but let's wait until next time. I know right where we're going and we seriously need to stick together," Max answered.

"This isn't just some lame excuse to hold my hand again, is it?" Cindy asked, as she batted her eyes and flashed a smile.

"No," Max retorted, as he took her by the hand, but he couldn't hide a quick grin.

He concentrated painstakingly on where they needed to go. "*Preseliva se*, Kleen." The porch vanished from beneath their feet and streamers zipped by them right before they slammed into the solid stone floor of the enemy gateway. This time they managed to only drop to their knees on landing.

"That..." Cindy tried to speak but Max yanked her quickly to her feet and pulled her towards a ridge a short distance away.

As they ran, Max's head jerked from side to side—looking for any indication they had been seen. Even though it was night, the red glow given off by the pools and rivers of lava made things bright enough to see two kids appear out of thin air. Once over the small rise, they dropped to the ground and rolled over on their bellies. After verifying that nothing was behind them, they observed the enemy gateway and the stone structures around it.

Max spotted the prison first. "Mom," he breathed quietly.

"What? Where?" Cindy asked.

Max pointed to the building to the left of the enemy gateway.

"Where do you want to start looking for the, for lack of a better word, library?"

"I'll bet it's one of those buildings straight behind the gateway," Max whispered, his eyes glued on the prison.

"We'd better hurry. Even with the roots, we don't know how long we can stay before we have to go back."

"Right." Max started to get up when a group of cloaked figures emerged from a building to the right of the prison. He hunkered down behind the ridge again.

The figures proceeded out onto the gateway structure and each went to stand in front of a stone slab forming the ring around the gateway. As soon as they had taken their positions, they began to chant.

"They're getting ready to start their gateway. That's the spell they use," Max said.

"It's a good thing we arrived a few minutes ago. We could have landed right in the middle of this."

Two more cloaked figures moved into the circle, one of them carrying the hourglass. The soft multicolored lights emitted by the trapped souls grew in intensity with each passing moment.

"Those poor things," Cindy gasped.

The cloaked figure with the hourglass held it high as he approached the stone archway with its three-way entrance in the middle of the structure. Then, turning it upside down, souls began to flow through the neck into the lower chamber as the figure slotted the hourglass into the hole under the archway.

As soon as he stepped back, a light appeared in the archway and grew until it engulfed the entire stone structure. Max and Cindy's mouths fell open and they remained frozen as Hudich stepped out of the light into the world of Kleen.

"We need to get out of here!" Cindy gasped in a horrified voice.

"Yes, you do!" someone whispered behind them.

19

The Arrangement

Max and Cindy rolled over quicker than they could think and tried to get up. A staff pinned Cindy to the ground while a boot secured Max.

"What are you doing here?" the stranger asked with a hint of surprise. "Do you know how much trouble you're in?"

Max exchanged a panicked look with Cindy.

"Does Joseph know you are here?" the figure asked.

"Whaaaa…" Cindy stammered, sounding as confused as Max felt.

"Who are you?" Max asked.

The figure released the hold it had on both of them and tapped Cindy with the staff to move over. "It's me, your self-defense instructor," Sky said, lying down between them. "So? Does Joseph know you are here?"

"Not really," Max said, relieved it was Sky, but terrified at the same time. He didn't know whether Sky's discovery of them would affect his plan to save his mother.

"Not really? That sounds like no to me."

"Okay, no," Max said. "What are you doing here?"

"I have been scouting this place for three days now," Sky said, peering over the ridge at Hudich and the enemy gateway.

When the chanting stopped and the light of the gateway went dark, Max returned to watching the scene. Hudich's servant, who had put the hourglass in place, retrieved it and then lowered his hood.

"Alan, of course," Max hissed, as he watched Alan bow low before his master, Hudich.

"I wish I could hear what they're saying," Cindy whispered.

"It does not matter," Sky said. "I was just about to call Joseph when I saw the two of you running to this ridge. So, where is the gateway?"

"We didn't come through the gateway," Max said.

"Really, you used magic? I am indeed impressed. Somehow I do not think your grandfather is going to be as impressed when he learns that you came here."

"Did you find the library?" Cindy asked.

"Not a library, a vault," Sky said. "Yes. And I am fairly certain that they do not know where it is yet. It lies in some catacombs under the prison. The entrance is hard to find and there are Haireens guarding it. These Haireens can change shapes like a chameleon."

"How did you get past them?" Max asked.

"Oh, you shall discover that I can get into just about any place I wish without being detected. It might take some time. Three days this time. Now that I know the way in, it will be even easier next time."

"Why didn't you just destroy everything in there?" Cindy asked.

"Did you see my mother?" Max asked.

"My mission was not to destroy anything, so I left it as I found it," Sky said to Cindy. "No, Max, I did not enter the prison, but there is at least one person still alive in there. A faint moaning can be heard when one is close enough."

"Will you tell us how to get into the catacombs without being detected?" Cindy asked.

"Only if you tell me why you are here unbeknownst to your grandfather." Sky said.

Max and Cindy exchanged another quick glance. Cindy shrugged her shoulders and put up her hands.

"See here, Max. You can tell me now, or I can tell your grandfather that I saw you here. I am sure I will learn what you are up to then. Your grandfather already knows the enemy wants you to steal the key."

"What? How?"

"He is a smart man." Sky gave Max a wink. "Let me see if I have understood everything. Your mother was kidnapped and you were taken for a short period of time. We know Hudich and his followers want to remove the collar. You have been a little secretive, to say the least. One need not be a rocket scientist, as your grandfather might say, to figure it out."

"I suppose not." Max debated what to do.

"Come now," Sky urged. "I know you are reluctant to trust anybody because of what happened with Marko, but you can trust me."

"It's not the Marko thing. There is a spy among us once again. They seem to know everything I'm doing," Max stressed, remembering the lock of his mother's hair Larry had given him at the beginning of summer.

"Yes, Joseph and Yelka suspect that too. But as I said, you can tell me what you are up to now, or after I tell your grandfather."

"Okay, I have to trust someone." Max told Sky everything he had been holding back from Grandpa. With every word he uttered, it was as if the vice that held him tight loosened a little. He told her about his mission and about the beast in the cave behind Larry's house. In that moment, a strong bond and a friendship formed between them. Somehow Max knew this relationship would last.

"I see. We need to come up with a good plan." Sky said, after Max had finished.

"Are you going to tell my grandfather?"

"No," Sky answered. "But if you are not going to, you had better create a very good plan in a hurry. Now that Hudich is here, I am certain those catacombs will not stay hidden for long."

"Will you help?" Cindy asked.

"Yes. In fact, I insist on it. Now, you had better return home."

Max looked at Cindy. "Ready?"

Cindy nodded and they both cast the return spell. When they arrived back home everything was the same as when they had left. The effects of the spell weren't very strong this time because of the special roots they had eaten.

"Max, do you think there could be any negative effects from eating too many roots?" Cindy asked.

"I'm not sure. If you notice anything strange let me know immediately, and I'll do the same."

"Okay."

"You'd better go home and I'll see you tomorrow." Max turned towards the front door.

"Okay," Cindy agreed and skipped down the first two steps and then came to a halt.

The sudden silence stopped Max from entering the house. Cindy stood on the bottom step staring out into the street. On the other side of the fence waited the creature, Grd, wearing human clothes. His scaly face split wide in a smile that revealed his vicious, hooked teeth.

"Uh, Max," Cindy stammered.

"Come on." Max opened the door. "I'll sleep on the floor and you can have the bed."

They hustled inside and closed the door on Grd. They climbed the stairs as a light from the hall below sprang to life, followed by Grandpa's footsteps coming down the hall.

"Hurry," Max whispered, and they sped up the steps and into Max's room. Through a crack in the door they watched Grandpa turn towards the third floor staircase.

The sound of the gateway filled the house a few moments later and then silence.

"Do you think Sky will tell him?" Cindy asked, as Max closed the door.

"I hope not."

"She's right, you know. I'm sure Grandpa is onto you."

Max got another pillow and blanket out of his closet and threw them on the floor. "I know but I'm not sure he would give me the key."

"What are we going to do?"

"I don't know yet," he said as he sank down to the floor and covered himself with the blanket.

"Max what are you... Cindy why are you here?" Grandpa sputtered as he entered the room early the next morning.

"Ah, we were up late talking last night and when Cindy went to go home, Grd was waiting outside the fence. We figured it was safer if she stayed here," Max said, as he tried to relieve a crick in his back by stretching. Sleeping on the floor had resulted in stiff joints and a sore back. "What's going on?"

"They've moved Hudich to Kleen and there's been another murder," Grandpa said with a grave expression as he looked at Cindy.

"Grandpa, you're scaring me," Cindy said, her face turning pale as Grandpa sat down on the bed next to her.

"No, it's not anyone we know. I'm just relieved that you decided to stay here last night. The thought of that creature. . ." He patted her hand. "They found the body in the Szepanski's yard this time. I'm going to check it out. If you want to come with me you'd better hurry. Breakfast is ready downstairs. Cindy, I'll let your mother know where you are."

"Was the body in the same condition as the others?" Max asked as Grandpa got up to leave.

"From what I've heard." Grandpa nodded and headed towards the door.

"Well, when did they move Hudich?" Max asked as an afterthought, trying to pretend as if he didn't know.

"Last night, but we can talk about that later," Grandpa called over his shoulder as he hurried from the room.

Max and Cindy went downstairs and inhaled their breakfast before joining Grandpa in the front room. They all left the house together and Grandpa led them through the new neighborhood towards a house surrounded by police cars. They joined a large crowd which was milling about outside an area cordoned off by yellow plastic warning tape.

Max's jaw dropped as he noticed people from both sides talking together. It was the first time he had seen such a thing. Everyone looked worried, confirming what Larry had told Max about why the enemy had imported the Zbal.

"It appears that some of the enemy, at least, is in the dark," Grandpa said, as he walked towards a tall blonde woman standing alone next to the police tape.

The sight of this woman shocked Max even more than the unusual co-mingling of friend and foe. It was Sky dressed in a tee shirt and blue jeans. Except for her pale skin, she looked like any human waiting for information the same as everyone else. As they weaved their way through the crowd towards her, someone grabbed Max by the collar, stopping his progress.

"We need to talk," Alan whispered in his ear, and escorted him towards the back of the crowd. "I'm sure you are already aware, because of that collar, that Hudich is no longer with the Zeenosees. Let me just inform you that he is very displeased with your lack of progress in bringing us the key. We have decided that perhaps you need a bit more, shall we say, persuading. If you continue to dawdle in this manner, life could get extremely unpleasant for your mother and your uncle. Am I being clear enough for you?"

Max's blood boiled as it pumped through his body. "Yes," he whispered through his dry mouth.

"Very good. Now, when can we expect the key? I suggest you give me a date, a date in the very near future."

"You'll get your key and you'll get it soon," Max hissed through gritted teeth.

"Is this man bothering you, Max?" Sky asked, as she appeared next to Alan.

"We're just having a private conversation, and it is none of your business," Alan shot Sky a wicked look. "I suggest you leave us alone."

Sky put her hand on Alan's shoulder. "Max is most certainly my business." She smiled pleasantly.

Alan's face turned a bright red and he looked like a volcano about to erupt. He tried to brush Sky's hand off but she countered like lightning. She caught his hand and pinned his arm behind his back.

"Let us set the record straight," Sky spoke in Alan's ear in a calm, controlled voice. "If you, or anyone, harms Max or his mother in anyway, I will come for you. You will not even have time to worry yourself ill about it because I shall be there to deliver your punishment before you know it." Sky released her hold on Alan so he could turn.

Alan's expression was one of a man on the verge of losing it. He started to utter what sounded like a spell. Sky's hand shot out like a striking snake clasping Alan's throat with a death grip, instantly preventing him from speaking.

"I did not believe you were really that stupid," Sky said softly, tilting her head and smiling menacingly. "If you ever try something like that again, I shall stop you from speaking forevermore." Sky pulled her hand away but then, in a blur of speed, it lashed out again, fingers jabbing Alan in the throat causing him to gasp for breath.

Alan staggered and fell to one knee.

Max couldn't move. Sky's actions had left him frozen, mouth agape in shock. He didn't know if this helped or hurt his mother. Sky winked at him and then walked away.

"Are you all right?" Max asked, before he realized the question had popped out. It was a reflex question and he struggled to keep a smile from crossing his face.

The look of bewilderment on Alan's face as he shifted his glare from Sky back to Max caused Max to snort.

"You won't think it's funny if you don't get me the key," Alan gurgled, enraged by Max's effort to keep from laughing.

"I'll let you know in a couple of days when we can make the exchange," Max said, his momentary joy gone.

"There will be no exchange, you foolish boy, or have you forgotten?" Alan had regained his composure.

"Well there's going to be one now. Here's something you can tell your master. Either we have an exchange or Hudich goes through life without any magical abilities whatsoever." Max left in search of Cindy, Sky and his grandfather.

When Max caught up to them, he received another surprise. Grandpa was conversing with the Sheriff while Sky and Cindy watched a short distance away.

"What's that all about?"

"Apparently, the police are baffled. They released the Verrellis a short while ago for lack of evidence, and the dental records of the victims have been sent out in hopes of finding their identities," Cindy said.

"While I have you alone, I have something to say." Max glanced around to make sure no one was listening. "I think we should get the records from Kleen," he whispered.

Sky and Cindy looked astonished.

"I think we should do this before I agree to take them the key in exchange for my mother. If something goes wrong, I don't want them to be able to build another gateway," Max said.

"When were you thinking of retrieving those records?" Sky asked with a smile.

"As soon as possible."

"It would be best if we use the gateway, you know," Sky stated. "You and Cindy were losing energy at a terrifying rate last night. I know you are getting better and stronger at casting that spell, but if we do this, I will need you around longer than a few hours."

"So, you're going to help us?" Cindy asked.

"Yes."

"It appears that the others are as confused as we are," Grandpa said as he rejoined them. "So, whatever was set loose on us, not everyone was in on it." Grandpa looked around and his eyes froze on Alan.

Max and the others followed his gaze.

"Alan will know."

"Alan does know," Max stated, drawing them farther away from everyone. "So do Larry and his friends. Or at least they know part of it."

"What are you talking about?"

Max proceeded to tell Grandpa about the blood-lusting creature in the cave behind Alan's house and what Larry had done to him there.

"Why would you let Larry do this to you?" Grandpa asked.

"I can't tell you everything yet," Max said, and Grandpa frowned. "I can say this: we need to move the records from the cave under the prison on Kleen, tonight."

"And how do you know about that?" Grandpa shot Sky a sideways glance.

"She caught Max and me there last night," Cindy spoke up. "That's the real reason I was at your house this morning. The part about Grd keeping me from going home was the truth though."

"Please, Grandpa, I know I'm being secretive for now, but trust me."

Grandpa studied the three of them for a moment. "I can give Max permission, Cindy. But you'll have to get it from your parents."

"Come, Cindy. I will go with you," Sky said, and she led Cindy down the street.

"So, when are you planning on telling me everything?" Grandpa raised his eyebrows.

"Soon, I promise."

Later that day, Max helped Martin work on his spells in the backyard.

"You're doing great," Max complimented Martin, after he had successfully stopped a whiffle ball Max had thrown.

"*Pridi*," Max called, and the ball flew back into his hand. He wound up his arm to hurl the ball again when Cindy and Sky returned. Cindy rushed through the gate with a big smile, showing her excitement.

"Sky did it! She actually talked my mom and dad into letting me go. I doubted she'd be able to, but she came up with some valid arguments." Cindy looked admiringly up at Sky, who grinned and winked at Max.

"Really?" Max returned her smile.

"Where are you guys going?" Martin asked, coming over to them.

"Uh, we're going with Sky on a little mission," Max replied.

"Can I come?"

"I'm sorry, Martin, but it's going to be dangerous and I have not yet had time to start your training," Sky said, and turned towards the house. "I will go inform Joseph."

"What are you going to do? Will you be using magic?" Martin's eyes shown with wonder.

"Maybe, but if everything goes right we might not have to. But I can tell you this: it is something that will help bring your dad home."

"My Da…" Martin's expression changed as if a dark shadow had settled over him, and tears welled up in his eyes.

"Sorry, Martin." Cindy put her arm comfortingly around his shoulder while scowling at Max.

"Do you think I'll really ever see him again?" Martin sighed, and wiped his eyes with his hand.

"Of course I do." Cindy patted him on the back.

"How's what you're doing with Sky going to help him?"

"Well," Cindy looked at Max and he shrugged his shoulders. "Can you keep a secret?"

"Yes."

"You have to promise not to tell anyone. Even your mother," Max warned.

"I promise," Martin agreed. The look of sadness took on a determined aspect.

Max scanned the area to make sure they were really alone. "We're going after some ancient records that the enemy is looking for. They're in a world called Kleen. The same place they're holding my mom and your dad."

"Wow," Martin said. "And that will help my dad?"

"It sure will," Cindy smiled.

Nervous anticipation distracted Max and Cindy for the rest of the day. No matter what Max did to try to keep his thoughts elsewhere, it didn't work. He and Cindy played catch for over an hour and even explored a few of the rooms in Grandpa's house for the first time this summer. Nothing they tried helped. Even the discovery of several interesting mechanical objects in the science room, which Max made a mental note to ask Grandpa about, couldn't distract them from their pending trip.

"Maybe we should pack our stuff," Max said, shortly before dinnertime.

"I think we should eat some more of the roots before we go. Sky did say there were Haireens guarding the entrance to the catacombs. We may be in for a fight," Cindy said.

"Good idea," Max agreed. "It's smart to be prepared in case we need our magic."

Cindy went to gather up supplies for the night's journey into Kleen.

The hour Max thought would never come finally arrived. He stood inside the force field with Grandpa, Cindy, and Sky, waiting for Grandpa to start the gateway.

"I hope you both know how to handle a gun," Sky said.

Max and Cindy exchanged glances and then nodded they did.

"Good, we always want an advantage." Sky handed each of them a chrome gun. "These are laser guns. If you have to use it, do so."

They took the guns and tucked them in their packs.

Grandpa turned on the gateway. "Just get the records and get out," he said to Sky. "You two," he said rounding on Max and Cindy, "make sure you do everything Sky says."

"We will," they promised.

"I still don't know about this." Grandpa shook his head.

"We'll be all right." Max gave his grandfather a hug.

"Let's go," Sky said and entered the gateway.

"Be careful," Grandpa said, as Max and Cindy stepped into the light.

Max and Cindy stepped down from the gateway onto the stony surface of Kleen. It took a moment for Max's eyes to adjust to the darkness. The half moons cast a small amount of light on their surroundings and a soft orange glow to the left suggested there was a settlement nearby.

"Is that the prison?" Max pointed to the light.

"Yes. Now, follow me and do not speak unless it is absolutely necessary," Sky whispered, glancing cautiously in all directions. She led them at an angle towards the right side of the prison. They moved at a good pace, one that allowed them to cover ground quickly, but not recklessly.

A fissure of steam escaped a crack in the ground to their left, causing them to jump. Sky seized Cindy by the wrist to stop her from falling into a thermal pool behind her. After regaining their composure, they hurried on. Sky took them around a small hill, and as they made their way, the ground gradually began to descend into a canyon. When they cleared the hill, the canyon opened up into an enormous gorge. Solid rock jutted skyward all around them, making spire-like formations. The air grew hot, and the rotten-egg stench of sulfur assaulted their noses. Pools of lava and water dotted the floor of the gorge, and steam obscured their vision.

Once in the gorge, Sky guided them through a crack between two rock towers, where a natural incline took them up to a small flat surface at their summits. The area resembled an observation point, as it sat nestled between the rocks, with openings to view the area in front of them.

"I want you to wait here, while I locate the creatures," Sky commanded, as she peeked over the edge. "The entrance to the cave is behind those three rock pillars right up against the cliff. The prison is on top of that. I will be back shortly."

Max and Cindy watched her leave and then located the spot where she indicated the cave would be. A small lake of steaming water spread out in front of the three tall columns as if to guard it from the rest of the gorge.

Sky returned shortly with a puzzled look on her face. "I cannot find any sign of the Haireens. I do not know if they have found a better hiding place or if they are gone."

"Why would they leave?" Max asked.

"Maybe they're out looking for food," Cindy offered.

"Perhaps," Sky said. "I cannot see any other tracks which might indicate that the cave has been discovered by someone else." She stared at the area around the entrance to the catacombs and Max and Cindy joined in.

Nothing stirred but the rising steam and the occasional splatter of lava as an air bubble rose to the top and popped. The glow from the lava mixed with the steam cast strange floating shadows everywhere.

"What do you want to do?" Max asked.

"We go in," Sky said, directing them back down the narrow crack onto the floor of the gorge. She guided them around and between pools of water, lava, and the towering rock formations.

As they approached the area Sky had designated as the entrance, the large pool of water completely surrounded the rock spires except for a narrow ledge along the right side. Sky's path took them to the left, away from the small walkway. She weaved around several boulders and lava pits before they stood in front of the pool almost against the cliff face on the left side of the rock towers.

Sky pulled them into a little huddle. "Take out your guns and be on the lookout. I still have had no sighting of the creatures, but something does not feel right."

"How are we going to get in?" Cindy asked, waving her hand at the pool.

"Ah," Sky smiled. "The secret to getting past the creatures. They were guarding the easy entrance on the other side, but there is another way. You will have to step exactly where I do. You need to understand that one misstep could cost you your life. Now, follow me."

Sky approached the pool and skirted along the water's edge. Her head bobbed and swayed as she peered at the water from different angles. Suddenly she froze and stared at a particular spot on the pool. Then she extended her foot and placed it in the water. Her boot only went in about a fraction of an inch before she hit bottom. Another step brought her legs together on what must have been a stone hidden just below the surface of the pool. While standing on the stone, she repeated the process and advanced to another rock hidden just below the water. Once there, she waved for Max to proceed out onto the first stone. "The water is extremely hot and very deep if you miss the correct..."

They moved along at a snail's pace. Sky would locate the next spot in the chain while Cindy and Max followed. After what felt like hours, they reached the base of the far left rock tower. Sky motioned them to wait and she circled to the other side of the spire and disappeared. After a few minutes, her head appeared around the pillar and she motioned for them to proceed.

Behind the towers, large rocks littered the ground so completely that they had to balance as they stepped from rock to rock. Max scanned the cliff face for the entrance of the cave, but he couldn't make anything out. They were directly behind the center tower when Sky's hand shot in the air, bringing them to a halt. She stood tall and unmoving for several moments before turning towards the back of the center rock formation. She worked her way behind a large boulder resting against the center tower. There, between the boulder and the side of the tower, was a narrow opening. "Be on your guard. Something is definitely not right," Sky cautioned as she slid through the narrow gap.

After the narrow entrance, the way opened up into a large cavern with stalactites and stalagmites forming what looked like strange rows of teeth. A flowing river of lava cast a strange reddish orange light over the entire place. Sky quickened her pace and led them in an almost straight line through the cavern to an opening on the far side.

This opening was a little too perfect to have been created by nature. The walls were smooth and the ceiling perfectly rounded. At the end of the hall another room opened up before them. Here were tables with a thick layer of dust covering their tops. Several shelves lined the walls with books, scrolls, discolored jars and cobwebs filling their surfaces. An old, thick rope hung through a round opening in the stone ceiling in the center of the room.

"What's that?" Max asked, pointing at the rope while staring up at the dark hole.

"The rope leads to a closet-sized room above. I checked it out last time I was here. It looked as if it had been an entrance at one time, but it is sealed off now," Sky responded.

"How do we know which book we want?" Cindy asked, eyeing the walls.

"That is simple," said Sky as she moved towards a small podium in the corner of the room that held a large opened, leather-bound book.

"Okay, I agree that's probably the book, but what if it isn't?" Max asked as Sky peered down at the book.

"There is a diagram of an hourglass on the open pages," Sky said, snatching the book up and bringing it to them.

"Well, if it's not, we should throw the other books into the river of lav…" Cindy froze.

A strange hissing sound echoed off the walls causing the hairs on the back of Max's neck to stand on end.

Out of the shadows around the room, four Grd-like creatures materialized, surrounding them.

20

The Feather in the Enemy's Cap

"We knew you'd come back," the Haireen closest to Sky hissed through his reptilian lips.

Max, Cindy, and Sky quickly formed a tight circle in the center of the room with their backs to each other. The Haireens began to close in around them, cutting off any possible escape routes.

"Did you think we weren't aware that someone had entered our domain? Did you think that we wouldn't wait for your return?" spat another.

Max's heart raced inside his chest as he tried to hold the futuristic ray gun steady.

A sudden flash of light filled the room, followed by a horrifying screech which echoed off the wall of the catacombs, as Sky shot and destroyed the closest Haireen.

Boom! Boom! Lights flashed and screams followed, as Max and Cindy eliminated two more creatures. The final creature backed away but his flexed posture indicated that he might attack at any minute.

Sky kept her gun aimed at the Haireen while guiding Max and Cindy toward the exit.

"Wait." Max pointed his gun at the shelves. Boom! Boom! Boom! Max annihilated the shelves and everything on them. The laser blasts disintegrated the old books and scrolls.

"Sky," Cindy yelled, as two more Haireens entered the room in front of them.

Sky didn't hesitate, and killed the first Haireen in line with another blast. "I suggest you keep back. I do not negotiate and I do not wait around for idle chit chat." She glared at the other two, who retreated a short distance away.

They growled with anger and snapped their jaws of hooked teeth, biting empty air, threatening the trio.

"Max, have your grandfather open the gateway on the far side of the pool in front of the three rock formations," Sky shouted, as she led them at a sprint through the small corridor and out into the main cavern.

Max struggled to take out his communicator as they dashed through the stalagmites. More Haireens joined in the chase and didn't show any fear of the guns still wielded by Sky and Cindy, who continued to shoot down the vicious creatures. Max managed to send the message and worked on stuffing the communicator back in his pocket. With his attention occupied by this task, Max didn't see the thing that he collided with and it sent him careening into a limestone spike. He dropped his gun as needle-like claws sliced a hideous gash in his forearm, which he had raised to defend himself.

"*Premakni*," Max screamed, sending his assailant into the air. A bright flash disintegrated the Haireen in midair as Sky blasted it with her gun before it hit the ground.

Max scrambled to his feet. "*Premakni!*" He sent more Haireens flying like bowling pins. He looked around in a panic. His attackers had succeeded in separating him from Sky and Cindy.

Cindy and Sky fired their guns nonstop into an onslaught of the lizard-like beasts scrambling to overpower them.

While Max fought his way back to Cindy and Sky using all the spells in his arsenal, he received several nasty bites and scratches, losing enough blood to drain his energy. They managed to gain the outside of the cave where yet more Haireens waited for them. Sky looked like a gunfighter in the old west as she gunned down a multitude of attackers.

The creatures resembled sharks in a feeding frenzy. The fact that their fellow Haireens were being destroyed had no effect. They continued to tighten the noose around Max, Cindy, and Sky.

The three fought their way out onto the walkway leading over the pool of boiling water. Haireens pressed in on them from both sides. Sky kept them at bay from the front and Cindy from the back. Max took the communicator out of his pocket and typed a new message. The response was almost immediate.

"How do we get out of here?" Cindy screamed.

"We jump!" Max answered.

"What?" Sky and Cindy asked in confused terror.

"Jump!" Max grabbed Cindy with one hand and Sky with the other. He leapt from the walkway towards the middle of the steaming pool, pulling Sky and Cindy with him.

They landed in a pile on the third floor of Grandpa's house with the gateway dissolving into the old mirror behind them.

"Is everyone okay?" Grandpa hustled to help them up.

"Incredible! I thought nothing could scare me," Sky said, "but you almost made me mess myself when you pulled me off that ledge. I had heard about the stunt last year where you opened the gateway on the side of a mountain, but I did not think I would experience it myself."

"Did you get what we needed?" Grandpa asked.

"I think so." Sky held out the leather bound book. "Max destroyed everything else, so if this does not contain what we need, we can rest assured that they do not have it either."

"Max, you look pale and you're bleeding!" Grandpa exposed Max's arm to reveal an ugly gash on it. "Your pants are shredded and your legs are bleeding. Let's get downstairs so I can tend these. Sky, help me get him down to the kitchen." Grandpa and Sky supported Max to the kitchen.

In the kitchen, they sat around the table watching Grandpa clean and wrap Max's wounds. "I'll contact Olik to come take a better look at these. We don't want them getting infected, or worse." Grandpa patted Max on the shoulder and smiled kindly at him. "Now, let's see what we can find in that book."

Sky pushed the book across the table towards Grandpa. He turned the book around and carefully opened its cover. The text was old and faded but still legible. Grandpa gently navigated the book's brittle pages, scanning their contents, while Max, Cindy, and Sky nudged closer to peer over his shoulder. Grandpa's page turning came to a halt on a page with an elaborate illustration of an hourglass. Aside from the book's alien-looking text, the page also had a good deal of hand-written annotations in the margins and empty spaces.

"Can you make out what it says?" Sky asked, after Grandpa failed to turn the page for a few minutes.

"Yes. It's an old language but I can translate most of it well enough to get the gist of it. I will need some help getting the entire translation, but this is indeed the book we wanted. The book Hudich wants. It is an evil object…" Grandpa paused as a sleepy looking Martin walked into the kitchen rubbing his eyes.

"Whaa? What are you guys doing up so late?" Martin asked, stretching his arms over his head.

"We were just discuss…" Grandpa tried to get out an explanation.

"Remember the thing I told you about?" Max interrupted. "The thing that will help us get your dad back? We got it!"

"Really!" Martin squealed with delight, his drowsiness disappearing as he hurried to the table.

"Max!" Grandpa shot him a stern look.

"I didn't tell him everything. Just enough to give him hope."

"He didn't. I was there," Cindy confirmed quickly.

"What is it?" Martin asked, eyeing the book in front of Grandpa. "A book?" His face screwed up in confusion.

"Yes, Martin, a book," Grandpa said.

"How can that help my dad?"

"Well, it contains powerful and important information that the enemy would like to have. Now we need to decide what to do with this book. Do we destroy it or hide it away."

"I think we should keep it for at least a little while," Max offered. "It could be a valuable bargaining chip."

"NO! We dare not keep it and run the risk that they might capture it somehow! This is too dangerous for the enemy to ever have," Grandpa declared, with such vehemence all eyes looked down at the book, expecting it to jump to life.

"Martin, did you need something?" Grandpa asked with a sudden smile, dialing down his tone instantly.

"Um, just a drink of water." Martin continued to stare at the book.

"Max, could you please get Martin a glass of water?" Grandpa closed the book as if trying to hide a secret.

After Max had escorted Martin to the stairs, he returned to the table.

"So, Max, what do you think our next move should be?" Grandpa asked, and all eyes fell on Max.

"Well," Max began.

Later that night, while everyone slept, Max snuck down to the study and took the key out of its hiding place. He went back to his room and attached it to a silver chain. He placed the key in a drawer before getting back in bed.

Max awoke the next morning with bright sunshine from the window prodding his eyelids. He stared up at the bedroom ceiling, allowing the previous night's events to parade through his mind. He tried to go back to sleep for a while longer, knowing he needed the rest. This lasted until he felt the vibration of the gateway through the walls of his room. Finally, accepting the fact he wasn't going to get any additional shuteye, he got out of bed.

Opening the top drawer of his dresser and pushing aside some shirts, he revealed the key to Hudich's collar. He took a deep breath before picking up the key and placing the cold silver chain around his neck.

Removing his backpack from the closet, Max dumped its contents onto his bed. Old granola bars, an empty water skin, a compass, some rope, a few remaining roots and the skeleton key spilled onto his covers. He picked up the skeleton key and stuffed it into his pocket. *Never know when you're going to need this. I'll eat the roots before I leave.*

He didn't know if he could pull his plan off or not. *What will Grandpa think? What if something happens to Mom? To Uncle Frank?* Max's emotions simmered at the surface. The full spectrum from fear to anger revolved inside him like a carnival ride.

He didn't have the desire to speak to anyone this morning. He knew what he had to do and wanted to get it over with. Stepping into his tied shoes, he twisted his feet until they slid on and then hustled down the stairs. He opened the front door with one goal in mind.

"Max," Martin called, as Max shuffled down the steps.

"I have an errand to run, Martin." Max tried to get on his way.

"Can I come?" Martin hurried to catch up to Max as he continued towards the front gate.

"NO!"

"Please," Martin pleaded.

Max wheeled on Martin. "You can't come today, so get lost before you get hurt," Max spat.

The enthusiasm in Martin's eyes dimmed like a candle flame being extinguished by a glass cover. Max hated himself at that moment. Martin had seemed frightened all summer and now when he finally had hope and some self-esteem, Max felt awful about crushing it. "I'm sorry, Martin," he added more gently. "I have something very important to do and I really have to do it alone."

Martin lowered his head. "Will it help my dad?"

"Yes, in fact, what I'm doing could be the most important thing in bringing your dad home." Max didn't wait for Martin to respond. He went out the front gate and headed down the street.

All the possible scenarios of what could happen tonight danced in the forefront of Max's mind. Things could go horribly wrong and cost people their lives or it could all go as planned. Even if everything went smoothly, Hudich would be free of the collar tonight. *I can't see any other way!*

Max paused at Larry's street. Several people working in their yards halted their chores to look up at him. *Dang! It's Saturday.* Max had lost track of the days of the week in all the flurry of events that had transpired, and he had hoped to get to Larry's house without a lot of fanfare. There was no way around it, though. He must go on. He took a deep breath and then started down the road. An eerie feeling crept over him with each step, as more people came out of their houses and lined the street.

"Abomination!" Several shouted as Max passed.

"Give up the gateway!" Another called.

Alan came out of his house, followed by Larry, and they met Max at the curb. Alan wore a sinister expression of arrogance while Larry merely smiled his usual smug grin.

Alan opened his mouth to speak when a scream of such madness filled the street that it stopped his utterance. He turned and with slitted eyes looked at Larry, who was sniggering behind his back. "Larry, what's so funny?"

"Nothing." Larry attempted to regain his composure.

It took every ounce of courage Max had to remain where he was. *The Zbal knows I'm near!*

"It seems as if our new pet is very interested in you," Alan sneered. "I haven't heard him this excited since the last time he was set loose to prey on…that. . ." Alan's expression changed to one of contemplation as he glanced sidelong at Larry again.

"Can we get on with this?" Max asked, not wanting to be there any longer than needed.

Before Alan could reply, the beast in the cave screamed its insane cry again.

"What's your hurry?" Alan smirked as if he could tell the Zbal disturbed Max, and he wanted to savor every second of Max's discomfort.

"I just thought you would want to free that loser, Hudich, as soon as possible," Max spat, feeling his anger starting to rise.

"What did you say?" Alan's face flushed and his jaw became rigid.

"You heard me. Anyway, tonight I'll sneak out. I figure about 11 p.m."

"Just make sure you don't waste our time," Alan hissed as the Zbal howled again.

"I won't." Max turned and strolled back up the street as if he didn't have a care in the world. He could feel everyone's eyes burning a hole in his back as he left.

Shortly after Max returned home, Cindy showed up. "Is everything ready?" She asked.

"I hope so," Max said, even though deep down in the pit of his stomach it felt like the constantly churning acid would eat right through him.

"What do you want to do now?"

"Anything to take my mind off tonight," Max said.

They spent a couple of hours playing catch with Martin to pass the time, but by noon the heat of the summer sun made it too hot to be out in the open. Even with no more pleasant distractions to occupy Max's thoughts, the time slipped away faster than he would have liked. Before he knew it, it was early evening.

"I hope I'm doing the right thing," Max mused, as he and Cindy sipped lemonade on the front porch swing.

"I'm sure it will all work out."

The porch swing gently swayed back and forth and they sat in thoughtful silence until it was time for Cindy to head home. "Good luck," she said, as she shuffled her feet down the steps.

"You too," Max added. He waited for her to reach her yard before he entered Grandpa's house and went upstairs.

He took the skeleton key out of his pocket. "*Izgine* key," he uttered and the key vanished. After stowing it back in his pocket, he cast the same spell on the key around his neck. He then waited on his bed until it was time to leave.

A little before eleven, he devoured the two remaining roots. He went to the upstairs bathroom and got a drink from the faucet. "Are you ready?" he said to himself, as he splashed some water on his face. After drying himself with a towel, he left for what he hoped wasn't the last time.

The night air was cool and felt good on his face. If it weren't for his destination, he would have enjoyed a night like this. As Max approached Alan's street, no streetlights were on, but there was plenty of light.

Burning torches bordered the sidewalks and black-cloaked people crowded the street, leaving Max little room to walk. That cocky feeling he'd had when he left Alan's presence earlier that day, was gone.

"You're going to die," some shouted.

"Hudich will soon rule all," others heckled. "Long live Hudich!"

"Well, you actually made it," Alan smiled, as the crowd continued to shout. A hysterical wail from the Zbal in the cave silenced the onlookers. "He does like you." Alan relished the moment.

"Let's get this over with." Max struggled to stop his voice from shaking.

"Yes," Alan said pleasantly, and waved Max toward a thin line of light between two torches.

Max watched the light flicker brighter in spots. It grew and stretched as he approached. He turned and glanced at Alan who was right behind him. Then he stepped towards their gateway while muttering under his breath and disappeared.

As Max landed in front of the gateway on Kleen, he fell to his knees.

Alan almost tripped over him as he came through. "Get moving, there's no turning back now," Alan spat, thrusting his knee roughly into Max's back.

Max scrambled to his feet. The chanting which had filled the air stopped, and the light of the gateway went out.

Hudich waited just a few feet away, his face hidden deep inside his hood as usual. Several figures scuttled around him, taking orders.

Cindy leaned over the gateway control panel with Grandpa. Grandpa showed her how to operate it while Yelka, Sky, Olik, and Jax and his men stood inside the five metallic stands.

"Now, do you think you have it?" Grandpa queried.

"Yes. After you all go through, I shut it down and wait for your call," Cindy responded.

"Okay everyone, it's time," Grandpa ordered. "Yelka, is Ell in position?"

"Yes, we moved him twenty minutes ago," Yelka responded.

"Jax, have men been sent to Alan's street?" Grandpa turned to Jax.

"Yes."

"Good, let's go then."

Everyone picked up bags of gear and lined up in front of the mirror. Cindy started the gateway and watched them leave, one by one.

"I'm sorry," Yelka said, before she disappeared into the light.

After everyone had gone, Cindy closed the gateway. Her anger and frustration from being left behind had ebbed a little since Grandpa put her in charge of the gateway. At least she had an important job to do, and that was something. *Why couldn't my mother let me go! This is my best friend's life, after all.* She went down the stairs to the second floor to wait.

A loud crash, like the sound of furniture being broken and splintered, froze Cindy to the bottom step. There was more smashing followed by a low growl. *Who's in the house?* Cindy realized all the lights in the large house were on when they hadn't been earlier. Peering around the corner, she saw debris littered the hall. Ripped clothes, torn books and damaged furniture lay everywhere.

"Where is it?" a deep guttural voice echoed through the house.

Martin! Donna! Cindy hurried along the hall as quietly as she could towards the other end of the house. Martin's door stood wide open and nothing appeared to be disturbed. She made a quick search of the room and found it empty.

Donna's room was the complete opposite of Martin's. Shelves had been pulled to the floor and the bed overturned. Cindy scanned the room but her eyes jumped to the door every few seconds as loud bangs and booms echoed through the house.

"Where is it?" the roar came again.

A soft groan under a pile of clothes caught Cindy's attention. Pushing the pile aside, she found Donna unconscious with cuts and bruises that resembled large bite marks all around her head. Cindy moved aside the clothes and examined the rest of Donna to reveal more of the same. She had several puncture wounds on her arms and legs, some bleeding quite severely. *GRD! How did he get in? Where's Martin?*

Cindy quickly bound the deeper, freely bleeding gashes with clothes lying around the room. Her heart pummeled her chest, and she knew she had to find Martin. She couldn't let him end up like the nameless victims that had been found in the neighborhood. Cindy hid Donna under some more clothes and a blanket before creeping to the door. The pounding of her heart in her ears muffled the sounds of destruction and the creature's angry bellows drifting up from downstairs.

###

"Where is the key?" Hudich growled.

Even with his hood on, Max could picture Hudich's red eyes glaring out at him. "You didn't think I would be stupid enough to have the key on me?" Max asked.

"Search him," Hudich ordered and several cloaked figures approached him.

"Look. Look," Max said before they started their inspection. Even though the keys were invisible, they were still tangible and a physical search might reveal them. He pulled out his pockets, lifted his shirt almost off, and then held his palms up with the invisible key setting on top. "See."

"You stupid child!" Hudich exploded, causing the searchers to back away.

"You told us you had the key. You filthy little liar," Alan shouted. "How dare you waste our time?"

Max held up his hands. "Wait. I don't have the key on me but it's here in Kleen. I hid it here the other night and I will get it for you as soon as you release my mother and my uncle."

"How do we know the key is here?" Hudich asked, the anger in his voice abating slightly.

"Because without it you wouldn't be willing to make the deal I'm going to offer." Max fought to maintain his composure.

Hudich was an unreadable statue. "Bring the mother and the uncle," he ordered, and two Night Shades hurried towards the prison.

A few minutes later, the figures returned escorting Max's mother and uncle from the prison. They looked half-starved and filthy. Tears welled up in Max's eyes at the sight of them and the thought of what they'd been through.

"Max! Max!" His mother tried to run to him, but one figure held her back.

"Mom," Max said, stepping towards her but a glance from Alan and Hudich told him to stay back.

"What's your offer?" Hudich hissed. "And before you answer, know this—if I don't like it you will watch them die."

Max swallowed the dryness in his throat. "You send my mother and uncle back. I give you the key, and I take their place."

"MAX, NO!" his mother cried. "GET OUT OF HERE! TAKE ME BACK TO MY CELL! LET HIM GO!" She continued to scream and struggle with the guard.

Hudich and Alan both appeared unconvinced, and Max realized that he needed more to sweeten the deal. "I will also give you the book you seek."

"What book?" Hudich asked.

"The one you've been looking for. The one with the blueprints to your hourglass. I have it and I will give it to you in exchange for my mother and uncle. We found it in caves below the prison." Max pointed to the stone structure.

"Humm." Hudich seemed to be considering the idea.

"I like it," Alan smiled. His eyes full of greed and wonder.

"I can live with those terms." Hudich nodded his approval. "So, where are the key and this book?"

"You start your gateway and then I'll show you," Max said, above the cries of his mother.

Hudich snapped his fingers and the minion holding the hourglass stepped forward. The members in the circle began to chant as the keeper of the hourglass turned it upside down and inserted it into the slot under the archway. The light of the gateway responded quickly.

The two guards dragged Max's mother and uncle to the edge of the gateway and stopped.

"Where are the items?" Hudich barked. Just then, an explosion off to their right rocked the ground. Everyone turned to see a battle between the ancient wizards' keepers and Grandpa and the others. "What is that old fool doing here?"

While everyone watched the fight, Max extracted the key to Hudich's collar, made it visible, wrapped the chain tight around his wrist and darted to a lava pit at the edge of the stone circle that housed the enemy gateway. "Hudich!" Max yelled, drawing everyone's attention. "Here's the key. Send them through the gateway and it's yours. Otherwise, live the rest of your life with as much magic as a baby." Max lifted his arm ready to throw the key into the molten rock.

Alan cast a spell stripping the key from Max's hand but the silver chain held it secured to Max's wrist. After the spell faded Max still retained the key. "Send them!"

Hudich's chest heaved angrily, but he gave a curt nod, and the guards shoved Max's hysterical mother and his uncle through the gateway.

"Give me the key," Hudich ordered, with his hand extended.

Max unwrapped the chain and tossed the key to Hudich as he moved away from the pit.

Hudich snagged it out of the air and handed it to Alan as the light of the gateway vanished. Kneeling down, Hudich lowered his hood so Alan could unlatch the collar. The collar dropped to the ground and Hudich stood stretching his arms high above his head, "YYYYEEEEEEESSSSSSSSS." A shock wave of released magic exploded outward from Hudich, knocking everyone within a quarter mile to the ground.

Max grabbed onto a rock protruding out of the stone floor to keep from being blown into the lava pit. As Max got to his feet, all eyes were on Hudich. Even the battle temporarily ceased and the ancient wizards' keepers fled in fear.

"Max," Hudich smiled wickedly, turning towards him. "Now, give me the book."

"I lied. It's safely out of your reach!" Max exclaimed.

"Not to worry, you will still bring it to me," Hudich laughed, shocking Max. "We have a bargaining chip you didn't know about. One that will keep you company in your new place of permanent residence."

"Huh?" Max's crinkled his nose in confusion.

"Hudich, you're free," Alan beamed with adoration.

"Bring me the hourglass," Hudich ordered, and Alan rushed to obey his master's command.

As Alan strutted back toward Hudich with the hourglass, *"PRIDI"* rang out, and the hourglass flew out of Alan's hands.

The hourglass soared towards Grandpa's outstretched hands. But before it reached them, Hudich cast a counter spell pulling the hourglass back towards him. Suddenly, spells filled the air as both sides tried to gain control of the hourglass. It floated, suspended in the air between the two groups.

Jax and his men launched an attack on Hudich's followers, drawing their attention away from the hourglass. A multitude of spells filled the air with colored sparks, fire, and other elements popping in every direction, while Hudich, Alan, and some of the others battled Grandpa, Yelka, and Sky for possession of the hourglass.

Max looked around to find a way to help; for now, no one was paying any attention to him. Max spotted what he needed as the hourglass inched closer and closer to Hudich. Knowing that part of being a good pitcher was deception, Max made his choice. He picked up a round stone lying on the ground, wound up, and threw the rock.

Hudich spotted the approaching stone and dragged the hourglass about a foot lower, out of the stone's apparent path. But this stone was one of Max's all-star curveballs, and it curved downward and collided with the hourglass, shattering the glass container. Time froze as pieces of the hourglass flew apart, half towards Grandpa and the other half towards Hudich.

"We're free! We're free!" Excited and ethereal voices broke the sounds of the battle, as a ray of light from heaven penetrated the night sky and shone down on the stone archway. The small multicolored lights of the released souls floated toward the beam of light and traveled up it in a spiral motion. When the last of the souls had entered the light, it faded away into the darkness.

"NNNNNOOOOOOOOOOOOOOOOOO!" Hudich roared ferociously, and another release of magic slammed like a lead wall into everyone in the vicinity.

Hudich spun on Max and held out his hand uttering a strange word. Max flew neck first into the opened vise of Hudich's large hand which clamped down on his windpipe. "You and your new roommate will pay for that," Hudich spat, as he threw Max to the ground.

Max dropped onto the stone floor, coughing and gasping for air, wondering vaguely what Hudich meant by roommate. "Never heard of a curve ball, have you?" He wheezed, trying to laugh.

"Kill them all," Hudich yelled, waving his hand in the direction of Grandpa and the others.

"Retreat!" The call sounded from the hill as Grandpa and the others fled from Hudich and his followers.

"Cowards!" Hudich growled. "Stand and fight!" He cast several spells at Grandpa and the others as they took flight.

"Why would they leave him?" Alan asked.

"Take him to the prison. Now!" Hudich rumbled. "They're up to something. They wouldn't give him up that easily. The rest of you—after them!" Hudich pointed in the direction of Grandpa and the others.

Two guards lifted Max off the ground and carried him towards the prison, with Hudich right behind him. "You may have had a plan, but you missed a very important piece. We still have leverage that you didn't know about. We will rebuild the hourglass after you bring me the book. Oh yes, you will bring me the book, after you've seen our bargaining chip."

"What chip?" Max asked in a harsh voice, still trying to recover from the chokehold Hudich put on him.

"You will see," Hudich chuckled wickedly.

They entered the prison and placed Max in the cell he had occupied earlier that summer.

"Bring in his cellmate," Hudich ordered.

The guards opened the door on the back wall from where the eerie wailing had come during Max's previous visit. A minute later they emerged, bringing Martin with them. They threw him into Max's mother's old cell and closed the door.

"Martin! What are you doing here? How did they get you out of Grandpa's house?" Max pressed his face against the bars of his cell.

Something was wrong. Martin looked worn, exhausted and thin. Tattered clothes hung on his small frame and his skin looked cracked and bruised.

"Max," Martin started crying. "Where are we? I want to go home!"

"How did they catch you at Grandpa's?" Max asked again.

"Grandpa's? They took me from my house." He continued to weep.

A very bad feeling started to steal over Max as if a shadow had filled the room, sucking the light and life from him.

"Martin, how long have you been here?"

"Since, since April, I think!"

21

Battles Everywhere

"You've been here since April?" Max gasped in total shock.

"That's right, Max. The Martin in your world isn't the real Martin, and since you already know what Grd is, I'm sure you can put two and two together." Hudich laughed and Alan and the guards joined in. "Enjoy your stay! Right now I have other things to take care of, but I'll be back to help convince you to retrieve the book."

After everyone left, Max pulled the skeleton key out of his pocket and made it visible again.

"How did you do that?" Martin stopped sobbing.

"It's a long story. Right now, we need to get out of here." Max unlocked his cell and then proceeded to free Martin.

Joe took out his communicator as he hustled up the hill on his tired old legs. Spells cast by their pursuers fell short as he typed in his message. He kept his eyes on the device as he negotiated a bulky rock formation at the top of the hill and then started down. After a few minutes of running, he reached the designated exit point but Cindy hadn't responded. "Come on, Cindy," he muttered under his breath.

"What's wrong?" Yelka asked, as she fell in beside him.

"I'm not sure." Joe shot Yelka a worried look. "Cindy's not answering."

"What could have happened to her?"

"Good question."

"Where is the gateway?" Sky asked, joining them.

"We don't know," Yelka answered. "Something seems to be keeping Cindy."

"Take up defensive positions," Sky shouted to Jax and his men. Joe and Yelka followed Sky to a clump of boulders to take cover.

The second they reached the rocks, they made themselves as flat as they could, hiding behind the stones as spells exploded all around them.

Columns of enemy fighters sprang over the hilltop sending all manner of evil at them. Not only spells—but also arrows, darts and bullets—whizzed past their heads. Sky seemed like a wraith, vanishing from one spot and popping up in another; casting spells deep into the midst of the enemy.

###

Martin fell into Max's arms, sobbing as the door swung inward. "How are we going to get out of here?"

"I'm not sure." Max propped Martin up against the cage for a moment and rushed to the entrance of the prison. He opened the door just a sliver in order to peep outside and see if the way was clear, but the door bumped into the back of a guard.

"What the…" the guard spun around.

"*Premakni*," Max screamed in fright, and the door slammed into the guard knocking him to the ground.

Max stood in the doorway and his eyes met Hudich's as the latter was giving orders from the center of the stone platform.

"MAX!" Hudich bellowed.

Max yanked the door shut and locked it with the skeleton key. Dragging Martin by the hand, he raced to the door opposite, where Martin had been kept. "Are there any doors beyond this one?" Max asked, as the skeleton key did its job.

"No," Martin cried, as they jumped into the next room. "There's no place to hide either."

Max tried to push the second door shut as the main prison door exploded inward in a shower of twisted metal and rubble, almost knocking Max and Martin off their feet. Dust poured into the chamber, choking the cousins.

"Help me shut the door!" Max ordered.

They scrambled to their feet and slammed the door shut just as a tremendous force blew it off its hinges, throwing Max and Martin against the back wall. A loud crunch echoed off the walls as the blast smashed the door into the back wall.

Through the cloud of dust, Max noticed the door had created a hole in the back wall.

"Out the hole!" Max pulled Martin to his feet.

"COME OUT!" Hudich's voice demanded through the haze, as Max and Martin squeezed through the crack into a small room with a hole in the floor and a rope descending through it from the ceiling.

"Quick!" Max thrust the rope into Martin's hands.

As Max and Martin reached the bottom, Max realized they now stood in the center of the ancient wizards' lair, from where Max, Sky and Cindy had retrieved the book. *No wonder Alan and the others didn't find this room with the entrance sealed.* Max didn't have time to worry about the guardians as spells exploded around them from above. They raced out of the room through the tunnel and into the outer chamber.

"You can't escape," Hudich yelled, as he landed on the floor.

Max and Martin started weaving in and out of the stalagmites in an effort to put something between them and Hudich's dangerous magic.

Suddenly, the guardians materialized from every direction, closing in on Max and Martin, and cutting them off at every turn. They snapped their jaws and hissed through their teeth in an effort to corral their prey.

Hudich sprang into the cavern, drawing the attention of the creatures that had protected it for the ancients. Hudich raised his hands high over his head, and lightning sprang from his fingertips, melting anything that got in his way.

The fierce hissing and growls of the reptilian creatures turned to howls of pain and shrieks of panic as they scrambled to get out of Hudich's way.

Max and Martin found themselves swept along toward the cavern entrance in a sea of fleeing guardians. Once, Martin disappeared below the wave of creatures, but Max managed to hold onto his shirt and yank him back to his feet. Bodies crammed together as they tried to squeeze out of the small opening of the cave. The Haireens' response to Hudich surprised Max. They were terrified, yet the other night it seemed as if nothing could deter them.

Hudich advanced across the cavern, destroying anything and everything in his path. His wrath hit the cave like the fury of a powerful hurricane.

Max and Martin managed to exit the cavern and fought their way through the guardians to the stone walkway. More spells rained down on them, this time from above, where Alan and a few others were waiting on the cliffs behind the prison. Enchantments from the cliffs threw the fleeing creatures from the spires and walkway into the boiling water of the large pool which guarded the passage to the cave.

"*Premakni.*" Max threw his hands over his head, striking one of the attackers on the cliff.

"Max!" Martin screamed, as a spell knocked him back into a rock spire.

Max rushed to lift him back up. He took Martin by the hand. "*Izginiva se.*" Max made the two of them invisible and moved Martin away from the rock tower as a slew of spells slammed into it, knocking the tower into the water.

"What happened?" Martin asked in a bewildered voice.

"We're invisible, so be super quiet!"

Creatures continued to pour out of the cave as Max led Martin out of their path and away from the walkway. He steered them towards the hidden stones on the other side of the pond. "Watch where my feet splash the water and step only on those exact spots after I say so," Max whispered.

Max and Martin had managed to get a few steps out into the middle of the pool when Hudich emerged from the cave. "Where are they?" Hudich roared.

"They went invisible, and we've cast spells to reveal them but they must have gotten across the walkway," Alan yelled over the cliff.

"Is there a way out of this canyon?" Hudich asked, through gritted teeth.

"Yes," Alan called back.

"Get there and make sure they do not escape!"

The guardians continued to scramble over the walkway to get out of Hudich's way. Max and Martin made it across the stones and sprinted around rock formations and lava pits.

"Max, I can see you again," Martin said.

"I know, I'm getting tired," Max said, as he gulped in mouthfuls of air. Sweat ran down his forehead, stinging his eyes. Max released the invisibility spell in an effort to conserve energy. He still had to get Martin to safety.

###

"Hey, something's happening," Jax called over the battle, pointing back to his left.

Joe turned to see the reptile-like creatures rushing out of a canyon behind them. "Something's coming up behind us," he said to Yelka.

"We don't want to be trapped in crossfire," Yelka added.

"Come on." Grandpa darted for another section of rocks in the direction of the canyon. Yelka cast a couple of spells to shield them for a few moments and then followed after him.

Joe and Yelka proceeded to jump from one section of cover to another, making their way towards the canyon. The Haireens continued to scramble out of the gap, only to find themselves trapped in the middle of the battle. They lashed out at anyone in the way of their efforts to break free.

Joe and Yelka launched several fireballs into the heart of the Haireens, scattering them away from Jax and his men. Sky continued her assault on Hudich's followers, able to keep them at bay single-handedly.

###

Cindy crept down the hall, her palms sweaty and her mouth dry. The chaotic noises from below continued to grow in volume and ferocity with each step she took. She had just reached the top of the staircase when she felt her communicator vibrating in her pocket, which was almost enough to stop her heart. Her fingers trembled as she took out the device and read Grandpa's message.

She started to enter a response and then realized everything was quiet. She glanced up from the communicator to see a creature walking upright like a person wearing a long thick robe but with a lizard-like head. It smiled broadly at her, revealing its rows of sharp, hooked teeth and its forked tongue flicked out, tasting the air. There was blood on its lips.

"Martin," she gasped. *What's happened to Martin?*

The Haireen exploded up the steps and Cindy dove out of the way as it crashed into the wall opposite the stairs. Cindy rolled to her feet and sprinted for the spiral staircase but the Haireen was too quick. It sprang at her and sank its teeth into her ankle.

Cindy screamed as she fell to the floor. The beast started to drag her back towards the stairs. She kicked its head several times with her free leg. The Haireen jerked her leg back and forth like a dog playing tug of war with a sock. Her ankle snapped and the agony caused lights to flash before Cindy's eyes, and she felt like her leg was about to come off completely.

"*Prizgaj*," Cindy screamed and held a ball of fire in her hand for a second before placing it on the Haireen's head.

The animal let out a high-pitched scream and released its hold on Cindy. It slammed back and forth into the walls trying to douse the flames.

Cindy gritted her teeth and got up on one leg. Blood soaked her pant leg and she felt an agonizing pain with each jolt as she hopped to the staircase. Holding onto the rail, she managed the stairs one by one, leaving a red trail behind her. When she reached the landing, the Haireen appeared at the bottom of the stairs, its head burnt in several spots.

Cindy launched herself across the room as the Haireen rushed up after her. She dove for the control panel and hit the force field button. The Haireen had not managed to get totally inside the barriers before the field was activated. The impact of its power caught the beast and flung it across the room into the wall.

Cindy responded to Grandpa's message, adjusted the dials and turned on the machine. The mirror started revolving and picked up speed.

Cindy's attacker got to its feet and tested the power of the force field one more time. After the second violent collision with the wall, it acted confused and paced along the perimeter, eyeing Cindy hungrily.

"Come on, Grandpa. Come on, please hurry," Cindy tried to will them through the gateway. She collapsed on the floor, unable to balance on one leg a moment longer.

The Haireen continued to watch her through the force field as if figuring out its next move.

###

Max and Martin continued to dodge Hudich's spells, but because of Martin's long prison stay and Max's extended magic use, they lost ground. They weaved in and out of rock towers and around lava pools as they followed the Haireens into the narrow canyon leading out of the valley. Sparks and lightning bolts exploded all around them as Hudich filled the air with all manner of spells in his effort to stop their escape.

Hudich's attack showed no mercy as his wayward spells struck down anything in their path. Fleeing guardians went down left and right as the enchantments meant to kill Max struck them instead.

Suddenly, the fleeing sea of creatures made an abrupt halt. Max and Martin found themselves squeezed relentlessly in the logjam of bodies running from the constant inundation of spells.

"What's happening?" Martin asked, as a Haireen smashed him into Max from behind.

"It looks like another battle up ahead." Max pushed his way through the Haireens as fire crackled through the air at the top of the canyon.

Joe and Yelka continued to direct the lizard-like beasts around Jax and the others with an array of spells.

"Cindy, at last," Joe said, fishing the communicator out of his pocket, almost dropping it in his haste.

"Is she all right?" Yelka yelled, as she continued her attack on the creatures.

"She's going to open the gateway," Joe shouted, as he read the message. As the communicator drew his attention away from the guardians, Yelka was unable to hold them back by herself, and they broke through.

Everyone braced to fight, but the Haireens didn't slow in their efforts to flee from Hudich. They bolted past Joe, Yelka and the others and ran on into the night.

Joe took out his crystal and waved it over the area in front of the mouth of the canyon. It flashed indicating the location of the gateway. "Sky, Jax, we're leaving now," Joe called, as he and Yelka raced towards the exit.

As the dam of guardians broke, Max and Martin fell to the ground and received several unintended blows as the remaining Haireens trampled them in their efforts to escape. Max's strength left him; it felt like he had gone thirteen rounds with the heavyweight boxing champ of the world. His knees shook as Martin scrambled to his feet then helped Max up.

Max shook his head to clear a buzzing in his ears. He was exhausted and leaned on Martin as they staggered up the canyon.

Suddenly, a tremendous force caught Max and Martin from behind and slammed them forward as if a bomb had gone off behind them.

"Max, look!" Martin pointed to a group of people gathering at the upper entrance to the canyon.

Max thought his eyes deceived him as Grandpa, Yelka and the others appeared at the entrance of the canyon. Max opened his mouth to call out as another spell bounced him and Martin along the ground like leaves in a strong wind. They rolled and tumbled over the canyon floor, hitting rocks and shrubs in their path.

"*Premakni*," Max screamed, as he caught sight of Hudich walking up the canyon behind them. Hudich raised an arm and swatted Max's spell away as if it were an annoying fly.

"Max, Martin," Sky called from the mouth of the canyon, drawing their attention. "Max and Martin are down there!" She motioned to the others.

Surprised voices asked, "What? Where?"

"Martin, run to her." Max pointed to Sky. "Run and don't look back. Run as fast as you can."

"What about you?"

"Don't worry about me. GO! GO NOW!"

Martin got up and rushed towards Sky as Max turned to face Hudich. "*Premakni*," Max called again as Hudich sent another spell up the canyon. Max's enchantment only lessened the blow of Hudich's spell as it tossed Max along the ground.

"Why aren't you running like the foolish coward I know you are?" Hudich barked as he advanced on him.

"I just needed to make sure Martin and the others got away first," Max said, too tired to stand and too exhausted to say anything but the truth.

"What?" Hudich said more to himself, as Grandpa and the others, with Martin, disappeared through the gateway. "They would not leave you behind," Hudich rumbled, as he lifted Max off the ground with one arm and held him aloft. "What are they planning? That old fool always has something up his sleeve."

"Only this, I didn't come through your gateway. *Vrnim se* Earth," Max said with a smile and satisfied sigh. Max could hear Hudich's outcry of wrath follow him as he sped away from Kleen. He hit the ground and nose-planted on the pavement in front of Alan's house.

All the people and the torches from earlier in the evening were gone, as Max clambered to his feet. He wanted to hurry home, but he had very little energy and only made it a few steps before a pain in his side dropped him to his knees. As Max attempted to run a second time, Larry and his gang turned onto the street.

They laughed and joked together about never having to see Max again. They continued to get closer, unaware that Max was kneeling in their street. Max put his head down, praying they would pass him by without spotting him. He held his breath as they approached, hoping the darkness would keep him hidden.

"Hey, what's that?" Jo called.

Max knew the jig was up. He took in a large gulp of air and used all the energy he had left. "*Premaknite*," he called, exploding to his feet. The spell blasted Larry and his group through the air as Max jogged away as fast as he could, holding his arms tight against the stitch in his side.

He reached the end of the street, and the sound of angry voices followed after him.

"I thought he was gone. How did he get back?"

Then a voice loud and clear rang out. "Release the Zbal!" It was Jo, and a chorus of agreement answered her proclamation.

Adrenaline rushed through Max's body like liquid energy, and his legs picked up speed. The thought of Larry and the horrifying Zbal destroying his plans of escape infuriated Max, driving him on.

###

"Martin!" Cindy said, as he stepped out of the gateway with Grandpa and the others. It was Martin, but he appeared thinner and worn.

Yelka rushed to Cindy's side and worriedly began to examine her leg. "Cindy, what happened?"

"That happened." Cindy pointed a finger at the Haireen on the other side of the force field.

Everyone looked upon the lizard-like beast staring at them from the other side of the barrier. From out of his robe he took out the leather-bound book from Kleen for all to see and flashed his hooked teeth in a wicked smile. It turned and raced down the steps as Grandpa's fist slammed down on the control panel, turning off the force field.

Sky sprang ahead of everyone in her pursuit of the imposter as it dashed through the house. Jax and his men followed as Grandpa and Yelka carried Cindy downstairs.

###

Max sprinted up Grandpa's street ignoring the burning in his lungs and the ache in his side. Fear of being devoured by an unstoppable, insane beast spurred him on. A high-pitched roar rang across the town, setting the hair on the back of Max's neck on end. He knew it was the Zbal that had made the sound, and that it was hunting him.

The Zbal's cry filled the air again. Closer now. Max reached the front gate and rushed into the yard. As he checked to make sure the latch was secure, a dark shadow appeared at the end of the street. Two lamp-like saucer eyes locked on him and advanced up the street at an incredible speed.

Max broke for the house while looking over his shoulder at the oncoming freight train of the Zbal. He raced headlong up the steps and collided with the lizard-beast that had been posing as Martin. They rolled down the steps in a heap of flying arms and legs. When they came to a stop, Sky was on the porch, a gun in one hand and her sword in the other.

The fleeing Haireen used Max to push itself off the ground, slamming him into the sidewalk as it darted out the gate. Sky's blasts followed the lizard-like creature into the street, throwing up debris at its heels.

"We must stop him," Grandpa said, as the others came out of the house.

Suddenly, a ferocious growl and then a wail of pain erupted out of the blackness as the Zbal attacked the fleeing imposter. The dark night made it difficult to follow the battle that ensued on the other side of the fence. The horrible screams and the tearing sounds swept fear over Max. As he got to his feet, the noise stopped.

Max felt cold, as if something was wrong. Everything started moving in slow motion. A loud sniff followed by another reached his ears. A defining scream of madness broke the silence. The dark beast leapt the fence in an effort to get at Max. It hit the ground and sprang towards him in one fluid motion.

Max put up his arms in a defensive position. A different growl echoed across the yard and something huge knocked Max sideways and caught the Zbal by the head in mid air. Ell materialized, shaking the monster violently by the neck, killing it. The Zbal's lifeless body flopped to the ground, and Ell nudged it with his foot. After he made certain it was dead, he went to Max, who wrapped his arms around Ell's huge head.

You saved my life!

Everyone but Yelka and Cindy gathered around the lifeless creature for a better view. Cindy was lying on the porch swing as Yelka tended her leg.

"A Zbal," Sky said with a note of awe, staring down at the beast.

Grandpa took a quick look and then hurried out into the street.

"What are you doing?" Max asked, as Sky and the others followed Grandpa.

Max and Ell joined the others in the street.

"It's gone." Jax returned from the alley between the houses. "The Haireen is wounded but still very mobile."

"Shall I go after it?" Sky asked.

"Yes, you must" Grandpa urged, with a grave look on his face, and Sky bolted in the direction Jax had indicated.

"What's wrong?" Max asked.

"It took the book."

"Martin's imposter?"

"Yes."

"How did the Zbal get through the spell protecting your house?" Max asked.

"It has no magic abilities. It's just an animal. The spell only works against magical beings," Grandpa stated.

"Max. Oh, Max," his mother called as she, his uncle and a few of Jax's men walked up the street towards them.

Max ran as fast as his exhausted body would go until he landed in his mother's arms.

22

Happy Reunions, Unfinished Business

Sky left, followed by Jax and few of his men. A joyous reunion commenced in the front room of Grandpa's house. Yelka and Olik took care of the wounded. Aunt Donna had several deep cuts and a concussion due to a severe blow to the head during her struggle with Martin's imposter, but otherwise she was doing well. Cindy's broken leg had to be reset and she also received over a hundred stitches. Max's mother, Uncle Frank, and Martin, while undernourished, were in relatively good health.

Max helped Grandpa prepare food for everyone while his mother sat at the kitchen table listening, as they discussed the day's events.

"I can't believe we actually pulled that off. We were lucky to only have Hudich get rid of the collar," Max said, as he carried a load of dishes to the table. "At least now we know who was giving information to the enemy."

"Yes, they had us fooled, again. Having one imposter convinced us there could only be one," Grandpa sighed, as he flipped pancakes.

"I'm just glad to be out of that horrible place," Max's mother added.

Max had been feeling rather proud of himself, but Grandpa's glum mood worried him. "What's wrong?"

"Nothing," Grandpa forced a smile.

"It's the book isn't it?" Max asked.

"What book?" Max's mother inquired.

"The creature who posed as Martin stole a book that Max, Cindy and Sky risked their lives to retrieve from Kleen, the world where you were imprisoned. It contains the spells and instructions necessary to build another gateway. That's what's troubling me. If that Haireen figures out how to use it, there will be trouble."

"I thought you said those creatures weren't aware of magic or how to use it." Max continued, setting the table.

"Well they weren't. But this one..."

Max froze. "We taught him!" Max now remembered the magic lessons, and how he and Cindy had given Martin all those roots from Svet.

"Precisely," Grandpa said. "I hope Sky and Jax can catch up to him, or we still have a lot of work to do. Let's hope Hudich doesn't find out about it, or he will devote all his energy to obtaining the book."

"What are we going to do if Sky isn't able to get it back?" Max asked.

"We'll talk about that if Sky returns empty-handed."

Sky and Jax returned two days later with grave news. They had indeed been unable to capture the Haireen and even lost its trail when it had made its way into Chicago. Max could tell by Sky's demeanor that she still didn't like having Jax around.

While Jax and his men returned to their own world, Sky set out in pursuit of the Haireen once again. Grandpa established a creature-tracking command center right next to the gateway. Sky now used the gateway to move quickly from place to place; tracking the creature on foot was not really feasible if they really meant to catch it. They pored over newspapers on the web and had the news channel on twenty-four hours a day. Any word of a mysterious disappearance or murder with strange circumstances did not go unnoticed, and Grandpa marked its location on a large map on the wall.

If not for the Haireen's escape with the book, Max's world would have been peaceful once again. The enormous weight that had been hanging over him all summer had vanished. He no longer felt the pressure of worrying about something horrible happening to his mother and his uncle. He did have a nagging conscious about the fact that he had set Hudich loose, however. He vowed to somehow rectify this, although he didn't have a clue as to how he would accomplish this goal.

A week after the rescue everyone sat together on the porch drinking lemonade. Uncle Frank, not wanting to be involved in what he called "madness," announced they would be going into hiding. He refused to tell anyone, even Aunt Donna, where they would be going.

"What about you?" Grandpa asked, turning to Max's mother.

Max almost dropped his lemonade as his head snapped up towards his mother.

"I want to fight," she said. "I can see how important this is and what these evil people are capable of doing. I think Max and I should be here, to help you."

"Of course. You are welcome to stay here," Grandpa said.

Max's eyes fell on Cindy, who was smiling.

"We do need to come up with a story about my disappearance," Max's mother said. "I mean, I just can't show up without an explanation, when you reported me missing to the police."

"I think you shouldn't even let the police know you're back," Mrs. Carlson said. "I mean, why do they need to know you've returned? If you and Max stay here and do not return to the city, there's no need to say anything to them at all."

"I concur," Yelka said. "It might be safer if you—how do they say—stay off the radar."

The next morning Grandpa prepared the gateway to take Uncle Frank, Aunt Donna, and Martin home so they could collect their belongings before disappearing. Grandpa had a hard time convincing Frank they shouldn't go directly to their house. It wasn't until Max and Yelka told him the stories of the shed that he finally agreed with Grandpa. They decided to exit into an empty field a half-mile from their house.

Max and his mother decided to go with them so they could say goodbye, in case this really was the last time they would see them.

"Just call me when you want to come back," Yelka said, before she started the gateway.

"I want to stay and fight," Martin pleaded, as the light of the gateway swallowed the mirror. Max smiled at the fact that the real Martin wasn't as timid as his imposter had made him seem.

"There's no place you can hide that they won't find you, if they want to," Grandpa said to Frank, as he led them through the gateway.

Uncle Frank merely grunted in response to this remark and then escorted Martin and Donna through. Max and his mother went last.

They stepped out of the gateway into a field with tall grass surrounded by trees. Grandpa made sure no one passing by had spotted them.

"Come on." Grandpa waved them to follow him into the shadow of some large cottonwoods.

"I don't think anyone's here," Frank complained.

"You never know. Besides, they've already used your house. How do you know they haven't set a trap for you? I'm sure they're angry about what happened, even though Hudich did succeed in removing the collar. Better safe than sorry."

"Oh, I've heard enough of this nonsense! Come on, Donna, Martin," Frank ordered, and pushed past Grandpa, pulling his family with him.

Grandpa turned to Max and his mother and shook his head. Frank marched towards his house at such a quick pace that everyone else had trouble keeping up. When he rounded the side street which led to their home, he froze.

Police cars and other emergency vehicles surrounded Frank's house. A string of yellow police tape formed a restricted zone, keeping unauthorized personnel out of the immediate area of their house. Onlookers lined the street on both sides, trying to get a glimpse at the commotion.

"What's going on?" Frank stared at his house.

"The shed!" Max exclaimed, remembering the stench.

Several coroners appeared, pushing body bags on gurneys around from the back of the house.

A group of people passed them on the street, talking to each other. "Did you hear? They said the bodies appeared to have been eaten."

"NO!" one gasped.

"We need to get out of here," Grandpa stressed. "If you're not the main suspect now, you soon will be."

"Yes, right," Frank stammered in a hushed voice, as the color drained from his face. He glanced in all directions with fear in his eyes.

"Come on." Donna took Frank by the hand and directed him after Grandpa.

They hurried back to the field and returned through the gateway to Grandpa's house. That night, Frank conceded to settle in the new subdivision behind Grandpa's house. They decided that it would be best to have a new last name, and Olik created some authentic looking identification documents for them. Frank's attitude underwent a dramatic change after that. He started to study magic and did his best to get involved, not only with the community, but with the ongoing war efforts against Hudich and his followers. It seemed the gravity of the situation had finally hit home.

Max and Cindy continued to go to the school for magic lessons but also had their own personal teacher in Yelka. They traveled to Svet at least two times a week to practice magic and to visit Yelka and Ell, who had begun to learn magic with them.

Not only did they have private magic lessons, but Olik went back to giving them math and science as he had the previous summer.

"I wish Sky could start teaching us more self-defense," Cindy commented one day, after a particularly difficult math lesson with Olik.

"Me too. I see the importance of this stuff but it just isn't as much fun. I hope she catches up to the Haireen soon," Max added.

Several weeks went by without a word from Sky, and it had been even longer since they had heard from Alan or Hudich or any of the others. Then one evening, a pale blond woman wearing a long black dress appeared in front of the gate to Grandpa's house. She held a handkerchief and had tears running down her cheeks. Two more women stood a short distance behind her, looking as somber as the first.

"Who are those women?" Mrs. Rigdon asked, peering out the front window.

"What? Who?" Grandpa lowered a map he had been studying.

"I don't know. I've never seen them before," Max said, standing up for a better look.

"Me neither," Cindy added.

"Why don't they come in the gate?" Mrs. Rigdon asked.

"Because they can't. That's Alan's wife, Larry's mother," Grandpa said, dropping the paper in the chair and heading for the door.

Everyone else followed him out the front door and to the gate. A melancholy Larry peeked his head out from behind a tree to the right of his mother. Larry's mother dabbed at her bloodshot eyes with the handkerchief and tried to compose herself.

"May I help you, Vicky?" Grandpa asked, as he reached the gate.

"I don't know how to ask this," she said, with a quivering bottom lip. "You see. After you destroyed the hourglass…" She lowered her head into the hanky and started crying. The women behind her wept as well.

"Oh," Grandpa said, and appeared to struggle with hiding a smile. "We trapped Alan in Kleen, along with their husbands too, I assume." He nodded in the direction of the other women, pulling at his white beard.

"Good," Max muttered to Cindy.

"I... We came to ask if you would bring them home. They can come home using magic, but they can't stay. And... Hudich..." She took several large breaths and hung her head. "Hudich doesn't want them to come home at all."

"That doesn't surprise me," Grandpa said, more to himself than anyone in particular. "Your husband is responsible for setting Hudich free. First from Pekel last summer, and then helping him to remove the collar."

"I know but, please..." she begged.

"He's learning a hard lesson," Grandpa said. "The devil, Hudich in this case, really never cares for anyone but himself."

"Will you help him? Them?" She nodded towards the women behind her.

"I might," Grandpa said, surprising everybody on the inside of the fence.

"What?" Max asked, a little louder than he intended, drawing everyone's attention. He felt his cheeks flush with heat, and he glanced at Cindy for support. She stood with her mouth open, and Max didn't know if it was a reaction to what he—or what Grandpa—had said.

Grandpa frowned at Max before turning his attention back to Larry's mother. "I'll give it some thought. I'll need to come up with a plan to remove them. Hudich can't know until they're already gone. You realize he won't be happy about it."

"Yes," she answered lifting her head. "I just want my husband back."

"I'm busy with something at the moment, but I'll contact you as soon as I'm ready."

"Thank you," she said, and the other women responded in the same manner before they departed.

"How can you help them?" Max demanded after they were gone.

"Did you like being separated from your mother?" Grandpa asked with a wry smile, as he eyed Max.

Max didn't know how to respond. His grandfather's words stung him. He wanted to be a better person than the enemy, and reluctantly admitted that helping Alan and the other men rejoin their families was the right thing to do.

They didn't hear from Alan's wife or anyone else from the enemy's side in the weeks that followed. Max and Cindy continued their lessons and prepared for the upcoming school year.

Late one night, while Max, Cindy and Martin were playing a board game, the sound of the vibrating gateway filled the house. They all exchanged confused looks.

"Who do you think that is?" Cindy asked.

"Let's go find out," Max suggested, and they hustled upstairs in time to see Sky step out of the gateway.

They stood outside the force field watching as Grandpa and Sky engaged in a conversation.

"We can't hear a thing!" Cindy said.

"I know," Max whispered. Grandpa didn't know they were there, and they couldn't hear a word of what Sky had to say. Grandpa turned to the control panel and made some adjustments. The gateway flashed as it changed worlds.

"Where's she going?" Martin asked.

"Who knows?" Max exhaled with disappointment.

"Hey," Cindy piped up, as Yelka emerged from the gateway.

Grandpa hit the off switch and the force field disappeared, while the mirror dematerialized out of the light.

"Oh," Grandpa gave a little jump. "Didn't know you were waiting there."

"We want to know what the news is," Cindy said.

"Don't worry, you shall hear it," Sky smiled. "In fact, this is going to require all of us."

They went downstairs and gathered around the kitchen table. Max and Cindy's mothers, who had become good friends, joined them.

"I tracked the creature, Kacha, to New York City," Sky said, before taking a drink of water.

"Kacha?" Cindy said with a confused look.

"Oh, I discovered its name at one of its victim's homes. It is learning to read and write and it had written its name on the wall. Not only is it learning to read and write, but also its magical powers are growing. I have also found evidence of spells being used on its victims. I think the creature is using magic to catch them."

"Is it still…" Max couldn't finish the sentence.

"What? Eating them? Yes," Sky said. "I think it has developed a real taste for humans now. We need to stop this vile beast and we need to stop it in a hurry. Doing that is going to take all of us. Kacha is going to have an array of spells in its arsenal that we have never seen."

"What makes you say that?" Yelka asked, with her eyebrows knit together.

"I caught up to it at one point. I was lucky to get away with my life. I think the creature could now give Hudich a run for his money."

"That's not good news. We should have destroyed the book the minute we took possession of it," Grandpa lamented.

"It's my fault." Max hung his head. "I convinced you to keep it for a bargaining chip."

"You didn't convince me. I was curious and wanted to study it a little. I should have remembered that when you play with evil, it burns you in the end."

"What do we need to do?" Mrs. Carlson asked. "I mean, what can we do if he is becoming that powerful?"

"We need a plan. A really good one," Sky responded. "We are going to have to outsmart Kacha. Even though it is learning, the beast still lacks the ability to plan ahead. That is how I was able to escape; I out—thought it."

"So, we need to out—think it, too," Grandpa stated, glancing around the room. "With everyone in this room, we should be able to do that."

Kacha shuffled its feet down the stairs to the subway. It ran its now human-male-formed fingers through its wavy blond hair and adjusted its silk tie. The creature flashed its human smile to an attractive woman in a red dress as it passed through the turnstile. It was in a rather good mood as it stepped onto one of the packed cars of a train heading downtown.

Kacha found an empty seat next to a small child playing with some toy cars in his lap. "May I sit next to you, my young man?" Kacha asked with a smile.

"Sure," the boy smiled back and returned to his cars.

"That's a neat car." Kacha pointed to a red sports car.

"It's my favorite," the boy replied holding it up for Kacha. "Do you like toys?"

"Yes," Kacha smiled, "only different ones."

"Like what?"

"Well, I'll show you when we reach the tunnel where the lights tend to flicker a little."

"Okay," the boy said with anticipation.

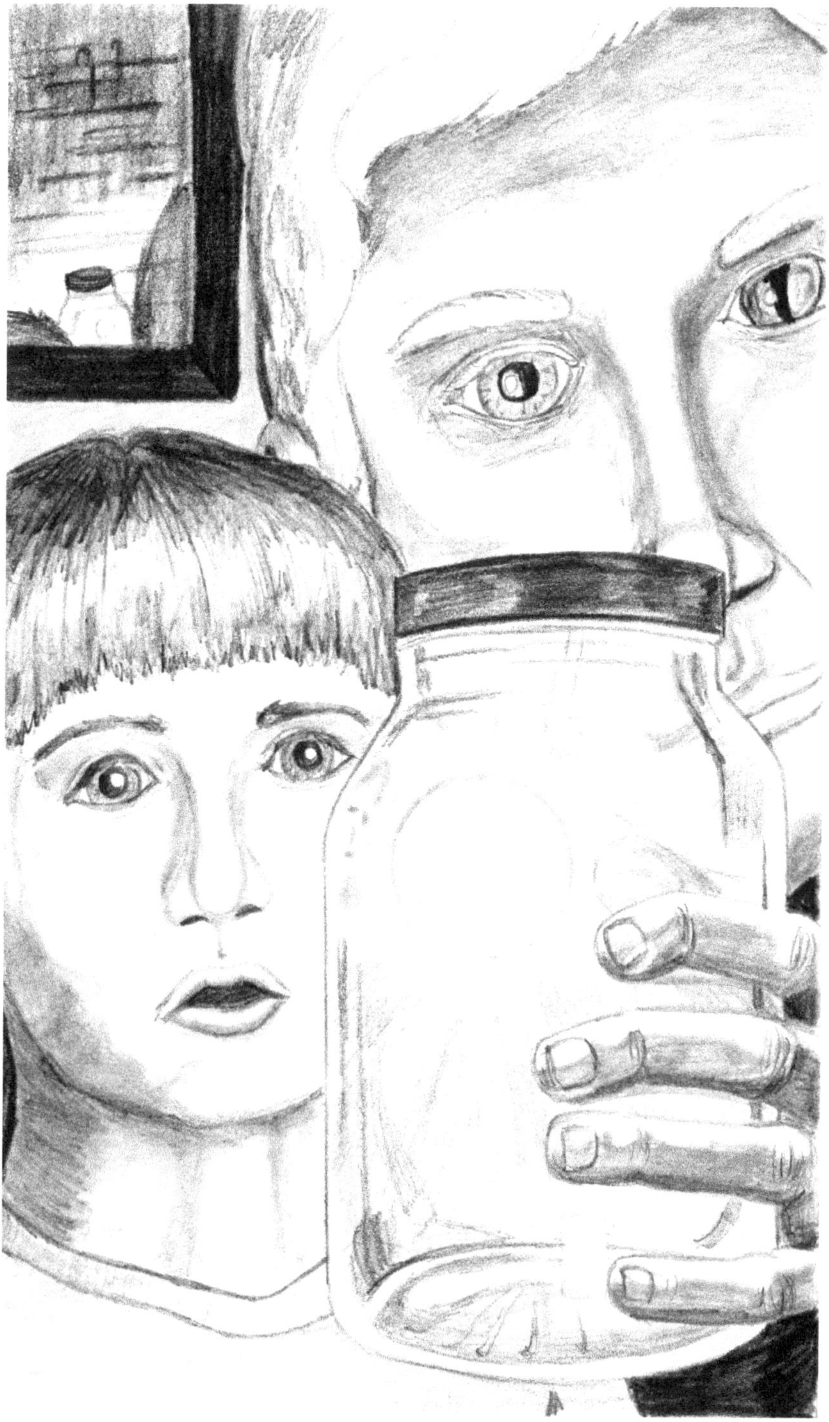

Kacha's eyes sparkled as they pulled out of the station. As the train sped along, it reached into its suit jacket and pulled out a small jar with the lid securely fastened.

"A jar," the boy frowned as he caught sight of it in Kacha's hand.

"Not the jar, but what's inside," Kacha winked, tongue darting out to wet its lips.

"It looks empty!"

"Yes, that's why we need the dark," Kacha said as the train light's started to flash. In the dark of the train car, a small, green light floated in the jar for the boy to see.

"Wow, what is it?" the boy asked, as the lights of the subway car came back to life.

"My first captured soul!" Kacha smirked.

Spell Pronunciations and Definitions

The following words are from the Slovene language

Stress marks: [bold type] indicates the primary stressed syllable, as in news·pa·per [**nooz**-pey-per] and in·for·ma·tion [in-fer-**mey**-shuhn]

pridi (**pri**·di) [**prē**-dē] – Moves objects towards you.
zaspi (za·**spi**) [zä-**spē**] – Causes sleep.
zbudi(**zbu**·di)[**zboo**-dē] – Awakes a sleeping person.
prizgaj (**pri**·zgaj) [**prē**- 3g ī] – Use to create fire.
ugasni (u·**ga**·sni) [oo-**gä**-snē] – Use to extinguish fire.
premakni (pre·**ma**·kni) [prā-**mä**-knē] – Moves objects away from you.
vstani (**vs**·ta·ni) [**oos**-tä-nē] – Stops moving objects.
pochasi (po·**cha**·si) [pō-**chä**-sē] – Slows moving objects down.
izginem se (iz·**gi**·nem·se) [ēz-**gē**-n äm- sā] – Makes one invisible.
prikazi se (pri·**ka**·zi·se) [prē-**kä**-zē-sā] – Makes one visible.
izbrisi znamenje (iz·**bir**·si·zna·**men**·je) [ēz-**brē**-shē znä-**men**yē] – Removes curses.
preselim se(pre·se·**lim**·se)[pre-se-**lēm-sā**] – Transports one to another world.
vrnim se(vr·**nim**·se)[vr-**nēm**-sā] – To return from transport.
odkri (**od**·kri)[**ōd**-krē] – Reveals something hidden.
razkrij zlo (raz·**krij**·zlo)[räz-**krē**-zlō] – Reveals a person who has been using evil magic.
razkrij dobro (raz·**krij**·do·bro)[räz-**krē**-dō-brō] – Reveals a person who has been using good magic.
unichi (u·**ni**·chi)[oo-**nē**-chē] – To destroy something.
vrtinchim se(vr·**tin**·chim·se)[vr-**tēn**-chēm-sā] – To twirl like a tornado.
zadravi (za·**dra**·vi)[zä-**drä**-vē] – To heal something.

Symbols and their examples:

ē b**ee**
ä f**a**ther
3 vi**si**on
ī p**ie**, b**y**
oo b**oo**t
ā p**ay**
ō t**oe**
e b**et**

James Todd Cochrane was born in California in 1969. He received his BA from Utah State University, where he majored in Business Information Systems with a minor in German.

A writer since elementary school, he published his first novel, Max and the Gatekeeper, in 2007.

The author writes part-time while working as a computer programmer. He now lives with his wife, Carol, in Juneau, Alaska.

BOOKS

Max and the Gatekeeper (Max and the Gatekeeper Book I)

The Hourglass of Souls (Max and the Gatekeeper Book II)

The Descendant and the Demon's Fork (Max and the Gatekeeper Book III)

The Dark Society (Max and the Gatekeeper Book IV)

Max and the Gatekeeper Book V in progress

NOVELLA SERIES (EBOOKS ONLY)

Centalpha 6 Part I

Centalpha 6 Part II

Centalpha 6 Part III

Centalpha 6 Part IV

Centalpha 6 Part V

Centalpha 6 Omnibus

Centalpha 6 Part VI coming soon